PENGUIN
ARKANA

The Cult of the
Black Virgin

Ean Begg is a Jungian analyst and writer of guidebooks to the western mystery tradition. These include *Myth and Today's Consciousness* (Coventure, 1984) and, in collaboration with his wife, Deike, *On the Trail of Merlin* (Aquarian, 1991) and *In Search of the Holy Grail and the Precious Blood* (Thorsons, 1995). He read modern languages at Jesus College, Oxford, and holds the Diploma of the C. G. Jung Institute, Zurich.

The Cult of the Black Virgin

Ean Begg

ARKANA

PENGUIN BOOKS

PENGUIN BOOKS

Published by the Penguin Group
Penguin Books Ltd, 27 Wrights Lane, London W8 5TZ, England
Penguin Putnam Inc., 375 Hudson Street, New York, New York 10014, USA
Penguin Books Australia Ltd, Ringwood, Victoria, Australia
Penguin Books Canada Ltd, 10 Alcorn Avenue, Toronto, Ontario, Canada M4V 3B2
Penguin Books (NZ) Ltd, 182–190 Wairau Road, Auckland 10, New Zealand

Penguin Books Ltd, Registered Offices: Harmondsworth, Middlesex, England

First published in Arkana 1985
Published with new material in Arkana 1996
3 5 7 9 10 8 6 4

Typeset by Datix International Ltd, Bungay, Suffolk
Printed in England by Clays Ltd, St Ives plc

To Our Dear Lady of Einsiedeln,
Madonna of the Hermits in the Dark Forest,
with gratitude

Contents

Contents

Illustrations

Preface

As the work of a part-time amateur with little opportunity for lengthy research in libraries, this book of necessity relies heavily on secondary sources. I hope I have acknowledged all these in the bibliography. I decided reluctantly that it would overburden the text to include references and footnotes. While accepting responsibility for any errors, I must point out that it has not been my concern to differentiate historical fact — always difficult to establish — from legendary material which may throw light on the way people have viewed the cult of the Black Virgin at various times.

The factual foundation on which this book is based, the result of much individual research and scores of visits to Black Virgin sites, is the gazetteer. It will help to ground the reader in the reality of the subject if he or she will devote some time to browsing in the gazetteer with reference to the illustrations and maps before embarking on the text.

E.C.M.B.
London, on the feast of St Sophia, 1984

Foreword to the Revised and Expanded Edition

When this book appeared in 1985 it was the first in English to consider the phenomenon of the Black Madonnas and the first in any language to attempt a comprehensive gazetteer of all the exemplars. Although there have been other books dealing with aspects of the subject since, no subsequent author has produced an international list of images of the Virgin held to be dark or black. My original catalogue was inevitably deficient since, in many important Black Virgin countries such as Spain, there was at the time of writing hardly any information on which to base my researches. It was not until after publication that I became familiar with the rich collection of books written by Juan G. Atienza, regrettably none of them available in English, that cover all aspects of mysterious Spain, especially the Templar tradition. He has not written about Black Virgins directly, except for a few pages in *Nuestra Señora de Lucifer* (Martinez Roca, 1991), but his work contains many valuable references to them. The same is true of an excellent book by Rafael Alarcón Herrera, *La Otra España del Temple* (Martinez Roca, 1988). Italy was another country where there were — and still are — few literary sources to be followed up, so I am indebted to a recent book by Lucia Chiavola Birnbaum, *Black Madonnas* (Northeastern University Press, 1993), for casting more light on some of them. But it is, above all, to interested readers who have taken the trouble to write to me with suggestions and comments that these additions owe their existence.

Here I must make a confession: I have not been able to visit all the sites in the Addenda to the Gazetteer, but have thought it worthwhile in the interests of comprehensiveness to include them. Increasingly, Black Virgins are being whitened, stolen, removed to museums or withdrawn from circulation so, before the evidence disappears of a popular cult that links us to the ancient world, I wish to preserve as much knowledge about it as possible.

My wife, Deike, whom I consider co-author of this book —
so many of the sites have we visited and worked on together
— has in the interim period written with me two books on
related but distinct subjects: *On the Trail of Merlin* and *In
Search of the Holy Grail and the Precious Blood*. We have
stumbled across, by serendipity, a number of Black Virgins
during our travels, as a result of which we realize that they are
far more numerous than we could ever have supposed when
the book was gestating.

To balance the disappearances, new Black Virgins have
entered the scene, especially in England and in North America.
The Carmelite Friars of Aylesford are proud to call their
modern statue of Our Lady the Black Madonna, and a number
of other images, Anglican as well as Catholic, have been
included without attaining this eminence, in memory of the
times when England was Our Lady's Dowry. Eastern Europe
and the Orthodox world remain, to my sorrow, largely *terra
incognita*. We don't speak the necessary languages, travel by
car is sometimes still difficult and the Church is often cagey.
When I asked a priest in Pelion about an icon of the Black
Madonna in a little chapel of his parish, he replied that in
Greece they came in all the colours of the rainbow and that
this had no significance.

Many of the Black Virgin sites in the earlier editions, which
I qualified as doubtful, such as Covadonga in Spain, I now
know, from their origins, are genuine. It would, however, I
feel, be too confusing to regrade them. Reader, please take this
into account and do not disdain Black Virgins of the second
and third categories. Please, too, write to us with any Black
Virgins you may find or know of, or any information you may
have on those already listed.

I have not graded the sites in the Addenda, as the fuller
entries are, in most cases, self-explanatory.

The new Michelin regional maps of Italy and Spain, with
their comprehensive gazetteers and sensible reference system,
are so good that I have not bothered to specify which province
each site is in or to add any plans of my own. The grid
reference follows the number of the map. Where two map
references are given, the first refers to the map of the whole
country (map-number followed by fold in brackets), the second

to a more specific region. The map references for sites in
England are all taken from A–Z maps, with the grid reference
first and the page number following.

Introduction

ARE THERE SUCH THINGS AS BLACK VIRGINS?

Oettingen for Bavaria,
Hal for the Belgians,
Montserrat for Spain,
Alba for the Magyars.
For Italy Loreto,
But in France, Liesse
Is their joy and ever shall be.

Quod Bavaris Ottinga,
Quod Belgis Hala,
Quod Serra Montis Hesperiis,
Quod Hungaris Regalis Alba,
Quodque Laurentum Italis,
Laetitia Francis illud est,
et erit suis.

This verse dating from 1629 catalogues some of the national shrines of Europe. At the heart of each is an ancient tradition of devotion to a statue of the Black Virgin. The poet could just as well have included Chartres, Le Puy and Rocamadour in France, Einsiedeln in Switzerland, Oropa in Piedmont, Our Lady of the Pillar in Zaragoza and Our Lady of Guadalupe and all the Spains. These are a few of the most famous among the scores of Black Virgins that have survived centuries of war and revolution, some in great basilicas, some in tiny village churches, others in museums and private collections.

If it is true that a large proportion of the ancient miraculous Madonnas of the world are black, why is such a surprising phenomenon so little known and what are the causes of it? Scholars are proverbially uninquisitive, especially about matters outside their own academic discipline, and the subject falls uneasily between art history and ecclesiology. To art historians many of the Black Virgins must appear crude, even grotesque, wormeaten, restored or replaced, of doubtful provenance, difficult to examine or date. Where they belong to a recognizable class, like the Thrones of Wisdom in Catalonia or the Auvergne, their dark colour has attracted little attention. The Black Virgin of Padua is well documented because it is by Donatello.

1. Montserrat (copy in Santiago de Compostela)

Theologians evince, if anything, even less enthusiasm for the subject than art historians. The still popular cult of wonder-working images is not only reactionary and non-scriptural, it also evokes memories of awkward subjects best left in obscurity like the pre-Christian origins of much in Christianity, the history of the Templars, Catharism and other heresies, and secrets concerning the Merovingian dynasty. So, blackness in statues of the Virgin tends to be ignored and, where admitted, is attributed to the effects of candle smoke, burial, immersion or fashion's passing whim. The contention, then, of the Catholic Church is that most such statues were not originally intended to be black, and only became so by accident later. The fact remains that they are black and to discuss the phenomenon in visual terms only is to disguise their deepest significance.

Over the last century, however, there has been an upsurge of literary and historical interest in Black Virgins, though this has largely been confined to France. Perhaps for this reason much prominence has been given to the twelfth-century origins of cult and statues. This has resulted in an arbitrary exclusion of many examples of the genre from consideration as genuine Black Virgin.

Since I am neither a historian nor a theologian and am no art expert, I shall be examining the subject from the viewpoint of archetypal psychology, treating legends and traditions as 'Just-So Stories' that are also of potential symbolic interest. I shall therefore not exclude from consideration *a priori* any site or image that has been associated with the cult of the Black Virgin.

From whatever viewpoint one examines the subject, however, and whatever the causes of the phenomenon may be, it is indisputable that some of the most famous statues of the Madonna in Western Europe have faces and hands that are black, by intention, and are known to have been so for many centuries. There are also approximately 450 images of the Virgin throughout the world, not counting those in Africa south of the Mediterranean littoral, which have been called black, dark, brown or grey.

SOURCES

The principal sources of information concerning Black Virgins are three general books on the subject, all of which confine themselves to France, with only brief references to images elsewhere. The first of these to appear was *'Etude sur l'origine des Vierges Noires'* by Marie Durand-Lefèbvre in 1937. Her extensive catalogue includes paintings, copies of statues from outside France, such as those of Einsiedeln and Loreto, and several items listed on the basis of unchecked information from private sources which subsequent research has failed to verify. She gives, where available, a detailed and comprehensive bibliography for each entry. Her main hypothesis is the iconographical and cultic continuity between pagan goddesses and the Black Virgins.

This theme is taken up independently by Emile Saillens, who was able to avail himself of his predecessor's work, though his

own researches began before 1937. His convincing and
systematic book 'Nos Vierges Noires, leurs origines', which was
not published, owing to the war, until 1945, contains a valuable
catalogue of 'places in France that possess, or have possessed a
statuette said to be of a Black Virgin' with a summary of
information using abbreviations about each entry, as well as a
number of useful maps.

Jacques Huynen in 'L'Enigme des Vierges Noires', 1972,
although he owes much to Saillens, copying his list of images
outside France verbatim, is particularly interested in the esoteric,
initiatory aspects of the cult. This leads him to focus on the
twelfth century, and the mysteries connected with alchemy and
the Order of the Temple. In the second part of the book he
examines in detail twelve French shrines and their symbolic
significance.

The essay by Moss and Cappannari, 'In Quest of the Black
Virgin', while informed by Saillens, is a precious introduction to
the Black Virgins of Italy, and the fruit of a collaboration that
lasted twenty years. Recent articles on the subject by Baigent and
Leigh in 'The Unexplained' and by Brétigny and Sérénac in
'Nostra' have also been taken into consideration. Large numbers
of locally published guide-books and brochures relating to
individual shrines have proved to be mines of useful
information. A predecessor to the present work from within the
field of depth psychology is 'The Black Madonna of Einsiedeln:
A Psychological Perspective', by Frederick R. Gustafson Jr.
André Pertoka's cryptic monograph, 'Recherches sur le
symbolisme des Vierges Noires, des dieux noirs, et des pierres-
noires dans les traditions religieuses,' though suggestive, has
proved, on the whole, too arbitrary and metaphysical for the
purposes of this book. No. 266 of the journal Atlantis, Jan./Feb.
1972, 'Mystérieuses Vierges Noires' contains several articles
with interesting insights.

Of the numerous works dealing with Marian shrines in
general, I am particularly indebted to Fr J. E. Drochon's
monumental 'Histoire illustrée des pélérinages français de la
Très Sainte Vierge' of 1890, though in stating that of 1,200
remarkable French Madonnas, only 50 are black, he succumbs, I
suspect, to the clerical tendency to minimize the phenomenon.

EVIDENCE FOR CONTINUITY OF THE
BLACK VIRGIN TRADITION

Early textual references to the blackness of images of the Virgin are rare, though Peter Comestor, the twelfth-century biblical scholar of Troyes and Paris, St Bernard of Clairvaux and Nicephorus Callixtus (1256–c1335), the Byzantine church historian, have been called as witnesses.

In a chronicle of the year 1255 it is written that St Louis, on his return from the Crusade, 'left in the country of Forez several images of Our Lady made and carved in wood of black colour which he had brought from the Levant'. The Virgin of Myans is referred to as 'La Noire' in a document of 1619, referring back to an incident of 1248. There is documentary evidence that the Virgin of Pézenas was black in 1340. Notre-Dame de Bon Espoir in Dijon is reported to have been black in 1591. The painting of 1676 in Bruges records the already ancient Spanish Black Virgin, Our Lady of Regula. Our Lady of Modène is known to have been black since 1623. The meticulous description and sketch of the Black Virgin of Le Puy given by Faujas de St Fons in 1778 is powerful evidence that the statuette was black by design, and had been so from its origins, which are no later than the twelfth century.

Even without historically verifiable examples there is an argument from common sense which merits consideration. Worshippers love the holy images familiar to them, regret their loss and resist any change in their appearance. This is attested by the ferocious revolts of the iconoclastic period in the Eastern Empire, as well as by the courage and tenacity with which local people strove to preserve their Madonnas during the wars of religion, the French Revolution and the Spanish Civil War. It is also noteworthy that Black Virgins, well-known as centres of pilgrimage in the past, lose much of their power to attract cultic enthusiasm once they have been painted over. That this fact was well appreciated by civil and ecclesiastical authorities is illustrated by the history of Our Lady of Einsiedeln. The statue was evacuated to Austria in 1798 to escape the designs of Napoleon. When the Madonna was returned in 1803, she was found, to the consternation of the Lords of the Capitol, to have been cleaned during her stay in Bludenz. It was promptly decided that she should be restored to her wonted blackness before being exposed once more to the gaze of the faithful. The copy of her in Fribourg was created black in 1690.

A further factor worth noting is the durability of local traditional names for objects, places and geographical features. We do not know when the Black Virgin, which has been the object of continuous veneration at Montserrat since the ninth century, though not necessarily in the same form, acquired her soubriquet of La Moreneta, nor when the Marseillais bestowed on one of their Virgins the title of La Bouéno Méro Négro, but such epithets as these, as well as the constantly recurring La Brune and La Noire, have a venerable ring to them and are unlikely to be of recent coinage.

Saillens estimates from the evidence that is available that by the middle of the sixteenth century, before the depredations of the Huguenots, there were 190 statuettes of the Black Virgin in France, mostly in the Auvergne, Bourbonnais, Pyrenees, Rhône, Provence and Savoy.

WHY IS SHE BLACK?

Spokesmen for the Church, when asked to explain the origin of Black Virgins, tend to invoke candle smoke or general exposure to the elements. After a time, they would say, as at Einsiedeln, the faithful become accustomed to a sooty image, and the clergy pander to their prejudice by the use of paint where necessary. Apart from the considerable contrary evidence of clerical antipathy to Black Virgins and disregard for parishioners' wishes, this rationalistic hypothesis raises two important questions. If the presumed polychrome faces and hands of the Virgin and Child have been blackened by the elements, why has their polychrome clothing not been similarly discoloured? Secondly, why has a similar process not occurred in the case of other venerated images?

There are, indeed, a few figures in addition to Mary and a handful of black Christs (e.g. St Flour, Mexico, Philippines, Lucca) who are occasionally represented as black. The other figures are interesting in that there seems to be a sound symbolic reason for blackness in their funerary, chthonic, sexual and occult associations. The list includes: St Anne, St Mary the Egyptian, The Queen of Sheba, Sara the Egyptian, St Catherine of Alexandria, the Libyan Sibyl, one of the Magi, the executioner of John the Baptist, St Maurice and his Theban legion, among whom Saillens includes St Ours and St Victor, whose cathedral houses the Black Virgin of Marseilles. The cult of St Martin de Porres is a recent one, but his image, improbably black for the son of a Spanish hidalgo and a South American Indian woman, has attracted a surprisingly strong devotion in the Dominican churches of Western Europe. Apart from Mary, however, black images are too rare to arouse much comment or controversy.

Black Virgins, on the other hand, are too widespread a phenomenon to escape curiosity, though until recently, this has been surprisingly muted. The aetiology that relies on exposure to the elements raises, as we have seen, as many problems as it solves, but there are other explanations, less current today than in the 1930s, both ingenious and disingenuous, which Saillens took time to refute.

1 Mary lived in a hot climate and would have been very sunburnt. The numerous portraits of her attributed to St Luke show this to be the case.

   Saillens points to the circularity of this argument. 'Why are the portraits brown?' 'Because Mary was brown.' 'How do we know?' 'Because of the portraits.'

2 Black Virgins were made by dark-skinned people of the Middle East in their own image.

   In fact there is no ancient tradition in Asia or Africa according to which Mary is represented as black. Even in Ethiopia she is generally shown as much lighter coloured than the majority of the indigenous population. Furthermore, Black Virgins, though often reputed to have been brought back from the Crusades, belong in most cases to the class of Auvergnat or Catalan Thrones of Wisdom and are considered to be of local workmanship.

3 The sculptors of Black Virgins naively supposed the inhabitants of Palestine to be dark-skinned.

   The reality is that contact between Western Europe and the Levant has been constant and considerable since 600BC, and the appearance of Jews and Saracens was perfectly familiar to the twelfth-century Frenchmen and Spaniards. A whole quarter of the city of Orléans (qv) was inhabited by Syrians from as early as the sixth century when the Irish missionary St Columbanus stayed with them, the Merovingian king, Gontran, being reputedly acclaimed by them in 588. The first Christian oratory in the Auvergne, dating from the fourth century was at Fontgièvre, near Clermont. The name 'fountain of Jews' refers, according to Pourrat, the foremost historian of the region, to Syrian Christians. From AD 768 to 900 Narbonne was actually a Jewish principality, and in the following centuries cross-fertilizing influences linking Islam, then in full occupation of Spain, with Judaism and Christianity, were particularly strong.

4 Prototypes of the Black Virgins were carved in black material such as ebony, basalt or metal, thus setting a precedent for future usage.

  In fact, almost all Black Virgins are carved in wood, either of indigenous timber such as oak, apple, olive, pear, or in cedar. Ebony was virtually unknown in Western Europe until the thirteenth century.

CHRISTIAN ATTITUDES TO THE BLACK VIRGIN CULT

Many Christians, both among the clergy and the laity, simply accept that the Black Virgins present us with a mystery for which there is no obvious explanation. In 1944, Leonard W. Moss, entering the church at Lucera in southern Italy, came across his first Black Virgin and asked the priest, 'Father, why is the Madonna black?' The response was, 'My son, she is black because she is black.' When, in December 1980, I visited Orcival, whose wonder-working Madonna figures in all the lists of Black Virgins, though her appearance belies the description, I asked the proprietress of the souvenir shop opposite the church why she was called black. The answer, in a tone which brooked no further cross-examination, was 'Because she is.'

The priest's answer to Moss may seem a charming example of holy simplicity, but there was no mistaking the open hostility, when, on 28 December 1952, as Moss and Cappannari presented their paper on Black Virgins to the American

Association for the Advancement of Science, every priest and nun in the audience walked out. My impression of the reaction of the clergy to the subject of Black Virgins has been one of helpful courtesy tinged with genuine disinterest in and ignorance of the subject. As a result, many cults are dying.

At Ballon near Le Mans, one of the many places in France that echo the name of Belenus, the Celtic god of flocks, and its suggestively named twin parish of St Mars-sous-Ballon, the priest knew nothing of any cult of the Virgin, black or otherwise, in the neighbourhood. None of the local inhabitants I spoke to could recall any particular Marian devotion. Yet Saillens writes categorically of the fifteenth-century Notre-Dame des Champs at Ballon as the only example of an earthenware Black Virgin in France, and states that it is now in a private collection, having been replaced in the nineteenth century at St Mars by a standing wooden statue of 150cm.

At Bollène (another Belenus town?) on the southern Rhône, in more typical Black Virgin country, and its neighbouring parish of Mondragon, six kilometres away, with the chapel of St Aries half way between them, another agricultural Madonna, Notre-Dame des Plans, is vouched for as black by Drochon, Durand-Lefèbvre and Saillens, all giving somewhat different information about it. The parish priest, who was again helpful and friendly, showed me the ancient and famous statue of the Virgin and Child, with carved draperies in red, and natural complexions with no trace of blackness. He had never heard it called a Black Virgin.

Our Lady of the Hollies at Arfeuilles, a druidic centre, is also noted as black, ancient and interesting by all three authors as at Bollène. Drochon writes of the statue: 'One of the most interesting images which Christian art has bequeathed to us, she was formerly completely black.' Regretting that she had been whitened in the middle of the nineteenth century, he adds, though he has no special interest in Black Virgins: 'God preserve our churches from these ill-advised restorers.' When I visited the church in 1980, the elderly woman sacristan knew nothing of any Black Virgin, but remembered the statue, which was badly worm-eaten, being taken away in 1938 and returning refurbished, repainted and gilded. The same fate overtook Our Lady of the Thornbush, or of Life, at Avioth near the Belgian frontier, which

had certainly been black at one time. Like her sister of Arfeuilles,
she specialized in resuscitating dead babies so that they might be
baptised and gain admission to heaven, and, as at Arfeuilles, the
cult seems diminished since her blackness was purged. At Dijon I
was told by a newsagent that the priest will not permit the sale of
postcards of Our Lady of Good Hope, one of the most famous
and ancient of French Black Virgins, though now considerably
paler than of yore.

These few examples, among many, of clerical opposition to
Black Virgins leading to diminution of fervour, are in sharp
contrast to the almost ferocious exclusiveness with which the
faithful in some communities guard the secret of their, still black,
Madonnas. The curator of the castle museum at Le Barroux who
held the key to the hill-top chapel where the local Black Virgin
was reputed to be situated, rudely refused both the key and any
information as to the image's whereabouts. The remarkable
Black Virgin of Belloc has been transferred from her abandoned
mountain sanctuary to the village church of Dorres. The
proprietress of the adjacent hotel who holds the key said the
church was now never opened under any circumstances, except
during Mass, which was not a frequent occurrence as the priest
had to serve five parishes and a large mental hospital. It may be
that the theft of the Black Virgin of Nuria, the most famous of
the Pyrenees and only a few miles across the frontier, and that of
the ancient Madonna of St Martin du Canigou, has helped to fan
the flames of suspicious protectiveness throughout the region.

Few original statues are left in isolated chapels these days, in
which a growing epidemic of thefts is proving the greatest
scourge of Black Virgins since the French Revolution, and, when
they are still in existence, the sanctuaries are firmly sealed
against anyone seeking entrance or even a glimpse of the
interior. Our Lady of the Oak-Tree on the Col d'Arès near Prats-
de-Mollo has been removed from public veneration to the safe-
keeping of the presbytery, as has La Belle Briançonne, removed
from the chapel of St Etienne-des-Grès near Tarascon. Even
famous statues in the middle of towns are not immune to eclipse.
At Manosque, in Provence, home of Our Lady of the Brambles
and of Life, whom Durand-Lefèbvre describes as 'the doyenne of
our Black Virgins', and to whom Huynen brought renewed
publicity when he consecrated a whole chapter of his book to

her, the church has been closed for some years for repairs and no one seemed to know either when it would reopen or where the famous image could be seen. There were no postcards or photographs of it on sale in the town, and no local guide-books referring to it. It seemed as though Manosque's most celebrated inhabitant was already half forgotten, while the local authorities write that she is hidden and may not be seen. Some 30 miles away, in contrast, at the other end of the Lubéron range, the little Santo Vierge Négro of Goult-Lumières, who outshines as a wonder-worker the more flamboyant Lady of Light on the high altar, has been replaced by a copy since her theft in 1978, but continues to attract a fervent following, thanks to the devoted work of the nuns who keep the pilgrimage centre.

It seems then that a remarkable cultural survival of great mystery and antiquity is ironically in danger of disappearing from all but a few well-protected sites just at the moment when the attention of a wider public is being directed towards it. The Black Virgins of France that survived the fury of the Huguenots and the Revolutionaries are now being subjected to a three-fold process of attrition from thefts of uncertain motivation, the indifference and neglect of a sceptical age, and embarrassed suppression by the Church, often disguised as protectiveness. Why should the Church feel so sensitive about its Black Virgins?

The cult has inevitably suffered since the Second Vatican Council from the prevailing animus against 'non-historical orthodoxy' and in favour of biblical truth and simplicity of worship. But another reason for clerical lack of enthusiasm when faced with the enduring popularity of the Black Virgins may owe something, not merely to liturgical trends, but to suspicion of the sort of people who are attracted by the phenomenon. Joan of Arc, now raised to the altars, and safely dead for five and a half centuries, was not in her lifetime a favourite daughter of the Church, though her special devotion to Black Virgins would not have been viewed askance in her day. More recent devotees have, however, included the writers, Anatole France, noted for his mocking and ironical wit, often at the expense of orthodox religion, and J.-K. Huysmans, frequenter of magicians, who, before his conversion was notorious for his tales of debauchery and occultism including his sensational description of a black mass. Neither of these nor the elusive alchemist, Fulcanelli, author of *Le Mystère des Cathédrales*, are the sort of people calculated to allay clerical hesitancy towards Black Virgin fanciers, but there have been other examples which are even less reassuring.

Not far from Domrémy, birth-place of Joan of Arc, there rises from the plateau an impressive 500 metre high table mountain with a blunt peak at either end, whose name, Sion-Vaudémont, fortuitously links the mountain of the Lord to that of Wotan. Huynen states that, from the Middle Ages to the Revolution, a Black Virgin reigned there, though which of the various statues associated with the shrine he is referring to is not clear. What is certain is that Sion, 'La Colline Inspirée' of Barrès, has had an eventful history since St Gérard of Toul placed a statue of Mary on the mountain in 994, in place of pagan Rosmerta. Through the vicissitudes of life in a frontier province, Our Lady of Sion has remained the tutelary patroness of Lorraine.

A piquant page of the mountain's history involves one of the great religious scandals of the nineteenth century. In 1838 the three brothers Baillard, all priests, more or less simultaneously established houses of a new Catholic religious order, the Brothers of Christian Doctrine, on the two holy mountains of Alsace and Lorraine, Mount St Odile and Sion, which they had somehow managed to acquire. From 1843 they fell under the spell of a magus and mystagogue known variously as Michel Vintras, the French Jeremiah, Elias the Artist and the Organ. Vintras preached the advent of the Age of the Holy Spirit, long prophesied by Joachim of Flora, which would coincide with a redemption wrought by the Virgin Mediatrix and her pre-destined priestesses. In this new dispensation the greatest sacrament was the sexual act, through which the original androgyny would be restored. Thus, on the mountain of Rosmerta, the love-goddess, the sacred prostitution of the old high places and the orgiastic communion of licentious Gnostics were celebrated anew. Another devotion was that to Joan of Arc, the star pointing the way to the Marian dawn, the salvific one who would introduce the great monarch, the lily whose mission was to unite herself in love with the greatest of the saints. Despite international support and interest, which included, apparently, that of the House of Habsburg, bishops and police had their way, and with the suppression in 1852 of the Baillard establishment, the great experiment came to an end. During excavations that took place towards the end of the century, a bronze statuette of a hermaphrodite, well endowed with both sexual characteristics, was unearthed at Sion and placed in a museum in Nancy where it so scandalized the conventions of the period that it had to be withdrawn from public view.

Even without the assistance of the Baillard brothers and their successors, the attention of a rational and progressive age is being directed towards the archetypal feminine. Strange things do happen. For example, between 1928 and 1972, 232 apparitions of the Virgin attracted sufficient interest to be reported in the press and be investigated by the Church authorities. Since 1972 many more apparitions as well as statues of the Virgin that weep and move have been reported. As recently as 1982 and 1983 a pagan Black Virgin made according to ancient rites was venerated in the course of Druidic ceremonies at St Georges Nigremont. So, perhaps, despite the countervailing spirit of the age it is too early to close the chapter of odd events connected with the cult of the Virgin. But apart from those supernatural interventions in favour of the Marian cult in general, the story of the Black Virgin may also include a heretical secret with the power to shock and astonish even current post-Christian attitudes, a secret, moreover, closely involving political forces still influential in modern Europe. Small wonder if the Church's public attitude to the subject is one of extreme caution.

THE PRIEURÉ DE SION AND THE BLACK VIRGIN

That early images of the Madonna and Child were based on those of Isis and Horus is generally accepted. That the cult of the Black Virgin is essentially a product of the twelfth-century Gothic renaissance, which was a period of religious novelty as well as of faith, is also well established. The legendary origin of so many of the statuettes in the baggage trains of returning crusaders, especially when they happened to be Templars, is no guarantee of the orthodoxy of their cult. That many legends of the period connect the twelfth-century Black Virgins with an earlier miraculous origin dating from the Merovingian period raises potentially disquieting religio-political questions.

There exists in France an organization that has been in continuous existence since the twelfth century, that has some features both of an order of chivalry and of a religious order, though it is not quite either; a secret society which does not spurn the right sort of publicity; a political grouping with specific aims that is also interested in ancient esoteric wisdom and hidden mysteries. Its full name is the Order of the Prieuré Notre-Dame de Sion, and its chief aim seems always to have been the restoration of the Merovingian blood-line to the throne. It is also passionately concerned with the cult of the Black Virgin and has a remarkable record of equal rights for women. One of its female Grand Masters (or Helmsmen), Iolande de Bar (1428-83) lived at Sion-Vaudémont. A detailed account of the Prieuré is to be found in *The Holy Blood and the Holy Grail* by Baigent, Leigh and Lincoln.

Two other authors who have links with the Prieuré, Deloux and Brétigny, suggest that its predilection for the town of Blois as a meeting-place is due in part to the Black Virgin that was venerated there until the Revolution, an exemplar of the one 'who in the era that is drawing to a close is called the Virgin Mary and who remains the eternal Isis'. The authors print a photograph of the Black Virgin of Goult, which they call, in contradistinction to the local guide-book, 'Notre-Dame de Lumière', with the caption 'a Black Virgin particularly venerated by the initiates of the Prieuré of Sion'.

The Grand Master of the Prieuré 1981-4, Pierre Plantard, is reported as saying that the Sicambrians, ancestors of the Frankish Merovingians, worshipped Cybele as Diana of the Nine Fires, or as Arduina, the eponymous goddess of the Ardennes. The huge idol to Diana/Arduina which once towered over Carignan, in north-east France, between the Black Virgin sites of Orval, Avioth and Mezières, near to Stenay, where the Merovingian king and saint, Dagobert II, was murdered in 679, points circumstantially to a link between the two cults. In this connection Plantard mentions that one of the most important acts of Dagobert, when he acceded to the throne after his Irish exile, was to continue the ancient tradition of Gaul, the worship of the Black Virgin. The Black Virgin, he insists, is Isis and her name is Notre-Dame de Lumière.

Why this emphasis on Isis who was, after all, a universal

goddess of countless names? She identifies herself with Artemis of the Cretans and with Cybele when in the *Golden Ass* she tells Apuleius, 'For the Phrygians that are the first of all men call me The Mother of the Gods at Pessinus.' Only the Ethiopians 'of both sort, that dwell in the Orient and are enlightened by the morning rays of the sun, and the Egyptians, which are excellent in all kind of ancient doctrine and by their proper ceremonies accustom to worship me, do call me by my true name, Queen Isis.' But in Gaul, Isis was no more prominent as a universal goddess than Cybele or Artemis/Diana, who have as good a right to be considered precursors of the Black Virgin. May the reason for the Prieuré's insistence on the primacy of Isis not be the importance attached to some Egyptian connection? Victor Belot in *La France des Pélerinages*, referring to Sara, the black Egyptian servant who accompanied her mistresses to Les Saintes Maries de la Mer, writes: 'Sara will give birth to the cult of Black Virgins particularly venerated in certain places, although many authors prefer to leave this privilege to Isis, the Egyptian goddess.' These two possibilities are not, of course, mutually exclusive. In other words, Sara, beloved of the Gypsies, may also be an avatar of Egyptian Isis.

The most important of the three Marys to disembark at what was then still the Isle of Ratis, on whose acropolis Artemis, Isis and Cybele had been worshipped since the fourth century BC, was St Mary Magdalene, whose cult is intertwined with that of another repentant harlot, St Mary the Egyptian. Now, at Orléans, where there is an ancient cult of the Magdalen, St Mary the Egyptian was one of the titles of the Black Virgin. If there is some mystery linking Isis, Egypt, Mary the Egyptian, Mary Magdelene and the Black Virgin, in what way does it involve the Prieuré? Kings often claim illustrious ancestry: the Mikado is the son of Heaven; the British royal line is descended from the gods of the north and the heroes of Troy; the founder of the Ethiopian Empire was the son of the Queen of Sheba and Solomon. What more likely than that the French monarchy should outbid its rivals with an even more dazzling progenitor? According to Lacordaire, who re-established the Dominican Order in France after the Revolution, Louis XI, the most enthusiastic votary the Black Virgin cult has ever known, with attested visits, often repeated, to more than a score of her shrines, regarded Mary

Magdalene as one of the royal line of France. The pious author does not elaborate on this theme, but the secret tradition unearthed by the authors of *The Holy Blood and the Holy Grail* is that the Magdalen brought with her to Les Saintes Maries de la Mer, like a new Queen of Sheba, the fruit of her womb and of the loins of the King of Kings, Jesus Christ. Somehow, this new shoot from the Rod of Jesse became the founder of the Merovingians, though that honour is usually accorded to Mérovée (*c.*374-*c.*425), who was the son both of King Clodio and of a fabulous aquatic beast from beyond the seas. Such is the Holy Blood, and also the Holy Grail (*sang real*) which qualified the Bouillon-Boulogne family to accede by right to the throne of Jerusalem after the first Crusade.

THE SURVIVAL OF THE GODDESS

This is heady stuff, but even if one accepts it literally, as the Prieuré and other contemporaries evidently do, it is difficult to know what to do with the information. It may be that Nostradamus will be proved right and that we shall have to await the outcome of the next war for a new ruler of the ancient root to reveal himself and lead the way to a new order in Europe. But meantime the story is rich in symbolic significance for the travails of our age. Let us look at the history of religion for a moment through the symbols of astrology. At the beginning of the previous epoch, called the Age of Aries, the Ram succeeded the Bull as the sacrificial and symbolic animal. Abraham discovered a ram caught by its horns in a thicket and sacrificed it in place of his son Isaac. Towards the mid-point of the age, Moses, versed 'in all the wisdom of the Egyptians', led his people out of Egypt, received the new commandments on Mount Sinai, and destroyed the Golden Calf. At the beginning of the age of Pisces, Jesus, as the Lamb of God and only begotten son, reversed the process of Abraham's sacrifice by offering himself consciously in place of the animal holocausts in the Temple. Now, as in the calendar of the Platonic Great Year we approach the Aquarian age, something from the Piscean era of Christ, still unrealized and unrecognized, needs to be acknowledged to inaugurate the new dominant of consciousness that a tired world awaits. 'Out of Egypt have I called my son' (Matthew 2.15). Like Abraham and Moses, Jesus, too, sojourned in the land of Egypt whose name means black. If the evidence adduced by Desmond Stewart in *The Foreigner* is to be credited, then his sojourn may have been long indeed, lasting well into young manhood. The wisdom of the Egyptians that he imbibed in Alexandria would almost certainly have been that of syncretistic Gnosticism, for whose adherents it was no mere abstraction, but a personified, divine, feminine principle, which could be experienced. To the feminine, earthy, cyclical stability of Taurus there had succeeded the fiery masculine dynamism of Aries and the aggressive expansion of the great empires. With, finally, Rome's loss of impetus, and its infiltration by mystical, other-worldly religions from across the sea, including Christianity, the Piscean influence strongly affected all strata of society.

Two things happened to interfere with this process away from the maleness of Aries towards a more intuitive, feeling, 'yin' approach. One was Christianity's need to differentiate itself from the increasingly amorphous, syncretistic mood of Hellenism, and distance itself from rivals that at times seemed all too similar to it. The other was the historical accident, or intervention of the Holy Spirit, which led to a merger between the Roman imperium and the Christian ecclesia to form Caesaropapism and make of it both state religion and party line.

By the beginning of the Christian era the cult of the Olympian deities was in decline. Worship of Jupiter, as of Caesar, belonged to the official religion and had little power to stir the hearts of those who sought salvation and the assurance of immortality. The cult of the great goddesses, allied to Olympus for a while, but antedating it, retained its old prestige and fervour in many places. The mysteries of Demeter and Persephone at Eleusis greatly prospered under the Roman Empire, while from Ephesus to Marseilles the prerogatives of Artemis remained unassailable, even by St Paul.

Such evidence as exists suggests that, throughout the Celtic world, worship of the Triple Mother (Deae Matres) and of the Mare-Goddess, Epona, remained of considerable importance throughout the Roman ascendancy. Furthermore, the three great goddesses from the east, Isis, Cybele and Diana of the Ephesians, all on occasions represented as black, had already established themselves in the west in pre-Roman times. The Phocaeans, from their base at Marseilles, founded in 600BC, spread the fame of their patroness Artemis, a replica of the Ephesian, far and wide along the Mediterranean littoral from Antibes to Barcelona and beyond, as well as into the Gallic heartland of their allies the Arverni, and wherever their traders forged or followed the tin-routes. This Massiliot sphere of influence happens to correspond to those areas where the greatest concentration of Black Virgins is to be found.

But in the later centuries of the rule of Rome, it was the more exotic cults of Isis and Cybele that aroused the greatest enthusiasm and the largest congregations. The west welcomed the great universal goddess as a phenomenon neither alien nor imposed from without. Lyons, capital of the Three Gauls, was already the city of Cybele by the third century, while in Paris Isis reigned until St Genevieve took over her attributes as the new patroness of the city.

As late as the fourth century it must have seemed probable to a contemporary observer that, if the Empire survived, a religion of consensus would predominate based on the worship of the universal Great Mother and her son/consort, sacrificed for the salvation of many. Protestant critics of Rome were later to aver that, Empire or not, this was precisely what had occurred. But the Christian Church that Constantine established was, for various reasons, undergoing a strongly masculine phase. First, the courage it had displayed under the persecutions of Decius and Diocletian, which had so greatly impressed Constantine, called for the defiant steadfastness and simple faith of Christian soldiers in both its male and female martyrs, rather than subtler, gentler, more ambiguous qualities. It was, furthermore, with just such qualities that the Church, by creeds and definitions, had been at grips for two centuries in the form of Christian Gnosticism, ever elusive and diffuse in its quest for feminine wisdom and subjective, experiential truth.

The Church that emerged had many of the characteristics of a suddenly victorious resistance movement and was, all too humanly, unsympathetic towards former foes, fellow-travellers and those who had shown little stomach for the fight. It also inherited the Roman virtue of sound organization, based on a powerful central authority, and preserved by strict legalism. One consequence of Caesaro-papism was that failure to toe the party line became a new crime, called heresy, which was vigorously suppressed wherever possible. In the far corners of the Empire, however, such as Edessa, the headquarters of Syrian Christianity, home of the first Christian Church and the first icon, freer reign was given to the imagination. From that area stemmed the earliest version of the Assumption of Mary, and the first liturgy and hymns in her honour.

The Marian stream flowing from Edessa became a torrent when, at Ephesus in AD431, in the interests of deterring heresy as well as of honouring the Virgin, she was declared Theotokos, the Mother of God. This occurred in the home town of the first and greatest temple of Artemis, as well as of Mary herself in her last years.

Thus, in the Empire of the East, the hyperdulia accorded to Mary, a step short of the worship of God but superior to the veneration that is offered to the saints, perpetuated the preceding cult of Wisdom and the Great Mother. In AD438 the Empress Eudoxia sent to her sister-in-law the Empress Pulcheria an icon of the Virgin painted by St Luke, which, with the possible exception of a second-century mural from the catacomb of Priscilla in Rome, is the first recorded image of Our Lady. Pulcheria became an enthusiastic collector of relics pertaining to the Virgin and helped to set the fashion for holy images which flourished wherever Byzantium held sway, until the iconoclastic controversy of the seventh and eighth centuries caused a temporary set-back.

HISTORICAL SURVEY OF THE BLACK VIRGIN CULT IN THE WEST

Eudoxia's image became known as the Nicopoeion, Creator of Victory, and, indeed, under the sign of Mary, 'terrible as an army with banners', the old Empire of the East was to maintain its integrity against foes within and without for a further thousand years. In the west, however, a very different situation prevailed. In 410 Rome was sacked, and, within half a century, the Visigoths ruled from the Loire to Andalucia, with Franks to the north, Burgundians to the east and Vandals to the south.

Neither the Celts nor the Teutonic invaders had a strong ancient tradition of anthropomorphic deities worshipped in temples built with hands. Once the Roman influence had been withdrawn, it seems probable that most rural areas were content to revert to simpler ways, whether Christian or pagan. The well-organized Christian groups under their bishops, many of them powerful personalities, became the representatives of their communities, replacing the imperial bureaucracy as a possible body with whom the new rulers could treat. Monasticism, which started in the east, was, by the time of the invasions, well-established in Gaul thanks to such pioneering founders as St Martin (AD 360), St Honoratus (410) and John Cassian (406/415). It helped to preserve learning and civilization, provided a training-school for effective leaders and, as in the case of Cassian's twin foundation for men and women in Marseilles, underlined the role of women in the Church and provided a focus for the cult of the Virgin. At some point during the fifth century the temple of Isis at Soissons was rededicated to the Blessed Virgin, and, in 410, Cybele processed in her ox-cart for the last time through the streets of Autun. Le Puy was already consecrated to Mary by AD 225, though her first apparition there (AD 46/7) rivals that of Zaragoza (AD 40). The irruption of the Christian, though heretically Arian, Visigoths into Gaul accelerated the decline of paganism in the lands they controlled and the transition to the Christian Goddess.

It is to the Merovingian period (AD 500-750) that many of the Black Virgin shrines of France trace their origins. Our Lady of Boulogne sailed into the harbour standing in a boat with no sails or crew, but containing a copy of the Gospels in Syriac, while King Dagobert I was attending Sunday Mass. The legendary date for the consecration of the crypt is AD 46 but, in its present form, it was built by St Ida, mother of Godefroy de Bouillon, conqueror of Jerusalem and founder of the Prieuré, whose tomb is there. The Black Virgin Cult of Mauriac dates from 507, when Theodechilde, daughter of Clovis, first Christian king of the Franks, found, haloed by light in a forest clearing, a statuette guarded by a lioness and her cubs. Clovis met his queen, Clotilde, at Ferrières, the first Christian village in Gaul, where the cult of the Black Virgin had its legendary origin in AD 44. Not long after the destruction of church and town by Attila (AD

461), the Merovingian dynasty lavishly restored and augmented the cult, and its last reigning members made it their place of residence.

The ninth century was an important era for the cult of the Black Virgin. In 888, not long after the liberation of Barcelona, the little, dark Madonna of Montserrat was discovered by shepherds in the mountain cave where, long before, a Gothic bishop had hidden her from the Moors. At roughly the same period another Virgin, destined to become the patroness of her people, Our Lady of the Dark Forest, was carried up by St Meinrad to the Hermitage where the Abbey of Einsiedeln now stands. A monk of Mont St Michel, where Louis XI was to found his order of chivalry, visited the Holy Land in 867, where he would have been in a position to acquire sacred images, though it is possible that devotion to the statue of Our Lady of the Dead at Mont-Tombe in the crypt of the abbey church dates from even earlier. In 876 Charles the Bald transferred the chemise (*chainze*) of the Virgin from Aachen to Chartres, where the cult of a holy well 'of the strong', and of 'The Virgin Who Will Give Birth', Our Subterranean Lady, has been attributed to the Druidic era.

But the age, *par excellence,* of Our Lady, when she began to be venerated by that name, was inaugurated when the Crusaders, with a new marching song from Le Puy, the 'Salve Regina', on their lips, embarked on the mission entrusted to them at Clermont, of winning Jerusalem back for Christendom. To the battle cry of 'God wills it!', Godefroy de Bouillon's army stormed Jerusalem in 1099 and on his death shortly afterwards, his brother Baldwin was proclaimed first Latin king of the world capital of the three great religions known to the west. Some eighteen years later a small party of knights appeared, ostensibly charged with the task of patrolling the Jaffa-Jerusalem road and protecting pilgrims, though it seems doubtful that a mere nine cavalrymen, mounted, according to tradition, two to a horse to emphasise their poverty, would have proved an effective police force for this purpose. In fact, however, their mission seems to have been more enigmatic, since they were housed in a wing of the royal palace on the site of Solomon's Temple. This setting, which appears needlessly lavish for knights vowed to a life of penury, as well as unsound tactically as a highway patrol barracks, earned them their name, the Order of the Temple. The

2. Guadalupe

Temple, it has been speculated, was indeed what they had come to investigate, and the object of their quest nothing less than the Ark of the Covenant, the very presence of God that tabernacled with the Children of Israel during the years of Exodus from Egypt, placed by Solomon in the Holy of Holies at the heart of the Temple he built for it, and which, perchance, still lay hidden in the foundations after the ravages of Nebuchadnezzar and the Romans. Unless, as the Ethiopian tradition maintains, Solomon had already bestowed it on the son he shared with the Queen of Sheba. I once asked a member of one of the Orders which succeeded the Templars at their dissolution what was the symbolic meaning of the Black Virgin. He answered by another question: 'What did the Templars go to look for in Jerusalem?'

Another quest object and sacred container, unheard of before the twelfth century, but universally famous by the time of the massacre of Montségur, was the Holy Grail. In its first literary manifestation, the author, Chrétien de Troyes, makes a bizarre connection, generally attributed to ignorance or inadvertency, when, into this Celtic fable, he introduces the wife of Solomon. Wolfram von Eschenbach, in his slightly later version *Parzival* claimed as his source Kyot de Provins, a troubadour and apologist for the Templars. Curiously enough, the last earthly guardian of the Grail was Parzival's nephew, Prester John, a mysterious Priest-King, like Melchizedek of Jerusalem, whose realm included India and Ethiopia. He is yet another phenomenon of questionable tangibility to emerge from the twelfth century. He had, however, by 1177, achieved sufficient prestige and reality for Pope Alexander III to address him in a letter as 'King of the Indies, most holy priest'. Prester John had previously written (1165) to his friends, 'The Emperor of Rome and the King of France'; describing himself as 'by the grace of God, King over all Christian kings'. He tells of his capital, which has many of the features of a Grail castle, and of the strange fauna and flora of his country, including a pair of Alerions, the heraldic birds of the House of Lorraine which Godefroy of Bouillon substituted for the Merovingian bees on his escutcheon.

Of the two chief candidates in the west to be considered the Castle of the Grail, one is Montségur, site in 1244 of the last stand of the Cathars, those heretical champions of the religion of Amor against Roma and of the civilization of Oc against the barbarism of the north. The other is Montserrat, home of La Moreneta, where Wagner was inspired to compose his *Parsifal* and St Ignatius hung up his sword. Glastonbury, where, according to legend, St Joseph of Arimathea built in AD 63 the first church in Britain and dedicated it to the Virgin, has long been associated with the Holy Grail. Joseph arrived on these shores with 150 followers on a miraculous shirt (*chainze?*), while the remainder of his retinue, who had been unable to keep their vows of abstinence during the journey, crossed the Channel more prosaically on a ship built by King Solomon. A possible predecessor of St Joseph's as a proto-missionary was Aristobulus, a name famous in early Alexandrian syncretism, but better known to us as Zebedee, the husband of Mary Salome and the father of St James of Compostela, who, presumably after the voyage with them to Les Saintes Maries de la Mer, though his name does not feature on the passenger list, continued northward to bear the good news to this island.

ST BERNARD AND THE RELIGION OF OUR LADY

These were potent legends in their day, and if viewed as part of the history of ideas that have stirred the imagination of our ancestors and influenced their attitudes, rather than as concrete historical facts, they merit sympathetic understanding. A passionate longing is at the heart of the matter — something is lost that by the twelfth century desperately needs to be found. If it is the Holy Grail, then it is to Christians a secret about Christ's new commandment of love, expressed in His passion, crucifixion and resurrection, and his nourishing presence with those of pure heart who ask the right question. But, as a symbol, it is also at one with the magic cauldrons of Cerridwen and the Dagda in Celtic lore, with Medea's vessel of transformation and the pot in which Odin spirited away the mead that inspires poetry and wisdom.

If it is the Ark of the Covenant we seek, we must first turn to Moses, trained in the Egyptian mysteries, who kept within it the tables of the law, summation of the new dispensation, and some of the daily, supersubstantial bread of heaven that fed the Israelites in the wilderness. It also housed Aaron's magic wand, which, like the Rod of Jesse and Joseph of Arimathea's staff, contains within itself an ardent shoot (Plant-ard?), a spirit of spontaneous regeneration potential to matter, that has the power to burgeon at unexpected times and places. But we must look back, too, to the Ark of Noah in which life was preserved on Earth during the Flood, and, since in twelfth-century Latin the words are one, up to the arch in the heavens, which was the solution to the Flood, as well as forward to the pointed arch that was the wonder of that surprisingly named phenomenon, Gothic art. In or off the great nave-vessels of the Gothic churches and cathedrals, or in the crypts below, we find the statues of Our Lady in whose name all this beauty was created. It is especially when she appears in her black form, as a Virgin of the Crusades, that we should meditate on the title given her in the Litany of Loreto, *Arca foederis*, Ark of the Covenant, a motif underlined in the symbolism of Chartres Cathedral. Finally we might do well to cast a sideways glance, since riddlers and puzzlers delight in the subtle word-play, sometimes called green language, or the language of birds, at Arcas, the bear, doubly constellated in the heavens, attribute of Artemis, Arthur and Dagobert II, a fabulous beast, evocative of Arcadia and its sacred mysteries.

Amid all the legends and riddles of the twelfth century one historical character stands out as incomparably the most important figure of his day, who provides a golden thread through most of the themes of which we have been treating, St Bernard of Clairvaux. Born at Fontaines, said to have possessed its own Black Virgin, on the outskirts of Dijon, where the ancient Lady of Good Hope already reigned, he received while still a boy three drops of milk from the breast of the Black Virgin of Châtillon. Inspired by this, he took the ailing new Order of Cîteaux, reduced to a handful of monks, and turned it into a vast multinational enterprise of civilization, spanning Europe and making it prosper through hundreds of Abbeys from Russia to the furthest west, each one dedicated to Our Lady. In 1128 he wrote the rule of the Order of the Temple. Among the Templars' founder members were Bernard's uncle, André de Montbard and Hugues de Payen, first Grand Master of the Temple and of the Prieuré. The Templars, imprisoned and awaiting death in the Castle of Chinon after the coup of 1307, composed a prayer to Our Lady acknowledging Bernard to be the founder of her religion. In addition to the numerous hymns and sermons he addressed to her, he wrote about 280 sermons on the theme of the Song of Songs, the epithalamion of Solomon and the Queen of Sheba, whose versicle 'I am black, but I am beautiful, O ye daughters of Jerusalem', is the recurring refrain of the Black Virgin cult. Marina Warner hints that Bernard's visit to Rome inspired the mosaic in St Maria de Trastevere, the first in Rome for three centuries, in which the Virgin is shown as the beloved Shulamite from the 'Song of Songs', bride of Solomon and Christ. He encouraged the pilgrimage to Compostela, sometimes called the Milky Way, star-studded with Templar commanderies, Benedictine or Cistercian hostelries and churches of the Black Virgin. From one of the four great starting-points, Vézelay, centre of the cult of the Magdalen and subsequent Black Virgin site, he preached the Second Crusade. After his death, this holy lover of Our Lady acquired, on his canonization, the same feast day, 20 August, as St Amadour, founder of Rocamadour. Canonization makes some strangely appropriate bedfellows, as we shall see later, especially in Chapter 4.

St Bernard was familiar with the Cathars and their doctrines, having carried out an arduous and unsuccessful preaching campaign in their midst. He also had much respect for and interest in Islamic lore in spite of launching the Second Crusade. St Malachy, the last of the great Irish holy men of the Middle Ages to make their mark on Europe, to whom were attributed the celebrated prophecies concerning all future popes, was his close friend and died in his arms. Although it is not explicit in his writings, it is plausible to deduce from his actions that Bernard cherished the vision of a new world order based on the three pillars of the Benedictines, the Cistercians and the Templars, under a King of Kings. Thus the theocratic ideal of Godefroy de Bouillon would have found fulfilment.

But in this monk, extraversion was always balanced by spiritual inwardness, and the divine harmony, potential within each individual, interested him no less than the affairs of Church and State. In this age of the troubadours and the courts of love Bernard could be seen as the first troubadour of Our Lady, whose favours he had received and whose image he carried in his heart. In this he was reverting to the tradition of a major source of troubadour poetry, Sufism, in which the beloved is symbolic and spiritual. In the west, La Dame, although physically real, was also the inspiring glorious presence, leading the lover along the path and protecting him in danger. She is Goethe's 'eternal feminine' and the muse of all true poets. Denis de Rougemont, the author of *Passion and Society*, surmises that La Dame is the anima, the spiritual part of man, the archetypal content which, according to Jung, may be the messenger of the Grail, linking a man to the inner journey of the individuation process. John Layard attests that Bernard, who at times seems almost possessed by the positive anima, had also a remarkable psychological understanding of her negative repressed aspect when he describes 'Eve within the soul', as 'that lady who lies at home paralysed and grievously tormented'.

Neither the cult of the Black Virgin nor the art of the troubadours died with the twelfth century, but the new flowering of the feminine principle to which it had given birth suffered a deadly blow. Rome allied itself with the King of France and the mercenary barons of the north to unleash against the heartland of southern civilization the Albigensian Crusade. Much more than Catharism withered in the ensuing blight: the courts of the inquisition replaced the courts of love; so-called heretics, men and women, were tortured and massacred; and, when the inquisitors' original victims were no more, they turned their attention to so-called witchcraft to fuel their fires for another half millennium. The mantle of courtesy passed from Languedoc to Italy as the terrible fourteenth century brought the slander and destruction of the Templars, the Hundred Years War and the Black Death.

The witch pyres of Europe were extinguished late in time by the cold douche of the Age of Reason. Less cruel and murderous than the age of superstition, it was hardly less inimical to all that is meant by the feminine principle. The revolutionary devotees of what they called the Goddess Reason were at one with their high-minded Protestant predecessors in seeing the little Black Virgins as an archetypal opposite to all they stood for, a symbol older and more formidable than King or Pope, of that elemental and uncontrollable source of life, possessing a spirit and wisdom of its own not subject to organization or the laws of rationality. In the nineteenth century, popular enthusiasm broke through the encrusting intellectual superiority of the clerisy in the direct experience of Our Lady manifest at Lourdes, La Salette, rue du Bac and Knock. This wave of devotion reanimated the ancient devotion to the Black Virgins, many of which were solemnly crowned by authority of the Pope during the period 1860-90. The twentieth century has witnessed further apparitions, some, like those of Fatima, Banneux and Beauraing, authorized as genuine cults by the Church, others, like Garabandal and Zeitoun, blossoming as unofficial roses.

Synchronous with these archetypal phenomena, whether they are viewed as hysterical mass hallucinations or as psychic realities, the most striking and influential sociological development of the past century in the west has been the sexual revolution — the emancipation of women through education, equal rights, divorce, birth-control, legal abortion and greater freedom of sexual choice. Such liberty, not unknown to the Celtic women of old, was repressed during the Christian era, and has had to struggle to re-emerge in the teeth of opposition by the Church.

The return of the Black Virgin to the forefront of collective consciousness has coincided with the profound psychological need to reconcile sexuality and religion. She has always helped her supplicants to circumvent the rigidities of patriarchal legislation and is traditionally on the side of physical processes — healing the sick, easing the pangs of childbirth, making the milk flow. She knows how to break rigid masculine rules, bringing dead babies back to life long enough to receive baptism and escape from limbo to paradise, looking with tolerance on the sins of the flesh as when she acts as midwife to a pregnant abbess or stands in for a truant nun tasting for a time the illicit pleasures of sin. Politically, she is in favour of freedom and integrity, the right of peoples, cities and nations to be inviolate and independent from outside interference. Nowhere is this more evident than in the history of the Queen of Poland, the Black Madonna of Czestochowa.

CHAPTER 1
The influence of the east

There can be no sure historical beginning to our story. The wheel, whether it be spun by Hindu Maya, Roman Fortuna, British Arianrhod or Christian Catherine of Alexandria, revolves in endless cycles between Yin and Yang. In spinning a tale, however, one must start somewhere, with a 'once upon a time', with a something that happened 'in illo tempore'. Once upon a time men, carried away by technological hubris and over-weening aggression against the heavens, constructed Babel. Excessive Yang provoked the Yin of the great waters and the one-sidedness was swept clean. Life re-emerged with a raven and a dove from the ark of the coupling, a rainbow linked the opposites, and the first wine was made. Once upon a time there were small townships that depended on horticulture. They were replaced by cities dependent on intensive farming to feed them and on great armies to defend them. Once upon a time Gilgamesh and Enkidu cut down the tree of the great goddess, and restless peoples from the north and east, Aryan followers of the headstrong ram, slew the bull of heaven and subjugated its mistress to their male deities, although never wholly.

Yet, if there is no beginning, there is at least a text — and a biblical one — which catches the spirit and essence of our story: 'I am black but beautiful' (Song of Solomon 1.5). Who is the beloved who sings this refrain to her lover? All we are told of her is that she is a Shulamite, that is, one who has found peace, perhaps the counterpart of Solomon whose name also contains the word 'shalom'. Jerusalem is the city of peace where Solomon built his Temple for the Shekinah, the feminine, indwelling, glorious presence of God, and Jerusalem will be the bride of Christ at the consummation of the aeons. Undoubtedly the black beauty is the Lady Anima, who has stimulated the fantasies and aroused the projections of men throughout the centuries. The stern moralists and champions of scholarly orthodoxy, Bernard and Aquinas, who both cast out nature with a pitch-fork in youth, devoted their most fervent later meditations to the love story of the dark lady. Sometimes she is Pharaoh's daughter, the wisdom of the Egyptians, but more often she is seen as Solomon's most famous lover, the Queen of Sheba, who came to try him with hard questions. Sheba can mean 'seven', i.e. the planets, or 'oath', a solemn vow or covenant witnessed and enforced by the heavenly powers. It is also the realm of the Sabeans, a people early synonymous with astrologers and later with Gnostics, whom Islam tolerated, along with Jews and Christians, as one of the peoples of the book. Jesus refers to her favourably (Matthew 12.42) as the Queen of the South who will rise up to condemn unbelievers at the Last Judgment. The Queen of the South is also the title of the Countess of Toulouse, city whose Black Virgin, La Daurade, was originally the goddess of wisdom, Pallas Athene. Meridiana, a noon-day enchantress from the warm south, seduced Gerbert of Aurillac (qv) and gave him such wisdom that he became the most learned man of his age, Pope of the year 1000, the first Frenchman to sit on the throne of Peter.

Differing accounts exist of the Queen of Sheba's true country. In one version the hoopoe, who taught Solomon the language of birds, described a wonderful land of which he knew nothing, the only part of the world not under his control. In the Qu'ran (Sura 27) Solomon learns that a woman reigns over this people, possessed of every virtue and of a splendid throne, but who worship the sun rather than Allah. He invites this Queen to visit him and she arrives at Sion accompanied by a camel-train laden with unparalleled riches in gold, spices and precious stones. Solomon is, however, suspicious of his guest's credentials: if she is a djinn she will have hairy legs like a wild-ass or a wild-goat. He therefore arranges for her to approach him in a room with a glass floor so that he can see under her skirts. In another version, he sits on the far side of a stream to see if she will use the bridge made of the wood of the true Cross. The Queen recognizes it, not surprisingly, since, in an earlier incarnation, it had been the tree of paradise and she the serpent, so she wades instead across the water, hoisting her skirts to reveal what Solomon wanted to see, her hairy legs. Neither of them seems much put out and Solomon restores the limbs to pristine comeliness by means of a special depilatory he has prepared. It would seem then that Solomon did not find her and the particular religious tradition she represented altogether unacceptable, a tolerance which accords with his reputation of introducing foreign ways into Israel.

In the Kebra Nagast, the Ethiopian 'Book of the Glory of the Kings' (c.13th century), the founder of the Ethiopian dynasty is named as Menelek ('son of the wise'), offspring of Solomon and the Queen of Sheba. (This tradition is enshrined in the Ethiopian constitution of 1955 which states that Haile Selassie was a direct descendant of Menelek.) The Queen's name here is Makeda, 'the fiery one', which might link her to that fiery, hirsute, wandering star, the comet (='hairy' in Greek). It was such a star that led the Magi, like the sons of Noah returning to the Ark, along with 'all from Saba' (Mass for Epiphany), to Mary, the new Ark of the Covenant who first displayed the precious content of her womb to the world in Bethlehem at Epiphany. In the Middle Ages the Magi were known as the Three Kings of Cologne, city of Roman, Celt and Teuton, where two Black Virgins reign. Since 1355 one of the Kings has been traditionally represented as Black. According to Michel Tournier the Black King is Caspar, the monarch of Sudanese Meroë (Mérovée?) the bearer of gold whose name means 'the white one'. More often the black Magus is considered to be Melchior, 'king of light', whose gift is myrrh, signifying entombment. Epiphany is also the feast of St Melanius, 'the black', a fifth-century Celt from Brittany, and the only saint of this name in the calendar.

The Queen of Sheba, in a legend from the borders of Ethiopia and Eritrea, was a Tigre girl known as Eteye Azeb ('queen of the south') who was tied half-way up a tree as an offering to a dragon. Seven saints, resting under the tree, alerted to her presence by tears falling on them, rescued her and slew the dragon by means of the Cross. She returned to her village where she was elected chief and chose another young woman as her deputy. But some dragon's blood had splashed her heel transforming it into that of an ass. She set off with her lieutenant to be healed by King Solomon, after which the story follows much the same course as the other versions except that she gives birth to Menelek, on whom his father, Solomon, bestows the Ark of the Covenant. In one variation of the saga from the

Christian west, Queen Sibylla, as she is called, the ancestress of all magicians, has the webbed foot of a water-fowl rather than a hoof. In this she resembles La Reine Pédauque, identified with Charlemagne's mother, the Merovingian princess, Bertha of the Big Foot. She conceived him between Liesse, home of the favourite Black Virgin of the French monarchs, and Laon (qv), where there is a Black Virgin and a statue of the Eritrean sybil who prophesies the end of the world. There, too, a phial of the Virgin's milk was venerated until 1789. Pépin le Bref later married Bertha in order to legitimize his usurpation of the throne. Other authorities have traced La Reine Pédauque's origins to Austris, 'south wind', wife of Euric, the Visigothic ruler of Toulouse, in whose church of the Black Virgin, La Daurade, she was buried. She is associated with a bridge, a subterranean aqueduct and a magic distaff, one of the symbols of Athene.

The distaff, sign of practical feminine wisdom, is woman's magic wand of transformation in that almost alchemical process, the production of linen from flax. The third of the riddles posed by the Queen of Sheba to Solomon had as its answer the word 'flax'. The mid-day demoness of the Wends, Pripolniza, appeared in the fields between midday and two o'clock to subject any people still foolish enough to be abroad to a searching examination on the cultivation of flax and the weaving of linen, punishing those who failed by cutting off their heads and carrying them away with her. Similar tales are told of the Pshesponiza of the Spreewald, near Berlin, and the Serpolnica of the Serbs. Freyja, too, from her name Horn, is a flax-goddess. Quite possibly two of the suggested prototypes of La Reine Pédauque, Bertha of the Big Foot and Bertha of Burgundy, tenth-century Queen of France, have become confused with the Teutonic mother-goddess, one of whose attributes was the distaff. De Sède suggests that the confusion between Bertha and the Reine Pédauque may stem from the punning association of Bertha and 'bertel', the word for a distaff in the language of Oc. The pun-language of birds familiar to Solomon through the hoopoe, who was the Queen of Sheba's father, was rediscovered by the troubadors of Toulouse. They would have appreciated the similarity between La Reine Pédauque, the queen with the goosefoot, and La Reine du Pays d'Oc. They would also have noted Reine de Saba, *reino sabo* (wise queen).

This queen of many disguises has had an extensive mythology within the Christian epoch. It may just be an amusing coincidence that the spirit of Epiphany in Germany is known as Frau Bertha, who has very large feet and an iron nose, a nursery demoness who lulls good children to sleep, but is the terror of the badly behaved. In England, the morrow of the Epiphany used to be known as St Distaff's Day or Rock Day, after an old name for the distaff. Marie-Louise von Franz identifies her with Maria the Jewess or Prophetess, the greatest woman alchemist. Honorius of Autun (early twelfth century) in his commentary on the Song of Solomon sees the Queen of the South as a figure of the Church which is the queen and concubine of Christ. To complete the equation, St Gregory the Great (540-604) relates the south and its wind to the unseen orders of angels and the heat of the Holy Spirit. A link is thus forged between the Queen of the South, the Queen of Sheba, the black Shulamite of the Song of Solomon and Maria the Alchemist. In a later chapter the connection between this underground stream of the repressed goddess and the cult of Mary Magdelene, whom the Gnostics saw as the lover of Christ, and the Black Virgin will be fully considered. In the camarín of the Black Virgin of Guadalupe, the Statue of Miriam, Moses' sister, is called Maria Prophetissa.

In her various forms, the figure we are discussing has always been a favourite of writers. Anatole France's alchemical novel is called *La Rôtisserie de la Reine Pédauque*. In Flaubert's *Temptation of St Antony* the Queen of Sheba represents luxuria, the deadly sin of lust (Venus, goddess of love, rides a goose and is drawn in a swan-chariot). A comparable image is to be found in the writings of Gérard de Nerval (1808-55), the troubadour of the anima and of the disconsolate Prince of Aquitaine whose tower has been destroyed. His fatal obsession with Aurélia gives a remarkable impression of the quality of this figure. He tells of 'the Queen of the South, such as I saw her in my dreams . . . crowned with stars, in a turban sparkling with the colours of the rainbow . . . her face is olive-tinted . . . one foot is on a bridge, the other on a wheel . . . one hand rests on the highest rock of the mountains in the Yemen, the other stretched out to the heavens holds . . . the flower of fire . . . the celestial serpent opens its maw to seize it . . . the Sign of the Ram appears twice in the zodiac, which reflects the face of the Queen as in a mirror, a face which takes on the features of St Rosalie . . . she appears, crowned with stars, ready to save the world . . . on the peak of the highest mountain of the Yemen a wonderful bird is singing in a cage . . . it is the talisman of the new ages . . . Leviathan with black wings flies heavily around . . . beyond the sea there rises another peak on which is written this name: Mérovée.' Nerval hanged himself from a lamp-post at dawn on 26 January 1855, with the manuscript of *Aurélia,* it is said, in his pocket. In 1862 Gounod produced an opera *The Queen of Sheba* based on this story.

Christianity reached Ethiopia in apostolic times when Philip the Deacon converted and baptised the eunuch-treasurer of Queen Candace (Acts 7.26-39). Candace seems to have been the title of the Queens of Ethiopia in Hellenistic times, as well as the name of a Queen of Tarsus who seduced Alexander the Great into a life of sloth, or accidie. This is one of the afflictions meted out by Meridiana, the noonday demoness. Candace is another manifestation of the Queen of Sheba archetype. As Nerval knew, her true country, in so far as it has a local habitation and a name, is neither Ethiopia nor Egypt but the Yemen, the Saba where flax was grown and gold abounded. Near the ancient capital of Marib stood the great shrine of Mahram Bilquis, one of the most strongly fortified sites of southern Arabia, probably designed by Phoenician architects between the eleventh and ninth centuries BC, when they also were building the Temple of Jerusalem. This seems to have been the Temple of the moon god Ilmuqah who, though masculine, is the same as the goddess Ishtar, and the Queen of Sheba, locally known as Bilqis/Balqis. Charles Nodier, Grand Master of the Prieuré de Sion and mentor of de Nerval, wrote of her as Belkiss in *La Fée aux Miettes.* His disciple, closest friend and successor as Nautonier of the Prieuré, Victor Hugo, called her by the name under which she is now presenting herself to the world, Lilith.

LILITH

Considering her successful literary career, Lilith remains surprisingly little known to the educated public. Alfred de Vigny, another friend of Nodier's, writes of her as the spirit of night, Adam's mistress, the rival and enemy of Eve and her children. Victor Hugo makes of her Satan's eldest daughter, the black soul of the world, the great woman of the shadow, the savage and eternal blackness of night, who is fate and Isis. Lilith and Isis have in common their knowledge of the secret name of God. Anatole France, the ironist and admirer of Black Virgins, who wrote a two-volume life of Joan of Arc, included among his novels *Thaïs*, the story of the repentant whore of Egypt who became a saint, and, in 1889, *La Fille de Lilith*. D. G. Rossetti tells of her vengeance on Adam and Eve, and Goethe finds a place for her in his description of Walpurgisnacht. She appears in Shaw's *Back to Methuselah* and as Sabine/Lily in *The Skin of Our Teeth* by Thornton Wilder, played seductively on the London stage by Vivien Leigh. Berg's opera *Lulu* and Wedekind's *Pandora's Box*, on which it is largely based, are both inspired by the myth of Lilith and her repression. George MacDonald's *Lilith* presents a faithful portrait of the archetype. Anaïs Nin consecrated one of her erotic tales in *Delta of Venus* to a character called Lilith. In films, Lilith has been played by Jean Seberg and Marianne Faithfull (in *Lucifer Rising*).

Who then is this figure who has come to stand for feminine rebellion against masculine denial of woman's right to freedom and equality? The earliest known portrait of her, dating from c.1950 BC, is the terra-cotta Burney relief in the British Museum. In it she is depicted as a beautiful, winged, naked woman with the feet of a bird (a cock, thought the cabbalists), standing on two lions and flanked by a pair of owls, with an ephah, for measuring grain, in her hand. Her turban is somewhat reminiscent of that of the Black Virgin of Meymac and her hands are raised hieratically to shoulder height.

As 'the hand of Inanna', the task of the young maiden Lilith in Erech was to gather men from the streets and bring them to the temple of the goddess. But she is best known as one of the Sumerian demons of storm and night. Her main function seems to have been that of a vampirish succuba. Originally her nest was in the middle of the Huluppu tree — probably a willow — a position later much favoured by Black Virgins. Like Wotan's Yggdrasil, Lilith's tree had a dragon at its base and a bird

3. Meymac

perching on top. The hero Gilgamesh, though his own father may have been a Lillu-demon, killed the dragon and cut down the tree, obliging the now homeless Lilith to flee into the wilderness. A seventh-century tablet from Syria shows her as a winged sphinx, a creature notorious for its riddles but in this case evidently more to be feared as a killer of new-born infants. It was above all in this role that she was most redoubted by the Jews from the eighth century BC, though she was also well-known as a seductive — and destructive — nocturnal temptress. Her main threat to Orthodox Judaism may have been the recurrent temptation to the cult of the goddess.

The explanation for such behaviour had to await an eleventh-century cabbalistic document, 'The Alphabet of Ben Sira'. According to this tradition, the first man and woman were created simultaneously from the same substance, with equal rights as the primal androgynous being, joined together at the rear. A conflict arose as to the best position to adopt during sexual intercourse. Lilith resented Adam's pretensions to superiority and her consequent relegation to a passive, supine role. In her despair she invoked the ineffable name of Yahweh, and was forthwith granted wings with which she flew from the paradise that had become her prison. Three angels were sent to recapture her, but she remained obdurate. She was sentenced to give birth to innumerable progeny, of which one hundred would perish daily. Crushed at the cruelty of the punishment, she cast herself into the Red Sea, at which the angels, pitying her sorrow, accorded her power over all new-born babies, for eight days in the case of boys and for twenty in the case of girls, while children born out of wedlock would be permanently at her mercy. Any infant protected by an amulet bearing the names of the angels would be immune from her attentions. Powers of life and death over new-born babies are attributed to many Black Virgins.

After the death of Abel, Adam abstained from Eve for 130 years, during which time he received the secret visits of Lilith. One of their offspring conceived during this period was a wise frog who taught the languages of men, animals and birds as well as the healing properties of herbs and precious stones. By the middle of the thirteenth century, when the cult of the Black Virgin was well-established, the vindication of Lilith reached the point where a Spanish cabbalist described her as 'a ladder on which one can ascend to the rungs of prophecy'. In the sixteenth-century cabbala she is seen covered with hair from head to foot, like Mary Magdalene, Mary the Egyptian and other repentant harlots, leading her band of demonesses in wild, sardana-like round-dances.

Repressed gods take their captors captive. Both Lilith and, as we shall see, Wotan, insinuate themselves into the cults that succeed them. Thus Lilith, from being an abhorred demoness, becomes the bride of Yahweh, the spirit of the diaspora, after the destruction of the Temple. In a notable case of divine wife-swapping, Lilith, wife of Samael/Satan, changes places with the Matronit, consort of Yahweh. In the contrast between Lilith and Matronit we might perhaps see a parallel with the opposing pairs, Mary, Queen of Heaven, and Mary Magdalene; White Virgin and Black Virgin; Church and Synagogue; orthodoxy and heresy. As goddess of the underground religious stream, Lilith fostered the development of the cabbala in Saracen Spain: the cabbala flourished mightily during Israel's sojourn there and fecundated the nascent mysticism of the Christian — and not so Christian — west.

Lilith has no mention in the Authorized Version of the Bible. In Isaiah 34.14 she appears as a screech-owl, a name still given to the witches of Italy and Switzerland, which is amended in the Revised Standard Version as 'night-hag', though the Septuagint, more familiar with such creatures, calls her 'Lamia'. The French Jerusalem Bible, in addition to the Isaiah references, has Lilith (Job 18.15) dwelling in the tent of the wicked. She appears also in the Bible in a number of other forms under other names. Of her identity with the Queen of Sheba in the cabbala, the Zohar and Arabic legends, there is no doubt. She is also associated with the concubine of Abraham, Hagar 'the Egyptian', whose son, Ishmael, having been begotten on the Black Stone of the Ka'aba, became the ancestor of the Arab peoples. It was Lilith and her companion, Naamah, who elicited the famous judgment of Solomon over the child whose ownership they disputed. One of her incarnations was no doubt Moses' first desert wife, Zipporah ('female bird'), and perhaps even his second, called 'the Ethiopian woman', whose dusky beauty distinguished her from other women. When asked by her father Jethro who had rescued her (Exodus 2. 19-20), Zipporah flew to the well and returned with Moses in her talons. Like Wisdom, possessed from of old by the Egyptians and the Children of the East, she dwelt at the bottom of the sea. Another Lilithian sea-creature, Rahab the Harlot, whose family wrought fine linen and who had lain with all the rulers of the world, married Joshua. She thus became ancestress of eight priests and prophets including Hulda the prophetess, which also happens to be one of the names of the Teutonic goddess of the underworld and of witches. Lilith even succeeded in seducing the prophet Elijah without his knowledge, and had a child by him. This may link her to the Shunamite woman, who alone knows the hiding-place of the invisible spirit of Elijah on Mount Carmel, where he waits for a second coming like Arthur and Barbarossa. The Order of Our Lady of Mount Carmel, founded on the mountain in 1154 by St Berthold and a group of Frankish hermits, claims continuity with and spiritual descent from Elijah and the sons of the prophets. Carmelite churches are not infrequently associated with the cult of the Black Virgin.

It is not only in the Jewish esoteric tradition that Lilith sometimes appears in a favourable light. The Gnostic Mandaeans, whose origins are not Christian but stem from John the Baptist, and who have practised their religion uninterruptedly for two thousand years in the swamps of the Tigris-Euphrates delta, know of her from their sacred book, the Ginza. In it Lilith-Zahriel is the daughter of the King and Queen of the Underworld whom they give in marriage to the King of Light, Manda d'Hayye ('knowledge of life'), the personification of Gnosis, or to his son. As a dowry to this marriage of heaven and hell, Lilith brings a magic mirror, a crown and a pearl. She instructs her husband in the secrets of darkness and presents him with a son who combines the wisdom of both realms. When Kushta, the way incarnate, tests him with hard questions, the son defends his mother against charges of being a child-stealing demoness to reveal her as a beneficent spirit who comes to the help of women in labour, sitting on their bed to comfort them.

Lilith has other, less direct, links with John the Baptist in the surprising setting of the Pyrenees, through the characters in the New Testament who most resemble her, Salome and her mother, Herodias. After they had engineered the execution of John, they were exiled along with Herod the Tetrarch, according to Josephus, to Ludgdunum (Convenarum) 'near Spain', now St Bertrand de Comminges (qv). Salome drowned while crossing a frozen river, but Herodias lived on in legend to become identified in the Middle Ages with Diana Nocticula, or Noctiluca, queen of the night-hags. She led her covens to midnight sabbaths where children were sacrificed in fields of wild flax, to be devoured, regurgitated and replaced in their cradles. Perhaps Salome and Herodias are the two Ethiopian maids of the Virgin Mary, Tarbis and Lorda, who founded the cities of Tarbes and Lourdes. Their memory may also have inspired the tradition of a Queen of Ethiopia who, defeated in a war with Moses, fled to exile by the waters of the Adour. According to yet another tale, Lourdes derived its name from the Arab commander of the last stronghold north of the Pyrenees to hold out against Charlemagne. In 778, Rorice II, Bishop of Le Puy (qv), persuaded the general, Mirat, to accompany him on a pilgrimage to the Black Virgin of Mt Anis, where he was baptised Lorus and made governor of the citadel, now renamed Lourdes in his honour.

Lilithian traditions seem to have lingered on in the Pyrenees until the twentieth century. Denis Saurat relates in *La Religion des Géants* that, as recently as 1900, groups of eight to ten girls, roaming in the mountains of the Haute-Ariège, would seize and overpower any unknown young man they chanced upon and use him for their amorous purposes until they decided to release him. Black Pyrenean fairies had a similar reputation.

LAMIAS AND SPHINXES

With the advent of the patriarchy, the dethroning of the great goddesses occurred throughout the ancient world. There are, therefore, many parallels, western and eastern, in addition to those already mentioned, to the negative, raging, demoniac Lilith. Lamia, the name used for her in the Septuagint version of the Bible, was originally a bisexual Libyan queen, daughter of Belus, beloved by Jupiter, who was robbed of her children by jealous Juno. The only offspring who survived was the sea monster, Scylla, guardian of the Straits of Messina, who could devour six men at a time through the wolves' heads that formed her loins. Lamia's own name means both 'gluttonous' and 'lecherous'. Lamia was probably the Libyan version of the Egyptian goddess, Neith, similar to Athene and Anath. She joined a gang of Empusas, shrieking bogey-women who ate their lovers, though retaining her own speciality of enticing and devouring young children. Libya was the early Greek name for the continent of Africa, and the Libyan Sibyl, depicted with her sisters on the marble floor of Siena Cathedral, is the only one shown as black. Lamias later became a separate species, beautiful women who were serpents from the waist down, and in the Middle Ages were synonymous with witches. Keats's poem *Lamia* describes how one such creature returned Melusine-like to her serpent form on her wedding night. That Lamia was also able to bestow wisdom is suggested by her power to pluck out and replace her eyes at will like the triple Graiae whose eye enabled Perseus to find Medusa. Robert Graves observes in this connection that her removable eyes 'may be deduced from a picture of the goddess about to bestow mystic sight on a hero by proffering him an eye.'

Of the various composite monsters in the ancient world known as sphinx (=strangler), that of Egypt was a symbol of Ra's kingship. Later sphinxes were female or hermaphrodite riddlers with animal attributes who carried off boys and youths to satisfy their lust or, like Valkyries, hovered round the scene of fatal combats. Lilith herself is shown as a mixture of wolf, lion and scorpion. Sirens, Rhine-maidens, mermaids, undines, nixies, the fairy Melusine and other water-nymphs tempt voyagers from their path and underline the fatality of desire. Gorgons and basilisks kill at a glance. The Harpies, fierce, starved-looking winged demonesses, of whom one is called 'Darkness', are, like Lilith, associated with storms and pollute everything they touch, emitting an atrocious stench, while the Furies, daughters of earth, pursue men vengefully and drive them mad. There are many dragons, dracs, wouivres (wyverns, vipers), including the Tarasque (cf. Tarascon) and the Graouly (cf. Metz) as well as the lizards of Moulins and Paris, to be found near to Black Virgin sites. They generally symbolize pagan religion and particularly the presence of a goddess and priestesses.

INANNA

To become acquainted with the goddess before she was demoted and demonized, we must return to the writings of the third millennium BC, in that cradle of civilization that was Sumeria. There Inanna was an universal goddess of the heavens, fertility, war, justice, sexual love and healing, whose throne was the world-tree and who bestowed the kingship on the mortal of her choice. When the hero, Gilgamesh, cut down her tree, and the sky-god, Enlil, dispossessed her, she became a homeless wanderer, like Lilith, the Shekinah of the exile, and like Jesus himself.

The bird has its nesting place, but I — my young are dispersed.
The fish lies in calm waters, but I — my resting place exists not,
 The dog kneels at the threshold, but I — I have no threshold.

Surely Matthew 8.20 echoes this: 'Foxes have holes, and birds of the air have nests; but the Son of Man has nowhere to lay his head.' Inanna's resemblance to the Christian saviour does not end here. She descended into hell to attend the funeral of the raging bull of heaven, her instrument for terrorizing the earth. In the underworld she was stripped, humiliated, whipped and hung on a peg. On the third day the deities of the upper world became aware of her plight and Enki, the god of waters and wisdom, engineered her release. When she returned to the world of light she had assimilated something of the power of Ereshkigal, the queen of the dead, who may represent Inanna's own occult qualities. One of these powers was that of killing with a glance. In psychological terms this motif may denote the quality of objective discrimination so essential to a woman's integration of her masculine element.

KALI

Inanna is the precursor of Ishtar, Astarte, Aphrodite, and Venus, goddesses whose powers are more specialized than hers. All now belong to the archaeology of myth, save the Venus of astrology. There is one contemporary of Inanna's still active today, however, who retains her awesome cultic power, and that is Kali, goddess of time. The Aryan invaders of north-west India no doubt encountered dark goddesses among the Dravidians of the Indus Valley, whose advanced civilization may have been related to that of the Sumerian Chaldaeans. It now seems probable that reed ships plied between Mesopotamia and India from the beginning of this period, so it would not be surprising if some cross-cultural, iconographical similarities should exist between Indian goddesses and those of the Middle East. One of Kali's names, as the first manifestation of being, is Lalita and Lilith returns the compliment when she acknowledges that Kali is one of her fourteen names. The philological evidence relates the Lilith stem to words of licking, swallowing, lechery and darkness, all consistent with the myth of Kali. Dark, sensuous lilac is derived from the Persian word for midnight blue indigo, itself an import from the Indus. It may carry echoes of the Hindu goddess Lila, whose name means 'play', consort of the blue Vishnu as Narayana, the primal being, moving in the waters.

According to Plutarch, there is also a mountain in India called Lilaeus which produces a black stone known as clitoris, with which the inhabitants of the country adorn their ears (see Pertoka p.25).

NEITH

The most direct influence on the cult and image of the Black Virgin derives without doubt from three goddesses of the ancient Near East, Isis, Cybele and Diana of the Ephesians, but because their influence came through the all-pervading universalism of the later Roman Empire, they will be discussed in the next chapter. There is, however, another goddess from Egypt, who conveys many of the qualities that are inherent in the essential significance of the Black Virgin. Neith was the oldest and wisest of the goddesses, to whom the gods themselves appealed for judgment. Originally the war goddess of Sais, she also presided over the useful arts, a double role which led the Greeks to identify her with Athene. That she was also considered a universal goddess similar to Isis is attested by the inscription on her temple which proclaimed: 'I am all that has been, that is, and that will be. No mortal has yet been able to lift the veil which covers me.' Her epithet, 'the Libyan', links her to the west, traditional home of Lamia and of the dead whose protectress she is. As well as guarding coffins and canopic jars, she is also patroness of marriage. A school of medicine called 'The House of Life' was attached to her sanctuary. She wears a red crown, whose name, 'Net', is in fact her own. As Nut she is the dark, star-studded night sky, arching over the earth, forming with her hands and feet the gateways to life and death. She was the primal androgyne, a self-fertilizing virgin bringing forth life from herself before all worlds. Her crossed arrows represent not merely her warlike nature, but the strife between the opposites, spirit and matter, life and death, which forms the framework of mortal destiny. Her other symbol is therefore, appropriately, the shuttle, with which she weaves the fate of individuals and the universe. The French word for shuttle, 'navette', also means incense-boat, and the roll eaten in honour of the Black Virgin of Candlemas in Marseilles. It is, finally, one of the key symbols of

Catharism. Neumann calls Neith a 'goddess of magic and weaving, unborn goddess, originating in herself', and points out that she was worshipped with mysteries and lantern processions' as are the Black Virgin of Marseilles and many of her sisters. Sir Wallis Budge writes of her as 'the personification of the eternal feminine principle of life which was self-sustaining and self-existent and was secret and unknown and all-pervading'.

ANATH

In her settlement of the dispute between the gods, Neith's judgment was that Horus, despite his youth, should be awarded the throne, while Set, diabolical deity of storm and desert, should be compensated with twice his existing property and two wives. They were the Syrian goddesses, Astarte, parallel to Ishtar, Innana, Aphrodite and Venus, and Anath, very similar to Neith herself and to Athene. Like other Near Eastern goddesses Anath unites within her being opposing qualities — virginal and whorish, maternal and destructive. With her sickle she cuts off the life of Mot, the harvest-god, El's favourite son, whom she grinds in her mill. Baal is her son, brother, lover and also, probably, her victim. One of her names is Qadesh, Holy, which she shares with the forest in which Baal met his death in a struggle with wild bulls. The ass, an animal associated with Set and Lilith, is sacrificed to her. The reborn Baal becomes her son-consort Aleyin or Amurra (Lord of the West).

The Syrian goddesses with their licentious rites were a constant temptation to monotheistic Jewish worshippers of the male god Yahweh. Geoffrey Ashe states that apostate Jews in Egypt at the time of Jeremiah worshipped divine wisdom in the form of the mighty virgin Anath. A stele of the cult under Rameses II, the Pharaoh of the Exodus, refers to her as 'Queen of Heaven and mistress of all the gods'. Jewish mercenaries stationed at Elephantiné near Aswan in the fifth century BC had a temple to Anath as well as one to Yaho (Yahweh). Thus she was associated to the Lord as a female companion, much as Christ and Mary Magdalene were to be linked by the Gnostics of Alexandria. Desmond Stewart argues that it was in this milieu that Jesus grew to manhood, and that the temple where he

debated with the elders was at Leontopolis, between Cairo and
Alexandria, rather than Jerusalem. Jeremiah (7.8; 44.15-19)
complains of the libations and sacrifices of incense and cakes
(navettes?) offered to the Queen of Heaven. Epiphanius 850
years later inveighed against assemblies of silly women called
Collyridians who worshipped Mary as Queen of Heaven and
offered bread rolls (*kollyrida* = cakes of bread) to her throne.

Anath comes nearer to home as a possible direct predecessor
of at least one Black Virgin, La Daurade of Toulouse, believed to
have been originally a statue of Pallas Athene, the Greek Anath,
whose legend becomes linked to that of the web-footed Queen of
the South, La Reine Pédauque. Gerard de Sède considers that the
most probable prototype for this figure is Anath, hellenized as
Aphrodite Anaxerete (queen of virtue). Anaxerete was a lady of
Cyprus at whose door her unsuccessful suitor, Iphis, hanged
himself, as she looked out, unmoved, from her window.
Aphrodite turned her to stone and the resulting statue was
known as Venus Prospiciens (looking forwards or out). De Sède
states that Anath was a goddess of fertilizing waters, though this
function belonged especially to her Persian equivalent, Anahita,
goddess of sacred prostitution, whose cult became assimilated to
that of Cybele and of Ephesian Artemis. La Reine Pédauque is
credited with building the aqueduct which supplied Toulouse
with water. According to de Sède, Venus Anaxarete or Anate
was turned into a duck, for which the Latin stem is *anat-*. *Nassa*
is one Greek word for duck, while the word for queen is *anassa,*
a *jeu de mots* which makes Anat a likely candidate for La Reine
Pédauque if, like the Celts, we do not differentiate too finely the
goose from the duck. Finally de Sède quotes a poem from Ras
Shamra which refers obliquely to Anat as Queen of the South,
and mentions a medieval planisphere on which Gallina, a Latin
name for Venus Anate, is shown as a goddess with her webbed
foot on the winter solstice, i.e. the south. Gallina, the hen, would
have feet similar to the Lilith of the Burney relief. It may be
worth noting that Queen Austris of Toulouse was a Visigoth and
that the Old High German for duck is *anut*.

Anath belongs to that widespread category of goddesses
whose names contain the syllable 'an', which generally signifies
nourishment and abundance, though it can have dark, sinister,
devouring connotations. In Christianity there is St Anne, the

grandmother of God. Nanna, a child's word for grandmother, is also the Greek word for aunt, an epithet for Cybele and the name of the wife of the dying god, Baldur, who goes to the pyre with him. Anus in Latin means 'old woman' as well as fundament, changing to 'nonna' in Vulgar Latin, from which our word 'nun' derives. As the old gods and goddesses declined into fairy-tale characters Anath, no doubt, turned into Mother Goose, the kindly nanny who soothes the nursery in the telling of tales, though her other side may appear as the wicked step-mother or godmother.

HATHOR

The fairy godmothers of the Egyptians, seven or nine in number, were known as Hathors and they appeared at a birth to prophesy the baby's fate for good or ill. Hathor herself, whom the Greeks identified with Aphrodite, was a sky goddess, Hat-Hor, 'the dwelling of Horus', within whom the sun-god resided. She was, like the cat-goddess, Bast, the bestower of joy and love, the celestial cow who nourished all living creatures with her milk, including the Pharaoh. She was even more solicitous for the dead as guardian of the Theban necropolis (cf. Arles, Marseilles, et al.) and shares with Neith the title 'Queen of the West'. In the last epoch of Egypt, so much did she cherish the dead that the person who had died became known as a Hathor rather than an Osiris. She was sometimes known as 'the Lady of the Sycamore' from the tree on the edge of the desert from which she would welcome souls on their way to the other world with gifts of bread and water. The sycamore, many-breasted with figs, is the Egyptian tree of life which gives forth a milky substance. Hathor shares it as a symbol with Nut, Diana of the Ephesians and with Zacchaeus/St Amador (who climbed one and received there an invitation to entertain Jesus to dinner). This story is told only by St Luke, but it seems to refer to the same occasion as that at which Mary anointed the feet of the Lord and wiped them with her hair. As well as a tree, Hathor was, like Lilith, the ladder on which the righteous could ascend to heaven. She was well-known on the Red Sea coast of Somalia, which may itself be the land of Punt which was originally her home, and that, in some versions, of the Queen of Sheba. She is also known as the Lady of Byblos, the city where the coffin of Osiris, enclosed within a tree after being washed ashore, was made the pillar of a temple. At Byblos she was a serpent-goddess whose cobra symbolized the eye of wisdom.

SEKHMET

The negative aspect of Hathor, the blazing, destructive sun eye of Ra has, like Cybele, Artemis, Medusa, Lilith and St Mary of Egypt, the lion as her symbol. She is, however, more bloodthirsty than any other warrior goddess of Europe and the Near East, a lion-headed deity who boasts 'When I slay men my heart rejoices.' She would have destroyed the race completely in a vengeful rage had not Ra diverted her by placing seven thousand vessels of beer and pomegranate juice on the battlefield, which Sekhmet, mistaking for blood, swallowed up until drunkenness overcame her. Her lion's head she shares with Aion, the time and destiny which devour all things, the wrath of God that is the working of the law of cause and effect. The Sphinx, too, is a lion, who kills the man that lacks the Gnosis to answer her questions about the nature and meaning of human life. Some modern astrologers see Saturn, the dark tester and teacher of wisdom, as an essentially feminine influence.

Isha Schwaller de Lubicz, analysing the etymology of Sekhmet, describes it as the personification of the chaotic darkness which brings light out of ignorance. Since Sekhmet symbolizes the putrefaction without which the spiritual life-force cannot be released at death, we may call her, like Kali, the merciful. Lubicz also depicts her as a sort of telluric lightning-conductor, attracting to itself the fire of Ptah and neutralizing it. From the interaction of these forces, the Egyptian Prometheus, Nefertum, arose. Sekhmet is the annihilating power which makes conception possible: one form must die before another can come into being. The beloved in the 'Song of Solomon' is black because she has been exposed to the sun. St Mary the Egyptian suffered the same fate from her long life of penance in the desert and, at death, a lion dug her grave. One of the reasons given for the blackness of our virgins is that Mary, too, was very sunburnt. The most important function of the Black Virgin is her power to stay the destructive hand of God, tempering justice with mercy.

Once upon a time, God's dove and God's raven were sundered, and the raven of the Ark became accursed. It, like the dove, had once been white and was blackened in performance of its Promethean role of bringing the light and fire of consciousness to mankind. Marie-Louise von Franz describes the raven as the light-bringer *par excellence,* the creative depression which is God's messenger. The process, however depressing it may seem, is the way.

CHAPTER 2
The classical tradition

In the first three centuries of the Christian era it seemed increasingly as though a generalized worship of the Great Goddess might establish itself as the dominant religion of the Roman Empire, incorporating even the cults of Mithra and the Unconquered Sun. Under a multitude of names she had held sway from east to west before the Hellenes arrived in Greece or the Romans in Italy. Now, despite the formalities of emperor-worship and official religion, a wave of popular devotion was sweeping her back into the pre-eminence she had enjoyed before the Olympian dispensation. There is a tendency for all the goddesses to merge into each other, which makes it difficult to be sure which qualities to attribute to which divinity. The process of merging accelerated during the period we shall be looking at. In Christianity the feminine principle was represented by Black Virgins, White Virgins and a host of female saints, each having her own symbol and specific nature. As Christianity gradually asserted itself, the great bronze and marble statues of the pagan deities were destroyed. Smaller, household images or votive offerings, hidden in the earth, in cleft rocks or hollow trees, survived, especially in remote country places. Some were lost, some, perhaps, still visited as fairy trees and stones, long after their true nature had been forgotten. The memory of them may have influenced a later generation of religious sculptors. In addition, at the time of the Crusades, original pagan statues, or images based on them, were brought back from the east by returning warriors, as Madonnas.

Apart from the candle-smoke theory, this is the simplest and most widely held explanation for the existence of Black Virgins in Europe. They would thus be a survival, and a continuation under a new name and a new religion of goddesses from the classical world. Of the multitudes of candidates available, three stand out by reason of their popularity in the Europe of late paganism and from the fact that each has at some time been represented as black: Artemis, Isis and Cybele. The first to arrive was Artemis.

ARTEMIS — IN ARCADIA

It is debatable how far the Artemis of Greece, the 'maiden huntress', should be identified with the many-breasted, fertile, Ephesian goddess. Between them they combine the paradox of virgin and mother which is at the heart of Christian Marian dogma. In pre-Hellenic times Artemis was universally worshipped in Greece, her name being commonly derived from *artamos,* slaughterer, a fact which provides a possible link with those Black Virgins who have special affinities with the guild of butchers (cf. Murat). As huntress she both preserves and destroys game animals, but she does not draw the line at animals. Human sacrifice, real or simulated, was offered to her, and she herself has a bloodthirsty record of killing her would-be lovers, or those of her nymphs. When Orion, the mighty hunter and beautiful giant touched her indiscreetly during the chase, she summoned up the great scorpion from the earth to despatch him. In another version she draws her silver bow and shoots him through the head as he swims towards her. This suggests she is a head-hunter, too, like Kali and, perhaps, also, like the Black Virgin of Einsiedeln, who stands atop the skull of St Meinrad. Although Artemis seems to have disliked all males, she particularly resisted heroes of the stamp of Hercules and Achilles.

The fate of Actaeon, who came too close to her and was subsequently torn to pieces by his own hounds, is well-known. In yet another tale, mistaking her for a bear, she slew her beloved other half, Callisto, the wolfish Lycaon's daughter, after she had yielded to the embraces of Zeus in the temple where he was worshipped in wolf form. Before Callisto died, however, the nymph bore a son, Arcas, from whom Arcadia, Artemis' land of predilection, took its name. The authors of *The Holy Blood and the Holy Grail* have pointed out the connection between the wolf tribe of Benjamin and the bear-land of Arcadia. In the first Book of Maccabees, Chapter 12, Jonathan, the High Priest, writes to the Spartans to enlist their help in the struggle against Antiochus Epiphanes. He encloses a letter sent to a previous High Priest (probably Onias I who held office from 323-300 BC) from Areius, King of the Spartans, offering non-military assistance and stating: 'It has been found in writing concerning the Spartans and the Jews that they are brethren and are of the family of Abraham' (v. 21). This may be relevant to our hypothesis that the Merovingian dynasty, a wolf god and the symbol of the bear are all involved in the history of the Black Virgin cult.

ARCADIA AND THE ARK

Many associations can be teased out of the word Arcadia. The Greek word in the Septuagint version of the Bible from Alexandria used *kibitos* for both Noah's Ark and the Ark of the Covenant, though a barge and a box are very different objects. The root word, *kibos*, also yields the diminutive *kiborion*. This is the seed-vessel of the Nile water lily or lotus, as well as our word ciborium, the covered chalice used to contain the eucharistic bread. (For the Ark in which Moses floated on the Nile among the bulrushes a different word is used, though from a more archaic version of the same root.) The name of King Arthur may be derived from the cognate Celtic *arto* meaning a bear, or *art*, a stone. Latin and Greek forms deriving from the radical *arc* include words meaning bow, rainbow, arch, arcane, enclose, coffin, prison, concealed and citadel, and also bear-like, keep safe and keep away. *Dia*, in Greek, is a poetical term for Zeus, and for Hera (she who belongs to Zeus). In Latin 'Dia' is the name of the mother of Mercury. Hermes, the Greek Mercury, is born in Arcadia, in a dark cave on Mt Kyllene, the son of Maia and Zeus. Maia (= midwife) was very close to Callisto, and when the latter was assumed to heaven as the Great Bear, looked after her son, Arcas. One of Maia's names in Rome is Maiesta, meaning majesty (this is a description given by art historians to the great majority of Black Virgins, particularly those to be found in the Auvergne). Maia is goddess of the merry but Virgin month sacred to Venus, Mary and the mercurial Heavenly Twins. When Artemis herself had to be fitted into the new patriarchal scheme on Olympus, it was necessary to assign to her parents, of whom the first are Zeus and Demeter, the Great Mother who was goddess of Greece before Zeus appeared on the scene. This parentage would make her akin to Persephone, the dangerous Virgin goddess of the underworld. In yet another version Persephone herself is the mother of Artemis, thus making the daughter a feminine version of the holy child of Eleusis. Isis and Dionysos are also, somewhat surprisingly, cast in the role of Artemis' parents (though the Bacchic connection appears to have continued in the tradition of ritually sponging with wine the Black Isiac Virgin of Le Puy).

The most generally accepted story of the birth of Artemis, however, is that she was the daughter of Leto, whose name may mean stone or lady, and whose father was Polos, the pole-star or axis of the universe. Leto came to Delos in the form of a she-wolf from Lycis, wolf-land, and brought forth Artemis without pain, a fact which made her, like the Black Virgin of Le Puy, a patron of easy births. A dragon, the Python, had tried to prevent Leto, like the heavenly woman of the Book of Revelation, from giving birth to the sun-god Apollo, who was Artemis' younger twin.

The secret of Artemis, she of the ark and the art, the androgynous product of sun and moon, cannot be confined by time, space or custom. The Ark/Grail is the symbol of the virgin whore, wisdom, who mixes all things in an orgy of syncretism, to bring forth the oneness of truth without diversity.

Robert Graves in *The White Goddess* provides further amplification of the motif 'Ark' that lends some weight to this proposition. He tells of the Roman Emperor, Alexander Severus (AD 222-235), the Arkite, born in the Temple of Alexander the Great at Arka in Lebanon. He developed his own syncretistic Arkite religion in which Abraham, Orpheus, Alexander and Jesus Christ were household gods.

Earlier Arkites, mentioned in Genesis 10.17 — a passage which contains a mention of Nimrod, who is the Old Testament Orion, and of several peoples connected with Saba — were worshippers of Astarte/Ishtar, the goddess to whom an acacia-wood ark was sacred. For the Jews the Ark of the Lord, also made of acacia wood, contained the most sacred objects and became itself the most sacred object, symbol of the Shekinah, God's presence among his people. To touch or approach the Ark is death, but acacia symbolizes resurrection and immortality. Some say the son of Solomon and the Queen of Saba/Sheba took the Ark to Ethiopia, others that it remained hidden in the Temple in Jerusalem. The acacia from which it is built is an incorruptible and ardent plant, which reveals, in masonic ritual, the tomb of Hiram, the Master Builder of the Temple, the one who holds the secret of the lost arcane tradition. The tomb depicted in Poussins's *Les Bergers d'Arcadie,* believed by many to point to secrets of the Merovingian blood-line, is in old Plantard territory near Rennes-le-Château, at Arques (see Paris 1). Could the other name for Poussin's pinating, *Et in Aracadia ego,* which is also the motto of the Plantard family, mean, in addition to the obvious translation, 'And in the Ark I am the God/Goddess'? Might we even guess that Joan of Arc, Art or Aix, friend of René d'Anjou of the Prieuré, an Artemisian warrior-maiden, inspired by a fairy tree and a devotee of Black Virgins, is somehow involved in the mystery?

Artemis of Ephesus

It is with Artemis of Ephesus rather than the Arcadian Lady of Wild Things that we must now concern ourselves in the quest for the origins of the Black Virgin. According to legend, she started as a black meteoric stone discovered in a swamp by Amazons. Such a stone, known in French as *bétyle,* from the Greek *baitulos,* both manifests the divine presence and signifies Bethel, the house of God. It was there that Jacob had his dream of the ladder and angels while resting his head on the Stone of Scone which lies beneath the throne of Britain. We may remember here that the Holy Grail is sometimes considered to be a stone, as well as a vessel.

Ephesus was where the Virgin Mary traditionally spent her closing years before her Dormition and Assumption, with St John, before his exile to Patmos. In Ephesus in AD 431 the Virgin Mary was proclaimed 'Mother of God', and her cult spread thence to the city of the she-wolf, Rome, and so to all the corners of the world, as, indeed, a thousand years earlier had that of her predecessor, the Black Ephesian. The best-known image of Artemis of Ephesus, a Roman alabaster and bronze statue of the second century, shows her with black face, hands and feet, multiple breasts, on her head a mural crown or tower, and on her dress images including bulls, goats, deer and a bee. It is probable that the image of the goddess which the Phocaeans brought to Gaul with them in 600 BC, where they founded Massilia, now Marseilles, was not dissimilar, since the cult travelled from there to Rome. Other goddesses were worshipped in Marseilles, but Artemis seems to have held her place in Massiliot hearts as the Lady of the City, which was to become the richest trading emporium of the western Mediterranean. The Phocaeans were great travellers, sailing as far afield as Britain in their quest for tin and other precious goods, and where they went they would no doubt have taken with them images of their patroness (cf. Banyuls). Furthermore, visitors to Marseilles, being impressed by the statues of various goddesses they saw there, may well have taken replicas home with them. It is striking that the greatest incidence of Black Virgins occurs in areas where the Phocaeans had settlements, or important trading partners such as the Arverni of the Auvergne. Thus it is possible that in such regions as Provence, the Rhône, Catalonia and the river valleys of the eastern Pyrenees, a custom may have grown up, during the long centuries of Massiliot influence, of venerating the goddess in her dark aspect.

Artemis and the tree
This face of the night is not always merciful, as we have already glimpsed. Artemis is hostile to love and punishes sexual transgressors severely. Unawakened little girls, brownies playing bears to her honour in the forest, are great favourites of hers, but boys fare less well at the hands of her devotees. In Sparta, youths were flogged in front of the statue of Artemis Orthia (upright), in a combination of fertility rite and painful puberty initiation. The sexual puritanism of the new goddess of Christianity, with its proliferation of monastic establishments based on Marseilles and Lérins from the early fifth century, would not altogether have displeased Arcadian Artemis.

The most notable cultic feature belonging both to Artemis and to the Black Virgins is the fact that they both tend to make their home in trees where they are later 'found'. Artemis Orthia, like the Black Virgin of Bourg, was found in a hollow willow tree, and hence is known as Lygodesma, 'willow-captive'. Other images of her were adored in a myrtle and a cedar. A third-century coin from Myrrha in Asia Minor shows the Virgin in a tree flanked by two axe-wielding figures, possibly Cabiri. From Scherpenheuvel in Belgium to Prats in the Pyrenees, via Chartres and Longpont, there are many examples of Black Virgins being associated with an earlier tree cult. Then too both Artemis and the Black Virgin demand to be worshipped in their own way, where they have been found. When moved against her will the Black Virgin resists by becoming insupportably heavy. Artemis too indicates her disapproval in this way, as when the flagellation of the young Spartans slackened, a phenomenon noted by the priestesses who carried her during the ceremony.

Artemis and the underworld

In her darker, Persephone, side Artemis is often confused and identified with Hecate, an underworld power (Notre-Dame de Sous-Terre), whose sacred trees are the graveyard yew, good for bows and for arrow poison, and the willow, the wicked witch tree. The triple goddess rules in all the worlds, but it is as the invincible Queen of the Dead that she most resembles our Black Virgins. Our Lady of Avioth, found in a hawthorn tree, still preserves outside her basilica a unique architectural feature, La Recévresse, where dead babies were offered to the Black Virgin (Artemis and Hecate both care for babies and bestow a quick death). In Marseilles, amidst the ancient necropolis, Notre Dame de Confession presides in a crypt over the tombs of the martyrs from whom she takes her name. One of these, sometimes met with elsewhere as a companion of Black Virgins, is St Maurice (Maurus = Moorish, black; Maurs = Mars) to whom one prays to be delivered from unwanted parents. Hecate presides over purification rites, so February, month of the dead which begins with Candlemas, the Feast of the Purification of the Blessed Virgin Mary, is especially her time. In 472 this feast succeeded to the torchlight procession in honour of Persephone, and that of the Lupercalia. At this feast a goat and a dog were sacrificed to the wolf-god, and young women were ritually beaten with goat-skin thongs. This tradition continues in our 'beating of the bounds'. The most famous and ancient Candlemas procession is that of St Victor of Marseilles, where the new light is brought up from the crypt with green candles. Candlemas, the oldest feast of the Virgin, also commemorates the presentation of Christ in the

Temple, a second epiphany at the home of divine wisdom. Persephone's name contains, etymologically, not only elements of destruction but of epiphany, the showing forth of the light. Her male equivalent, the Roman god of February purifications, Februus, is a form of Dispater, god of the dead, who, as Pluto, rapes Persephone into the underworld. As Plutus, he is born from Demeter or Irene, Peace (the Black Virgin, Notre-Dame de Paix, in Paris, is compared in 'Horizons Blancs' to a statue of Irene holding Plutus). The companion to the Lady of Candlemas in the Christian calendar, and to the Black Virgin in many of her shrines, is St Roch, shown with a dog at his heels. The dog is also the sacred animal of Hecate, as both devourer of corpses and the guide of souls to the underworld.

Diana, the Artemis/Hecate of the Roman world, the wood-goddess of the golden bough, whose name means 'shining one' or 'dual-Ana' (i.e. the goddess of both earth and moon), is also the feminine form of Dis/Dianus/Janus. She degenerates but persists in the Christian era as the goddess of witches, and queen of the night. Something of her tradition lives on in Black Virgins, making them much prized by modern necromancers. Black Annis/Dana, a Celtic parallel to Diana in her destructive mode, may have given her name to Mont Anis, home of the Black Virgin of Le Puy, but Anis also reminds us of the favourite drink of those who talk the *langue d'oc*, which is made from a flower belonging to the genus artemisia. No wonder St Bernard selected for his first abbey in the valley of light a site by the stream called Absinthe (the 'wormwood' on the sponge at the Crucifixion). The great feast of the Virgin, the Assumption, which occurs on 15 August, probably originates in a festival of Diana. Metz Cathedral (qv) was built on top of a Temple of Diana (see also Calatayud, Manfredonia, Le Puy).

CYBELE

Cybele is the Phrygian mother of the gods whose prototype has been traced back to the neolithic matriarchal civilization of Çatal Hüyük. She was first worshipped as a black stone, and it was thus that she journeyed to Rome in 205 BC, sent by King Attalus of Pergamum at the request of the Senate. It had been advised in the Sibylline Books that only she could save them from the showers of stones and the inroads of Hannibal that beset them. She was carried by matrons to the Palatine site of what was to be the Virgin of the Ara Coeli (qv), and placed in the Temple of Victory. Annually, on 25 March, the Christian Lady Day, her statue, whose head consisted of a black stone, was bathed in the River Almo (Almus = nourishing, cf. Alma Mater). To the Romans she was simply 'Magna Mater', the Great Mother, and the earliest Phrygian name for her consort was Papas, father, which· is still the Greek word for priest. In Pessinus, the black stone, which in Rome became the head of the goddess, was considered to be her throne. Can it have been a memory of this tradition that led Hincmar, the ninth-century Archbishop of Rheims, to assert that the appropriate colour for the throne of the Virgin was black? The name Pessinus, though presumably from the old Phrygian language, awakens echoes surprisingly relevant to the significance of Cybele through the only two Greek words with the root *pess*. *Pessos* is an oval stone especially used in playing draughts, a cubic mass of building, the dark edge of the pupil of the eye, and a pessary. *Pesso* means to bake, ripen, ferment or digest.

By the third century AD Cybele was the supreme deity of Lyons, capital of the three Gauls, where a Black Virgin cult flourishes today. Julian the Apostate favoured her cult and composed a beautiful prayer in which he apostrophized her as the Virgin: 'Wisdom, Providence, Creator of our souls'. Bulls were sacrificed to her at the Vatican in the last years of the fourth century and, as late as 410 AD she was still publicly honoured in Gaul. Originally a mountain goddess, generally accompanied by lions, she became the tutelary deity of cities and frontier citadels, protecting her people from war and pestilence, and speaking to them in subterranean oracles and ecstasies. Her name is etymologically linked with the words for crypt, cave, head and dome and is distantly related to the Ka'aba, the cube-shaped holy of holies in Mecca that contains the feminine black stone venerated by Islam. Her youthful companion was the lesser consort-god, Attis, who was castrated and transformed into the pine-tree. In his memory and to honour the goddess, her priests, the Galli, were also eunuchs.

The word Galli, which also means Gauls (and those Gallic birds, cocks), reminds us that Phrygia was invaded and partly occupied in 278 BC by Gauls who called their new homeland

Galatia. The Gauls had reservations about a castrated god but, being accustomed to the worship of the goddess, were not slow to welcome Cybele, and assimilate her into their own divinities of water, fertility and victory. She was worshipped from the fourth century BC at Ra, which became Les Saintes Maries de la Mer, along with her sisters and rivals Artemis and Isis. Examples of the Black Virgin sites that have been associated with her include Aix-en-Provence, where her consort has become St Mitra, and Madrid, where she presides from her chariot in the famous fountain over the traffic of the Plaza de Cibeles in the capital of the bull cult. (See also Agde, on the Golf du Lion, Arles, Auxerre, Avignon, Beaune, Chartres, Clermont-Ferrand, Grande-Chartreuse, Laon, Limoux, Marseilles, Mauriac, Mézières, Mont St Michel, Monte Vergine, Patti/Tindari, Périgueux, Rocamadour, Rome, Tarascon, Toulouse, Tournai, Valence/Cornas, Vence/St Paul and Vichy.)

Lyons, city of Cybele

Although her cult was slow to establish pre-eminence there, the city of Cybele in France is without doubt Lyons, where her huge temple (86 by 53 metres) has been supplanted by the great basilica of Notre Dame de Fourvière (the old forum) and the oratory of the Black Virgins. Her lion is still on the arms of the city surmounting three fleur de lys. Of the cult of Cybele little now remains at Lyons; the foundations of the temple have been excavated; the mask of the statue of the goddess with red hair, and her altar, are preserved in the magnificent Musée de la Civilisation Gallo-Romaine; the bust of Tutela, protectress of cities who holds a horn of plenty, is probably an aspect of her; the rue du Boeuf may commemorate the crowned bull led in procession on her great feast. In AD 177 the coincidence of her feast of Hilaria, 25 March (Lady Day) with the Christian Good Friday was the cause of public rioting and the repression of the Christian community. It is curious in this connection that at Le Puy (qv) whenever Lady Day and Good Friday coincide, a jubilee is declared, to which pilgrims flock from all nations.

An interesting souvenir of Cybele persisted in Lyons until the sixteenth century in the form of a statue of the goddess Copia (Abundance) in the Church of St Etienne, where on Christmas night (the Vigil of St Stephen), women presented candles and offerings of fruit and animals to the goddess, and departed walking backwards. The local name for the statue was Ferrabo, believed to be a corruption of Farrago, a word meaning a mixture of different grains in a hotch-potch, an excellent description of Lyons, city of Cybele where so many traditions meet. According to Saillens the cult of the Black Virgin of Fourvière dates from the destruction of this idol from the pagan past.

We do not know for certain the colour of the original Virgin of Fourvière, destroyed by the Huguenots in 1562, but Louis XI, whose predilection for Black Virgins is well known, stated that he had always had from his earliest youth a 'great affection for the glorious Virgin Mary, mother of God, and for her chapel of Fourvière on the mount of Lyons'. He spent five months in the city in 1476, between two pilgrimages to Le Puy. His first gesture was to climb up to the shrine and make an offering to Our Lady, whom he endowed richly with the town of Charlieu and 84 parishes.

In the year AD 186, during the golden age of Gallo-Roman Lyons, on Fourvière, Julia Domna, known as the philosopher, second wife of the Emperor Septimius Severus, gave birth to the Emperor Caracalla. Syrian, and initiate of Astarte, she was a passionate disciple of Apollonius of Tyana, a contemporary of Jesus, who died at a great age, in Ephesus (like John). His life's work included a syncretistic and esoteric missionary journey to Babylon, Persia, Alexandria, the source of the Nile, Spain and Provence, purifying the rites of all the shrines he visited. Of his books on *Sacrifices, Astrological Predictions* and *Pythagoras* (whose successor he was considered), almost nothing has survived, and he himself, unjustly accounted a rival to the Christian God, has faded on the palate of history.

The Christian church in Lyons prided itself on its own direct link to the Ephesus of St John through Irenaeus, its second bishop, who complained of the many foolish women attracted to Gnosticism in the Rhône Valley. He was a pupil of that Polycarp who, according to Irenaeus, 'had intercourse with John'. He probably died in the destruction of Lyons by Septimius Severus in 197. The relics of the first bishop Potinus, martyred after the quarrel with the followers of Cybele in 177, were thrown into the Rhône along with those of his fellow martyrs, but it seems likely that they were commemorated in the church of the Maccabees on the plateau of Sarra, which it shared with the church of St Irenaeus. This highly unusual name for a Christian church is that of the Old Testament apocryphal book in which mention is made of the link between Israel and Sparta (Arcadia).

In the Church of the Maccabees was venerated the body of a fourth-century Archbishop, St Justus, who retired to the ruins of Thebes to lead a cenobitic existence amid the remnants of Egyptian syncretism. From the Thebaid, monasticism spread to Marseilles with Cassian. The district of St Just is now next to that of St Luc, who might be expected to be a favourite of the Lyonnais, given the similarity of his name to that of Lug, their divine founder.

The Maccabees yielded place to the monastery of St Just where Clement V was crowned Pope on 14 November 1305. As he and King Philippe le Bel were passing in procession by the convent of La Madeleine, a huge block of masonry detached itself from the building, killing the Pope's brother and the Duke of Brittany and narrowly missing pontiff and monarch. It was this king, with the reluctant collusion of the Pope, who brought about the destruction of the Templars in 1307-8. Their quarter in Lyons, a veritable forbidden city, was larger than that of Paris, and may have been the heart of the mercantile operations of the whole order. The Templars might still be here today if they had heeded the recommendations of the Council of Lyons in 1274, at which Pope Gregory X proposed a merger with the Knights of St John. He also tried to reunite the Churches of East and West by reforming the morals of the clergy and liberating the Holy Land. The first of these aims was realised in twentieth-century Lyons in the form of the Orthodox Catholic Church founded in 1939 at 16 rue du Boeuf by Fr Kovalewsky who rejected the Great Schism. The Liberal Catholic Church, an off-shoot of the Theosophical Society, which said Mass in French and believed, like Apollonius of Tyana, in reincarnation, also flourished in Lyons between the wars, despite excommunication. Another heresy, that of 'the poor men of Lyons', which claimed to preserve a pure and uncorrupted pre-Constantinian Christianity, was founded in the city in the twelfth century and still survives in the Piedmont across the border from the Black Virgins of Modane and St Martin de Vésubie.

That Lyons is a city of occultism, Templars, Tarot and heresy cannot be laid at the door of the Black Virgins of Fourvière or that of their neighbour, Cybele. Yet Lyons is also a city, where, despite the depradations of the past two thousand years, nothing is forgotten. In the painting by the nineteenth-century artist Orsel in the basilica, Mary is shown enthroned in the sky, saving her city of Lyons just discernible below. Under her throne a lion is lying.

Lionesses lick their cubs into shape and life. One of the endearing features which various Black Virgins share with Cybele Fatua is to help infants to speak, to awaken the word in them. Then, too, as a lioness protects her cubs, Our Lady of Victories and Cybele/Andarta fight for their cities and protect them against the foe. Cybele, as Fortune, also brings peace and prosperity between wars. A second-century BC relief from Rome shows her enthroned, stately and matronly, looking for all the world like the later Queen Victoria, holding a shield like Britannia, being drawn on a processional cart by two lions. In this matriarchal role she is very much the confidante of women, reflecting the present and the future in a comforting light, Our Lady of Perpetual Succour and Good Hope. It is however in her initiatory aspect as sibylline hierophant of the mysteries of death and rebirth, whether her youthful consort be Attis, Dionysus or Mithra, that her influence on the cult of the Black Virgin is of greatest interest to modern votaries.

ISIS

The Prieuré, as we have noted, insist that the Black Virgin, whether worshipped under other names, such as Diana or Cybele, is in fact Isis, the true goddess of France, now known as Our Lady of Light. Some 500 years before Dagobert II reputedly set about restoring the cult of the Black Virgin she had already, in *The Golden Ass* of Apuleius, claimed to be *the* universal goddess, subsuming the attributes of all the others.

'I am Nature, the universal Mother, mistress of all the elements, primordial child of time, sovereign of all things spiritual, queen of the dead, queen also of the immortals,

the single manifestation of all gods and goddesses that are.
. . . The primeval Phrygians call me Pessinuntica [i.e.
Cybele], Mother of the gods; the Athenians, sprung from
their own soil, call me Cecropian Artemis; for the islanders
of Cyprus I am Paphian Aphrodite; for the archers of
Crete I am Dictynna, for the trilingual Sicilians, Stygian
Proserpine [Persephone]: and for the Eleusinians their
ancient Mother of the Corn [Demeter].

'Some know me as Juno, some as Bellona of the Battles;
others as Hecate, others again as Rhamnusia [Nemesis?],
but both races of Aethiopians, whose lands the morning
sun first shines upon, and the Egyptians who excel in
ancient learning and worship me with ceremonies proper
to my god-head, call me by my true name, namely, Queen
Isis.' (trans. Robert Graves.)

So how are we to differentiate Isis from all the other goddesses
she assimilates? She tells Lucius one thing he must do in order to
be saved and become human. While her priests offer her the first
fruits of the new sailing season by dedicating a ship to her, he
must follow the High Priest and eat some blooms from the
bouquet of roses attached to his sistrum. Here she associates
herself with the rose, though she shares that symbol with
Aphrodite, her indigenous flower being rather the lotus, or Nile
water-lily, that rises from mud through water to reflect the sun.
The other symbol, the boat, is also the prerogative of Aphrodite
as protectress of sailors, but the barque of Isis bears more
explicit connotations such as that of caring for the dead on their
night-sea journey. In her care for Osiris she tends all the dead,
but she also nurtures the living. More than any other goddess,
Isis is shown as a nursing mother, with the infant Horus at her
breast or the infant Harpocrates on her lap, enjoining silence,
though she also suckles Pharaohs, as the Black Virgins of
Chartres and Châtillon granted their milk to Fulbert and
Bernard. In these images lie the origins of Madonna and Child.
The ankh which Isis carries as supreme initiatrix may account
for some of the oddly shaped sceptres carried by the Black
Virgins who, like Isis, often favour the colour green. Their
greenness and blackness point to the beginning of the opus
whose secret, according to alchemists, is to be found in 'the sex

of Isis'. As the whore wisdom, she spent ten years in a brothel in Tyre. She alone knows the secret name of the god Ra, through which she wields her power. Her own name is considered by many scholars to mean 'throne', while to others, when combined with Maat, it signifies 'ancient wisdom'. Every living being is a drop of her blood, to be protected under her wings in death and lovingly restored to life. Though the greatest danger to the Church, she has never entirely lost her popularity and prestige in the west. Diana is the queen of the night for witches, Isis for Masons and Rosicrucians. Of the great Black Virgin cities of France, Lyons is devoted to Cybele, the patroness of Marseilles is Artemis. Toulouse of Pallas Athene in its very essence *is* the Queen of the South, home of a Gnostic wisdom school in the sixth century. It was left to Paris, eventually the greatest of them all, to be selected by Isis, greatest of the goddesses, as her sacred capital.

Isis in Paris

There are many etymologies of the name 'Paris'. Its older name, 'Lutetia', has been derived from Lucus, the descendant of Noah who became a Celtic king, but also from the Greek word for light and from Lug/Luc, the god of light who lent his name to Lyons and other Celtic cities. It has even been derived from mud.

Hercules, on his way from Asia Minor to the garden of the Hesperides, was accompanied by some Parrhesians who abandoned the journey to settle on the Seine, where they became the Parisii, the ruling clan of the area. Of the Parrhesians little is known, but a clue as to their true identity may be found in the Greek word *parrhesia,* which means frankness. There was also a fourth-century BC Ephesian painter, Parrhesius, who accorded royal honours to himself and whose paintings of divinities on wood and paper became, like those of St Luke, models for later artists. It is to the Franks, however, that we must once again return. Like the founders of Rome and London, they claimed descent from Troy through Francion, son of Hector. Paris, the new capital, simply commemorates their unfortunate country-man, who, in the beauty contest of the three goddesses, awarded the golden apple to Aphrodite, and later abducted Helen, sparking off the Trojan war. The Franks, profligate with clues to their origin, would have arrived in Paris via Troyes.

Another etymology stresses the importance of the syllable 'is', a pre-Celtic word for a holy place where there is a subterranean current of water or telluric energy called a wouivre, which creates special conditions favourable for divinatory and initiatory purposes. This sacred syllable may account for the suffix -is or -es to be found in the name of many French towns.

Isis can easily assimilate such diverse explanations within her all-accommodating universality, but that which honours her most is the derivation of Par-Isis, 'grove' or 'barque' of Isis, and the Île de la Cité certainly bears a close resemblance to a Nile felucca. In Roman times her temple was at the western limits of the city, on the marshy left bank of the Seine, later the site of the famous abbey and church of St Germain-des-Prés and of St Sulpice. Some time during this period, Paris was evangelized by Dionysius, St Denis, who is joint male patron of France with St Michael. Donald Attwater writes of Denis that in the ninth century 'a very strange legend had grown up around him in which three different people, living in different ages, were made into one man'. The first, a learned Athenian converted by St Paul, was martyred on Montmartre, hill of Mercury, martyrs or, more prosaically, pine-martens or sables. The second was a sixth-century theologian who wrote three books: *The Celestial Hierarchy*, an account of how the nine choirs of angels mediate God to man, *The Divine Names*, on the attributes of God, and *The Mystical Theology*, which describes the ascent of the soul to God. Denis's great achievement was to synthesize Neo-Platonic thought and Christian dogma. The third St Denis was said in the sixth century to have been sent to Paris in 250, where he was martyred as the first bishop. *En route* he visited the image of the Virgo Paritura, later to become the Black Virgin of Longpont (qv), where he explained to the people that the Virgin had now given birth. After execution he carried his severed head to the site of the present basilica of St Denis.

Another St Dionysius was the great third-century Bishop of Alexandria and head of the Catechetic School there in succession to Origen, who was accused of tritheism by Dionysius of Rome, and tried to reconcile warring factors within the Church. The god Dionysus may also have a part to play in the legend through the sojourn which the third St Denis made in the Faubourg St Jacques, a suburb, where, until the Revolution, there stood a church dedicated to Our Lady of the Vines. A suggested etymology for Jacques is Iacchus, Dionysus as the divine child of the Eleusinian Mysteries, and it is not immediately obvious why it should be a pet-name for John. A pilgrim on the milky way to Santiago de Compostela is also known as a 'jack'.

The cult of St Denis owes much to St Genevieve and the Merovingian dynasty. Between the time of these two saints, Lutetia had enjoyed a brief period as capital of the Roman Empire under Julian the Apostate (332-63) who loved the place, which he saved from the incursions of the Salian Franks. His attempt to restore the cult of King Helios and the Mother of the Gods proved short-lived, as did his effort to keep out the Franks. It would not be long before Paris was turning to them for fear of an even worse fate. Meanwhile they had Genevieve.

She was a shepherdess, like other Arcadian saints, born of a rich family in Nanterre around the year 420. St Germain of Auxerre, *en route* to Britain to combat Pelagianism, met her while she was still a child, foretold her future sanctity and received her vows. Another who recognised her worth was St Marcel, Bishop of Paris, whose feast is on All Saints' Day (1 November), who turned water into wine and delivered the city from a dragon whose lair was in a harlot's tomb. Genevieve lost her parents at fifteen, and went to stay with her godmother in the city. From there she undertook charitable journeys to Meaux, Laon, Tours and Orléans, all of which have been associated with the Black Virgin cult. In 450, when Attila and his Huns were at the gates of Paris, Genevieve stopped the tide of panic by announcing that they would not attack. She was proved right, and, shortly after, they were defeated at the Catalaunian Fields by Aetius, with his mixed army of Gallo-Romans, Franks, Burgundians and Visigoths.

Soon it was the turn of the Franks from Tournai, under their King, Childeric, son of Merovée/Merweg and father of Clovis, to besiege the city. To relieve the starvation of its inhabitants, Genevieve organised and led an armada of ships to Troyes and Arcis (the Is of the Ark, or the Ark of Isis?), which returned laden with corn. When the city eventually fell to the Franks, Childeric did not hold this act of defiance against Genevieve, whose character and sage counsel he much respected. Perhaps his native ferocity had been mitigated by his Thuringian wife Basine who had made him stand outside the door of the palace on their wedding night. During his chaste vigil he had a vision of wolves, bears, lions, leopards and unicorns. Their son, Clovis, the first King of France, and his sainted queen, Clotilda, were friends of Genevieve, and at her behest inaugurated a programme of church-building. The cult of St Denis was especially close to Genevieve's heart. She and Clovis died within a short time of each other in 511 and 512, and were buried close together in the church which became the Pantheon. According to an old custom the reliquary of St Genevieve is never exposed without that of St Marcel.

Clovis was succeeded by Childebert I, 'King of Paris', who brought back with him from an expedition to Toledo the tunic of St Vincent with a number of chalices and vases from the treasure of Solomon. St Germain, Bishop of Paris (494-576), advised him to build a church and abbey worthy to house such relics. The site chosen was that of the old temple of Isis. A black statuette of the goddess, 'slender, tall and upright, naked save for some wisps of garment around her limbs', was venerated as the Virgin in the Church of St Germain-des-Prés until broken up on the orders of Abbot Briconnet in 1514. The Benedictines of St Germain are, like the priests of Isis, 'wearers of the black'. The seal of Abbot Hugh III, 1138, shows her holding what seems to be a long lotus or fleur de lys in her right hand. Today, the Black Virgin is still at St Germain, though hard to find. All the Merovingian kings were buried there until Dagobert I removed the royal mausoleum to St Denis. According to P. Saintyves, the successor to Isis is not only St Genevieve, patroness of Paris, but also St Gudule, patroness of Brussels (qv), present-day capital of what was once the old Frankish kingdom. St Theodosia, whose statue is in the Chapel of St Genevieve in St Sulpice (Paris) may be a third.

Isis in Black Virgin sites
About Isis at Le Puy (qv) much has already been said. Santa Sabina, mother house of the Dominican order, and the most perfect example of a Roman Christian basilica, had already in the fourth century, after the Council of Ephesus, been built over a Temple of Isis, near the temples of Juno and Diana. Also in Rome, the oldest Madonna in the world, the brown Virgin of the

4. Paris (Neuilly)

catacomb of Priscilla, is considered by some authorities to be Isis. In the cathedral of Metz (qv), the coronation church of the Lorraine dynasty where St Bernard preached the Crusade, a statue of Isis was also venerated as the Virgin until the sixteenth century. The effigy of the Graouly, a dragon drowned by St Clement in the Seille, can be seen in the crypt. The worship of Isis, introduced into Lucera (qv Italy) by sea-going Apulians, may have been one influence in the rise of the cult of the Black Virgin there.

The Black Virgin of Boulogne-sur-Mer illustrates the special relationship linking Isis to Merovingian France. In AD 633, during the reign of Dagobert I, king of all France, who may have been attending Sunday Mass there at the time, a ship sailed into the harbour, without oars or sails, containing nothing but a statue, three feet high, of the Black Virgin and a copy of the Gospels in Syriac. These last would almost certainly have been the version known as 'The Gospel of the Mixed', based on the Diatessaron of the second-century Gnostic, Tatian. In another legend, illustrated in a fifteenth-century church window, the boat is drawn by swans. The French *cygne* is homophonous with *signe,* 'a sign', which points us to the Swan Knight, Lohengrin or Helias, the son of Parzival, the Grail Knight, and the putative grandfather of Godefroy de Bouillon, who was born in Boulogne. St Ida, Godefroy's mother, built the old crypt of the cathedral, where there is a replica of Godefroy's tomb. From 1104, shortly after Godefroy's capture of Jerusalem and the foundation of the Latin Kingdom there under his brother, Baldwin, another Black Virgin began to be venerated at the church of Our Lady of the Holy Blood in Boulogne. Louis XI, perhaps recognising the precedence of an older line, but mainly motivated by shrewd political reasons of state, bestowed the suzerainty of the Boulonnais into the hands of Notre-Dame de Boulogne. (See also Valenciennes and Vichy.)

Who is the invisible helmsman of the barque of Isis? The Grand Master of the Prieuré de Sion has exactly this title, Nautonnier. In the *langue des oiseaux, bateau* is linked not only with *batelier,* boatman, but also with Le Bateleur, master of the Tarot, trickster, juggler and controller of the elements. By a stretch of the imagination it could yield us *le batisseur,* the builder or mason.

OTHER GODDESSES

Aphrodite/Venus

Venus was a rustic garden goddess with little cult in Rome until taken over by Aphrodite of Erice (cf. Custonaci) whose temple was built in the city in 217 BC. After that she became popular throughout the Empire. In her native land Aphrodite is sometimes represented as black, as a small votive statue of her in Cyprus, swathed in a star- or rose-covered robe proves. Geoffrey Grigson who reports this exhibit, speaks of the existence of an Aphrodite of Darkness in Egypt and Crete and of Black Aphrodites at Mantinea in Arcadia, in a cypress wood on the outskirts of Corinth and at Thespiai. The Christian Saints Melanie ('black') may derive from this Aphrodite Melainis, whom Grigson considers to be mixed with Isis. Probably it is through Isis that some of the cult and attributes of Venus have been assimilated by Christianity, since her sexuality was too explicit to be borrowed directly by carvers or painters of Black Virgins, though towards the end of the classical era she became increasingly identified with heavenly love. Durand-Lefèbvre writes of a Black Virgin that still existed before the Second World War at Sainte-Vinère in Bucharest, whose silver face, turned coal black, aroused the enthusiasm of the faithful. Valvanera (Spain) is the Valley of Venus, and there was a temple to her at Montserrat. It is a curious coincidence that Phryne, the most beautiful of Greek courtesans, the model for Praxiteles' statues of Aphrodite, should bear a name on account of her dark complexion which means 'toad', the animal symbol of the Merovingian dynasty, transformed by some love goddess into the fleur de lys. The main survivor of the Venus cult in Christianity is probably that of the Magdalen and allied saintly penitents.

Athene/Minerva

The name of the goddess was remembered by the followers of the goddess of wisdom in the Cathar castle of Minerve, where Simon de Montfort burned to death 180 parfaits in 1210. The little carving of an owl that brings good luck on the outside wall of the Church of Notre Dame of Dijon, home of the Black Virgin, Notre-Dame de Bon Espoir, may be another souvenir. In

Toulouse, the Church of La Daurade was built on the site of a temple of Pallas Athene, whose statue was consecrated as that of the new Christian Virgin. She also had an important temple in Marseilles. In the middle of the seventh century, St Eloi, Bishop of Tournai, who had been master of the mint in Marseilles, warned the faithful against invoking Athene before weaving flax into linen. (See Lucera, Italy, and Vichy.)

Bona Dea
Michel Bertrand sees the origins of the Black Virgin in the cult of this goddess, but it is not certain with which 'good goddess' she should be associated. In Rome her proper name was Fauna or Damia, and her nocturnal orgiastic ceremonies were restricted to women. She is closely related to Maia. The various Black Virgins called 'la Bonne Mère' may well derive from her, as would Sicilian St Agatha (good). Her place in the calendar (5 February) makes her part of the Candlemas cycle that replaced the Lupercalia over which Faunus, husband of Fauna and son of Picus, presided. Bertrand also identifies her with St Martha. Both Bona Dea and Maia had a cult at Marseilles. In Sicily Bona Dea was probably an epithet for Demeter.

Ceres/Demeter
Demeter, a corn-goddess and minder of children, is sometimes shown as black (cf. Bona Dea). (See Authezat, Bucharest, Lucera and Monte Vergine, Italy.)

Fortuna/Fors
First-born of Jupiter, she is linked through her name and attributes not only to the wheel of fate (cf. St Catherine) but also to ports and the forum (cf. Clermont-Ferrand and Lyons). Roman emperors always kept a golden statue of her where they slept (cf. also Cybele).

Juno/Hera
Hera ('Lady'), the goddess of marriage and childbirth, is sometimes shown as black. She is often shown as enthroned, carrying a pomegranate and a flower. (See Crotone, Ragusa.)

Vacuna
Along with Bellona, Vitula and Victoria, one of the goddesses

chiefly associated with Mars, she is known to have been worshipped in Farfa (Italy).

Vesta/Hestia (Shining One)

Vesta derives from the Sankskrit root 'Vas', light, a word which, in Latin, means a vessel. She was a virgin fire goddess and every hearth had its own Vesta, which no doubt became blackened by smoke. In the few extant representations she is always shown as veiled. A statuette was found in the ruins of her Temple on a hill called Le Verrou (bolt) at Montpellier, where the Black Virgin, Nostra Dama des Taoulas, has many fiery connections (cf. also Couterne and Valenciennes). One of Vesta's close associates, Tellus Mater, Mother Earth, is shown on a Roman bas-relief with an ox and a sheep beneath her feet, and two children on her lap, flanked by one woman with a swan and another with a sea-monster. Vesta symbolizes ideal motherhood. The Vestal Virgins in Rome offer an example of pre-Christian chastity vows.

GODS

Apollo

The worship of the sun-god in Gaul is generally connected with that of Abellio/Belen. (See St Bertrand-de-Comminges.)

Hercules

Hercules has an important cult in Chipiona (qv Spain). As Hercules the wanderer he is of major interest in the cult of the Black Virgin through his courtship of Pyrene. His road, the Via Herculea, from Cadiz to Rome, leads through areas rich in Black Virgins (cf. especially Manosque). The Gallic Hercules is a very different figure from the Greco-Roman divine hero. (Cf. The Dagda/Sucellus, Chapter 3. See also Paris.)

Hermes/Mercury

Although in many of the sites connected with this god he is chiefly to be seen as a Gallo-Roman version of Wotan or Belen christianized as St Michael (cf. Le Puy), there are still many instances of place names deriving from Hermes or Mercury in near proximity to a Black Virgin. St Hermes shares a feast-day,

28 August, with St Augustine, learned doctor of the Church and former Gnostic.

Janus

Janus is one of the most important Roman gods. His two faces illustrate not only his role as deity of beginnings, looking to past and future, but his essential duality as the original bisexual chaos and the form which emerged from it. Diana/Jana and Saturn are especially associated with him. He may have been gallicized into Jean (John), one of the companions of the Black Virgin.

Jupiter

Jupiter, the father of the gods, is generally too public, official and heavenly to be much associated directly with the cult of the Black Virgin, but he does look down from his mountain sites onto a number of her shrines. (See Arpajon Great St Bernard, Valenciennes, Laurie, Monjou, Boëge and Vichy.)

Mars

Probably quite important under various names in the Black Virgin cult, he overlaps with other gods such as Wotan and Belen. Sts Maurice and Martin may well be among his successors. His animals are the wolf, the horse and the woodpecker, the bird held by the Child on the lap of Notre-Dame de Verdelais and possibly of the Black Virgin of Einsiedeln. In Italy he was a god of agriculture as well as war, and had as companions the cow-like Vacuna and Vitula. (See Boulogne and Valenciennes.)

Saturn

For the most part he is best approached in France through his Celtic and Teutonic equivalents, but the Merovingian holy place of Stenay is connected with him, and the Saturnalia began on 23 December, feast-day of St Dagobert, who was murdered near by.

CHAPTER 3
Natural religion: the Celtic and Teutonic sources

Dame Nature and Mother Earth; stones hurled from heaven or the volcanic depths or washed up on the shore with shapes that evoke the feminine; mountains that resemble the breasts of the goddess; springs, hot or cold, that flow as water of life from her womb; wells and caves that lead to the mysterious realm of birth and death; dark forests where the way is uncertain and wild things dwell; corn-fields and gardens, flocks and herds — these are the theophanies of the goddess. The classical world worshipped her at one remove from her origins as a statue in a man-made temple, often in a city. This separation of cult and nature grew deeper and wider in Christianity. The old nature gods like Pan became the new devils; nature herself became suspect and woman was repressed.

The Celtic world in its own way was just as civilized, if less urban, than the Roman. In it women retained many of their matriarchal rights and freedoms in relation to men, and the goddess was worshipped in her own natural forms in her own natural habitat. Again and again in the stories of the Black Virgins, a statue is found in a forest or a bush, or discovered when ploughing animals refuse to pass a certain spot. The statue is then taken to the parish church, only to return miraculously by night to her own place, where a chapel is then built in her honour. Almost invariably her cult is associated with natural phenomena, especially healing waters or striking geographical features such as extinct volcanoes, confluences and subterranean lines of force. The Romans had taken over and adapted many of the sacred sites of the Celtic world, which the Christians were later, in their turn, to sanctify, but the spirit of the place remains Celtic, and still whispers something of its origins through the cult associated with it.

The Romans renamed the Celtic and Teutonic gods after their own, and Christianity converted them into its saints and angels.

As a result, it is difficult to recapture the essence of the original deity. Furthermore, the divine names differ according to the various Celtic peoples who utter them, though the archetypal patterns, such as the triple goddess, remain constant. Since most of the Black Virgins are to be found in the land of the Gauls rather than Britain, or Ireland, it will often be simpler to use their names for the gods. Another complication is the influence of Teutonic cults, pre- and post-Roman, and the weight that should be accorded to them. The similarities between Celtic and Teutonic deities are, however, such as to make their cults often indistinguishable.

The Celtic influence on the development of the Black Virgin cult was further, though indirectly, reinforced by six centuries of missionary activity and fraternal visits by Irish monks in Western Europe. The first of these, St Columbanus (550-615), sojourned in the Syrian quarter of Orléans, with its cults to the Black Virgin, St Mary of Egypt and the Magdalen. The last, St Malachy of the prophecies, died in the arms of his friend and biographer, St Bernard, at Clairvaux in 1148. Among Irish links with the Merovingians, it should be noted that St Dagobert, their last king, spent his formative years in refuge in Ireland.

Few Celtic cult objects have been preserved from the pre-Roman period. The standing stones, whether arranged in elaborate temples as at Avebury and Stonehenge, or isolated menhirs and dolmens, were erected by earlier peoples, though the Celts held them in awe and no doubt used them for their religious ceremonies. A small number of sites believed to be those of pre-Roman Celtic temples have been discovered, but, more typically, worship took place in sacred places that were unenclosed. The Monster of Noves (qv) is a rare stone figure from the third century BC, phallic and devouring, in an area (see also Vacquières and Maillane) where there are a number of Black Virgins, including one associated with Hecate, goddess of death and rebirth. The original Black Virgins of Chartres and Longpont probably started life as Celtic fertility idols. It is not unlikely that many others may have either originated as pagan statuettes or have been inspired by them. In 1984 nearly two hundred small wooden statues were excavated from a pool in the sanctuary of Sequana, near the source of the Seine. In contrast to the Greeks and the Romans, the Celts considered rivers to be goddesses rather than sons of Okeanos and manifestations of Neptune. Not only river sources but also wells, lakes and springs were consequently honoured by images of the feminine, life-giving spirit, sometimes in the form of a single goddess and often in that of the triple Matres.

Of the many Black Virgins found in trees it is difficult to be sure whether the underlying influence is more likely to be Celtic, Teutonic or one deriving ultimately from the cult of Artemis/Diana. The symbolical value of the tree is hermaphroditic: it is the manifestation of the phallic power and firmness linking earth and heaven, but the life-force oracularly interpreting the divine will speaks with the voice of the goddess.

Although, in general, throughout their centuries of wandering, the Celts seem to have adapted to and assimilated the spirits of the places where they found themselves, there are a number of deities, specifically Celtic, which have connections in place or time with the cult of the Black Virgin. The Celts themselves committed none of their religious lore to writing during the pre-Christian period. Theirs was an oral culture, and wisdom was passed by word of mouth from generation to generation in the colleges of the bards and Druids. The texts on which most of our knowledge of Celtic religion and myth are based are either Roman or Christian, from a period not later than the eighth century. Neither Romans nor Christians were interested in the profundities of Celtic religion, and were content either to formulate it in their own terms or to comment on the more striking racial features: the independence of Celtic women, the drunkenness of Celtic men, the savagery and intrepidity of the warriors, male and female, and curious practices like the ritual copulation of the kings of Ulster with a mare. It is, however, generally agreed that the basis of Celtic religion was a belief in reincarnation. Tir nan Og, the land of eternal youth where warriors disport themselves, awaiting rebirth or eternally freed from its chains, has much in common with Wotan's Valhalla. The long years of Druidic initiation, the oral inculcation of bardic lore and the intricacies of the Ogham script, ensured that the religion was an esoteric one, preserved through the secret knowledge of a spiritual elite. When Ireland eventually embraced Christianity as it did, without the fertilising blood of martyrs, it was a Christianity based on the experiential know-

ledge of holy men and women, nuns, monks and Culdees that
kept the flame of the spirit burning in the west and re-
evangelized Europe. The Celtic Church long clung to the
customs and tonsure of St John and maintained the Greek
liturgical calendar over against that of Rome. In the peaceful
transition between the old faith and the new, most of the feasts
and divinities of Gaeldom were accommodated within the
Christian framework.

THE CELTIC DIVINITIES

The Dagda/Ogmios/Gallic Hercules/Sucellus/Dispater/Orcus
The second-century Greek philosopher, Lucian of Samosata,
commented on the strange image of Herakles current among the
Celts. He is an old man at the end of his life, balding, white-
haired, burnt by the sun, more like Charon than the classical
hero, but bearing the same accoutrements. He leads a considerable crowd by means of gold and amber cords linking their ears
to his tongue. Though he wears the lion-skin and wields the club
and bow, his power is evidently that of the word.

The oldest of the Celtic gods, father of all and lord of perfect
knowledge, was known to the Irish as the Dagda. His grotesque
appearance, garbed as a peasant, ugly, pot-bellied and coarse,
with a gargantuan appetite, probably marks him out as inherited
by the Celts from an earlier people. His son, Ogma Sun-Face or
Ogmias, god of literature and eloquence, was the inventor of
Ogham, the Celtic alphabet. The Dagda's club, so large that it
would have taken eight men to carry it, dealt death at one end,
and life at the other. His second most prized possession was a
magic cauldron that could never be emptied. It has much in
common with the magic cauldrons of Wotan and the black
goddess Cerridwen, though in their case the inspirational aspects
of the contents are emphasized, but it is, no doubt, one of the
early prototypes of the Holy Grail. Herakles is also associated
with a cauldron-shaped vessel which he borrowed from the sun
in order to make his voyage to the west. Bran the Blessed had a
cauldron which could restore the dead to life, but without the
power of speech, and it is probably this aspect of the vessel,

symbolizing both death and rebirth, that made it and its possessor so popular among the Celts.

The chief feast day associated with the Dagda, when he consumed a huge meal of porridge from a hole in the ground and mated with the Morrigan, a black mermaid goddess of water and the underworld, took place at Samain, 1 November. This is the season of witchcraft and the dead, Hallowe'en, All Saints and All Souls. The decline of the year, however, is also the time of the new wine, Martinmas fairs and sausage feasts, as hams are salted away for the long winter months. Pluto/Dispater is the god of riches as well as the underworld and, in astrology, rules Scorpio (24 October-22 November). In Gaul he is known as Sucellus, and is represented as a mature figure with a massive mallet, proffering a large drinking cup. All Gauls claimed to be descended from him. Some representations of St James the Greater are evocative of Sucellus.

At the feast of Samain, which was the Celtic New Year, when one looked both forward and back on a day which belonged to neither year, the boundaries between the world of the living and that of the gods and the dead were blurred. Similarly, in Christian times, those who have died in the parish during the year walk in procession to the graveyard on All Soul's Day, before returning to the earth.

Symbolically, at this end and beginning of the year, the lord of the dead and the dark goddess unite to ensure that the earth will once more be fruitful after the dead season, when they will reemerge as the new light and blessed greenness of early February. The Church's calendar for the period of Samain includes, as well as All Saints and All Souls, the following feasts: Christ the King, the Holy Relics, St Hubert (the wild huntsman of the Ardennes), the black St Martin de Porres, St Malachy of Armagh, St Flour and a number of others with Merovingian, Teutonic and Black Virgin associations.

Lug

One of the four major feasts of the Celtic year was Lughnasad, Lammas, held on 1 August to commemorate the death of Lug. The fact that to the Anglo-Saxons it was 'loaf-mass' suggests that Lug represented, as the first fruits of the grain harvest, the sun as it enters upon its annual decline. His many-sidedness precludes any possibility of seeing in him nothing but the dying and rising god of a vegetation cult. He gives as his chief occupation that of carpenter, which links him to Joseph, Jesus, builders of arks and chariots, and all constructors of frameworks. That he is armed with a magic spear, sired a hero, practised sorcery, poetry, horsemanship and the blacksmith's craft, as well as having a raven as his familiar, points to a strong association with Wotan. His consort in the ancient capital and Black Virgin site of Lyons, which takes its name from him, is called Rosmerta, who at Sion-Vaudémont (qv) is Wotan's queen (see also St Bertrand de Comminges). Lug's sling and his harp remind us of King David. The lion, too, belongs to both of them as it does to Cybele, the Lady of Lyons. The Greek root of his name, *luk* wolf, links him to Apollo, Arcadian Zeus and the tribe of Benjamin, but also has connotations with dawn and dusk, and the path of light, the sun's annual course. The Latin words which may be connected with him are *lux*, light, and *lucus*, a sacred grove. He is also, like his homophone St Luke, a historian. Robert Graves suggests both an identification with the three-fold Geryon and a possible derivation from the Sumerian word for 'son'. Irish mythology makes him the offspring of the triple goddess, a point well taken by the Church, which celebrates on 1 August the feast of Sts Faith, Hope and Charity, daughters of St Wisdom. Lug's other major city in France, Laon, the Carolingian capital, boasts a Black Virgin, a Templar Commandery and a bull-festooned cathedral. There is a Luc-sur-Aude between Rennes-le-Château and Limoux (qv) and a Luc-sur-Mer next to La Délivrande (qv). The comparative rarity of the name in France has led some to believe it was the unnameable name of God.

Bel/Belen/Belenus

Belen is another Celtic god of light, important for the study of the cult of the Black Virgin. Beaune is named for him or his latinized consort Bellona, later assimilated with Cybele. An image of him was found at Beaune in 1767 and her likeness appeared on the ancient arms of the city. Mont St Michel, where the Black Virgin was once known as Notre-Dame du Mont Tombe, was originally Tombelen. Nearby was a temple of Cybele. Bollène and Ballon no doubt owe their names to the god as do the many villages called St Bonnet to be found near Black Virgin sites. It seems improbable that the 28th Bishop of Clermont, who died in Lyons in 710, and whose body was brought home sewn up in the skin of a billy-goat, could have inspired such a large number of Church dedications if there were not some other motivation at work. The St Bonnet three kilometres from Riom had a temple to Belen, while at St Bonnet near St Germain l'Herm, where there was a temple of Diana, a phallic stone surmounted by a cross still survives. St Bonnet shares a feast-day, 15 January, with St Maurus (Mars). Belen, the Gallic Apollo, or Abellio, may also be the inspiration for Notre-Dame des Abeilles, the Black Virgin of Banyuls.

Belen seems to have been a more erotic god than Apollo. His feast is May Day with its Beltane fires when the licentious rites of the maypole were performed in honour of Flora/Maia/Venus, the May Queen. According to Saillens, Mont Saint Michel may have been in pagan times a resort of sacred prostitutes where the rites of Bacchus and Venus were celebrated at all seasons. 1 May, now the feast of St Joseph the Workman, was once that of St Amador in his own shrine of Rocamadour, where the Black Virgin succeeded to Sulevia, Minerva, Iduenna, a triple goddess integrated by Cybele. The eve of May Day sees the feasts of St Catherine of Siena, the bride of Christ, and one of a number of saints called Sophia. Belen's daughter, Arianrhod, who as lady of the silver celestial wheel (the Corona Borealis) is related to that other Catherine, of Alexandria, became the bride of Gwydion, considered by Robert Graves to be a Welsh form of Wotan. A daughter of the Greek Belos, ancestor of the Danaans, whom some associate with the Tuatha de Danaan in Ireland, was the bi-sexual, child-stealing Lamia.

Cernunnos

If Lug and Bel are translatable more or less interchangeably into the Gallic Mercury and Apollo, Cernunnos is less easily assimilated to classical modes. Robert Graves associates him with Actaeon. Joseph Campbell equates him with the Dagda. He is represented as the central god of a trinity, flanked by Mercury and Apollo, naked, effeminate youths in comparison with the powerful, mature, horned figure, seated cross-legged on a throne, beneath which a stag and a bull feed on the plenteous fodder which flows from his lap. On the Gundestrup Bowl, where he assumes the semi-lotus yoga position, he is surrounded by animals and holds a ram-headed serpent in his left hand. A figure riding a large fish is swimming away from him. A stele from Beaune museum shows him as the three-headed central figure of a triad of naked seated gods. Another carving found under Notre-Dame de Paris in 1911 shows the god with rings on his horns, glancing fixedly sideways. He almost certainly stems from the shamans to be seen weaving their hunting spells in prehistoric cave-paintings. Emma Jung and M.-L. von Franz relate him to Wotan and Merlin as well as to Christ, who in the Grail legends appeared to his disciples as a white stag. He lingers on in Christian hagiography as St Hubert, patron of hunters, and St Eustace whose emblem is also the stag. In England he may be remembered as Herne the Hunter, who had a great oak at Windsor, in the Abbots Bromley horn dance and as the Cerne Giant. In Scotland he is shown on a stone-carving as a merman with two tails.

Horned gods are by definition cuckold gods. Franck Marie suggests the hypothesis that the cuckolded god is one belonging to an earlier age. If Belen belongs to the age of Aries which ended with the coming of the Piscean saviour, Christ, Cernunnos harks back to the Taurean era of the great goddesses. Marie sees Cernunnos as the eremitic spirit of Mt Bugarach, the sacred Cathar mountain, halfway from Montségur to the sea. A stream called La Blanque flows from Bugarach to be joined by the Fontaine des Amours and another, variously called La Gode (a title of Freyja/Frigg/Hel) or La Madeleine which rises on Mt Serbairou. The confluence of these streams with the Sals takes place at Rennes-les-Bains, and all journey on together to the Aude, passing the Black Virgin of Limoux.

The Abbé Boudet of Rennes-les-Bains, mentor of the Abbé Saunière of Rennes-le-Château, wrote a strange book, published in 1886, *La Vraie Langue Celtique et le cromlech de Rennes-les-Bains* which was apparently much appreciated by Queen Victoria. Amidst a farrago of humorously false etymology and questionable history, he asserts that the Celtic inhabitants of the area (including Toulouse), the Volscian Tectosages, were the ancestors of the Franks and the sons of Gomer. Gomer was the son of Japhet, who came from Ceylon and India to the west via

Troy. Through him the Merovingians can thus claim to be descended from Noah. There are indeed some surprising place names in the area, like Goundhill, with its curious echoes of Goonhilly in the far west of Cornwall (one French euphemism for to be a cuckold is 'to go to Cornwall'), an odd neighbour for such Balkan-sounding peaks as Bugarach and Serbairou.

Perhaps some of the esoteric teaching associated with Cernunnos persisted in the Christian era. Marie hints at a mystery surrounding the nick-name 'Coucoupierre' given to Peter the Hermit, preacher and leader of the First Crusade. He was reputedly one of the Calabrian solitaries who settled in the Black Lands of the Golden Valley (see Orval, Belgium) where he became the tutor of Godefroy de Bouillon. The Latin *cuculus*, a cuckoo or adulterer, is very close to *cucullus*, a cowl, a similarity which no doubt accounts for the unusual cognomen of the monk. Did he perhaps introduce some teachings from the past that were not wholly orthodox into his woodland classes in the Ardennes? Joachim of Flora (1132-1202), who taught the imminent coming of the age of the Holy Spirit, a notion which was condemned by the Church, was from the same syncretistic southern Italian tradition as Peter the Hermit and experienced a conversion to the interior life in the Holy Land before becoming a Cistercian. He is named for St Joachim, who with his wife, St Anne, must be the most pre-Christian of saints. He shares his feast-day, 16 August, the day after the Assumption, with St Roch (qv), the companion of Black Virgins. St Anne's day is 26 July. On the 25th the memory is venerated of St Christopher, a Canaanite giant who carried the world on his shoulders in the form of the infant Christ, and affords Templar-like protection to pilgrims and wayfarers. The same day is the feast of St James the Greater of Compostela and of the curiously named St Cucufas. ('it is right to be cuckoo'?), also known as Quiquenfat, Guinefort and Cugat, called a Prince of Scotland in his chapel at Le Puy.

Teutates, Esus and Taranis
Lucan (AD 39-65) of Cordoba, nephew of Seneca, whose Stoic views he shared, writes of this trinity of Celtic gods in his *Pharsalia:* 'Mercury, among the Gauls, is called Teutates and is propitiated by immersing the victim head first in a cauldron of water until he is drowned; to satisfy Mars, called Esus, they hang

the victim on a tree and quarter him. For Taranis they offer burnt sacrifice in a wickerwork idol, filled with men.'

Marie traces modified survivals of such cults up to modern times in the traditions of carnival at Limoux (qv). The similarity of the name Esus, the woodman god, associated with hanging on a tree, to that of the crucified carpenter, Jesus, may have furthered an ease of transition between the two religions. A first-century AD bas-relief shows Esus cutting down a willow-tree containing a bull's head and three marsh birds, a scene comparable to that of the hero Gilgamesh cutting down the tree, also probably a willow, of the goddess Ishtar. Christians enthusiastically felled the sacred trees of Germany, but already the trees of the Taurean divinities had been hewn down by the votaries of the age of Aries. Julius Caesar had personally axed an ancient sacred grove at Marseilles, because all others feared the retribution of the goddess (cf. Chapter 2, Artemis — the coin of Myrrha). It thus seems possible that the placing of images of a goddess in a tree may be a cultic practice, dating back to the age of Taurus, which has survived to this day in numerous traditions relating to the Black Virgin. The Black Virgin of Neuerburg (qv Germany) was not removed from her tree until April 1984. It would seem that, like Zeus at Dodona, the gods of the Celts and Teutons may have taken over trees sacred to an older goddess without totally banishing her presence.

The Matres

Triads of gods are, as we have seen, an important feature in Celtic and Teutonic religion. There are, in addition, representations of three-headed deities, bulls with three horns, boars with three tusks, a bull with three cranes, the three sacred birds that guard the Isle of Man, etc., but the most widespread devotion among the Celts seems to have been the cult of the triple-goddess. Like triple Hecate, she rules over the three realms of sky, earth and underworld, presiding over birth, life and death. Wells and springs are the openings of her womb, and her moon governs the growth, flow and decay of all that is on earth. The triads are shown in different forms and venerated under a variety of names, as maiden, bride and crone. Typically they carry horns of plenty. Their distribution is wider than that of the male gods and they appear to date from an earlier period, being particularly popular among the poorer sections of the population, always more resistant to cultic novelties.

Rosmerta

This goddess is usually considered to be the consort of the Gallic Mercury and has been represented carrying the caduceus herself. Her cult was particularly prevalent in eastern Gaul, though images of her have been found as far west as Gloucestershire. At Sion-Vaudémont (qv), where she is the consort of the universal god Wotan, an *ex-voto* plaque erected by Carinius, thanking her and Mercury/Wotan for the safety of his son, Urbicus, was discovered in 1817. There is also a statue of her in Sion museum. At Lyons she was accounted the companion of Lug. She has been seen as a personification of fruitful mother earth, but her form and her name could also be suggestive of Venus, as could the sexual cult of the Virgin and the Holy Spirit which flourished at Sion in the mid-nineteenth century. To judge by her chief location in old Lotharingia, Rosmerta partakes, as an intermediate figure, of both the Celtic and Teutonic worlds. The Gaelic *ros* means either 'wood', or 'prominence', 'peninsula', 'headland', while the Germanic *hros* signifies horse. The Latin roots yield 'rose' and 'dew'. Merta is a puzzle. Most other *mart*-words find their ultimate origin in Mars, like Wotan, the god of War, or Martha, 'lady'. The Sanskrit root *mrt* means dead. The myrtle, on the other hand, sacred to Aphrodite/Venus, is a symbol of the feminine principle, associated with happiness, victory and initiation into the divine mysteries. The Greek *murtos* means both myrtle and clitoris. At the end of the last century a beautiful androgynous statue was excavated at Sion, reminding us that Venus carrying a caduceus might well be considered as Hermaphrodite, and that Gnostic sexual rites, of which those carried out at Sion were a late echo, were designed to restore the primal androgyny. In this borderland of Teuton and Celt one may also suspect the influence of Nerthus, androgynous mother, by her brother, of the love-goddess Freyja. According to de Sède, who sees her as the origin of the Black Virgin of Avioth, Rosmerta was attended by a cortège of dead children (p.23).

Epona/Rhiannon/Macha

Epona enjoyed a more widespread devotion than any other Celtic goddess, having been adopted as the patroness of Roman cavalry stables and carried by the legions to all parts of the Empire. She is shown riding side-saddle wearing a diadem and a long robe with a curious swirling, circular, four-fold halo or banneret of material billowing behind her head. She carries a key, a symbol also associated with Hecate, and gazes fixedly in front of her. This bas-relief was found at Gannat, a dozen miles from the initiates' church of Thuret (qv) where there is in addition to the famous Black Virgin, a remarkable font around which a uroboric horse bites its own tail. Sometimes Epona's horse or mare is accompanied by a foal (cf. stele in Beaune Museum). The Kings of Ulster used to mate ritually with a mare and the Queens of India with a stallion.

Horses, symbols of libido and death, are associated with a number of Black Virgin sites: Einsiedeln is the oldest and most

5. Thuret

famous centre of horse-breeding in Switzerland and the stud-farms of Saumur and those near Sion-Vaudémont are well-known in France. In England, Lady Godiva and the White Horse of Uffington testify to the durability of the goddess, though it should be remembered that the horse is sacred to Wotan and Freyja too. Perhaps the white horse of Belgic Kent, invaded by Hengist and Horsa ('stallion' and 'horse'), belongs to both Celt and Teuton. In Christian iconography, the horse is associated with St George, a Christianized figure from pagan myth, recently demoted by the Church. He doubtless owes his rulership of England to his resemblance to Wotan. St James also appears on a white charger at Compostela to rout the Moors. In Ireland, Macha and Mabd are equivalent to Epona as protectors of horses and chthonic divinities. The Welsh mare-goddess Rhiannon was queen of Dyfed, whose central point was the 'Dark Gate', entrance to the underworld.

Brigit/Anu/Danu/Dana

According to the *Larousse Encyclopedia of Mythology* it seems probable that all these deities are different concepts of the same mother-goddess figure. In Saillens's view the Black Virgin of Tarascon (qv), one of whose titles is 'La Belle Briançonne' is a combination of Brigit and Ana/Anu. Brigantia was the epony-mous goddess of the powerful tribe of the Brigantes, the most populous in Britain, whose capital was York. Further south her name extends from Briançon (the Gallo-Roman Brigantium) in the Alps to Brigantia (now Corunna) in the far north-west corner of Spain. The neighbours of the Brigantes in Yorkshire were the Parisii, founders of Paris, evidence of the Celtic capacity for wandering.

Brigit is especially associated with the cult of the Black Virgin through the feast Imbolc, one of the Celtic quarter days, which occurred on 1 February, now the feast of St Brigid, the Mary of the Gael, which coincides with Candlemas. Like Candlemas it was the celebration of the reawakening of the secret fire that would purify the land and herald the return of spring. The trial marriages that took place on that day, which lasted by mutual consent for a year, illustrate the comparative freedom of Celtic women to decide their own fate. At Beltane, on 1 May, Brigit, representing the Tuatha de Danaan, the people of the goddess

Danu, with whom she is probably identified, married Bres, who was half African, a giant Fomorian descended from Noah's son Ham, whose people were the earlier inhabitants of Ireland. Brigit (Irish 'Brig' = 'power') was a goddess of poetry, knowledge and the arts of civilization. Her shrine of the sacred fire at Kildare was continued by her Christian namesake, St Brigid or Bride (c.450–c.523). Bridewell, the chief women's prison in London, was once a convent of hers. Other features which St Brigid shares with many Black Virgins are her ability to raise the dead and the healing power of the cloth that has touched her, especially when applied to women suffering from barrenness and illnesses of childbirth.

St Bridgit, patron saint of Sweden, shares her feast day, 8 October, with three penitent whores, Margaret, Pelagia and Thais, as well as with St Bacchus. In 1346 she founded an order devoted to learning, the Brigittines, whose members were organized in double communities of men and women, like Cassian's foundation in Marseilles and St Brigid's at Kildare. In the new order, however, the prioress was the superior of both houses. Syon House was their headquarters in England. According to Robert Graves, some houses of the order 'reverted merrily to paganism'. The dark-faced St Mary of Egypt is associated by Graves with the Brigid/Bridgit archetype.

The syllable most commonly found in the names of goddesses throughout Europe and the Middle East is *an*. The Indo-Germanic root signifies 'to breathe', from which are derived *anemos* (wind), *animus* (spirit) and *anima* (soul). The Hebrew 'Hannah', name of the mothers of Samuel and the Virgin Mary, means, like John, 'God has favoured'. In Greek *ana* means 'O King', a form restricted to invocation of the gods, though Sappho is said to have used it as the vocative of *anassa*, meaning 'queen, lady or mistress' as applied to goddesses. *An* in Sumerian means 'heaven' while the Latin for a duck is *anas*. In general, throughout the Indo-European languages, the most prevalent associations with *ana* have to do with plenty and motherhood. This aspect of her is illustrated by the twin hills called the Paps of Anu in County Kerry. The Aryan conquerors of the Himalayas consecrated one of its great peaks to Anna Purna.

But the goddess also had a dark, devouring side, well illustrated in the legend of Black Annis or Cat Anna of Leicester, who lived in a cave she had clawed out for herself in the Dane (Danu?) Hills. She used to lie in wait for children by a huge pollard oak where she would hang their skins to dry after clawing them to death, sucking their blood and flaying them. She had a secret passage in later times leading from her lair to the cellars under the castle, and as late as 1941 a small girl evacuated from the city reported that you could hear her grinding her teeth five miles away. Black Annis may seem a far cry from the Christian goddess until one recalls that the speciality of Black Virgins is to grant eternal bliss to dead babies offered to them (cf. Avioth). This death aspect is also illustrated by the Irish great goddess, the Morrigan, especially associated with war and destruction, who hovers near the battle-field as a crow or raven.

The Roman goddess Anna Perenna was considered to be the sister of Belus the father of Danaus and Lamia, though Beli (Belen) was also said to be the son of Anna, 'Empress of Rome'. It is as St Anne that this potent symbol persists in Christianity. To the Bretons, according to Saillens, she largely replaces the Black Virgin (but see Guingamp). Her window in Chartres, the biggest image in the Cathedral, has been black since its donation by St Louis in the thirteenth century. Jean Markale talks of the submerged princess of Breton legends, the ruler of hell, who has dared to resist authority, and so is necessarily 'a bad and lewd woman'. Like Hecate, she rules the cross-roads by night and, like Lilith, she is the Devil's consort. Markale goes on, 'Yet surely she is the reflection of the goddess of ancient, pre-patriarchal societies . . . who haunts every corner of life, but reveals herself only very reluctantly, sometimes even as a Black Virgin.'

The Loathly Damsel

Perhaps it is this submerged princess who, at the very end of the Celtic era, seeks to bring about the redemption of an imprisoned maiden from the stately castle on a lofty mountain. According to the Mabinogion, a maiden came to King Arthur's court at Caerleon to reproach Peredur/Pereceval for not having asked about the streaming spear in the Castle of Wonders (the Grail Castle) where there is also a bleeding head. She rode a yellow mule and 'blacker were her face and her two hands than the blackest iron covered with pitch'.

THE TEUTONIC DEITIES

The possible influence of the Germanic tradition on the cult of
the Black Virgin has received little attention. Yet the vast
majority of Black Virgins are to be found in those areas of
Europe which, at the break-up of the Roman Empire, came
under the domination of the Arian Burgundians and Visigoths.
Certain factors made a transition from paganism to the heretical
Christianity of Arius easier than the acceptance of orthodox
Catholicism.

The gods of the Germans were not far removed from the
world of men. They were viewed as ancestors, heroes and kings
of old, in whom shone the light of the absolute, and who still,
like Wotan, rode the night-skies on wind-fast steeds or wandered
in the forests of middle earth befriending those in need. The idea
that Jesus Christ could have been consubstantial with the
absolute godhead and begotten by him before all worlds would
have been thoroughly alien to Teutons who claimed descent
from, and kinship with, their own high god. Arianism, on the
other hand, denying as it did, the full divinity of Christ, was
welcomed by the Goths and Burgundians. Much in the gospel
would, in fact, have been quite familiar to them. The rune for
Wotan, strongly resembling a crucified man, recalls the similarity of his sacrifice, hanging nine days on a tree to bring saving
knowledge to mankind, with that of Jesus (known to the Goths
as Frauja). Wotan, too, received his initiation into the waters of
wisdom through the mediation of a relation of his mother's,
Mimir, who, later, like John the Baptist, lost his head.

Wotan embalmed the head of Mimir, and cast spells upon it so
that it could continue to tell him of hidden things. Wotan also
brought the speaking head of Minos, Lord of the Underworld, to
Scandinavia. In later history, speaking heads were associated
with Gerbert of Aurillac, Roger Bacon, the Portuguese giant
Ferragus, and St Albertus Magnus, Dominican alchemist whose
tomb is in the Black Virgin city of Cologne. The 'wonderful
head' of the god Bran, buried under the Tower of London until
excavated by King Arthur, together with the ravens that are the
tutelary spirits of London, offer further parallels to the Wotan
cult. Darcy and Angebert associate a triple head from Bornholm,
sacred island of the Burgundians, with a wotanic ritual, and

point to a possible continuity between it and the head Baphomet used in Templar initiation ceremonies. The Baphomet carved by the Templars awaiting death at Chinon assumes, according to Yvon Roy, different faces when looked at from different angles and in varying lights. One possible example of a Baphomet may be found on a capital of the Templar church of Eunate (Spain), where a prophet, inverted, becomes a goat. Unquestionably the most dynamic and tenacious successors to the Templars were the Teutonic Knights, a highly wotanic order and faithful servants of the black eagle, whether with one head or two.

Wotan/Odin/Woden

Wotan offers a unique example of a European god in opposition to Christianity who, far from being a spent force, was beginning to reach his apogee during the first millennium of our era, being cut off in his prime and thoroughly repressed by the terrorist tactics of Charlemagne. If the cult of the Black Virgin attracts to itself elements from other, submerged, cults, it would be surprising if Wotan, the master of disguise and infiltration, were not represented in it. Indeed, his involvement with the ambiguous traditions of Sion-Vaudémont (qv) are undeniable. It seems likely that Einsiedeln (qv), with its dragon fountain, in the heart of old Switzerland, where Wotan still rides the sky with his retinue of souls, 'the holy people', preserves memories of the usurped god. The ancient *dalle du cavalier* at Rennes-le-Château is believed to represent the young King Sigebert IV and his knight Mérovée Lévi. May it not be that these two figures, Templar-like on one horse, stem from an iconographic tradition celebrating Wotan the saviour's rescue of his protégé, Hadding, from the hands of his foes?

The Romans identified Wotan with Mercury/Hermes. Both are tricksters and guides of souls who are often depicted wearing a broad-brimmed hat. With St Joseph they share the same day of the week, Wednesday (though in Germany the neutral Mittwoch has been tactfully substituted) and all three bestow a fortunate death. This, however, is only a small part of the repertoire of a god who was well on his way to attaining universality through assimilation of the attributes of his competitors, much as Isis was doing at the same period. His similarities with the war-god Mars/Ares are particularly strong. His name means 'rage'

('Wotan, id est furor', Adam of Bremen, eleventh-century archbishop), he is bearded, carries a spear and wears a helmet. As lord of hosts he throws into battle his irresistible, frenzied shock-troops, the Berserkers. Like Jupiter/Zeus, whose eagle he shares, he is the all-father, notorious for his amorous escapades, presiding jovially over a table of good cheer.

A raven-god like Saturn/Kronos, Wotan's great feast is Saturnalia or Yuletide, twelve nights at least which, disguised as St Nicholas, he has wrested back from the encroachments of Christianity, replacing the cross with his world-tree. *Larousse* compares Wotan as a sky-god to Varuna and Uranus. It is curious that Uranus, who has very little mythology, is increasingly seen by astrologers (as he was by Gustav Holst) as the magician, whose sudden strokes of fate turn everything upside down in revolutionary fashion. Such is Wotan, who raises up his favourites, only to cast them down at the height of their glory. If Wotan is assimilating Uranus, the ruler of the coming age of Aquarius, then it is important that the world should recognize Wotan's depth and wisdom. The Wotanic frenzy is essentially that of the shaman and seer rather than the warrior with which he is generally associated. He is a wine-god, like Jesus and Dionysus, and takes no other nourishment than the fermented juice of the grape. Wotan brought wisdom and Gnosis from the underworld and is, like Pluto, the lord of the dead.

In his chthonic role he is no doubt succeeded by Blaise, consort of the Black Virgin of Candlemas, whose name in Celtic means 'wolf', the animal most closely associated with Wotan. The crossed candles of Blaise applied to the throat remove blockages and assist communication, but they also resemble the cross of St Andrew, the saltire of Scotland and Burgundy. This symbol is the Teutonic rune of the eagle.

As lord of Minne (love) he vies with Eros and Christ and, perhaps, since he can change his sex, with Venus herself, Freyja. It is this repressed aspect of Wotan that especially relates him to much in the cult of the Black Virgin. His beloved Brünnhilde, whose disobedience ushered in the new age of humanity, had a daughter, the last of the Volsungs, Aslog. She lived on in Norway as a sooty-faced kitchen-maid whose name means 'raven'. Another female raven, according to Marion Bradley, was a priestess of Avalon, founded by Wotan's British counter-part, Merlin.

Frigg

Frigg is Wotan's second wife (the first being Jord/Erde), the goddess for whom Friday is named, identified by the Romans with Venus, but more strongly associated with marriage and child-bearing, and invoked by women in labour. Friday used to be considered a lucky day for weddings in Germany. Frigg was a powerful intercessor who prevailed upon Wotan to spare the Lombards to whom he had decreed defeat at the hands of the Vandals. She also persuaded Wotan to grant the request of King Rerir and his wife for a child. In these ways she fulfils functions very characteristic of the Black Virgins. Perhaps she is associated with Rosmerta, who at Sion, combines features of the mother, lover and bringer of victory.

Freyja

Freyja and Frigg are often confused and sometimes in-distinguishable, but Freyja possesses a number of important individual traits. Snorri, writing in *c.* 1220, calls her the most renowned of the goddesses and the only one still alive i.e. still the object of cultic veneration. If Frigg is Hera, protectress of married love, Freyja is Venus, goddess of love affairs and, in her own mythical tradition, the northern representative of the whore, wisdom. Her wisdom, like that of Loki and Wotan, is shamanistic: assuming the form of a bird, she can fly through the nine worlds bringing back knowledge and power to her petitioners. Thus she became identified by Christians with the queen of the night and of witches, and as such she is represented, like Diana, naked, her cloak flying behind her as she rides her broomstick through the air, on a twelfth-century wall-painting in Schleswig cathedral. As Gertrude ('spear-strength'), one of the Valkyries who were once her priestesses, she shares a feast-day, 17 March, with a number of interesting saints. These include St Gertrude of Nivelles, a city reputedly named after the Niebelungen, situated between the Black Virgin sites of Hal and Walcourt, where giants and a magical horse called Godet are still celebrated at carnival time. It is also the feast of St Joseph of

Arimathea, who brought the Holy Grail to Glastonbury. One pilgrim to Glastonbury was that man of many voyages, St Patrick, who has made 17 March famous wherever the Irish have travelled.

Freyja has much to do with horses, and may well be the original nightmare. Her devotees could assume the form of horses and were also accused of riding men to death on their beds. As a flax-goddess, Freyja is clearly related to the Slav Serpolnica, who also rapes men to death. One of Freyja's names, Mardoll, suggests a connection with the sea and may link her with Nehalennia, the goddess of Walcheren in the Scheldt estuary. This was the homeland of the Franks, where Mérovée/Merweg was engendered. Nehalennia is sometimes represented standing in the stern of a boat, like Isis and the Black Madonna who sailed in Merovingian times into the harbour of Boulogne. Boulogne is a great deal closer to Middelburg than to Alexandria, the home port of that other, more celebrated ship-goddess, Isis, star of the sea. Nehalennia is also represented, like St Roch and Hecate, with a dog, which may relate her to Freyja in her aspect as goddess of the dead. Freyja's other feast-day, 2 February, coincides with Candlemas, St Brigid's Imbolc festival, and day *par excellence* of the Black Virgin. Freyja's car is drawn by swans and doves.

Hel
Hel/Hella refers both to the place of the dead and to the goddess who presides there though, like Hecate, she has power, granted by Wotan, in all the worlds. Her head hung forward, partially disguising the fact that she possessed only half a face (cf. Champagnac-lec-Mines). The Belgian Black Virgin city of Hal (qv) has also been etymologically connected with Hel.

CHAPTER 4
The whore wisdom in the Christian era

There is nothing in the New Testament that offers much justification for a cult of the feminine principle as divine wisdom, mother of God or queen of heaven. Mary's role is dealt with in a few lines, and, after the narrative of the nativity, seems sometimes at odds with her son's mission. So how is it that little more than a century after the conversion of Constantine, the triumph of Mary Theotokos, the God-bearer, was celebrated on the altars of Christendom from the Rhône to the Euphrates?

There are two main reasons for this phenomenon. One, the great expansion during the later Roman Empire of the religion of universal goddesses such as Isis and Cybele, was discussed in Chapter 2. The other is more complex, and concerns the effect on Christianity of its first three centuries of struggle against Gnosticism, its hydra-headed adversary.

By the beginning of the Christian era, a fusing and blending of traditions had already been in progress for some centuries in the great mixing bowl of Alexandria. The vast Jewish population, worshipping one masculine, invisible God, and abhorring graven images, was surrounded on every hand by the deities and philosophies of Greece and Egypt. The translation of the Hebrew Bible into Greek in the third century BC had a subtle but profound effect on the way Jews came to think about God and the world. One of their greatest writers, Philo of Alexandria (*c.*20 BC–AD50) contributed to the development of a symbolic understanding of scripture that was later to be the hallmark of the Christian catechetical school led by Clement of Alexandria (*c.*150–*c.*215). Philo coined a word, 'archetype', to denote an exemplar, pattern or model, literally 'first-moulded', to refer to certain principal ideas, not far removed from those of Plato. They were not quite the same as the pagan gods of popular religion, but neither were they mere abstractions or dead concepts. A good example of such an archetype is 'the Word' used in the prologue to St John's Gospel to mean an intermediary power between God and the world. In the period separating Philo from Clement, Christianity in Egypt was dominated by the Gnostic tendency, which emphasized the importance of such influences emanating from the godhead. Many of these semi-personified abstract nouns, which demand to be capitalized, are feminine: Wisdom, Silence, Truth, Thought, Faith, Grace, Life, Church and Gnosis itself — intuitive, experiential knowledge or insight.

The Gnostics thus counterbalanced a slide, in both Judaism and Christianity, away from the feminine. St John's 'Word', for example, the unambiguously masculine 'Logos', borrows its attributes from the feminine 'Wisdom' who was with God before the creation. Similarly, 'Spirit', neuter in Greek and masculine in Latin, is, in its original Hebrew form, feminine, a fact which the Gnostics never forgot. Furthermore it was not just feminine words which played an important part in Gnosticism; women were leaders and teachers in their groups and could even act as deacon, priest or bishop if it fell to their lot. No doubt this is the reason St Paul, or someone using his name, forbade women to speak in church.

To the Gnostic, the importance of objective phenomena lies in their underlying symbolic significance, and the preoccupation of the later Church with concrete, literal, historic facts is quite alien to them. As a result, it is often difficult to be sure whether they are talking about real people or archetypal forces. Thus, Simon Magus, a contemporary of Christ's and an early Gnostic teacher, known to the Church as father of all heresies, was also acknowledged by his followers as the Great Power of God. His chief companion was Helen, whom he rescued from a brothel in Tyre and who is also Ennoia, the First Thought of God, Divine Wisdom, who fell into matter, suffering ever greater degradation with each incarnation, until the Great Power redeemed her. Similar claims are, of course, made concerning Christ, who came to redeem the lost sheep of the house of Israel, and whose biography is hardly less shadowy. Concerned as they were with the sufferings of fallen Sophia, Gnostics discerned a pattern in the relationship between Jesus and Mary Magdalene similar to that between Simon and Helen. Here is how the Magdalen is described in the Gnostic Gospel of Philip:

THE WHORE WISDOM IN THE CHRISTIAN ERA 95

As for the Wisdom who is called 'the barren', she is the
mother of the angels. And the companion of the Saviour is
Mary Magdalene. But Christ loved her more than all the
disciples and used to kiss her often on the mouth. The rest
of the disciples were offended by it and expressed
disapproval. They said to him, 'Why do you love her more
than all of us?' The Saviour answered and said to them,
'Why do I not love you like her? When a blind man and
one who sees are both together in darkness, they are no
different from one another. When the light comes then he
who sees will see the light, and he who is blind will remain
in darkness'. . . . His sister and his mother and his
companion were each a Mary.

The Gospel of Philip also reveals that 'It is by a kiss that the
perfect conceive and give birth.' In the Gospel of Mary she is
represented as being in communication with the risen Lord,
endowed with knowledge, vision and insight far exceeding
Peter's and the other disciples'. In 'The Dialogue of the Saviour'
she is described, in terms worthy of Isis, as the 'woman who
knew the All'.

The dictionary definition of 'magdalen' is 'reformed prostitute' and Sophia is called 'Prunikos' (= lewd). One of the titles of
Aphrodite, who is also Queen of Heaven, is 'Porné', the whore.
Why should wisdom be portrayed as a whore? Perhaps because
she is there for all who want her, crying on the roof-tops and
displaying her wares for those who can afford them. Wisdom is,
then, accessible, but in a despised and unexpected guise. To
Gnostics and Christians alike what tended to be disregarded was
the world of matter. Catholics saw it as the good creation of a
good God, but, thanks to a literal understanding of Genesis,
were hostile to its most dynamic manifestation, sexuality, as well
as to woman, who made it possible and tempting. Gnostics, on
the other hand, considered the phenomenal world to be the
creation of the inferior, foolish demiurge, whom they identified
with the god of the Old Testament. Nevertheless, matter
contained spiritual seeds or sparks which needed to be discovered and liberated before the mystery of conjunction between
Christos and Ecclesia could be consummated. One view
characteristic of many Gnostics, was that sex was permissible

and even beneficial to those who understood its symbolic significance i.e. the restoration of the essential androgynous unity of being that existed before the Fall. For Catholics, on the other hand, who, as seen by Gnostics, literalized everything, and were still intent on fruitfully multiplying, the use of sex merely compounded the original demiurgic error. To Gnostics, seeking freedom from error, ignorance and unconsciousness, but little concerned with moralizing notions of sin, it was procreation which was the mistake, not copulation, which some sects practised freely as part of their public religious observance.

The word 'whore' has come down in the world, like many another pertaining to female sexuality, and at first meant probably no more or less than 'lover'. This prejudice against female sexual expression stems from Judaism, always on guard in case the temples of Astarte and her hierodules should lure the faithful into apostasy, and from its successor, mainstream Christianity. Christ himself seems to have been well-disposed towards women. He pardoned the woman taken in adultery and cast seven devils out of Mary Magdalene. Jesus himself comes from a long line of wise whores, according to the Gospel which St Matthew called 'the book of the genealogy of Jesus Christ'. One, Tamar, dresses as a harlot and sits in the gateway to seduce her father-in-law, Judah. A later Tamar, the daughter of David, was raped by her brother. The second ancestress, Rahab, mother of Boaz, bears the same name as the harlot of Jericho, through whose wisdom the Israelites were able to enter and take possession of the Holy Land. She is also the fabulous sea-monster from whose body the world was fashioned and, in Psalm 87, a synonym for Egypt. Ruth, a Moabite, at her mother-in-law's instigation, seduced Boaz, who was an elderly relative of her late husband's as well as Rahab's son. The elders bless his marriage with the words 'may your house be like the house of Perez, whom Tamar bore to Judah.' Bathsheba, wife of a goddess-worshipping Hittite, is mentioned only obliquely: 'And David was the father of Solomon by the wife of Uriah.' Finally there is Mary herself, who was the object of scandalous gossip among the opponents of Christianity. She was accused of being a hairdresser who turned away from her husband and bore Jesus to her paramour, Pandira. In Alexandria the story went that she conceived Jesus by her brother. To the Gnostics, however, the archon Christ was the offspring of Sophia (Wisdom) and Bythos (Depth).

MARY MAGDALENE

The Gnostics, we have already seen, venerated the Magdalen as the favourite disciple, who experienced the highest Gnosis of the redeemer. It is related in the 'Panarion' of Epiphanius that Jesus took Mary with him to a mountain, where he produced a woman from his side and had intercourse with her 'until the semen flowed freely' to show what should be done 'that we might have life'. This demonstration, reminiscent of tantric yoga, no doubt symbolized the engendering of wholeness through union with one's contrasexual 'other half'. In the 'Gospel of Mary' she expounds to the apostles at Peter's request what is hidden from them in the words of the Saviour. Her speech, much of which is missing, shows that she is still in touch with Christ through visions, and discloses that it is in the mind, an intermediate area between soul and spirit, that visions are received. Peter angrily rejects her teaching and is rebuked by Levi: 'Peter, you have always been hot-tempered. Now I see you contending against the woman like the adversaries. But if the Saviour made her worthy, who are you to reject her? Surely the Saviour knows her very well. That is why he loved her more than us.'

Few biographical details can be deduced about Mary from the Bible or the Gnostic writings, but this has not prevented a wealth of material from coming down to us. The main source is the Blessed James of Voragine (c.1230–c.1298), Dominican Archbishop of Genoa and author of The Golden Legend, for centuries a best-selling 'lives of the saints'. His feast-day falls fortuitously on 13 July, the day on which black Sara the Egyptian, who accompanied Mary to France, is also celebrated.

According to Voragine, Mary was of royal blood, the daughter of Syrus (Syrian) and Eucharia (from eucharis, 'gracious' — a term applied to Aphrodite). She, her brother, Lazarus, and her sister, Martha, owned seven castles, in addition to the village of Bethany and much of Jerusalem. Her own dwelling of choice was Magdala (tower), a mile from Gennesaret on the Sea of

Galilee. The only place of this name mentioned in the Bible is Migdol in Exodus 14.2. Here, near the sea — Reed or Red — the Israelites camped for the last time on Egyptian soil before God destroyed Pharaoh's-army and Mary the prophetess led a dance of triumph.

It was near Magdala that Jesus questioned Peter about the quality of his love and said to him concerning John, the beloved disciple, 'If I will that he tarry till I come, what is that to thee?' Mary and John, the two beloved of the Lord, had been engaged to be married and the celebrations were actually in progress in Cana when John broke it off to follow Jesus instead. Mary was so chagrined that she threw herself into a life of promiscuity. She was freed from this at a dinner party given by Simon the leper, when Jesus cast seven devils out of her. She and Jesus then became close friends and he defended her against charges of impurity (the Pharisees), laziness (Martha) and extravagance (Judas and the Jews). He stayed with her at Bethany, where her tears over the apparent death of Lazarus, another beloved disciple, moved him to weep.

The leading role played by Mary at the Crucifixion and Resurrection needs no re-telling. Fourteen years after the Ascension, most of which time she spent with the mother of Jesus and, presumably, St John, she was put to sea by the Jews in a leaky boat without oars or rudder, accompanied by her servant, Martilla, who had once called to Jesus, 'blessed is the womb that bore you and the breasts that gave you suck' (Luke 11.27). Other passengers included Cedonius, a blind man healed by Jesus; Maximinus, one of the 72 whose feast-day, 8 June, coincides with that of St Melania (black) and precedes that of St Pelagia (a penitent whore); Lazarus, Martha, Mary Salome, Mary the mother of James, and Sara the black Egyptian servant.

They landed at Ratis, later Les Saintes-Maries-de-la-Mer, and Mary preached against idolatry in the neighbourhood of Marseilles. The ruler of the country came to pray to the idols for a child. Mary dissuaded him and appeared to his wife in a dream on three successive nights threatening the wrath of God unless the saints were looked after. The wife then became pregnant and the ruler set off with her and the new-born baby to discover whether Peter preached the same truth as Mary Magdalene, on whom he bestowed all his worldly goods. During the voyage his

wife died, and, after praying to the Magdalen, the ruler left her
on a hill with the baby, covering them with his cloak. He then
journeyed on to Jerusalem where St Peter took him on a tour of
the city. Two years later he returned to the hillside where he
found the baby alive, still sucking its dead mother's milk. He
prayed once more to the Magdalen and his wife was restored to
life. They returned to Marseilles and were baptised by
Maximinus who became the first bishop of Aix. Lazarus was
created the first bishop of Marseilles and Martha settled in
Tarascon (qv) where she quelled the Tarasque, the dragon of the
Rhône.

   Mary, after her life of activity, decided to choose that better
part that was her due and retired to Ste Baume, a name that
recalls the holy balm with which long ago she had anointed the
body of the Lord. There in a grotto she spent the last thirty years
of her earthly existence in prayer and solitude, where the rising
sun looks west over Aix and Marseilles. She was buried at St
Maximin, where, from the early fifth century, Cassianite monks
from St Victor of Marseilles were the guardians of her tomb.
Thus the cult is ancient, although many of the relics confirming
the legend were not discovered until the thirteenth and fifteenth
centuries. Those that were at St Maximin were transferred
during the Saracen invasions to Vézelay, which then became one
of the sacred high places of the west. Thence her cult spread to
ever more Madeleines, whose number increased from 33 to 125
between the eighth and twelfth centuries. Some fifty centres of
the cult of the Magdalen also contain shrines to the Black Virgin.

   How are we to interpret this story? It hardly requires the eye
of faith to see, in the seven demons and the seven castles, the
planetary stages on the journey of the soul into and out of
incarnation, according to the religion of Ishtar/Astarte/
Ashtoreth, a teaching which was assimilated by some Gnostic
groups. Astarte, among her many roles, is the goddess of love, in
whose temples sexual rites were performed. One clue to the
possible identity of the Magdalen in Gnostic eyes is to be found
in her parentage. If we put together Syrus and Eucharia
(Aphrodite) what we get is Dea Syria, Atargatis, a form of Ishtar,
who was worshipped with doves and fishes. If Mary Magdalene
was not herself a priestess or initiate of Astarte, then the
tradition she represents, closer to John than Peter, may be seen

as a syncretistic and esoteric one, thoroughly congenial to the Gnostic outlook.

To Gnostics there was one all-embracing feminine wisdom, including both the virgin and the whore, which they called Sophia or the Holy Spirit. They identified her with the vision granted to John on Patmos of 'a woman clothed with the sun, and the moon under her feet, and upon her head a crown of twelve stars' (Revelation 12.1) and they invoked her as 'Lady'. Later the Cathars, who used the name of John to signify the neophyte undergoing initiation in their rituals, were accused by the Inquisition of using the term 'Our Lady' to refer to their own church of love and to the Holy Spirit. The only parts of the Bible which they accepted were some of the prophetic books and the writings of John, especially Revelation.

Catharism, whose symbols included doves, fishes and a star, was brutally repressed, but ideas cannot be killed. Even when apparently dead and abandoned, like the Princess of Marseilles, the eternal religion of the great feminine spirit continues to nourish its children. An illustration from the Sforza Book of Hours (1490) speaks mutely of such a faith. It shows, in the sky, the huge figure of the Magdalen, as penitent, with hair completely covering her down to her bare feet. Apart from four angels attending her at each corner, like the 'World' in the Tarot, the picture contains a boat whose occupants gaze up in wonder at the heavenly portent, as does a bearded man in prayer on the land. Finally there is a rocky, brown mountain with a cave, outside which are a woman and child.

According to Runciman, the only Occultist child of what he calls 'Christian Dualism', i.e. Catharism, is probably to be found in the symbolism of the Tarot, which appeared in northern Italy, Marseilles and Lyons in the fourteenth century, after the repression of the Cathars and the Templars. There is, however, one other arcane tradition that has recently come to light, which is relevant to our story, that of the Holy Blood and the Holy Grail. Not all Cathars perished after the fall, in 1244, of Montségur, under what they called Mount Tabor, after the Gnostic mountain of the Holy Spirit. Le Roy Ladurie has shown that, up to eighty years later, they were still living their religion in an extensive area of the eastern Pyrenees. Apart from

Montaillou, the greatest concentration of Cathar families was to be found between Arques, source of one of the two major Parisian Black Virgins, Notre-Dame de Paix, and Limoux, home of the black Notre-Dame de Marceille. A mile or so from Arques stands the village ˙of Rennes-le-Château, former Visigothic capital of the region, where the most curious cult of Mary Magdalene has its centre. The church there, not, presumably, the first, was dedicated to her in 1059 shortly after the Razès had been acquired by the Counts of Toulouse, at a time when Catharism was beginning to sweep through Europe like wildfire. It was to Rennes, as we have noted, that Sigebert IV came with Merovée Lévi on 17 January 681 to seek refuge at the court of his Visigothic relations. He thus perpetuated the Merovingian blood-line, which, according to Baigent *et al*. stemmed from the union of Jesus Christ and Mary Magdalene.

The church was lavishly rebuilt at the expense of the Abbé Saunière, who was priest of Rennes-le-Château from 1885 to his death in 1917. Such was his veneration for the Magdelen that he also built for himself a large villa which he called Bethania, and a neo-Gothic fort, the Tour Magdala, which he intended using as a library. Some time in the nineteenth century the name of a spring at Rennes-les-Bains, below his tower, was changed from La Gode (the Gothic woman, a title of Freyja — cf. Daroca, Spain) to La Madeleine. Perhaps this alteration was the inspiration of the Abbé Boudet (1831–1915), Saunière's mentor and the author of *La vraie langue celtique*. Deloux and Brétigny mention another spring called La Madeleine in the churchyard of Rennes-le-Château which weeps drop by drop like the fountain of St Germaine, which heals afflictions of the eyes, outside Notre-Dame de Marceille.

The interior of the church offers many surprises. At the entrance, a winged, horned demon, Asmodeus, with a red body and a green dress, holds the water-stoup on his shoulders. (It was Asmodeus, son of Lilith, who tricked Solomon out of his ring of wisdom, through which he knew the language of birds, but it was fortunately returned, like that of Orval, by a fish.) He specialized, like the North African Lilith, Karina, in preventing intercourse between newly-weds, and, in the Book of Tobit, after killing seven of Sara's husbands on their wedding-nights, was finally banished to Egypt by Tobias, by means of a fish's liver. The other church in France where I have seen a modern coloured image of a single devil is that of Stenay (Satanacum), Merovingian stronghold and shrine near Orval, whence Sigebert, escaping his father's assassins, set out on his long journey. Curiously, in one of the statues of Jesus in the church, his posture, kneeling on one knee, eyes and face cast down sideways, is a mirror image of Asmodeus. In place of the holy water stoup, a baptismal vessel is held above his head by John.

The other contents of the church at Rennes merit no less attention. To begin with, many of the saints we shall shortly be discussing as companions of the Black Virgin and favourites of the Prieuré are represented. St Roch, like Amfortas the Fisher King, points to the unstanchable wound in his thigh. St Germaine Cousin de Pibrac releases a shower of roses from her apron, symbolizing, perhaps, the descendants of the Magdalen's womb who continue to flourish, against all odds, through the generations. There is a second statue of Jesus preaching from a mountain-top, which, like St Germaine's apron, is cascading with roses. St Anthony the Hermit from the sacred masonic city of Memphis, who overcame hallucinatory temptations in the desert, no doubt owes his place at Rennes to the coincidence of his feast-day, 17 January, with the arrival of Sigebert at Rennes. He is holding a closed book, signifying a mystery, possibly a stage in the alchemical process. His namesake, St Anthony of Padua (qv), invoked for finding that which is lost, and usually depicted holding a child, carries in his hand a fleur-de-lys, symbol since Merovingian times of the French royal family, and the flower which grows outside the Grail Castle. There are two images of the Magdalen, one holding a vase, perhaps containing balm or ashes, and one, under the altar, which shows her praying outside a cave. In a unique arrangement the Virgin Mary, here called 'the Virgin Mother', is carrying a child on one side of the choir, while St Joseph carries a second one on the other side. Against the exterior wall of the church a stucco statue of Our Lady of Lourdes is placed on top of a magnificent Visigothic pillar. The decoration of the lintel, which consists of crosses and roses, may point to a Rosicrucian influence.

ST BERNARD OF CLAIRVAUX

If Rennes-le-Château provides striking testimony to the persistence of the tradition still linking the Merovingian blood-line to Mary Magdalene, what of Vézelay (qv), the great centre of her cult in the Middle Ages? It was there, on Easter Sunday 1146, in front of King Louis VII, his troubadour queen, Eleanor, and some 100,000 nobles, knights and commoners, that St Bernard preached the Second Crusade. The great basilica of St Mary Magdalene was begun in 1096, the year of the First Crusade, when Godefroy de Bouillon set forth to claim the Kingdom of Jerusalem that was his by divine right. In 1217, Francis of Assisi, the troubadour saint of love and peace who, according to Runciman, caught something of the Cathar spirit and doctrine in his teachings, founded at Vézelay the first house of his Order in France. His Cordeliers and Capuchins are sometimes guardians of the Black Virgin.

Much has already been written about St Bernard in the Introduction. There can be little doubt that he plays a vital part in our story, as he did in almost all that happened in the twelfth century. He was deeply involved in the politics of his time, which was largely concerned with the relations of Church and State and the possibilities of uniting Christendom. Descendant of knights who had fought the infidel in Spain, Bernard, as a romantic boy, would have responded strongly to stories of the First Crusade and the vision of great armies setting forth from Clermont and Le Puy with the 'Salve Regina' on their lips. His uncle was one of the original nine Templars who spent nine years in Jerusalem on their enigmatic mission. On their return Bernard wrote the rule of their order and commended to them the 'obedience of Bethany, the Castle of Mary and Martha'. Meantime he had taken over the ailing young Cistercian Order and turned it into a power-house of civilization. Whatever his vision for Christendom, it seems to have included a unity in which Pope and Emperor each had his part to play, with the Kingdom of Jerusalem providing a symbolic rallying-point. Vast multi-national corporations like the Benedictines, Cistercians and Templars provided the infrastructure vital to the unity, efficiency and progress of Europe.

It is, however, as a great saint and mystic rather than as a statesman or polemist that Bernard is chiefly remembered today. He attached much importance to safeguarding Jerusalem, capital of Godefroy de Bouillon, but his real goal was the spiritual Sion, the bride of God, where lasting treasure can alone be found. In one of the many letters he wrote to Queen Mélisande, daughter, wife and mother of Kings of Jerusalem, Bernard advised: 'The Queen of the South came to hear the wisdom of Solomon to learn to be ruled and to rule in the same fashion. Now there is one greater than Solomon. Abandon yourself then to the Lord of Sion.' The heart of Bernard's spirituality is his devotion to Jesus as lover of the soul, a devotion that even today has a steamy, erotic quality that is somewhat shocking. 'I do not want your blessing, it is you I want,' he cries to the one he referred to as 'the husband' or 'the Word'. It is for this reason that the passionate, poetic imagery of the Song of Solomon is so much to his taste, as, identifying himself in soul with the black Shulamite, he abandons himself to the spiritual caresses of the divine lover.

The joys of spiritual love are androgynous, and it was no contradiction for Bernard to be also the greatest cavalier, servant and votary of Our Lady. In a prayer for the Nativity of the Virgin, 8 September 1308, addressed to 'Saint Mary, Holy Mother of God', the Templars awaiting death at Chinon besought her: 'Defend your religion which was founded by your holy and dear confessor, the Blessed Bernard' (Roy, p.235). Bernard's love of Notre Dame goes hand in hand with his dislike of the modernist, rationalizing tendencies which he attacked in the theology of his day, especially in Abelard. It also accords with a tendency towards nature mysticism: 'You will find more things in forests than in books; the trees, the stones will teach you what the masters cannot. Do you think that you cannot suck honey from the stone, oil from the hardest rock? Do the mountains not distil sweetness? Are the hills not flowing with milk and honey? There is so much I could tell you. I can hardly stop myself' (Letter 106). Is this a memory of his boyhood at Châtillon, with its woods, hills and springs, where he tasted the sweetness that distilled from the breast of the Black Virgin?

Of his other encounters with Black Virgins little is known for sure. He visited Aachen, Clermont-Ferrand, Dijon, Hasselt, Longpont, Paris, Rocadamour, Rome, Toulouse, Tournai and

Valenciennes, in all of which he would certainly have revered Our Lady. The Black Virgin of Affligem returned his 'Ave Maria' with a 'Salve Bernarde' and advised him to get on with his writing. He founded the Abbey of Orval, where the modern Black Virgin may well be continuing an older tradition. His links with Rocadamour are curious. In 1170, seventeen years after Bernard's death, the first document relating to the events there was produced by Robert de Thorigny, Abbot of Mont-Saint-Michel, who also first mentioned the Plantard motto 'Et in Arcadia ego'. In 1166 the Benedictines had found a well-preserved body in a tomb next to the chapel of the Black Virgin, which was claimed to be that of Amador/Zacchaeus/Sylvanus, of Jericho, Sinai and Lucca. He is not mentioned in Butler's five-volume *Lives of the Saints,* but the *Penguin Dictionary of Saints* assigns him as a feast-day 20 August. When Bernard was canonized on 18 January 1175 this also was the day that he was given. Thus, whether consciously or not, the Church emphasized a link between these two lovers of the Black Virgin. The remains of Clairvaux-on-the-Absinthe are now a prison, but in the small village church a painting of the Black Virgin was in a place of veneration when I visited it in 1981.

Bernard no doubt visited Rocamadour on his return from an exhausting and unsuccessful preaching mission against the Cathars of the Toulousain in 1145. He had already advised the use of troops against their co-religionaries in Germany, and would doubtless have pursued a similar course in the Languedoc if the Count of Toulouse had been amenable. But Bernard, too, was a child of his age, and not wholly immune to the spirit which favoured the Cathar phenomenon. Like the Gnostics, he based his spirituality on direct experience rather than on syllogisms. In the chastity which is the sign of absolute fidelity to God and Notre Dame, he is indistinguishable from a Cathar parfait. He wrote: 'God lives where continence endures. Chastity unites man to God. Continence makes man very close to God.' René Nelli has pointed out that this last proposition figures almost word for word in the Cathar ritual.

Apart from his orthodox detestation of Catharism, as a doctrine, though he admired the parfaits, Bernard must have found it a thorn in the flesh, hindering the great plan, spreading disunity among nations, attacking the Church in the rear, weakening it and bringing it into disrepute. It is not impossible that, faced with such an obstacle, irremovable by either political or religious means, Bernard should try to beat the Cathars at their own game. Dominic and Francis were to try much the same tactic — being just as holy, chaste, self-denying and poor as the parfaits. To reforge Christian Europe in the twelfth century, however, the piety of Bernard's Cistercians was not enough. The whole people of God needed to be inspired to lead the symbolic life. Such an inspiration was found from two sources — the building of the great Gothic cathedrals under the impetus of the new Templar/Cistercian architectural principles, and the making of pilgrimages. On the long route to Compostela, festooned with Black Virgin churches, between 500,000 and 2 million pilgrims journeyed every year. A Poitevin monk, Aimeri Picard, published a tourist guide of the various itineraries to Compostela in 1130, with the sights to see on the way. Benedictine and Cistercian guest-houses were placed at easy stages along the various roads, which were guarded by Templars and the other military orders. If the Cathars, beset by foes all round, made their religion even more mysterious than Gnosticism always is to the rational and orthodox, why not take the wind out of their sails? One means might be gently to promote the mystery of the Black Virgin, throned in the crypts and chancels of new churches rich in enigmatic carvings that expressed the inner pilgrimage. If such was the idea, it was only partly successful. Some of the guardians of the faith themselves, Templars, Franciscans and Dominicans, perhaps influenced by the power of the symbols they contemplated in their chapels, were visited by strange ideas and individual revelations. For the simple people, on the other hand, the Black Virgin no doubt continued to be what she had been for some thirty millennia, the manifestation of the Great Goddess.

CATHARS, TEMPLARS AND THE GRAIL

The following is a summary of the important connections, some of which have already been referred to, that can be made between Cathars, Templars, the Holy Grail and the cult of the Black Virgin.

1 Both Cathars and Templars were reputed to be the guardians or possessors of the Grail.

2 The last guardian of the Grail, Prester John, the nephew of Parzival, called himself the Priest-King of India and Ethiopia and probably represents an eastern Manichaean or Nestorian tradition. Through Ethiopia there is a connection with Solomon, the Queen of Sheba and the Ark of the Covenant.

3 Both Cathars and Templars were accused by the Inquisition of denying the validity of the sacraments, of renouncing the Cross, and of sodomy. The same Dominican inquisitor, Bernard Gui, went straight from oppressing Cathars in Toulouse to torturing Templars in Chinon and Paris.

4 Both had special extra-ecclesial rites which they kept secret, and avoided the priests and practices of conventional Christianity.

5 The Templars refused to take part in the Albigensian Crusade and, on occasion, offered Cathars refuge. They may even locally have taken up arms for the Cathar cause. Many Cathars became Templars at that time.

6 The Templars were particularly strong in the Cathar regions (e.g. two important Templar houses within three miles of Rennes-le-Château) and hoped to create a Templar state consisting of Provence, Languedoc, Aquitaine, Roussillon, Catalonia, Navarre, Majorca and Aragon, whose rulers were generally sympathetic to both Templars and Cathars. Black Virgins are numerous in these regions.

7 According to Charpentier, the Templars' spirituality was inspired by the mysteries of Egypt and they themselves were distant descendants of the Valentinian Gnostics of Alexandria.

8 The two centuries during which Cathars and Templars flourished and declined almost exactly coincide. Most Black Virgins date from this period (1100-1300), as does the cult of the Holy Grail.

9 A considerable proportion of Black Virgins are reputed to have been brought back from the Crusades, many by Templars.

10 Cathars and Templars both maintained secret contacts with

eastern heterodox religious groups, as well as with Jews and Arabs.

11 The troubadour movement, also repressed by the Church, forms a link between Cathars, Templars and the Grail.

12 The Cathar symbolism of figures with disproportionately large hands is a common feature of Black Virgins.

13 The great festival of the Templars was Pentecost, day of the Holy Spirit, as opposed to Easter or Christmas. Pentecost is also the high feast of the Arthurian Grail legends. The Cathars saw the coming of Jesus as just a stage, prefiguring the coming of the Holy Spirit.

14 Four hermaphrodite Gnostic statues, which had been discovered in Templar houses in or near Vienna, came to light there during the second decade of the nineteenth century, and were for a time in the Imperial Museum.

15 Both the Holy Grail and the Templar Baphomets (heads with one, two or three faces) protected, nourished and brought fertility to the land. The Black Virgin has similar powers. The Baphomet was said by the Templars to be 'the principle of beings created by God Trinity'. It has also been seen as the symbol of divine wisdom and Hugh J. Schonfield has demonstrated that, in the Hebrew Atbash cipher, Baphomet converts to Sophia. One of the few Baphomets ever discovered was the head of a woman. Girart de Marsac, on becoming a Templar, was shown a small image of a woman and was told that all would go well for him if he put his trust in her.

16 According to one legend, the lead Grail vessel containing the holy blood of Christ was washed up on the shore at Fécamp, where it hung from a fig-tree and worked miracles. Perhaps, like the lead coffin of Osiris, which suffered a similar fate, it is the real secret of alchemy. Mary Magdalene's arrival in France might be seen in a similar light.

17 The Order of the Temple was reputedly the creation of the Prieuré Notre-Dame de Sion, the guardian of the Merovingian blood-line and deeply involved in the cult of the Black Virgin.

SOME SAINTS OF THE HIDDEN ORDER

St Dagobert (651-79)
Dagobert II, son of Sigebert III of Austrasia and grand-son of 'le bon roi Dagobert I', last Merovingian king of all the Franks, was born in 651, heir to his father's throne. On the latter's death in 656, Dagobert was abducted by the usurping Mayor of the Palace, Grimoald, and entrusted to the Bishop of Poitiers, who took him to Ireland and left him at the monastery of Slane. He married a Celtic princess and was able to convince St Wilfrid of York by 'certain signs' that he was indeed the rightful king. His first wife died in 670, giving birth to their third daughter and he remarried Giselle de Razès, niece of the King of the Visigoths, at her home, Rennes-le-Château. In 676, their son Sigebert was born, and, soon after, he established himself on the throne, in his capital, Stenay. On 23 December 679 at midday, while resting at the foot of a tree during a hunt in the nearby Forest of Woevre, he was lanced through the eye by his godson, under the orders of Pepin of Heristal, and killed. Sigebert IV, it was alleged, was rescued and taken to Rennes-le-Château.

Dagobert was the first king of France to be canonized, two centuries after his death, in the reign of Charles the Bald, and a church was dedicated to him at Stenay. A verse account of his martyrdom in Latin was discovered at the Abbey of Orval (qv) in the mid-nineteenth century. His feast-day 23 December, also belongs, according to Robert Graves, to Benjamin, 'The Ruler of the South', whose totem animal is the wolf. It is also the beginning of the Saturnalia. Dagobert receives no entry in the dictionaries of saints and no trace of him is on public view at Stenay.

Ste Roseline de Villeneuve (1263-1329)
Ste Roseline's feast-day, 17 January, is also the great date in the calendar of the Merovingian blood-line. Indeed, her very name may symbolize that line. She was the daughter of Arnold of Villeneuve and Sibylle de Sabran. The Arnold of Villanova or Villeneuve known to history was a Catalan alchemist, mystic and physician (1240-1311), who knew the secret of sweetening the soluble salt of the sea, which was known in the art as the Virgin Mary or Stella Maris. Saint-Sabran was the quarter of

Toulouse associated with La Reine Pédauque, whose mother was called Rosala. Roseline had a brother, Helios, an unusual name evocative of the sun-god, Elijah and Lohengrin, who is sometimes called Helias. He was a crusader whom Roseline miraculously freed from his prison on the island of Rhodes (see Pézenas). As with Ste Germaine at Rennes, and other saints, a miracle of roses is attributed to her. Her body lies in the chapel near her family castle of Les Arcs (!) in Provence. It was so incorrupt, even to the brightness of the eyes, that Louis XIV, during a visit, ordered his physician to stick a needle into the left pupil, which still bears the marks. Perhaps in thus re-enacting the martyrdom of Dagobert, the Sun-King was taking the unconscious vengeance of a monarch of dubious rights on a symbol of the true blood-line. Deloux and Brétigny consider that Ste Roseline is Gerard de Nerval's 'Queen of the South'.

St Sulpice (d. c.647)

This contemporary of St Dagobert also has his feast day on 17 January. He was the second Bishop of Bourges, which is on the zero meridian of Paris, like Rennes-les-Bains, and was successful in converting all the Jews of his diocese. He was the protégé of the goldsmith St Eloi, Grand Vizier of Dagobert I. The famous seminary and church dedicated to him in Paris contains the obelisk with the copper line down the centre marking the exact point of the meridian. St Sulpice, in the grounds of St Germain-des-Prés (qv), had connections with the Prieuré from its foundation in 1642. (See also Villefranche-de-Conflent *et passim*.)

St Vincent de Paul (c.1580-1660)

Monsieur Vincent is a famous historical figure whose life abounds in enigmas. He left his flocks in the Landes and studied for the priesthood in Toulouse. In 1605, five years after ordination, he borrowed a horse, sold it and disappeared for two years. During that period he claimed to have been captured by Barbary pirates near Marseilles and sold into slavery in Tunis. One of his owners was an alchemist, whose secrets he seems to have learnt. He awakened to religion a woman, whom he described as a 'natural Turk', who helped him to escape. He set out with a Moslem convert from Nice in a small skiff, and they landed safely at Aigues-Mortes after a voyage of more than 1,000 kilometres. It was not only Molière with his 'que diable allait-il faire dans cette galère?' who found this tale hard to swallow. Deloux and Brétigny have suggested that for Marseilles we should read Marceille, home of the Black Virgin of Limoux, where Vincent met Jean Plantard the Alchemist, Count of Saint-Clair. According to this theory he was taken not to the Barbary coast but to the Chateau de Barberie, near Décize (qv), the 'occult bastion of France' and seat of the Merovingian descendants since the tenth century. It was utterly destroyed on the orders of Cardinal Mazarin in 1659. To complete this tale told in the *langue des oiseaux,* for 'les Maures' (Moors), who captured Vincent as alleged in his letter to M. de Comet, we could understand 'les morts' (the dead), indicating the death and rebirth initiation he must have undergone.

Those two years had an electrifying effect on the career of this poor priest with no connections and a dubious reputation for horse-trading and extravagant traveller's tales. In 1608 he journeyed to Rome where he reputedly demonstrated alchemical processes to the Pope, before returning to France on a secret mission to King Henry IV. He was taken up by Cardinal Bérulle, who arranged a good post for him with the family of Emmanuel de Gondi, Director-General of the Galleys. In 1617 he went to Bourg-en-Bresse (qv), where he has a chapel in the Church of the Black Virgin, and evangelized the countryside. On his return he became confessor to the Queen, Anne of Austria, and attended her husband Louis XIII on his death-bed. A fresco in his chapel in St Sulpice shows the Queen at the foot of the bed comforting two children, while Vincent, at the head, points the dying king to heaven. The problem is that Queen Anne had only one child, the future Louis XIV, whose 'miraculous' birth after twenty-three years of fruitless marriage gave rise to much ribald speculation concerning his legitimacy ('was Richelieu or Mazarin the father?'). It also gravely disappointed the hopes of the House of Lorraine, the claimants to the throne who represented the Merovingian blood-line.

If the mysterious second child stands for the 'lost king', ever ready and waiting to assume the throne, perhaps this is also how we may interpret the lost child with whom St Vincent is sometimes shown in iconography. He certainly seems to have had the interests of the blood-line at heart. A disciple of his was J.-J. Olier, the founder of the Society of St Sulpice, who had been healed of blindness and loss of faith by the Black Virgin of Loreto. He and Olier were the two clerical heads of the Compagnie du Saint-Sacrement along with Nicholas Pavillon, Jansenist Bishop of Alet, a town half-way between Rennes-le-Château and Limoux. This secret society, or 'cabale des dévots', satirized by Molière in *Tartuffe* was, it has been suggested, the form taken by the Prieuré to further the interests of the blood-line between 1627 and 1667, in opposition to the policies of Mazarin.

In 1633 St Vincent received from the Canons of St Victor the Priory of St Lazarus, which became his home and the mother house of the new congregation he founded to care for the needy, especially orphans and galley-slaves. He called it his Noah's Ark. The Missionaries of St Vincent de Paul were placed in charge of the pilgrimage to the Black Virgin of Marceille in 1873, and a large stone statue of their founder still bears mute testimony to his extraordinary career. St Vincent is known to have had a fervent devotion to both extant major Black Virgins in Paris. Notre-Dame de Paix, which was once the possession of the Joyeuse family at Arques, was made the object of a forty-days' indulgence in 1642 by Jean-François de Gondi, the first Archbishop of Paris and the brother of Vincent's patron. An illustration of the scene shows St Vincent praying in paradise on the same level as Our Lady, half-way between God and the people of France. He entrusted all his multifarious projects to Notre-Dame de Bonne Délivrance and it was planned that his body should make a station in the Chapel of the Black Virgin in 1806. A medal was struck to commemorate this event which never took place, with the Virgin on one side and a bust of St Vincent on the other. The Virgin made her final home in the Boulevard d'Argenson, family name of a well-known member of the Compagnie du Saint-Sacrement and author of its annals.

There are some sequences of saints' days that seem to have a special significance within the context of the hidden order. For instance, the feast day of St Vincent de Paul, 19 July, inaugurates an interesting octave: 20 July, St Margaret or Marina, 21 July, St Victor of Marseilles; 22 July, St Mary Magdalene, 23 July, St John Cassian, founder of St Victor de Marseilles (also the

Roman Neptunalia); 24 July, St Loup of Troyes; 25 July, St Christopher, a Canaanite giant and devil-worshipper, and St James the Greater (Santiago); 26 July, St Anne.

Gerbert of Aurillac, Pope Sylvester II (c.940-1003)

Although this unorthodox and Gnosticizing Pope exuded the odour of sanctity from his incorrupt body, he was never raised to the altars of the Church. The first Frenchman to be Pope, he acceded to the throne of Peter in 999, fortunate inversion of 666, the number of the Great Beast, at a time when the world was awaiting the dreaded millennium. He had much in common with St Vincent de Paul. Both were poor shepherds of Aquitaine, though from opposite corners of the province. Each had a liberating experience with a pagan woman and was apprenticed to an alchemist during an alleged journey to the world of Islam. On their return, both rapidly rose to positions of decisive importance in Church and State.

Gerbert was born in Aurillac, home of a Black Virgin and of a golden statue of St Géraud whose idolatrous splendour rivalled that of St. Foy de Conques (qv). Aurillac was noted for its golden fleeces, sheepskins left in the River Jordanne to attract particles of gold, and for its strong, ancient links with Compostela. The Benedictines of St Géraud, recognizing Gerbert's genius, sent him to study mathematics at Vich in Catalonia, on the road to Compostela, and other subjects at the great Arab universities of Toledo and Cordoba. According to one legend, he seduced the daughter of his alchemist master in order to learn the secret of secrets and was expelled from Spain. In another version he met a maiden of marvellous beauty, brilliant in gold and tissues of silk, who told him her name was Meridiana ('lady of the south'), and offered him her body, her riches and her magical wisdom if he would trust her. Gerbert agreed to the bargain and in a short time became successively Archbishop of Rheims, where Clovis was anointed, Archbishop of Ravenna, where Mérovée spent his youth, and Pope. As well as being the first Christian alchemist, credited with achieving the great work, he also had a talking head, which seems to have operated like a primitive computer. He introduced Arabic numbers to the west and invented the clock, the astrolabe and the hydraulic organ. In the realm of politics, he attempted to raise a crusade for the liberation of the Holy Land and established the Church in Hungary, ancient

6. Aurillac

Sicambria, making Stephen its first king. Perhaps the remarkable
career of Gerbert is a demonstration that trust is the price
demanded by the whore wisdom for her favours.

Ste Colombe and companions

According to Butler's *Lives of the Saints* there are, in addition to
the first Abbot of Iona, two female saints called Columba. One,
St Columba of Cordoba, the great centre of eastern Jewry in
Arabic Spain, was a nun beheaded by the Moors in 853. Her
feast-day, 17 September, coincides with that of St Hildegard of
Bingen, 'the Sibyl of the Rhine', who corresponded at length
with St Bernard. The following day belongs to St Thomas of

Villeneuve or Villanova, who curiously has a second feast on 22 September. That is also the feast of St Maurice (who has his individual feast on 21 July, the day before the Magdalen) and his companions, including Ursus ('bear') and Victor. Maurice, a Manichaean from Egypt, held the spear of Longinus until his dying breath to keep it from the Emperor Maximian. The spear of destiny is the masculine complement to the Holy Grail. Following Maurice's example 6,666 legionaries died with him, without offering resistance. Thomas of Villeneuve, with whose Sisters the Black Virgin of Paris resides, cares especially for lost children and was Bishop of the Grail city of Valencia. His views on the encounter of the Magdalen with the risen Christ are identical to those of St Bernard. He shares his first feast with St Methodius of Tyre (city of King Hiram, master mason of the Temple) or of Olympus (abode of the gods), who wrote a hymn to Christ as bridegroom of the Church. 19 September sees the feast of St Januarius of the famous liquefying holy blood, once preserved at Monte Vergine (qv), which is the pride of Naples (qv), fief of the Anjou dynasty. The two following days belong respectively to the wild huntsman St Eustace, patron of Madrid, whose relics are at St Denis, and St Maura, a dark lady from Troyes. 21 September is, however, better known as the feast of St Matthew, author of Christ's genealogy.

The second Ste Colombe is a virgin martyr from Sens, whose feast-day 31 December, which looks back to the old year and forward to the new, is shared with St Melania (the black) and St Sylvester. Perhaps it is she who gave her name to a village on the Seine, a mile away from St Bernard's Châtillon.

Who then is the Ste Colombe referred to in *Nostra* (March/April 1983)? She apparently crossed the Pyrenees from Spain, accompanied by a bear, and settled first at Colombiès in Aveyron, near Rodez (qv), a village on the zero meridian. She was nourished for twenty-eight days by manna, served on a miraculous shield, before making her home at Finestret, where her church contains a Black Virgin and, above the porch, a statue of the saint and her bear. A second village of Ste Colombe, some twenty miles to the north-east, just the other side of the meridian, attests to her fame in the eastern Pyrenees, where the cult of the Black Virgin is widespread. Her own cult was fostered by St Sulpice of Bourges, whence, according to de Sède, two

Princes, Bellovesus and Segovesus, set out to conquer the world *c*.400 BC. The first founded Milan (Mediolanum) and sacked Rome. The second led to the east an army of Volscian Tectosages from Toulouse. Their descendants sacked Delphi and founded Galatia.

The authors of *The Holy Blood and the Holy Grail* report a recent visit by members of the Prieuré 'to one of Sion's sacred sites, the village of Sainte-Colombe near Nevers, where the Plantard domain of Chateau Barberie was situated'.

The dove (*colombe*), the symbol of both Venus and the Holy Spirit, is the bird which brought La Sainte Ampoulle, the vessel that contained the oil used to anoint the Kings of France. In astronomy the constellation Columba flies just ahead of the ship Argo. Joseph is chosen by Mary among a host of suitors, when a dove flies from his rod and lands on his head.

St Roch and companions

One of the saints whose statue is most frequently found accompanying the Black Virgin is St Roch (Rock). This is surprising, since, at his death in 1327, aged about 32, most of the Romanesque Black Virgins had long been installed in their shrines. He was born in Montpellier in what had been Visigothic Septimania, in the shadow of Notre-Dame des Tables, after his mother, Liberia, prayed to La Nègre. He travelled as a healer in northern Italy, the main centre of Catharism at the time, caught the plague in Piacenza, recovered and was imprisoned as a spy. He also found time to make the pilgrimage to Compostela. According to another account he returned home and was imprisoned there when his relatives failed to recognize him. After his death, a miraculous cross was found imprinted on his body, similar to one of the physical signs by which the Merovingian blood-line can be recognized. In iconography he is almost always accompanied by a dog, the animal of Hecate, Hermes and Tobias. His other symbol is the terrible wound to which he points on the upper thigh, reminiscent of the Fisher-King's. St James is shown with such a wound in a painting at Santiago de Compostela. In 1913 the Church superimposed on his feast, 16 August, the day after Assumption, that of St Joachim, father of the Virgin Mary, who gave his name to the prophet of the coming spiritual church, Joachim of Flora. Saints who are remembered in the week between the Assumption and the Feast of the Immaculate Heart include Sts Bernard, Amadour, Louis d'Anjou, the twin temple-builders, Florus and Laurus, and John Eudes (1601-80). The last was a member of the Oratory, founded by St Vincent de Paul's benefactor, Bérulle, worked with fallen women, and, inspired by the Black Virgin of La Délivrande, founded his own congregation dedicated to the hearts of Jesus and Mary.

If 15 August commemorates the journey to heaven of the great mother of Christ, 18 August celebrates the discoverer of the Cross and the great mother of Christianity, Helen, whose son, Constantine, established it as the religion of the Empire. As the great goddesses of paganism were accompanied by sacrificial son-lovers, so two boy martyrs, Tarsicius and Mamas, whose relics are at Lucca, have their feasts on 15 and 17 August respectively. It is curious that Jacko of Cracow, 17 August, the doughty 'light of Poland', has come down to us as St Hyacinth, name of the beautiful youth slain by Apollo, especially as the Greek *hyakinthos* means 'fleur-de-lys'. (See Arfeuilles, La Chapelle-Geneste, Halle, Mayres, Mende, Meymac, Murat, Ribeauvillé, Saumur, Thuir *et passim*.) At Meymac St Roch's companion is not a dog but a tiny lady in black.

St Blaise

The historical existence of St Blaise is much less likely than that of St Roch. If Roch is the consort of the heavenly Virgin of the Assumption, Blaise accompanies the Lady of the Underworld, whose feast, Candlemas, 2 February, precedes his by one day. His popularity in the west as a saint to be invoked for sick animals and humans is no doubt due in part to the similarity of his name to Blez, a wolf-god identified with Dis, the father of the Gauls. This figure has been called, like Saturn, a sort of earth-mother of the masculine sex. In legend, Blaise forced a wolf to disgorge a poor woman's pig. He also saved the life of a boy by removing a fish-bone from his throat, giving rise to the ritual blessing of the throat still performed today. His symbols are a comb, the instrument of his martyrdom, and two crossed candles similar to St Andrew's saltire and the rune signifying the name of God. After his death, seven women collected his blood. Huynen states that Blaise, Anne, John the Baptist, and Michael are the saints most closely associated with the cult of the Black Virgin (see Blois). Blaise is the name of Merlin's master, who saved him from the Devil, and also his scribe who told the story of the Holy Grail. He was united with the Wardens of the Grail and dwelt thereafter in perpetual joy.

St Brice

St Brice or Britius (d.443) occasionally occurs as a place-name near Black Virgin sites (see Avioth *et passim*). He was a lost child, exposed on the banks of the Loire and rescued by St Martin to whom he was a constant thorn in the flesh. Martin even exclaimed: 'If Christ endured Judas, why not Martin Brice?' He nevertheless succeeded his benefactor as Bishop of Tours, though his pride made him unpopular and he was driven from his see for thirty years on grounds of immorality. Saillens thinks his popularity stems from Briccia, Celtic deity of springs. It is also worth noting that the Bryces of Pannonia, Hungary, who fought Tiberius and defeated Decius, were the ancestors of the Franks. Pyrene, beloved of Hercules, for whom the Pyrenees are named, was the daughter of Bebrycius, aponymous founder of the Bebryces, a powerful tribe in the area. St Brice shares a feast-day, 13 November, with St Bonhomme, the usual designation for a Cathar Parfait. The Cathars fasted from 13 November to Christmas.

Sts Amadour and Veronica

Amadour (lover), eponymous saint of Rocadamour, was born according to legend in Lucca, where his relics are venerated. He was the owner of a field in Sinai where corn miraculously grew to protect the Holy Family from Herod's troops during the flight from Egypt. As Zacchaeus, he was the diminutive publican who climbed a sycamore in Jericho to see Jesus and became his host for dinner and the night. The story of Zacchaeus occurs only in St Luke's Gospel (19.1-10). The old spelling of Lucca is Luca, the Italian for Luke. The passage in which Mary anoints Jesus's feet occurs much earlier in St Luke (7.36) than in the three other gospels. In Luke it comes immediately after the Zacchaeus episode. Matthew and Mark place the dinner-party at the house of Simon the Leper, while to John the setting was Bethany, at the house of Mary and Martha. John specifically mentions that

Lazarus, their brother, whom Jesus had raised from the dead, was at table with them. The next event is the triumphant entry of Jesus into Jerusalem.

We thus see Jesus favouring with his presence an outcast, whether by reason of his leprosy (and Lazarus, too, has come to signify a redeemed leper), or his occupation of tax-collector. This figure is also, by association, a beloved disciple who underwent a death-rebirth initiation and became in legend the first Bishop of Marseilles. The part of this tradition called 'Zacchaeus/Amador' came from the eastern Mediterranean, not to Provence, but to Soulac (qv) near the mouth of the Gironde. Thence he journeyed to Souillac which, like Soulac, means place of wild boars or *solitaires* (one of the physical characteristics peculiar to the Merovingian Kings was a line of bristles, like those of a boar, along the spine). He arrived at length at Rocamadour, whither he was guided by angels to the shrine of Sulevia (Cybele) whom he replaced by a Black Virgin carved by St Luke. His influence extended to the Auvergne (see Billom and St Nectaire). His body, as we have seen, was discovered in 1166 in the cave where he had placed the original Black Virgin. In Berry he was venerated as Silvanus, Latin name for the uncanny god of uncultivated land beyond the village boundaries, a synonym for Faunus/Pan and sometimes for Mars. His first feast-day at Rocamadour was 1 May, the day once sacred to Belen and the May Queen which is now the Feast of St Joseph the Workman. The name Zacchaeus/Zaccai means 'pure', the exact translation of Cathar. In St Luke's version, the man who invited Jesus to dinner on the occasion when a sinful woman of the town anointed the feet of Jesus was Simon the Pharisee. Pharisee also means 'pure'. Amadour has also been associated with the Arabic Amad-Aour, 'the just'.

Zacchaeus travelled to Aquitaine with his wife Veronica. Her name may derive from Verus Iconicus, 'true as of an image'. Lucca was famous for its images of 'the Holy Face of Lucca', Vaudelucques. The Holy Face was that of a black Christ in St Martin's Cathedral, carved by Nicodemus, to whom Jesus revealed the secret of rebirth (John 3.1-21) during a conversation by night. The statue arrived miraculously in Lucca in 782. Veronica is also the name of the saintly maiden who handed her napkin to Jesus on his way to Calvary, and found it imprinted with a true image of the Saviour's face after he had wiped the sweat from his brow. It is now preserved in St Peter's, Rome. Veronica may be the woman with an issue of blood who touched the border of Jesus's garment and was healed at once, although she had been haemorrhaging for twelve years. This story is interpolated in the middle of the miracle of the resuscitation of Jairus's ('God enlightens') daughter (Luke 7.40-56). Only Luke tells us that the girl was twelve years old. Before leaving Veronica of Lucca, let us note that San Frediano or Finnian, from Moville, a sixth-century Irish saint, was Bishop of Lucca in Merovingian times. His feast-day, 10 September, is also that of the Empress Pulcheria, first known possessor of an image of the Virgin, painted by St Luke, the Theotokos Hodegitria, some of whose copies are ranked as Black Virgins. William Rufus, who never broke an oath sworn by the Holy Face of Lucca, was sacrificed, according to Hugh Ross Williamson, in strange circumstances in 1100, at Lammas-tide, 1 August, the feast of Lug/Luc. Ross Williamson considers that the Holy Face of Lucca may be a Cathar devotion (p.33), but also states that Rufus may have been swearing by the Great Bull of paganism. The bull is the animal of St Luke, the reputed painter or sculptor of so many Black Virgins.

Other derivations of Veronica include Berenice, from the Greek 'Pherenike', bringer of victory, one of the attributes of the Virgin herself as Nikopoieon. Berenice was a Jewish princess of the family of Herod, born in AD 28, whom Titus brought to Rome with the intention of marrying, but changed his mind for fear of offending the Romans. Another Berenice was the sister-wife of Ptolemy Euergetes, King of Egypt (247-224 BC). She vowed her hair to the gods to bring her husband victory, but it was stolen from the Temple of Arsinoë at Zephyrium on the first night. Conon of Samos told the king that the winds had blown it to the stars. There it remains as the Coma Berenices, part of the constellation of the Virgin, between the Ox-Driver and the Lion. The corn that hid the Holy Family in Amadour's field during the Flight to Egypt is itself the hair of the Virgin. This scene is depicted at Avioth and in other Black Virgin churches. St Veronica shares a feast, 12 July, with St Nabor, the christianization of Neptune.

Does the story of Amador and Veronica indicate that the pure lover of the Church, not of Roma but Amor, born of the spirit, is wedded to the true image of the good God imprinted within the soul?

SOME HARLOT SAINTS

A number of Egyptian or Levantine harlot saints figure in the Church's calendar alongside Mary Magdalene. Mary the Egyptian is depicted next to her as black in a window of the church of St Merri in Paris and their iconography is sometimes very similar. Mary came to Alexandria in the hope of earning her fare to Jerusalem, where she wished to venerate the true Cross. With this end in view she prostituted herself to sailors for seventeen years before retiring to the desert to live a life of penitence as a hermit, clad in nothing but her hair and progressively blackened by the sun. After forty-seven years of solitude, now with very short, white hair, she met Zosimos, and asked him to return the following year and bury her, which he did, with the help of a friendly lion. Mary the Jewess or Prophetess was an important alchemist in the Egyptian tradition of Isis. Zosimos, writing c. AD 300, was a major successor and probably a contemporary of Mary's who developed her work. According to Saillens, the Black Virgin of Orleans was known as Ste Marie l'Egyptienne. Robert Graves calls her the patron saint of lovers and associates her with Walsingham (qv) and Compostela (qv). Her feast (2 April) is also that of the patient St Theodosia, whose statue is in the chapel of St Genevieve in St Germain-des-Prés.

There are various Pelagias who are known as penitent harlots or virgin martyrs who died to escape a fate worse than death. One, nick-named Margaret, settled on the Mount of Olives, near Bethany. She shares a feast-day, 8 October, with Thaïs, a beautiful, fourth-century Egyptian whore, about whom Anatole France wrote a novel. The most famous St Margaret, also called Marina (feast-day 20 July), was forced by her father to tend the sheep. She refused to marry the local prefect who had her imprisoned and tortured. The Devil swallowed her in the form of a dragon, but was forced to disgorge her by the cross she was wearing. Eventually she was beheaded. She is very often to be found in Black Virgin shrines, mostly in the company of St

Catherine of Alexandria, whose cultus, Attwater notes, bears some points of resemblance to hers. These two saints appeared constantly to Jeanne d'Arc, and advised her in all her heroic undertakings (though some say it was St Margaret of Scotland, not Antioch, who inspired the Maid). 'Marina' and 'Pelagia', which both mean 'of the sea', are titles of Aphrodite. The role of Marina in *Pericles, Prince of Tyre* suggests that Shakespeare may have been familiar with aspects of the esoteric, 'redeemed whore Wisdom' tradition.

St Theodata, the repentant whore of Philippi, shares a feast, 29 September, with St Michael who cast the dragon into the deep and is usually found near the Black Virgin. St Afra of Augsburg, a German repentant whore, converted by St Narcissus, shares her feast (5 August) with the Black Virgin of Rome, Our Lady of the Snows. The next day is the Transfiguration. St Euphrosyne spent thirty-eight years in a monastery disguised as a monk called Smaragdus. Lilith is Queen of Smaragd (emerald). The wisdom of Hermes Trismegistus was inscribed on emerald tablets.

ST CATHERINE OF ALEXANDRIA

St Catherine, another frequent companion of the Black Virgin, was for centuries one of the most popular saints in the calendar, whose fame was brought to the west by returning crusaders. A native of Alexandria in its third-century Gnostic apogee, royal, beautiful, rich and learned, she was, according to *Everyman's Book of Saints,* courted by the Emperor Maximian. She refused his advances and confounded a multitude of scholars assembled by him to overcome her scruples. Enraged, he had her broken on a wheel, scourged and beheaded, at which milk flowed from her veins.

It was Maximian who massacred the mutinous Theban Legion under St Maurice and resettled the Salian Franks in the Rhine-Scheldt delta. He married his daughter Fausta to Constantine in 307, the suggested year of St Catherine's martyrdom. He then led a revolt against Constantine in Gaul, which was defeated, and committed suicide at Marseilles in 310. His son Maxentius, the 'Emperor' of the story according to *The Penguin Dictionary of Saints,* was killed at the Battle of the Milvian Bridge which established Constantine and Christianity. In Butler's *Lives of the Saints,* however, Catherine's suitor is Maximinus, Caesar of the East from 305, who tried to revive paganism. It is also the name of Mary Magdalene's companion in Marseilles.

The name 'Catherine' is generally derived from the Greek root, *cathar-,* meaning pure, which may have earned her a certain popularity among Gnostic sympathisers. While she was in prison, she was fed by a dove and received a vision of Christ, which may, as in the case of her namesake from Siena, have culminated in a mystical marriage. Her body, hidden by angels, was discovered on Mount Sinai *c.*800 where the famous monastery, home of many texts from the early days of Christianity and also, reputedly, of a Black Virgin, was dedicated to her.

It is possible that the story of St Catherine's martyrdom may have been influenced by memories of the beautiful Hypatia ('highest'), subject of a historical novel of that name by Charles Kingsley. She was a philosopher and mathematician, the glory of the Neo-Platonic School of Alexandria, who was stripped naked and torn to pieces by the Christian mob.

As the patroness of young women, philosophers and scholars, Catherine symbolizes that highest feminine quality, wisdom. Is she also the tradition of the pure, Christian Gnosis of Alexandria, forced underground after the victory of the Cross at the Milvian Bridge, to re-emerge at the Crusades? In the Catherine wheel, her sign, she is one with Fortuna and de Nerval's Queen of the South. Her feast-day, 25 November, is shared by St Mercury.

ST ANNE

The cult of the mother of Our Lady was late in coming to the west and climaxed, according to Marina Warner, at the end of the fifteenth century. Her festival was not imposed by authority until 1584. In Brittany, writes Saillens, her cult generally replaces that of the Black Virgin. According to one legend, Joachim was only her first husband, the second being Cleophas, who has the same name as the father of St James and husband of

Mary who stood at the Cross with the Magdalen (John 19.25). His name is also given, in Matthew 10.3, as Alphaeus, and is that of an Arcadian river-god, the son of Thetis, who fell in love with Artemis and pursued her to Delos or Sicily. The third husband is surprisingly called Salome ('perfect'). Her body, according to Routledge's *Miniature Book of Saints,* was found in France at the time of Charlemagne by a dumb boy exclaiming, 'Here lies the body of Anne, mother of the Blessed Virgin Mary.' Her head was sent to Cologne (qv). The thirteenth-century stained glass window of her in Chartres Cathedral, next to that of Solomon, is the oldest image known to have been continuously black since its creation. Her Church in Jerusalem, built in the pure Cistercian style, was the subject of correspondence between St Bernard and Queen Mélisande. Its site by the Sheep-Gate, reputedly that of the birth-place of Mary, was the Asklepion of Jerusalem and later, under Saladin, a school of Qu'ranic wisdom. There Jesus healed a man who suffered, like Joachim, from impotence. Most of the information concerning the life of Anne and Joachim in Jerusalem derives from the apocryphal 'Protevangelium of James'. There are three characters called James in the New Testament, and it is often difficult to distinguish them in later legend. St Anne's day in the east is also that of James the Greater, Christopher and Cucufas.

ST JOHN THE BAPTIST

If, as seems likely, John was an Essene, influenced by the school of the Dead Sea Scrolls at Qumran, then he is part of a new mystical climate in Judaism, encompassing Philo's Alexandrian Therapeuts, in which the Gospel of the Kingdom was to grow and thrive. The Gnostic tradition that he represents has proved the most durable of all and still survives in Mesopotamia among the Mandaeans, also known as Nasoraeans and Christians of St John. The Merovingians, like the Nasoraeans/Nazarenes of old, never cut their hair. The Templars, too, were sometimes considered to be Christians of St John. They commemorated his feast, 24 June, which was also that of the Celtic goddess Dana, with great ceremony, as the lord of the interior church. Despite the divinity of Christ, it was John who remained the master, whose knowledge was the greater. Esoterically speaking, John and Jesus, born at the poles of the year, symbolise our two natures, mortal and immortal, like Castor and Pollux. The soul descends into matter in John's sign, Cancer, home of the Crib and the Asses, and journeys back to its source through Capricorn, the sign of Christ and the winter solstice. Soul and spirit, ego and self, ride the same horse of the body, but, for salvation, one must wax and the other wane. Jesus reveals that his cousin John is Elijah, who, with Moses, was also present at his Transfiguration. The feast of the beheading of John the Baptist, 29 August, is the day after that of an Ethiopian robber of the fourth century, St Moses the Black, who became a monk at Wadi Natrun in the Nile Delta. The executioner of John is, according to Saillens, regularly shown as black. We do not know what became of the head of John the Baptist after Herodias and Salome played with it and pricked its tongue. Was it the proto-Baphomet? John's name in Oc sounds the same as Janus/Dianus, to whom Robert Graves likens him. It no doubt looked both ways, back to Aries, whose sacrifice Christ fulfilled as the Lamb of God, and on to Pisces, with the symbol of the baptismal waters.

According to Rudolf Steiner, it was not only Lazarus who returned to life when Jesus said, 'Come forth.' John the Baptist also returned nineteen months after his beheading to dwell with Lazarus in one body. In his return he became one with St John the Divine, the author of the Gospel and Revelation. Thus 'he whom the Lord loved' was both John and Lazarus. The head of St Lazarus is at Andlau, close to the enlightening shrine of Mt St Odile in Alsace. Odile is the patroness of the knights who sought the Grail. Avallon also once claimed the relic and Autun still venerates its version.

CHAPTER 5
The symbolic meaning of the Black Virgin

How shall he watch at the stroke of midnight
Dove become phoenix, plumed with green and gold?
Or be caught up by jewelled talons
And haled away to a fastness of the hills
Where an unveiled woman, black as Mother Night,
Teaches him a new degree of love
And the tongues and songs of birds?

Robert Graves

There can be few people in the world interested in the poetry of myth who have not been profoundly affected by Robert Graves's inspired book *The White Goddess*. His work *Mammon and the Black Goddess* is less known. In it he states (p. 162): 'Provençal and Sicilian 'Black Virgins' are so named because they derive from an ancient tradition of Wisdom as Blackness.' He sees in her, over and above her role as ultimate inspirer of poets, the symbol of a new relationship between the sexes:

> The Black Goddess is so far hardly more than a word of hope whispered among the few who have served their apprenticeship to the White Goddess. She promises a new pacific bond between men and women . . . in which the patriarchal marriage bond will fade away . . . the Black Goddess has experienced good and evil, love and hate, truth and falsehood in the person of her sisters . . . she will lead man back to that sure instinct of love which he long ago forfeited by intellectual pride.

It is paradoxical that so old an image should be seen to represent such a new and radical departure. But then it is strange, too, that the Black Virgins which have been with us so long and in such great numbers, so often hidden and rediscovered, should now for the first time become widely recognized as a separate category within the iconography of the Virgin in the west. 'We are living', wrote Jung (*The Undiscovered Self*, pp. 110f.), 'in what the Greeks called the Kairos — the right time — for a "metamorphosis of the gods", i.e. of the fundamental principles of symbols.' If this is the right time or high time for us to discover the Black Virgin, how can we know what she is trying to say to us?

We have traced her history from the great goddesses of the pre-patriarchal period, especially Inanna and her handmaiden, Lilith. One of the striking characteristics of such figures is their extraverted, uninhibited sexuality. Whether women, other than, perhaps, queens, were accustomed to dominate their lovers as Inanna with Dumuzi can only be a matter for conjecture, but if they did, it is not surprising that the pendulum should have swung to its opposite. Lilith, on the other hand, in what is admittedly a very late tradition, appears to symbolize the demand that absolute equality and a degree of independence for woman be recognized by man. Her successors in the literally patriarchal world of the Old Testament went some way towards achieving these goals, though more in the non-scriptural legends than in the Bible itself. According to these, Zipporah was able to fly off with Moses in her talons, whereas in Exodus her most notable act is to save the life of Moses, threatened by the angel of the Lord. She performs the priestly function of circumcising their elder son and blooding Moses's penis with the foreskin, perhaps as a prefiguration of the saving of the first-born of the Hebrews through the blood of the paschal lamb on the door lintels. In the story of the Queen of Sheba, although Solomon is clearly represented in the superior position, he treats his guest with great respect and near-equality, as well as giving her all that she desired.

Even the glory of the Annunciation cannot obscure the almost wholly subordinate role played by women in the New Testament. The Lilith-like Herodias and Salome have a certain seductive, manipulative power, but it is negative and destructive. Only Mary Magdalene stands out as an active, heroic figure, the first to brave official displeasure by seeking Jesus in the tomb. The name Magdala, as we have noted, means 'tower'. It is curious that, in the Litany of Loreto, the Virgin is invoked twice as 'tower' — first as 'Turris Davidica', second as 'Turris eburnea'. That the Virgin Mary, through whom, according to the genealogy of Luke, Jesus is of the line of David, should be called 'Turris Davidica', is quite appropriate. The second appellation is somewhat more surprising. Tower of Ivory is a reference to the beauty of the neck of the black Shulamite in the Song of Solomon (7.4), and in this it matches the belly of her lover (5.14). A further possible connection between Old Testament references to ivory and the history of the Black Virgin is to be found in I Kings 10.18, immediately after the departure of the Queen of Sheba, where it is given as the material of Solomon's unique bull (or ram, II Chronicles 9.21) and lion throne with its six steps.

Ivory is an arcane substance with the property of rendering flesh incorruptible. When calcined in a closed vessel, however, it yields a fine soft pigment from which the shiny ivory-black paint is made. So is what we have in the Litany two Marys, the official white and the unofficial black one? A small, further point in favour of this hypothesis can be derived from a closer look at 'Davidica' and 'eburnea'. Two towers and two cities traditionally symbolize an opposition, at least since the time of Augustine. Geographically the tower of David could only be Jerusalem, home of the Temple. Might the Greek word for ivory, *elephantinos,* yield a rival? It is generally held that there was only one Temple, but in fact a syncretistic form of Judaism flourished in the Egyptian city of Elephantiné, where there was a temple of Yahweh alongside a cult of Anath in the fifth century BC, if not earlier. Elephantiné, as a feminine adjective qualifying the understood noun *polis,* would mean city or citadel of ivory. That the Judaism there was very different from that of Ezra or Nehemiah is demonstrated by the Elephantiné papyri. We may surmise that the orthodoxy of the temple of Leontopolis at the time of the Holy Family in Egypt was equally suspect, enlightened as it would have been by the Gnostic wisdom tradition of Alexandria. It seems likely that most of the so-called wisdom literature including the Song of Solomon, the Epistle to the Hebrews and many of the finest Gnostic writings, are of Alexandrian inspiration or origin. Alexandria is also the main source of the Gnostic works linking Jesus with Mary Magdalene. According to this tradition it was through the Magdalen, rather than through Peter and the male apostles, that Jesus transmitted his secret doctrine.

It is, of course, most unlikely that the Litany of Loreto, whose use in the shrine of the Black Virgin and the Holy House is first attested in 1558 during the Council of Trent, at the height of the Counter-Reformation, should be guilty of such a heretical play on words, though the study of Greek was fashionable at the time. The early origins of the Litany of Loreto, however, date back to the twelfth century when such enigmatic associations would have been by no means improbable.

Elaine Pagels has drawn attention to the polarity that was seen to exist from the second century between Mary Magdalene and Peter. All the writings that extolled the role of Mary were ultimately excluded from the canon. In the Pistis Sophia, Mary tells Jesus of her fear of Peter: 'Peter makes me hesitate; I am afraid of him, because he hates the female race.' If we think of this polarity not in personal terms but as two traditions within Christianity, what we see are the church of Peter, catholic, orthodox, male dominated and victorious, and the rival church of Mary, Gnostic and heretical, worshipping a male/female deity and served by priests of both sexes. In the legend of the Prince of Marseilles (Chapter 4) Peter's role is that of a guide to the historical sites of Jerusalem, while Mary has the power of life and death. Triumphant Rome tried to exterminate the Church of Mary, but only succeeded in driving it underground. The rights of women were likewise repressed, though in the Celtic world they retained many of their considerable ancient freedoms. They even, according to Jean Markale, took part in the celebration of the Mass in Ireland prior to the Norman conquest. The Celtic Church long maintained many of its original practices as well as links with eastern Christianity, only yielding gradually to Rome following the Synod of Whitby (664).

It was this Celtic Christianity that re-evangelized Europe from Aachen to Lucca in the so-called Dark Ages. From the same lands came the quest for the Grail that revivified the spirituality of the twelfth century. Markale writes of the Grail quest that it is inextricable from the quest for woman (p.200). At the same period the alternative church of love resurfaced in the form of Catharism. It is resurfacing again today, partly through the interest in Gnosis that the translation of the Nag Hammadi library has aroused, partly through the new attitude towards the feminine that is one of the major characteristics of the time we live in. The main contention of this book is that the rediscovery of the Black Virgin should be seen, along with the many apparitions of the Virgin that have occurred in recent years, as a further manifestation of this same process.

Such a contention is, of course, unprovable, since all the evidence is circumstantial and associative. There is no written account of the intentions of a carver or painter of the ancient Black Virgins. Theological references to them are scant, though St Bernard took the blackness as a symbol of humility. We can only infer from this silence that, for some unknown reason, the Church was reluctant to comment officially on the phenomenon save in simplistic terms. It is, however, no longer shocking to suggest that the images represent a continuation of pagan goddess-worship and that some may have once been idols consecrated to Isis or other deities. It is also undeniable that a remarkably high proportion of Madonnas over 200 years old, that are credited with miraculous powers, are black, as are the traditional patronesses of nations, provinces and cities.

It is characteristic of Black Virgins that they resuscitate dead babies long enough to receive baptism and escape limbo, and in this they adopt a subversive posture *vis-à-vis* the rules of male-dominated theology. They are also numerous in many areas where paganism lingered or where the Cathars flourished. Quite often there is a cult of Mary Magdalene and a Black Virgin in the same place. The interest apparently shown by the Prieuré in Black Virgins, Lilith and the Queen of Sheba, and literary figures connected with them encourages the speculation that the cult of the Black Virgin has indeed links to hidden, dark secrets of the past. That past, it should be remembered, if the principal conclusion of *The Holy Blood and the Holy Grail* has any justification, includes the descent of Mérovée from the child of Jesus and Mary Magdalene.

No appeal to reason by means of such evidence as can be produced carries much weight in comparison with the appeal to the imagination that the images themselves make. The first glimpse of an ancient statue of the Black Virgin shocks and surprises. Five minutes in contemplation of her suffice to convince that one is in the presence not of some antique doll, but of a great power, the *mana* of the age-old goddess of life, death and rebirth.

For those who are able to make a leap of faith, our Black Virgin in the west has much in common symbolically with the other great goddess figures of the world. In her subterranean darkness she could be compared with the terrifying maw of death, Kali. The circles of wax dedicated to her at Moulins, Marsat and elsewhere remind us that in our end is our beginning and vice versa, of the uroboric prison of Maya and Karma, the measure of whose round-dance we must tread. She is also the ancient wisdom of Isis-Maat, the secret of eternal life that is the gold at the end of the alchemical process, as well as the initial blackness. In short, she is the spirit of evolutionary conscious-ness that lies hidden in matter. But evolution rejects the closed circle for the open spiral; new planets do swim into our ken, and things are not always as they have been.

The Black Virgin is a Christian phenomenon as well as a perseveration of the ancient goddesses and compensates for the one-sided conscious attitudes of the age. The Age of Pisces idealized and concretized its opposite sign, Virgo. Chastity was admired, sexuality denigrated and repressed. As the temples of the goddesses were destroyed Lilith the Leviathan languished forlornly on her ocean bed. Penitent whores became favourite cult objects, while the Virgin Mary, like Athene before her, was promoted to be the statutory female on a patriarchal board essentially hostile to woman and nature. Against the frenzied fashion for denying, defeating and transcending nature, the Black Virgin stands for the healing power of nature, the alchemical principle that the work against nature can only proceed in and through nature.

After long, slow maturing in the earth something new emerged with the buried Black Virgins in the twelfth century, something like a quantum leap in consciousness, an understanding of the symbolic significance of the relationship between the sexes. The true meaning of love had nothing to do with possessing another person, settling down, marrying and having children. Tristan tells of tragic, adulterous love, transcending the protagonists' will and giving them their journey. The troubadours came near to intuiting that the myth was the way of soul-making. But courtly

7. Marsat

love was to prove an idea whose time had not yet come and, after Dante and Petrarch, the allegorical inspiration ran out of steam, to become little more than a literary convention. The pendulum swung back and the feminine principle experienced five centuries of heavy repression.

Whatever the Black Virgin symbolizes is, to judge from her miracles, not contrary to marriage and children. At a concrete level, fertility and the home are her major concerns. They are part of the way of nature, but human nature demands more for its entelechy than the fate of beasts. The breast that nourished St Bernard fed French literature in its infancy. Roland's sword, Durendal, rightly reposes in the vulva-cleft of Rocamadour and brings fertility to brides. The poetry of the period tells of love: love of homeland ('douce France'), of companions in arms, the art of love between men and women, and the love of the Rose — not contradictory to this — that is the meaning of all love.

The Black Virgins are often associated with esoteric teaching and schools of initiation. Wisdom has always cried on the roof-tops or at the street corners, and the spirit of this world always punishes those who buy her wares. The great age of the Black Virgin is the twelfth century, but legends about her hark back to the dawn of Christianity, the dynasty of the Merovingians and the age of Charlemagne. Like the Sleepers of Ephesus, ideas go underground for a few centuries to re-emerge when times are more propitious. The idea that the meaning of life has to do with the projection and reintegration of the soul, sketched in early Gnosticism, twelfth-century poetry and in later alchemy, was not made conscious until Jung, at the same time as he was beginning his researches into Gnosticism, formulated his principle of the anima/animus.

Of the many hundred apparitions of the Virgin which have been reported as collective phenomena over the past 150 years, some, it is said, have been black. But there is now no need for her secret to be hidden, at least in the west, where sceptical indifference is a greater danger than persecution. Indeed, the secret of the Virgin must be made as widely known as possible while the conditions are relatively favourable, or the world may slip back into an age darker than those which began in the fifth or the fourteenth centuries. The one-sided patriarchal system is dying, and to cling to it is now a psychic sin. Yet it seems unlikely that a return to the matriarchate is either possible or the way ahead. In those countries of the west where starvation and tyranny are not the major problems, the great search is for meaning, and it is above all in relationships that people look for significance in their lives. Increasingly they are disappointed.

Our ancient, battered, much-loved, little-understood Black Virgins are a still-living archetypal image that lies at the heart of our civilization and has a message for us. The feminine principle is not a theory but real and it has a will of its own which we ignore at our peril. It is an independent principle and cannot be forced against its will to go anywhere or do anything without bringing retribution on the perpetrator. She brings forth, nourishes, protects, heals, receives at death and immortalizes her children who follow the way of nature. This is no different from the law of their own nature, the logos in psychology, biology, cosmology, and yet, paradoxically, it is also a work against nature. The light of nature tells us that life is a pilgrimage, a journey to the stars along the Milky Way, her hero-path, a voyage across the great water in which she is ship, rudder and guiding star. As the spirit of light in darkness she comes to break the chains of those who live in the prison of unconsciousness and restore them to their true home. In the trackless forest she is both the underground magnetism and the intuition that senses it, pointing the traveller in the right direction. She is, traditionally, the compassionate one.

If she brings forth from her treasury things both old and new, we need to be wise to what possibilities are now on offer, before it is too late. There is clearly no return to the twelfth century, the third century or the third millennium BC. Inanna, Sophia, the Holy Grail and the Church of Amor are no longer available as living realities for us today. There are signs that the goddess now requires to be worshipped in spirit and in truth through the law written in our hearts, rather than in temples built with hands. One old truth is that man and woman, though different, are equal parts of a consciously androgynous whole that is each persons's potential reality. Many people, shown photographs of the Black Virgin for the first time, comment on how masculine some of them look. Certainly Our Lady of Rocamadour is at the far end of the spectrum from the simpering examples of sacristy art that purport to represent the Virgins of Lourdes and Fatima.

Men need for the good of their souls to relate consciously to the power of the feminine or they become overwhelmed and possessed by it through their own unconsciousness. Kings, Popes and the mighty ones of the world came humbly to venerate the Black Virgins of Le Puy, Rocamadour, Montpellier and Chartres, and carried images of the powerful feminine in their hearts. Today the impression created by the infant's experience of his mother is undeniably as strong as ever, but a vision of the transpersonal Queen of Heaven, Earth and the Underworld no longer awes and inspires the imagination of adult males.

Feminists justifiably object to the sexual stereotypes by which children and indeed the whole of society are conditioned. Yet, if we have no Kali, Isis or Brigit to lighten our darkness, we have witnessed in recent times a phenomenon whose symbolic and practical importance should not be minimized. In three import-ant nations, by the democratic will of the people, women have been raised to the position of supreme power and successfully wielded it. The authority of women is a fact of life to which the people of the west are having to accustom themselves, not just at home or in schools and hospitals, but in an ever-expanding range of occupations.

Europe had, of course, experienced female sovereigns before. There was a veritable romantic cult, by no means confined to England, that saw Queen Elizabeth as the new Astraea. She was the goddess, sister of Leto and daughter of Themis, who, when pursued by father Zeus, turned herself first into a quail, then into the island of quails, Delos, where her nephew Apollo was born. She was a goddess of the Golden Age, but when evil began to prevail on earth she was translated to the heavens, where she became the constellation Virgo. The best-selling novel in France for thirty years following its publication in 1607 was d'Urfé's *Astrée*. In Lanson's piquant phrase he 'took the arcadian pastoral and made of it a Merovingian historical novel'. Clearly the appeal of the Virgo archetype belonged to the spirit of the age.

It was, however, in Occitania, the land of the Cathars and the troubadours, that men in the Latin, Christian west first learned to honour and obey women, though not in marriage. As C. S. Lewis has shown, courtly love is adulterous and is characterized by humility and courtesy, within the context of the religion of love, though, surprisingly, he makes no reference to Catharism. Obedience to 'la Dame' and acquiescence in her rebukes had to be absolute. The phenomenon of courtly love developed at the end of the eleventh century and was formally condemned by the Church in its poetic expression by the troubadours in 1277.

C. S. Lewis proposes as the main cause of this radical new phenomenon in the history of humanity the large numbers of dependent, landless knights available in the châteaux of Languedoc to act as disciples apt to learn courtesy at the hand of the châtelaine and her ladies. This was no doubt an important factor; but surely a deeper, intrinsic attitude belonging to the time and place is at the heart of the matter, and that is the attitude of Cathars towards women and the feminine principle. One of the most remarkable and distinctive features of Catharism, which it shared with some early Gnostic groups, was that women were admitted to their priesthood of parfaits and parfaites. A celebrated example is afforded by Esclarmonde of Foix, the owner of Montségur and inspirer of its resistance, who bore eight children before, with her husband's agreement, she became a parfaite.

Cathars and troubadours, no less than Templars, exercise a powerful romantic attraction, and it is important not to idealize them. Cathar husbands at Montaillou were just as likely to beat their wives as any other peasants. There is a vein of misogyny that runs through the poetry of the troubadours from first to last, counterbalancing the extravagant service of praise accorded to the Lady. Nevertheless, Catharism and courtly love, which grew together as part of the same phenomenon, acknowledged, in theory and practice, women's freedom to take a lover. This world of incarnation was punishment enough, and the just God would not inflict further pains on those who followed the promptings of nature. To be passion's slave, however, might well entail further incarnations, and to have children would certainly prolong the time of waiting until the final purification at the end of the world. The parfaits and parfaites, who trod the path of enlightenment avoided identification with the world of matter in all its forms, but, for the simple hearers, sexual peccadilloes were not considered any worse than other deviations from that path. Indeed Cathars agreed with Plato and St Bernard that salvation began with love of bodies. Troubadours even went so far as to suggest that one must tend towards heaven through the love of women. Although both marriage and fornication were qualified as 'adultery', extra-marital union, undertaken freely, was preferable to the conjugal bond. It might even symbolize the return of the soul to its spirit after death. Nelli states categorically that Cathars and troubadours were perfectly in agreement that true love — from the soul — purified from the false love associated with marriage. The troubadour who wrote 'Flamenca' between 1250 and 1260 juxtaposes the 'Mass of Love' and the sacramental office, and made his hero serve God for the love of his lady. We are not so far in spirit from the sexual rites of Sion-Vaudémont six centuries later or from the licentious love-feasts of the Gnostics 900 years before.

Once women are free to bestow their favours and affections where they will, the whole structure of patriarchal society starts to crumble. In the long spiralling progress of the history of ideas this seems to be the point that we have once again reached. Now it is an idea whose time has come and no crusades have so far been launched by Church and State to quell it. If the Black Virgins really do carry a charge from the goddesses, perhaps, now that they have been 'found' yet again, they are whispering in our ears like the female serpent of Eden, 'You won't really die.'

Those who stress the esoteric, hidden, initiatory aspect of the Black Virgin cult are quite correct to do so in terms of the opposing orthodoxy of the Middle Ages. Now, in one sense, there are no secrets any more and wisdom cries from every paperback shelf. In another sense, everyone has to find his or her own secret, though the times may be more or less propitious for such an undertaking. The fact that so many of the Black Virgins are 'found', generally by pure serendipity, and are called Notre-Dame la Trouvée, is not without significance. The word in Oc for 'find' or 'invent' is *trobar,* from which 'troubadour', i.e. 'one who has found', is derived. But this does not by any means exhaust the possibilities of a term so rich in nuances for the practitioners of the *langue des oiseaux.* Basically, *trobar* is to express oneself in tropes, i.e. use words in a sense that differs from their normal usage. So the language of the troubadours is rich in multilingual puns, double-entendre, allusions both classical and biblical, paradox and allegory. In this language of *gay saber,* playful and tricksterish, nothing can be taken at face value. So, if a troubadour sings of his wife and his mistress, he may well be referring to the Church of Rome and Catharism. She is nagging and dangerous, this Lady, Rome, and one should not eat her meal (i.e. the Eucharist). Amor, the dark mistress, hidden underground, is the true source of light and inspiration. The most characteristic example of the hermetic *trobar clus,* elucidated by de Sède, is called 'The Death of Joana' or 'Lou Bouyé', 'the herdsman'. This song, which has become almost the national anthem of Oc, is a secret lament for the Cathar Church. Joana — Jeanne — the name given to a woman in the Cathar rituals — is found 'al pé del foc', at the foot of the fire, dead. She has gone to heaven with her goats (not sheep!). Did the pilgrims to Compostela who sang this refrain know what they were singing as they passed through the disconsolate lands? If Joana was translated to the heavens, perhaps, since the Cathars cherished astrology, we should seek her in Virgo whose wing touches the foot of the Herdsman, Boötes, where Arcturus, the bear-keeper, King Arthur, is the brightest star. On the other side of the Virgin is Crater, the cup that is both the Holy Grail and the mixing bowl in which our three natures are blended through incarnation.

The constellation Virgo, Isis to the Egyptians, is sometimes represented as a woman holding a wheatsheaf (Spica) and occasionally as a mermaid holding a child. There is, in fact, a duality at the heart of Virgo, echoing, in the age of Pisces, the contradictory nature of the two fishes. A glance at the Tarot card Justice, generally associated with the star-maiden Virgo, shows her with a sword in her right hand and a pair of scales in her left, reminding us that Virgo and Libra were once one. Now, Venus-ruled Libra has been sundered from Virgo, whose lord is androgynous Mercury. Balance, mercy, harmony, equilibrium have been split off from Justice, who, now, wields Spica, the spike or point, rather than Spica the ear of corn, or Triptolemus the fruit of the womb of the Eleusinian Virgin. Rákóczi writes of this card:

> To the more licentious it represented the 'virgin quality' that is gained, not by pure living, but by plunging into the abyss of sexual indulgence; here we have the exaltation of

the prostitute as a saint and the saint treated as one who is 'impure'. Hence, Gypsies often call this the Magdalene card and say that it is under the patronage of Sara, the Negress Saint of the Romany.

To the Cathar troubadour as to the psalmist it seemed as though there was little justice. The innocent were punished and the wicked flourished like the green bay-tree. These suffering righteous ones point to the unacceptable paradox at the heart of Christianity — a religion of love imposed by force. Virgo as the opposite sign to Christian Pisces, represents its beloved ideal, its bride and the reflection of the blind-spot in its soul. To Albertus Magnus it was Christ's rising sign. The literalization of the virginity of Mary, like the literalization of Eve's role as the wicked temptress of Genesis, broke the heart of Christianity and works of reparation to the Sacred Heart of Jesus and the Immaculate Heart of Mary have still not wholly healed the wound. Thus the dichotomy of the virgin and the whore, the good mother and the witch, continues to gnaw like an unresolved canker at the soul of modern man. The author of the Book of Revelation suffered severely from this split. The Great Woman of Heaven, the sign Virgo, the Holy Spirit and Mary Magdalene, brings forth a son who is to rule all nations with a rod of iron. She is at war with her neighbouring constellation of Hydra, the adversary of Hercules in his Cancer labour, associated here with the Great Whore of Babylon, who holds a golden cup 'full of abominations and filthiness of her fornication'. This may refer to the menstrual blood and semen consumed sacramentally by some Gnostic groups.

Like all true symbols, the glyph for Virgo ♍, is a meditation instrument capable of yielding many meanings. Some see in it the girdle of hymen and the promise of the immaculate conception of a Messiah. To others it is the wavy symbol of the primal waters attached to the cross of matter. Can we see folded wings, a fish-tail, the double 'M' of Mary Magdalene, the 'MR' of Maria Regina, or M followed by the healing symbol of pharmacopoeia? Pertoka interprets ♍ as the symbol of water and the Black Virgin, corresponding to the principle of differentiation. He gives it the phonetic value 'UR' ('primal' in German), which he explains as follows: (1) Waters in movement, in differentiation, the ear and the symbol of sound. (2) The idea of one thing covering another, or developing from it. (3) The sound of waves. (4) The moon in its various aspects. (5) The Hindu god Varuna, whose emblem is a fish, venerated with salt water and related to ideas of surrounding, enveloping, covering. Davidson relates it to the Hebrew letter 'Mem', signifying the feminine principle.

Astrologers confirm that the two open arches succeeded by a closed one in the sign Virgo are coiled chthonic energy held back by a locked door or closed circle from full manifestation in the phenomenal world. They see in it the untouched vagina and generative organs or the coils of the digestive tract, ruled by Virgo, where the process of refinement and differentiation occurs. Virgo is the sixth sign, at the end of the first half of the zodiac, the last of the six steps leading to personal achievement and a transition to the second circle where the individual learns to relate to the greater whole, including the transpersonal world. It thus has to do with the natural processes that are also mysteries of transformation which we experience as birth, sex and death. In Egyptian paintings the dead are swallowed by a viper to be reborn in the form of a scarab from its tail. The viper thus plays the role of the transforming alembic in alchemy. In whisky-distilling the indispensable copper condensing-pipe of Isis and Venus is known as the worm, which is also the old English word for dragon or great serpent. The wouivre (viper) is a telluric current, perhaps an underground stream, a geological fault, a vein of metal or a ley-line — a prehistoric track joining two prominent points in the landscape. It is generally invisible, but can be detected by sensitives or dowsers. It is the flow of our own life-current and the energy of the cosmos. Often a Black Virgin marks the site of a wouivre.

Virgo is not only the perpetual flux of Heraclitus but the principle that contains the flux. The containing transformer belongs to Maria Prophetissa, the alchemist, who is credited with inventing both the still and the bain-marie, whose heat, like that of the womb, is gentle and steady. In this sense Virgo is the great mother, Demeter, from whom Virgo borrows her wheat-sheaf. She looks, sorrowing, for Persephone in the underworld, as the Magdalen sought Jesus in the tomb, as Isis searched for

Osiris, Freyja for Frey, Orpheus for Eurydice and Dionysus for Semele.

Sophia that is above hovers over the waters, awakening her daughter and counterpart that is below. The Virgin Mother Isis has a second major arcanum in the Tarot, Temperance, called by Sally Nichols 'the heavenly alchemist'. She is a winged figure in red, blue and gold, holding a vessel in each hand, between which a double stream of silver — or perhaps quicksilver — liquid flows. The trump signifies transformation, or light in darkness, and is connected with Aquarius, the spirit of the coming age. It comes immediately after 'Death'.

There is a third trump connected with both Venus and Aquarius, 'The Star'. Its number, 17, associated with the Prieuré and Noah's Ark, also plays a part in the story of Mary the Egyptian. Paul Huson claims that 'it hails the rebirth of Dionysus.' It comes as a ray of hope after the salutary disaster of 'The Tower Struck by Lightning', the destruction of Babel or, perhaps, the massacre of the innocents after the fall of Montségur. The Star-Woman, the first human form to appear naked in the Tarot, pours the waters of life and truth from two vessels into a river. She kneels on one knee like Jesus and Asmodeus at Rennes, and is crowned with stars like Isis and Nerval's Queen of the South. The two trees (rose and acacia?) which frame her remind us of the trees of Knowledge and Life in Eden and the water, which flows from near her womb, emphasizes the feminine source of all life on earth. But there is another source and home in the sky. The seven stars above her symbolize the planetary stages in the soul's journey. The eighth great star, at their centre, which transcends them, is either Uranus, ruler of Aquarius, or the Ogdoad, where freedom from the lower spheres may begin, the realm, to the Gnostic Ophites, of the Mother. The soul's spiritual essence is starry and falls into matter through the planetary spheres. To the Valentinians, the Ogdoad was formed from the Supreme Being, called Depth, and the First Thought, Ennoia, also named Grace or Silence. From these were born Mind, the 'Only-Begotten' and Truth. The two other syzygies completing the divine eightsome are Logos (Word) and Life, with Anthropos (Man) and Ecclesia (Church, or assembly summoned by a crier).

Lest we should seem to be straying too far from our main theme, let us recall that the Tarot is a product of that fourteenth century that saw the destruction of the Order of the Temple, the eradication of Catharism in the Languedoc, the Black Death and the Hundred Years War. It presents in symbolic form the concentrated doctrine of heretical, dualist Christianity, particularly Catharism, though it is also associated with the Gypsies and, through its 22 Trumps which correspond to the letters of the Hebrew alphabet, with Cabbalistic Judaism. In such circles, astrology was held in high esteem, and systems, like that of Joachim of Flora, which predicted the coming of the age of the Holy Spirit, were closely studied. Not for nothing is 'The Star' believed to be that which led the Magi and the Three Kings of Cologne to the manger at Bethlehem and will lead the Wise Ones again to the source of meaning and redemption. But to see Gnosticism principally in terms of divination and prognostication is to fail to understand it. When examined from the standpoint of depth psychology the account it presents of the mystery and tragedy of life is far from ridiculous. Perhaps Gnostics might prefer the term 'Height Psychology', but then 'altus' in Latin means both 'deep' and 'high'.

As it was, the stream of knowledge had to flow underground for a time. The Tarot could be presented as just a game or a relatively harmless way of fortune-telling, though the churches have always looked askance at it. In the fortress of Toursac (see Monjou) which was inhabited by Templars well after the dissolution of the Order, a Jesuit in 1687 discovered in a hiding-place a remarkable Tarot deck with portraits of contemporary figures from the fourteenth and fifteenth centuries. These included Joan of Arc, her companions-in-arms Dunois and La Hire, the alchemist pope of Avignon, John XXII and Philip van Artevelde who led the Flemings against France and captured Bruges on the Feast of the Holy Blood.

Apart from the Tarot there were two other related forms in which heretical Gnosticism continued to flourish clandestinely in the west. Astrology kept the images of the pagan gods and goddesses alive in the minds of the people and spoke, through the horoscope, of an individual path for each person as a microcosm here below reflecting the macrocosm above. Alchemy, in its essence the art of psychic transformation, the 'yoga of

Gnosticism' as Quispel has called it, was recognized by Jung as the chief precursor of modern depth psychology. Of secret societies which exist alongside official religion and have generally been hostile to it, two relevant to our theme are the Freemasons, founded in the twelfth century under the patronage of St John the Baptist, and the Rosicrucians. Both have been associated by the authors of *The Holy Blood and the Holy Grail* with the Prieuré.

The underground stream, called by Coleridge Alph, is Alphaeus, 'the leprous one', which disappears at Arcadia to rise again in Sicily as the Fountain of Arethusa ('the waterer'), a goddess of springs, like Briccia, and one of the four Hesperides who form Venus, the evening star. Alphaeus, as we have seen, is also father of the Apostle James the Less, or Shorter, of whom little is known other than his feast-day, 1 May which is also that of Belen, Venus, Siegmund the Arian, Joseph the Workman and, formerly, Amadour. He is confused in Butler's *Lives of the Saints* with 'the best-known of all the apostles, son of Zebedee and a kinsman of Our Lord', James of Compostela. More commonly he is identified with James the Just, the brother of the Lord, one of the characters in the Gnostic writings whom Jesus kissed on the mouth. In the Gnostic Gospel of Thomas a remarkable claim is made for him: 'The disciples said to Jesus, "We know that you will depart from us. Who is to be our leader?" Jesus said to them, "Wherever you are, you are to go to James the righteous, for whose sake heaven and earth came into being."' It is likely that he represented the original Judaeo-Christian Gnostic teaching, which was also associated with Mary Magdalene, and which saw itself as betrayed by the later orthodox Catholicism that claimed to be the Church of Peter and Paul. The Gnostic saint lives on in England in 'The Court of St James', named after a twelfth-century leper hospital dedicated to him.

Is the Black Virgin a symbol of the hidden Church and of the underground stream? The Laffont *Dictionnaire des Symboles* defines virginity as the unmanifest and unrevealed. Blackness redoubles this significance. Concerning the symbolism of Black Virgins the *Dictionary* sees them as the virgin earth, not yet fecundated, thus emphasizing the passive quality of virginity. They are the womb of the earth or of the soul like those goddesses that are also sometimes shown as black — Isis,

Athene, Demeter, Cybele and Aphrodite. The *Everyman Dictionary of Non-Classical Mythology* simply sees in Black Virgins the continuation of the cult of Isis, as Christianity took over her chapels and her images. It adds: 'In . . . Les Saintes Maries de la Mer, Isis has been demoted to the rank of a serving-maid with the name of Sara, in which capacity she is still the divinity of the gypsies.' So the Great Goddess is now unmanifest, save as mother of the outcast gypsies.

Depth psychology has shown that the unmanifest has two levels, the personal unconscious and the collective unconscious. The unconscious, however, is not completely dark. The alchemists observed a stage in the opus which they called variously the leprosy of the metals or the blessed greenness. After an individual has poured his or her energies outwards into the world there may come a point at which the thirst for a new source of meaning begins to make itself felt. Virgo is the end of the first half of life that belongs to the conscious ego. John the Baptists's task, undertaken in Cancer (24 June), where souls come into incarnation, ends its first phase in Virgo with the sacrifice of his head (29 August). Then he is at one with the leper Lazarus and Elijah the green with his fiery soul-chariot, Elijah who in the Middle Ages became Helyas the Artist, the master of alchemy. The great work of the second half of life must be based on the Virgoan virtue of discrimination between the way of the world and one's own inner truth.

The Black Virgin reminds us that we have an alternative, and that not all roads lead to Rome. Isis the alchemist, in whose myth are contained all the elements of the art, is still with us. The real name of Egypt and alchemy both derive from Khem, 'black earth'. The Greek *chemia* means 'transmutation' and has been confused with *chumeia,* a mingling and *chuma,* 'that which is poured'. Not only are we, in the Gnostic view, a mixture of three elements — body, soul and spirit, as different as the salt, sulphur and mercury from which the alchemists prayed a fourth would emerge, we are also the result of the blended genes of all our ancestors and of the disparate factors in our conditioning that have formed our personalities. Underneath all our conditioning, hidden in the crypt of our being, near the waters of life, the Black Virgin is enthroned with her Child, the dark latency of our own essential nature, that which we were always meant to be.

Sometimes she comes to us in dreams and visions, in sickness cured, in rescue from catastrophe and in chance encounters with the numinous. The legends of her shrines are full of such experience.

Historically, the Black Virgin cult seems to point in the direction of two alternatives in particular. One, the alternative Church of Mary Magdalene, James, Zacchaeus, Gnosticism, Cathars, Templars and alchemists, we have circumambulated many times, peering at it from different angles. It contains much of the wisdom of the old religions as well as certain new phenomena that reached consciousness in the twelfth century, such as the Holy Grail and courtly love. If guilt by association is an admissible form of evidence — and it is all we have — then the Black Virgin can by no means be absolved of associating with some strange companions belonging to the alternative Church. The problem of the once and future king in exile, posed by the Prieuré de Sion, presents a different problem which has not yet been solved, but it may be significant that their mother-house in Jerusalem was adjacent to Bethany.

Books about Black Virgins prior to 1982 did not concern themselves with the Prieuré de Sion or the fortunes of the Merovingian dynasty, and it was not my original intention to break with this precedent. The Holy Blood and the Holy Grail made no mention of Black Virgins, but one of the authors alerted me to a possible correlation between them and the Prieuré. Then I read Rennes-le-Château in which Brétigny and Deloux refer to the Black Virgins of Blois, Limoux, Marseilles, Goult-Lumières and Sion-Vaudémont in the context of the Prieuré and its history. As my researches continued, it became increasingly obvious that the cult of the Black Virgin and the history of the Merovingian blood-line were inextricably linked.

The significance of this link is as mysterious as everything else to do with the Prieuré. That they should work for the restoration of the Merovingian dynasty, possibly at the head of a united Europe, is comprehensible, if somewhat eccentric. If they believe, and the point is left unclear in The Holy Blood and the Holy Grail, that the blood-line pretender is a descendant of Mary Magdalene, then her shrines, of which there are many in France, would seem to offer an appropriate symbol and rallying-point for the order without any need to symbolize her as the

Black Virgin. That they may also be interested in pursuing their aims by occult means should afford no surprise. Hitler's new order depended, he is reputed to have believed, on the magical power of the Jewish Spear of Destiny from the Hofburg in Vienna. The Compagnie du Saint Sacrement and the Rosi-crucians seem to have been inspired by political as well as spiritual goals. The role of the Black Virgin, if any, in the furtherance of these ends is, however, far from clear, unless we conclude that the Prieuré chooses to see in her the alternative Mary, the Magdalen, and all she stands for.

It is not only Christianity that is divided into two Churches, with the hidden one sometimes represented as the synagogue. Mary may stand for something else which we have not yet considered and that is heretical Judaism. It is here that the origins of Gnosticism as a historical phenomenon are to be found, and it is here that Jew and Christian are at one. Always in the background of our story is the hidden history of Judaism, with its back-sliding tendencies in the direction of the Goddess. The Merovingians claim descent from Noah and from the heretical, outcast tribe of Benjamin — sodomite sons of Belial — who emigrated to Arcadia and thence, like Alphaeus, to Sicily. It then formed the sacred dance sodality of the Salians in Rome. The Salians were also the priestly tribe of the Ligurian peoples, Provençal worshippers of the Goddess, whose descendants Mary Magdalene no doubt encountered. Many interesting references are to be found in *The Holy Blood and the Holy Grail* to the presence of Jews in Languedoc and Roussillon, where the words Goth and Jew were confused and frequently interchangeable. Dagobert's Visigothic father-in-law's sister married into a family called Lévi, one of whom no doubt brought the young Sigebert to Rennes-le-Château. Rennes itself has for its coat of arms the six-pointed star of David or seal of Solomon, and ancient Jewish inscriptions have been found in the area. The blood-line, it is claimed, continued through the rulers of the Jewish principality based on Visigothic Septimania with its capital of Narbonne, whose boundaries correspond to the later projected Templar realm north and south of the Pyrenees.

In the north, too, the Jewish connection is all-pervasive. The nearest village to Stenay is Baalon. According to de Sède, this commemorates the Syrian god Baal, whose worship Solomon reintroduced to Israel by dedicating a temple to him on the Mount of Olives, near Bethany. Stenay probably owes its name to Baal. It was his devouring Saturn/Moloch aspect to which children were sacrificed, especially at Yule-tide. The Church of St Dagobert was built on the site of the temple of Saturn/Moloch. The nearest Black Virgin to Stenay is at Avioth, a Hebrew word meaning 'ancestors', where children were also sacrificed. Shortly before the establishment of the Jewish/Merovingian principality of Narbonne an event of major importance occurred at the opposite end of Europe. In 740 the powerful empire of the Kazars adopted Judaism as its state religion under the guidance of Spanish Jews. Arthur Koestler argues that it is these Kazars who formed the great Jewish population of eastern Europe and thus constitute the majority of Jews, the Ashkenazim, throughout the world. He suggests that the German word for heretic, *Ketzer,* is derived from Kazar, and produces evidence that Yiddish is derived from Crimean Gothic. The emigration route from the east taken by the Kazars is strikingly similar to that taken by the Goths and Sicambrian Franks centuries before, though some Kazar incursions in eastern Europe dated from the mid-fifth century. The heretical Karaite Jews, whose name probably means 'dark', and who spend the sabbath in darkness, are aware of these secrets and have links to both eastern and western Jewry.

The old Jewish communities which had existed from the days of the Roman Empire along the Rhine and in France were, after much suffering, destroyed or exiled during the thirteenth and fourteenth centuries. Philippe le Bel confiscated their goods and expelled them on the feast of Mary Magdalene, 1306, a year before he arrested the Templars. The expulsion of the Jews from Spain and Portugal in 1492 and 1497, where they had formed an important part of the population, created vast numbers of forcibly converted Jews, constantly suspected of heresy by the Inquisition. These Jews either stayed where they were as part of the hidden Church, or spread their beliefs to other parts of Europe. The great wave of Jewish emigration from Poland and Russia to the west did not begin until 1648. It seems quite possible, however, that the links between western Jews and eastern Kazar/Jews, forged in the eighth century, were not totally broken in the intervening millennium and that those claiming descent from the Kings of Israel in France would have been aware of this 'heretical' Jewish secret. The Merovingians were accused of being *rois fainéants*, that is sacred rulers who did not occupy themselves with the day-to-day work of government, which was left to the Mayors of the Palace, who eventually usurped their throne. It is remarkable that a similar division of divine and secular power prevailed among the Kazars in the tenth century, a division symbolized by the king and queen of the chess-board. It seems that the passive role of the Kagan, or sacred king, dates from after the conversion of the Kazar Empire to Judaism. The idea of two rulers is not a new one to Judaism though Jewish kings were far from *rois fainéants*. At Qumran, however, in the Essene Jewish community that produced the Dead Sea Scrolls and may have had a distant influence on the heretical Nestorian Church, there was a strong tradition of two Messiahs, priestly and secular. John the Baptist and James the Just, both members of the priesthood and both influenced by the Essene tradition of Qumran, were considered to be the Priestly Messiah or Teacher. Jesus, on the other hand, was claimed to be the Messiah, son of David. The only person who called him by this title was blind Bartimeus ('son of the honoured one' — Timaeus was Plato's Pythagorean interlocutor). He was healed by Jesus immediately prior to the Zacchaeus episode, just after James and John have asked Jesus for places on his right and left hand when he enters into glory. Perhaps Bartimeus is the same person as Cedonius, the companion of Mary Magdalene on the voyage to France. Nathaniel/Bartholomew who also hails Jesus as King of Israel, was flayed in Armenia like St Blaise, and, like St James, is associated with St Philip. When Pantaenus (*c.*180), founder of the Catechetical School of Alexandria, visited India he was told Bartholomew had preached the Gospel there.

Some of the Church fathers state that James was both High Priest and of the line of David. Like the Merovingian kings, he never cut his hair. The Teacher of Righteousness, Zadok, whose name means 'just' or 'righteous', has been associated with John the Baptist. According to the 'Clementine Recognitions' two of John's closest disciples, who succeeded him as leaders of the Zadokites, were Simon Magus, 'father of all heresies', and Dositheus, a Samaritan heretic whose disciples held that he had not really died. According to other accounts, the Dositheans were a sect dating back to Maccabaean times. The Maccabaeans proved a great disappointment to the righteous, who withdrew to desert caves like Qumran. It is perhaps significant in this connection that in Lyons, hotbed of second-century Gnosticism, the Church of the Maccabees, near the present church of the Black Virgin on the plateau of Sarra, was rededicated to St Just, who had withdrawn to the Egyptian desert. Two other people referred to as 'just' in the New Testament are Joseph of Arimathea who possessed the Grail and Joseph Barsabbas ('son of man, or Sheba'?), defeated in the election to the Twelve by Matthias. A saint called Dositheus traditionally brought the Virgin of St Luke to Valvanera, valley of Venus.

Disappointed apocalypticism is commonly transmuted into mysticism, and that of Qumran seems to have been no exception to this principle. At the end of a millennium, however, or of a platonic great year, and when danger threatens, people long once more for the coming of the Messiah, Saviour or once and future king. As we approach the year 2000 and the age of Aquarius, amid prophecies of impending nuclear doom, Messianic hopes are once more stirring in many hearts, including, perhaps, those of the Prieuré. After the last battle the Grand Monarque will arise and reign from Avignon, ancient city of Cathars and Popes, watched over by a Black Virgin. This is foretold by Nostradamus, Merovingian propagandist as well as prophet, descendant of converted Jews who adopted a masculine form of Our Lady as their name. Nostradamus learned his wisdom at Montpellier and Orval, before settling at Salons, the city of the Salians. The Grand Monarque, of 'Trojan blood and Germanic heart' who is also 'King of Blois' and 'Belgic', is presumably of the Merovingian blood-line. He will restore the Church 'to pristine pre-eminence', though Rome and the Barque of St Peter will be destroyed. As all this is scheduled to happen before 1999, when Nostradamus predicts what seems to be the end of the world, it is no wonder that a sense of urgency should have motivated the Prieuré, after so many centuries of secrecy, to reveal itself and its aims to the world. Meantime let us hope that the Virgin turns towards us her 'most merciful face of night' as we recall that, to the Sufis, blackness is the final stage of the journey of the soul towards beatitude.

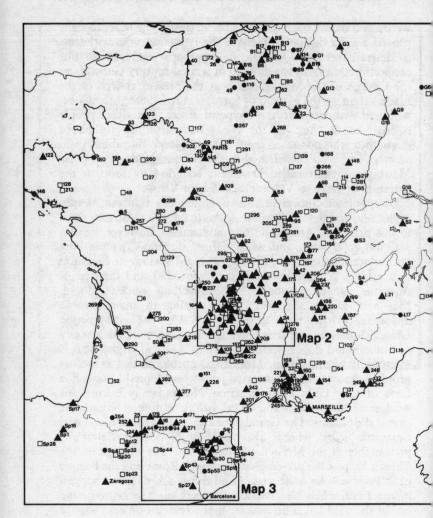

Map No. 1

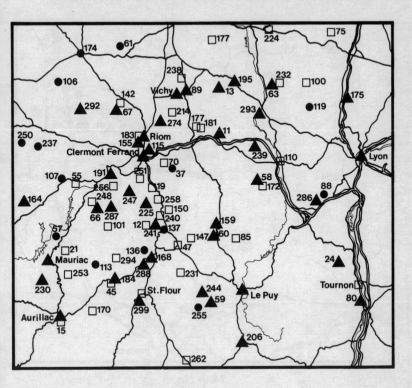

Map No. 2

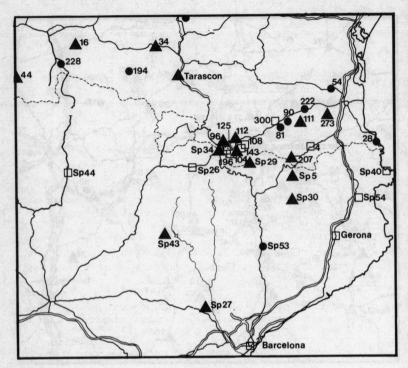

Map No. 3

Gazetteer

(The author would be glad to hear of any other information relevant
to the Gazetteer. Please write c/o the publishers.)

Bold Type   Site where an image generally acknowledged to be a Black
Virgin is still venerated, even where the original image has been replaced
or is no longer black. ▲ On the map.

Normal type   Sites where (1) a Black Virgin was formerly venerated,
(2) where the existence of a Black Virgin cult is probable but has not
been confirmed, or (3) where the image is a copy of an extant Black
Virgin. ● On the map.

Italics   Sites that have been associated with a Black Virgin cult, but
about which information is lacking or doubtful, or where the image is in
a museum or private ownership. □ On the map.

The map references are all taken from Michelin maps unless otherwise
stated, with the number of the map first and the number of the fold in
brackets.

Abbreviations: attr. – attributed to; BV – Black Virgin; Ch. – church;
cm – height of statue in centimetres; C. – century; Cattle – found by
cattle or sheep; D – destroyed or disappeared; ins – height of statue in
inches; Mer. – Merovingian connection; Na Sra – Nuestra Señora;
N-D – Notre-Dame (Our Lady); O. L. – Our Lady; Pag. – former
pagan cult in the area; Rev. – French Revolution; SD – site designated
by image's return to original position until shrine is built; Standing –
standing statue (if there is no mention the statue is seated or there is
no information); Water – holy well or spring nearby.

ALGERIA

Algiers   N-D d'Alger or Our Lady of
Africa, bronze, dark-hued standing
Virgin of the Annunciation from
Lyons, in Basilica resembling that of
Fourvière. Mgr Dupuch (from Verde-
lais before going to Lyons and Algiers)
wanted her to be considered the pro-
tectress of the various races of Africa.
Crown donated by Pope Pius IX. Our
Lady of Africa succeeded a statue
found in a chest with no name during
the early days of the French conquest

which Dupuch called N-D des Victoires. It was soon joined by the copy
of N-D de Verdelais. At one time the
image enjoyed a considerable cult
among Moslem women who venerated her as Lala Meriem. No information about present status of cult.

AUSTRIA

Mariazell Styria; 987 (39). The most
famous place of pilgrimage in Central
Europe, religious heart of the old
Austrian Empire, much favoured and
frequented by the Hapsburgs. Saillens
reports a BV there, but the Abbot only
refers to a copy c.1960 of Our Lady of
Montserrat. The ancient statue of Our
Lady now appears to be in natural
wood, though formerly painted. The
Virgin carries the Child on her right
knee; lime-wood; 22ins; no signs of
decay. According to tradition it is this
statue that a Benedictine monk called
Magnus took with him when he left
the Abbey of St Lambrecht in 1157 to
retire into the wilderness (cf. Einsiedeln).
When his path was blocked by thickets
or rocks, he prayed to the Virgin and
they opened to make way for him. He
set the statue on a linden tree and
became the priest of shepherds and
hunters, who helped him build a little
chapel round the tree. The first Ch. of
1200 was replaced by a larger one in
1340 by Louis the Great of Hungary
whom the Virgin of Mariazell inspired
in a dream to defeat the Turks and
Bulgars. From the favours bestowed
on her peoples she is revered as 'The
Great Mother of Austria', 'The Great
Lady of the Hungarians' and the
'Mother of the Slav Peoples'.

Mondsee Upper Austria; 987 (38);
copy of BV of Einsiedeln (Switzerland)
brought by St Wolfgang (c.925-994),

feast-day Hallowe'en, 31 October;
whereabouts of statue now unknown.

Nieder-Ranna Upper Austria; 987
(38); on Danube between Passau and
Linz; BV reported by Saillens; next to
Marsbach.

Sossau-an-der-Donau BV reported
by Lechner. I have been unable to
trace its whereabouts.

BELGIUM

B1 *Affligem Abbey* Hekelgem.
Brabant; 409 (F3); 6 km E of
Aalst; in Abbey Ch. open daily,
Onze Lieve Vrouw van Affligem
or van Vrede; polychrome crowned
statue of Virgin and Child with
bunch of grapes of 1605 replacing
stone statue of 14 C. destroyed in
1580. If there was a BV at Affligem
(Saillens and Huynen) it was almost certainly the original miraculous talking Madonna of the 12
C. which returned the greeting of
St Bernard who was venerating her
in 1146 with a 'Salve Bernarde'. St
Bernard then founded a Cistercian
Abbey there. That this may be the
case is hinted at by Coppens when
he quotes the authority Heer Graff
J. de Borchgrave d'Altena as
follows:

The present Virgin of Affligem recalls
the Madonna whom St Bernard
greeted through the medium of a
Gothic Virgin created at the end of the
14 C... A case similar to that at
Affligem is to be found at Tongeren
(qv) where a 15 C. statue of the Virgin
has replaced a Sedes Sapientiae now
kept in the treasury, which is of a
totally different type [and is black].

There is a 17 C. alabaster relief in St Catherine's Ch., Brussels (qv), showing St Bernard and other monks all in white stone venerating a statue of OLV van Affligem in golden brown.

Bon-Secours See Condé (France).

B2 Bruges/Brugge West-Vlaanderen; 409 (2); (1) in the Ch. of Our Lady of the Pottery attached to the Pottery Museum; painting of Moeder van Regula van Spaignen; BV dated 1676; 162.5 by 107.5 cm; formerly in the Augustinian Ch. in Bruges; badly placed to left of Chapel of St Anthony; Virgin with totally black face and hands holds white Christ Child. Influenced by Augustinian cult of Our Lady of Regula near León and at Chipiona in Spain, though the statue of the latter bears little resemblance to the painting.
(2) Small (18in) standing statue of Mary Mother of God, without Child, in courtyard of Capuchin Ch. in Boeveriestraat, recently restored and repainted; ⌐ourist Office says it was 'blackened by time and the elements'; now behind glass screen. First Chapter of Order of the Golden Fleece after founding in Dijon (qv) 1429 in Bruges.

B3 Brussels 409 (4); (1) in Ch. of St Catherine (open daily 7-7), 'De Zwerte Lieve Vrouw' (the black beloved lady); 14 C.?; 100 cm; white stone painted black; images of Sts Anne interceding for boatmen, Roch, Catherine, Mary Magdalene, John the Baptist and John the Evangelist; statue once in nearby Rue de la Vierge Noire. Under the altar in the Chapel of St Anne there is an alabaster carving of St Bernard and other monks being greeted by the Virgin of Affligem (qv).
(2) A copy of the BV painted 'by St Luke' in St Mary Major's, Rome, existed for centuries in the chapel of N-D de la Délivrance in St Michael's Cathedral until destroyed in the religious wars of the 16 C.

B4 Chèvremont Liège; 409 (15); 9 km E of Liège, SW of Fléron by N 3 and N 421, NW of Chaudfontaine; Carmelite Priory and Basilica with older Chapel of Our Lady on hillside. Fr F.-X. Georges, priest of nearby Verviers (qv) in his work *Notre-Dame de Verviers,* Verviers, 1913, p.37, after listing a dozen of the most famous BVs in Europe adds 'and nearer to us, Chèvremont and La Sarte-Huy'. The recent guidebook to Chèvremont makes no mention of a BV and the Carmelite sacristan knew nothing of one. Assuming Fr Georges is correct, the BV may have been destroyed during the bombardments of 1914, 1940, 1944-5, but more probably it has been restored and repainted more than once during this time, and is the small, white-faced N-D de Chèvremont, of uncertain date (crowned 1923), in the hillside chapel. Chèvremont was a Roman camp with a temple to Mercury and later one of the most important Merovingian citadels with walls 1 km in circumference and home of Ste Begge, great-great-grandmother of Charlemagne, who is still venerated at Chèvremont. The cult of N-D du Château-Neuf dates from her period (7 C.) but had been forgotten when revived by the English Jesuits in the 17 C. who used to walk to the hill from their noviciate house in Liège (they later returned to England to found Stonyhurst), which was a veritable school for martyrs. Inscribed on Chapel altar is 'Sancta Maria, ora pro Anglia', dated 1688 (exile of James II). In the monastery there is an unusual dark wood statue N-D de l'Encrier, which shows N-D holding an ink-well, and the Infant Jesus a pen and book. There is also a statue of St Roch of 1599. By 1914 7000 ex-votos bore testimony to the miraculous powers of the Virgin. Among the many cures, one miracle is that of a voice calling in the night to a prostitute telling her to climb as a bare-foot penitent to Our lady of Chèvremont. In 1919 20,000 pilgrims paid tribute to Our Lady for the preservation of Liège during the Great War, and in 1944, just after First Vespers of the Feast of the Nativity of the Virgin, the patronal feast of Chèvremont, Liège was liberated by the Americans, after an unexpected withdrawal by the Germans. Prehistoric cave dwelling of Bay-Bonnet near by. Statue of Virgin on site of former gibbet of Liège.

B5 *Dinant* Namur; 409 (14); the BV reported by Saillens and Huynen almost certainly refers to N-D de Foy in the sanctuary of Foy-N-D, 6 km E of Dinant between the N 36 and the N 48; statue discovered by a woodcutter in the heart of an ancient oak on 6 July 1609 and crowned 1909; famous for miracles of healing, especially of the eyes, paralysis and nervous diseases; von Rundstedt's offensive in Dec. 1944 stopped at Foy. According to the priest it is not a BV.

B6 **Hal/Halle** Brabant;   409 (13); 15 km SW of Brussels; in Ch. of St Martin, Our Lady of Hal, BV in majesty suckling the Infant Jesus; early 13 C.; 92.5 cm by 26 cm; walnut; Child on left arm and breast; statue belonged to St Elizabeth of Hungary (d.1231) whose husband Ludwig IV of Thuringia died at Otranto en route to the Crusades after sending home four statues associated with the cult of the BV (the others being 's Gravesande, Haarlem and Vilvoorde) though the BV of Hal is considered to be of local craftsmanship. Elizabeth gave it to her daughter Sophie of Brabant who in turn left it to her daughter Matilda, Countess of Holland, who gave it to the Ch. of Hal in 1267. In the crypt of 1402 an ancient oak-trunk can still be seen, perhaps the pedestal of an older statue or the relic of a pagan cult. There was a well near by. Images of Sts Roch, Mary Magdalene,

Catherine (co-patron), Joseph, Crispin and Moses and the Burning Bush. BV saves town from attackers (the cannon-balls which she intercepted in her lap in 1580 can still be seen in Ch.), heals sickness and restores dead and buried to life. Joachim, Dauphin of France, son of Louis XI buried in Ch. 1459. Edward III of England and Ludwig IV of Bavaria members of Confraternity of O-L of Hal. Philip the Bold, Duke of Burgundy, died in the Hostellerie du Cerf opposite the Basilica in 1404. Henry VIII gave a silver monstrance in 1513 in gratitude to the Virgin for victory over Louis XII. Hal was a refuge for English and Irish Catholics during penal times. Pilgrimage and procession 1st Sun. in Sept.

B7 Hasselt/Hasque Limburg; 409 (6); in Ch. of Our Lady; wooden, standing statue of Virgin with Child on left arm; early 14 C,; c. 100 cm; kept in glass cylinder to left of high altar; venerated as Virga Jesse (the rod of Jesse); crowned 1867; heavily restored and repainted recently with doll-like red daubs on cheeks. Claimed as BV by Durand-Lefèbvre, Saillens and Huynen. Tourist Office denies this, but recent postcards on sale in main bookshop still show her as dark greenish-brown with golden backcloth. The *Michelin Guide* to Benelux of 1962 still refers to her as a BV, which the Tourist Office enigmatically agreed was correct.

The first meeting of the Guild of St Mary of Hasselt was in 1308. The two statues either side of the high altar are of the Virgin and St Bernard (by Del Cour, 1707). Hasselt is the home of Belgium's finest gins. A fortnight of celebrations and processions in honour of the Virgin is held every 7 years.

B8 Huy (-la-Sarte) Liège; 409 (15); in sanctuary of La Sarte on hill-top S of Meuse (funicular or steep, winding motor road); N-D de la Sarte; walnut; seated; 15 C.? (Chapel to the Virgin on 'montagne du Sart' which had existed for a long time and where Mass was celebrated, attested in archives of 1501); large right hand of Virgin holds unusual tiered sceptre-like Roman standard with wings on top; very large golden key hangs from Child's right hand before Virgin's womb; captured Turkish standards either side of altar; ex-votos and candles. Fr F.-X. Georges in *N-D de Verviers*, 1913 (see Chèvremont), claims it as BV and its dark grey colouring supports the claim, but the priest in charge knows nothing of this. Huy, a stronghold on the Meuse between France and Holland, was often besieged and destroyed. After the Wars of Religion in the 16 C. the chapel was in ruins with the statue, a plaything for children, standing disfigured on one wall. In the summer of 1621, with the town still occupied by the Dutch and raided by bands of Spaniards and Liégois, Anne Hardy was passing the chapel on her way home with a bundle of faggots. She had the idea of taking the statue and becoming a devotee of the Virgin, so she hid it in the middle of her fire-wood and tried to pick it up. This she was quite unable to do, even with the help of two passers-by, so she returned the statue to its niche. The news of this miracle spread and three sworn affidavits were obtained from witnesses. Other miracles were reported, and in 1624 a new sanctuary was built. Saved at Rev. Sanctuary became Dominican Priory 1860; 26 June 1896 statue crowned. Exvotos, candles. Merovingian sarcophagus at Amay (7 km E).

B9 **Lier/Lierre** Antwerpen; 409 (4); in Kluizekerk (Dominican Ch.) 'De Bruine Lieve Vrouw', 'OLV ter Gratiën (Our Lady of Grace) Nigra sum sed formosa'; open daily 8-12 and 15-17; 17 C.; 115 cm; oak; standing; large right hand; Child held on left; crowned; the image originates from the Chapel of Our Lady of the Holy Repose in Lier; first miracle of healing attested 1632. St Gummarus, patron of Lier and its cathedral, is depicted with a flowering staff. Cathedral has images of Sts Catherine, John the Evangelist and Michael. Miraculous Virgin in Ch. of Sts Joseph and Bernard in Lisperstraat.

B10 *Louvain/Leuven* Brabant; 409 (13) (14); BV reported by Saillens and Huynen; Durand-

Lefèbvre states that Candlemas is held on 6 Feb in Louvain. Romanesque majesty considered as belonging to Congregation of Augustinian Sisters of Leuven now in St Elizabeth's Clinic, Uccle, Brussels, but not considered BV.

B11 Mechlin/Mechelen/Malines Antwerpen; 409 (4); (1) in Cathedral, OLV van Mirakel, painting attr. to St Luke; bust only; no Child; Virgin holds closed book in left hand. 15/16 C. copy of BV of Aracoeli, Rome. Only image acknowledged as BV by City archivist.
(2) Seated sculpture of the Virgin in St John's Ch. reported by Durand-Lefèbvre (Ch. closed for repairs 1984).
(3) Our Lady of Hanswijk in Ch. of Our Lady, Hanswijkstraat, continuation of Onze Lieve Vrouwstraat; reported as BV by Durand-Lefèbvre; statue above high altar not black now; crowned; standing; Child on left arm; ex-votos lead down to (closed) crypt.

B12 **Orval** Luxembourg belge; 409 (25), 26 km SE of Bouillon, 10 km NW of Avioth (qv, France); in Cistercian Ch. of N-D d'Orval above entrance to Chapter House modern dark metal statue of Virgin and Child entitled 'Stella Maris' by the Frères Jacques, goldsmiths, exhibited at the Exposition Internationale in Paris in 1937 before taking its place in the restored abbey. Symbolic waves reach to the waist of the Virgin who holds to her left Jesus, shown with dark curly hair and a toy yacht. The 5-pointed star above the Virgin's head, a symbol of the Queen of Heaven since Ishtar and Venus, formerly shown with the point downwards, denoting witchcraft and black magic, has now been righted. Visit only during Mass: 4,7.10, 11,17.40, 19.30. In 1070 some monks from Calabria in S Italy arrived near the present site of Orval and lived as hermits in the Forest of Merlanvaux under the patronage of Matilda of Tuscany, Duchess of Lorraine, aunt and foster-mother of Godefroy de Bouillon. In 1076 she was sitting by a spring lamenting the death of her only son and her husband when the ruby ring he had given her at their marriage fell into the water. She prayed to the Virgin, and at once a trout surfaced with the ring in its mouth. 'Here is the gold I was seeking,' cried the lady, 'happy the valley that restored it to me. It shall be known henceforth as the Golden Valley (Orval).' The alchemical flavour of the legend is enhanced by the title 'Terres Noires' bestowed since time immemorial on lands belonging to the Abbey of Orval. In 1070 Godefroy de Bouillon was 9/10 and might well have been tutored by one or more of the Calabrian hermits, whose leader, according to Gérard de Sède, 'La Race Fabuleuse', bore the name of Ursus, and whose number included Peter the Hermit, tutor of Godefroy, preacher of the First Crusade, leader of his own proto-crusade in 1096, who entered Jerusalem with Godefroy, and ended his days as Abbot and founder of the Augustinian Abbey of Huy (qv). The hermits left the area by 1108; on 9 Mar. 1131 St Bernard established Orval as a Cistercian Abbey. Further links with the Prieuré de Sion concern the sale of land to the Abbey of Orval in 1281 by the Abbot of the little priory of the Mount of Sion in Orleans (qv). Orval is on the Franco-Belgian border and 20 km from Stenay, where St Dagobert II was murdered and which Godefroy de Bouillon captured in 1077, to become its Seigneur.

B13   *Scherpenheuvel/Montaigu*
Brabant; 409 (5); 6 km W of Diest; OLV van Scherpenheuvel/N-D de Montaigu; national shrine of Belgium; open daily 6.30-19.30 (winter 7.30-18.30); 16 C.; 30.5 cm; oak, dark silver-grey colour; pilgrimage to sacred cruciform oak with statue of Virgin since before 1200 (documented 1304 by Lodewijk van Velthem, Priest of Zichem). *c*.1415 a passing shepherd, noticing the statue had fallen down, tried to take it away but remained crushed under its weight until his master, appearing on the scene, replaced it (cf. Huy *et al.*). Small sanctuary built there, D. during revolt against Spain, 1568. New Ch. built 1609-27 by Archduke Albert; town planned symmetrically around it. Paintings of the Life of St Anne and the Virgin by van Loon. Virgin crowed 1872; Ch. raised to Basilica status

1922. Large replica of oak reaches above altar towards dome, relics of oak under altar. Sichem is French for Shechem, where Joshua made his covenant. See Bargemont, Charlemont, Gray, Jussey, Mièges, Montciel, Nancy, Ornans, Tournon (France). Annual procession spring; not considered BV locally. In 1604 the Bishop of Antwerp had the ancient oak which bore the miraculous statue cut down. Of the numerous small statues carved from its wood Ornans and Jussey are acknowledged as BVs.

B14   Tongeren/Tongres Limburg; 409 (15); the original BV, 12 C.; Sedes Sapientiae, Our Lady in Labour, now in the treasury (No 72), acknowledged by citizens as black; visits in winter by arrangement with the Dean and the sacristan (who alone holds the key). The present miraculous crowned statue of Our Lady of Tongeren, Cause of our Joy; 1497; 150 cm; dark walnut; Virgin standing with Child on left arm holding bunch of grapes from which Child has picked one; living cult — flowers and candles; crowned 1890; frees prisoners (Turkish shackles behind altar); finds lost child; ends famine; Ark of the Covenant and Star of the Sea below altar; it is claimed (wrongly according to the Guide) that the Virgin wears a sword under her gown. Images of Sts Anne, Catherine, John the Baptist, John the Evangelist, Joseph, Luke and Mary Magdalene. St Materne early co-patron (cf. Walcourt). Tongeren, together with Tournai, claims to be Belgium's oldest town, with Roman and pre-Roman remains.

B15   Tournai 409   (11);   in Cathedral of N-D statue of N-D la Brune, N-D Flamande or de Tournai; local craftmanship; gift of Spanish officer in 1568 replacing in popular devotion the Old Madonna destroyed in 1566 by the Protestant iconoclasts; large brown standing statue in arched black marble niche on pillar on right of nave; living cult; statues of Sts Bernard and Amand look towards the BV from either side of the Chapel of St Catherine. Other chapels to Sts Michael, John the Baptist, Mary Magdalene, Martha, Margaret, Genevieve and Louis; relief of St Anne and Mary. Zodiacal west window transposes Gemini and Libra. Tournai shares with Tongeren (qv) the honour of being the oldest city in Belgium and was the capital of the Franks. Childeric died there (his body was discovered in 1653 covered in a mantle embroidered with golden bees) and Clovis, founder of the Merovingian dynasty, was born there. Many of the Kings of Europe visited Tournai, including Louis XI, Henry VIII, who occupied it for six years, René d'Anjou and the Emperor Charles V who held the 20th Chapter of the Order of the Golden Fleece in the Cathedral. Joan of Arc invited the inhabitants to the crowning of Charles VII at Rheims. N-D de la Treille reported to be BV; formerly in Ch.

of St Margaret (now closed), whereabouts unknown. Statue of goddess (Cybele?) holding lion cub, in museum.

B16 Verviers Liège; 409 (16); in Ch. of N-D des Recollets, Vierge Noire des Recollets or Mère de Miséricorde (Mother of Mercy); 1674; 200 cm; made of two sandstone blocks painted black; standing. On 18 Sept. 1692, at 2 p.m., when two severe earthquakes (60,000 people were killed in Sicily) occurred, the population ran into the Place des Recollets to avoid falling masonry. All 4,000 were astonished to see that the figures of Mary and Jesus in the statue, which at that time overlooked the square, had changed position. Whereas before both had looked to their front, the Virgin extending a sceptre in her left hand, the Christ Child standing on a pedestal with his right hand raised, now they had turned towards each other to adopt a strikingly different pose with her left hand and his right touching on her breast and his body twisted towards her at an awkward angle. This phenomenon, for which no satisfactory rational explanation has been offered, was confirmed in legal depositions undertaken from 104 witnesses and in a drawing 'before and after' by Jacques Silvius the sacristan. It was believed that the virgin was holding back the hand of God from punishment. During the French Revolution and the subsequent wars the statue underwent two blackening processes, being hidden in the chimney of the sacristy which was turned into a forge (possibly apocryphal) and in the fire of 1810 in which the Ch. was burnt down. In 1855 Fr Meunier had her scraped and painted uniformly black. Now in gallery at entrance to nave. Every seven years there is a festival lasting a fortnight around 18 Sept. in which a replica of the BV is carried in procession (next one in 1988). Very living cult, exvotos and candles. Crowned 1892. Also cult and statue of St Rita with silver bees attached to her dress (Merovingian symbol appropriated by Napoleon at his coronation). Country of coal mines and mineral waters (between Chaudfontaine and Spa) where the linguistic boundaries of French, German and Dutch meet, Verviers has two contiguous villages of Clermont immediately to the N and, 15 km to the W, Banneux, scene of the famous and now recognized apparitions of the Virgin which occurred in 1933.

B17   *Vilvoorde/Vilvorde* Brabant; 409 (4); 7 km N of Brussels by N 1; in Carmelite Convent (Troostkerk) Ch. in Leuvensestraat OLV van Troost/ N-D de Consolation; early 13 C.; one of a group of four statues — 's Gravesande, Haarlem (both D.) and Hal (qv for details of history), it was the parting gift of Sophie of Thuringia, Duchess of Brabant, before leaving for Germany in 1247; oak; 63 cm; totally restored and repainted in flesh tints in

Brussels recently (in 1879 there was nothing but a bust placed on a pedestal), though there is no evidence for Durand-Lefèbvre's assertion that this is a BV, save possibly in her reference to 'Intermédiaire des Chercheurs et des Curieux', 7 Aug. 1899, p.95, which I have been unable to trace. Although she has been compared to Our Lady of Hal, the external resemblances are minimal. They have, however, much in common when it comes to miraculous defences, and Our Lady of Vilvoorde appeared on the walls to deter attackers, became so heavy that she could not be carried away and put out a fire intended to destroy the Ch. and convent. She also liberates prisoners and resuscitates new-born babies among many other miracles of healing. Wall shrine to St Roch in Ridderstraat opposite entrance to convent. Dark statue of Virgin in nuns' recreation room.

B18 **Walcourt** Namur; 409 (13); 15 km S of Charleroi in Basilique St Materne, 4 C. Bishop of Cologne and Tongeren who placed a statue of the Virgin on the altar of an oratory in Walcourt where a pagan goddess had been worshipped; Ch. built 992 (consecrated 1026); present miraculous BV dates from this period which would make it one of the oldest statues of the Virgin in the west; 62 cm; wood; covered in silver 11 C.; plaques reinforced 13 C.; mask added 1626; popular legend says statue blackened in

8. Verviers

fire of 1220; Child (not an infant) sits sideways on Virgin's lap facing left like the Essen madonna; crowned 1875; living cult — candles and ex-votos; statues of St Bernard, Catherine (2), Anne, Margaret Michael, John the Baptist (3), John the Evangelist, and James the Greater; BV saved from fire by doves which carried it to Le Jardinet monastery which became a Cistercian Abbey in 1232; village of Clermont 5 km W. Silver Virgin of 1300 in treasury with sapphire placed on right breast is connected with the medieval cult of the Virgin's milk.

BOLIVIA

Copacabana Virgen de Copacabana, Dark Virgin of the Lake or Virgin of Candelaria (Candlemas). On shores of Lake Titicaca, in Basilica of the Sanctuary of Our Lady, Protectress of Bolivia; 4ft; standing statue of maguey, wood and stucco; plaster face and hands, Indian features; large sickle moon beneath Virgin's feet; carved *c.* 1576 by Francisco Yupanquie, a descendant of a noble Inca family. Origin of cult — Inca fisherman saved from storm on Lake Titicaca by Virgin who led them to safety. Chapel built 1583. Pilgrims leave Ch. walking backwards. 'Copacabana' = beholder of the blue horizon or beholder of the precious stone.

Sucre   Copy of BV of Guadalupe (Spain). Great devotion.

BRAZIL

Aparecida do Norte   São Paulo. In Sanctuary Ch. (there are 2 Basilicas), Nossa Senhora de Aparecida, formerly de Conceição. Brazil's most venerated religious image; terra cotta; 39 cm; standing on crescent moon in prayer; no Child; found in two parts by fisherman in Paraíba River in 1717, who after that never lacked a good catch. Black washed off in alcohol bath during restoration in 1950. In 1978 a madman attacked the statue and smashed it into 165 pieces. It has now been repaired and restored to its place and is a dark natural clay colour. Many miracles; living cult. The Brazilian

goddess of the seas and mother of the earth, Jemanja, is represented as black.

CANADA

Montreal   In Jesuit Ch., statue of N-D de Liesse; 1877; contains relics of old BV of Liesse (France, qv). The oldest Ch. in the city, N-D de Bon Secours, contains a Santa Casa of Loreto.

COSTA RICA

Costa Rica   Virgin of Costa Rica reported as BV by Moss and Cappannari.

CZECHOSLOVAKIA

Albendorff   Silesia. One of the chief pilgrimage sites of Silesia ('Silesian Jerusalem'). Statue; wood; 14 C.; 27 cm; Virgin holds apple; Child holds dove. The cult originated when a blind man sitting under a lime-tree was healed, and a statue of the Virgin was found in the tree. First chapel of 1263 built of wood by angels; closed by Hussites; cult re-established 17 C. Durand-Lefèbvre states that the statue is similar to N-D du Port at Clermont-Ferrand (qv).

Brno (Brünn)   Black Madonna of Brno; painted on cypress wood; 82cm x 47cm; gift of Kaiser Karl IV to new Augustinian monastery in Brno 1356; crowned 1736; attr. to St Luke; Child holds closed book in left hand. Saved in World War II. Said to be back on the altar of the Augustinian Ch. Copy in Aachen (qv).

Prague 4 BVs reported by Durand-Lefèbvre (1937). (1) Madonna of Loreto; (2) Our Lady of Monserrat; (3) Our Lady of Visherat, 16 C. copy of Salus Populi Romani in Rome; (4) Stare Mesto (Celetna Ulice), statue, 50 cm.

ECUADOR

Quinche In sanctuary Ch.; Na. Sra. del Quinche, or la Pequeñita (the little one). There may be darker Madonnas in Ecuador, but none is more beloved by the Indians who consider her their protector. In 1586 the Indians asked the sculptor Diego de Robles to carve them an image out of native cedar like that of Guadalupe (Mexico). The statue is constantly on tour, visiting the Indian communities throughout the country.

EGYPT

The ancient icon of St Catherine's Monastery in the Sinai is regarded by some as a BV. Some European BV's trace their origin to Egypt, home of Isis who provides the major iconographic model for the genre. A recent apparition of the Virgin took place at Zeitoun, on the outskirts of Cairo during 1968-9.

ENGLAND

Downside Abbey Stratton-on-the-Fosse, Somerset. Standing wooden statue in dark wood; Strasburg c. 1470, attr. to Nicolaus Gerhaert van Leyden; in N aisle of Abbey Ch. Obtained for Downside by Cardinal Gasquet at the turn of the century. Often referred to as the 'Black Madonna'.

Feering Essex. In private possession; BV; 16 C. Baroque in original costume and case; 7ins; only heads and one hand each sculpted; bought 1895 by Adrian Stokes RA 'somewhere down the Danube'. Child on right arm. Clearly intended to be black by design. Probably a copy of BV of Altötting (Germany, qv).

Glastonbury Somerset. The great church of Glastonbury had a Loreto chapel, presumably with an image of Our Lady of Loreto, added by Abbot Bere c.1500. The original statue of Our Lady of Glastonbury, traditionally carved by St Joseph of Arimathea, was one of the few objects to have survived the fire that destroyed most of the Abbey in 1184. Both images were presumably destroyed at the Reformation. At Glastonbury, images or cult of Sts Anne, Michael, John the Baptist, Margaret, Joseph of Arimathea and Brigid. According to legend,

Glastonbury is the site of the first Christian Ch. in Britain, dedicated to the Virgin by Joseph of Arimathea, who brought the Holy Grail there. It is also an island of the dead, Avalon, Merlin's temple of the stars, the true round table, and resting-place of Arthur, the once and future king.

London In Ch. of Our Lady of Hal (formerly the Belgian Ch.), 165 Arlington Road, Camden Town, NW 1, open 7.30a.m.–9p.m. (closed 1p.m. Bank Holidays); wooden statue of Our Lady of Hal (see Hal, Belgium); 1934; 3ft. Parish founded by a Belgian community of priests after the Great War — first service 1922. Present Ch. opened 1933.

There are copies of Our Lady of Czestochowa in London and throughout the country in churches where the Polish communities congregate.

Malmesbury Wilts. In Catholic Ch. of St Aldhelm's; painting of Our Lady of Guadalupe (Mexico); 9 by 4ft; early 17 C.? copy of original, unique in England; at Bradenstoke Priory c.1838; donated to St Aldhelms's in late 1920s; one of the treasures of the Clifton diocese.

Mayfield Sussex. Convent of the Holy Child. This former manor house of the Archbishops of Canterbury, now a girls' public school, possesses two BVs, and is included by Gustafson in his list of 13 famous BVs throughout the world.

(1) The statue in the chapel to the left of the altar was given to one of the nuns, Mother Mary-Veronica, by the heir of the Rev. C. Walker of Brighton in the 19 C. It stayed for many years in a little wooden shrine in the grounds until rescued by Sr Mary-Paul O'Connor. She took it to the Victoria and Albert Museum who declared that if English it was unique, if Flemish, rare and good. The *Blue Guide to England* dates it at c.1460. It was repaired by Hilary Pepler of the Ditchling Community. The statue in very dark wood is crowned, c.2ft 6ins, standing on a crescent moon, with Child on left arm holding ball under Virgin's chin. Sr Mary Evangelist liked to imagine that, since it had a hand missing, it might have been Our Lady of Boulogne, whose hand is still venerated in the Cathedral there.

(2) Seated madonna in courtyard room, wood, c. 2ft 6ins, crowned, slightly less dark than (1), Child on right knee, naked, with halo; found in ruins of farmer's storage room during restoration of buildings by Pugin in the 1850s.

Walsingham Norfolk. England's National Shrine of Our Lady. Saillens reports devotion to Our Lady of Loretto from 16 C., but Walsingham itself is England's Nazareth, whose story pre-dates Loretto's by more than two centuries. In 1061 Dame Richeldis de

Faverches, Lady of the Manor of Walsingham Parva, had a vision while her husband was on pilgrimage to the Holy Land, in which she was thrice taken in the spirit to the house of the Annunciation in Nazareth by the Virgin and told to note its dimensions well, since she must make an exact reproduction of it in Walsingham. There was some difficulty in choosing the correct site, and eventually the Blessed Virgin assisted by moving the foundations, which were constantly collapsing, some 200 feet to what became the site of the shrine until the Reformation, and one of the most famous sanctuaries of Our Lady in Christendom, whose pilgrimage route, like that of Compostela, was called the milky way. The major relic in Walsingham was, in fact, a phial containing some drops of the Virgin's milk. But the Lady Chapel with its wonder-working image, twice visited by Erasmus who described it as a 'rudely carved image with a crapaudine under its feet', and 'a counterfeit Ephesian Diana', but dedicated a poem to it, was the real goal of the pilgrimage, the one whom kings visited barefoot. There were also statues of Our Lady in gold and silver. Henry VIII, the last royal pilgrim, destroyed the Priory and had the statue burnt at Chelsea in 1539, but bequeathed his soul to Our Lady of Walsingham. The Slipper Chapel dedicated to St Catherine of Alexandria and Mt Sinai, which marked the final mile of the pilgrimage, formerly served by Benedictines of Conques, was bought in 1897 by Miss Charlotte Boyd and given to the monks of Downside. The first recorded pilgrimage since the Reformation took place that year, and in 1934 the chapel was recognized by the Catholic Bishops of England and Wales, with Papal approval, as the National Shrine of Our Lady. The statue in the 14 C. chapel is painted, but the replicas, based on the seal of Walsingham, are dark. In the Anglican shrine, where the cult of the Virgin recommenced in 1921, the year of the fire and restoration of the BV and Santa Casa in Loreto, a dark statue of the Virgin, based on the seal, is enthroned in replica of the original sacred house of the same dimensions, above the holy well. Richard Southwell, Thomas Cromwell's commissioner, claimed to have discovered in 1535 a secret room under the Priory used for the purposes of coining, alchemy and black magic. Royal pilgrims included Richard I, Henry III, Edward I (13 times), Edward II (twice — once after Bannockburn), David Bruce, Isabella of France, Edward III, and the Duke of Anjou.

FRANCE

1 *Agde* Hérault; 82 (15); (1) 2 km S of Agde, E of R. Hérault by D.32e; N-D du Grau; D; attr. St Luke; Pag; Ch. of La Genouillade contains stone with left knee-print

of Virgin, where she halted tidal wave. At Rev. man who damaged eyes of Virgin struck blind. Agde founded by Phocaeans 2,500 years ago as Agathé. 'The Good Goddess', in honour of Cybele, also echoes the name of Cybele's rock, Agdos, outside Pessinus, whence she was born in her androgynous form as Agdistis. Volcanic area; vines; olives; fishing; nearest hill Mt St Loup.

(2) Durand-Lefèbvre claims N-D de Bonencontre, terra cotta statue found 1523, as BV. *Nostra* 31/3/83 shows miraculous extant, healing BV at Agde. Tourist Office says there has never been a BV at Agde, but that La Genouillade is dark volcanic stone.

2 **Aix-en-Provence** Bouches-du-Rhône. 93 (13). (1) Ch. of La Madeleine; N-D des Grâces; 12/13 C.: standing; wood; 115 cm; now flesh coloured except for Virgin's disproportionately large, black, claw-like right hand; brought from Italy in 1274, traditionally by St Bonaventure, who died in Lyons that year; water; Pag.

(2) N-D de Seds, BV in old Cathedral of La Seds, both D. in 16 C.

(3) N-D d'Espérance, reported from various sources in Cathedral of St Sauveur as 80 cm, 1521 copy of (2), with devil as dog under feet. 13/2/82 Sacristan knew nothing of any notable statue of the Virgin, black or otherwise, in the Cathedral. The famous triptych by Nicholas Froment of the Virgin

sitting in the Burning Bush, commissioned by Good King René (d'Anjou) recalls the many BVs found in bushes. René was Grand Master of the Prieuré de Sion, titular King of Jerusalem; descended from the Merovingians and reputed patron of Joan of Arc, also known as Jeanne Daix.

2 (a) *Albert* Somme. 59(9). N-D de Brébières; 11C; reported as BV by local resident.

3 *Ambrus* Lot-et-Garonne. 79 (13) (14); a km S of Damazan. Vierge brune reported by inhabitant of Marmande; 16 C.; Madonna of the Landes; cork-oak; 11 C. Ch.; devotion since 5 C.; miraculous spring; statue stolen and found 1982; not black now.

4 *Amélie-les-Bains* (Els Banys, and formerly Bains d'Arles.) Pyrénées-Orientales 86 (18); N-D del Coll (hill or neck); very hard wood 80 cm; cattle; water; Pag.; found by ox 9 C. by Roman baths still frequented for respiratory and rheumatic complaints; Virgin noted for miraculous cures of throat diseases; ruins of old Ch. still visible 1952 founded by St Quentin (= ? Kantae Niskae, White Nixies or Water Nymphs) and destroyed to make place for garage of Hôtel des Thermes; Ch. first mentioned 869; Megalithic cult — carved stones found 1940 near old ford; carvings effaced 5/6 C.; feast days 8 Sept. and Sun. nearest 24 May (Our Lady Help of Christians);

Virgin frees captives — ex-voto chains on wall too high to be destroyed at Rev. Tourist Office says there is now no BV at Amélie-les-Bains.

5 Angers Maine-et-Loire; 64 (11), 63 (20); (1) in crypt of Ch. de la Trinité now attached to the École des Arts et Métiers on W Bank of R. Maine. N-D du Ronceray (bramble) or de la Charité; 12 C.; 18 cm; enamelled copper statue with silver crown and fleur-de-lys; Child on left knee with bare legs; Virgin holds curiously shaped sceptre in right hand; found in long-shut crypt in 1527; saved at Rev. by nun; returned to crypt 1882; stolen 1977. Benedictine Abbey built by Foulques Nerra, ferocious Count of Anjou (972-1040), whose wife Hildegarde, whom he had unjustly accused of adultery and thrown down from the castle walls, miraculously landed safely across the Maine by a bramble bush in which a statue of the Virgin was found. A bramble grew ever after by the window of the subterranean chapel. A later Foulques, Count of Anjou, an 'honorary' Templar, who married Godefroy de Bouillon's niece, thus becoming King of Jerusalem, a title to which René d'Anjou was to succeed (see Aix), restored the Abbey after Norman depredations, and, in 1119 Pope Calixtus II reconsecrated the high altar and presented a piece of the Virgin's girdle.

(2) Another Virgin, N-D Sous-Terre was discovered by Yolande d'Aragon, mother of René d'Anjou, thanks to a rabbit which jumped on to her lap to escape the hunt. Yolande found the statue in the bush where the rabbit had been hiding.

(3) In the Ch. of St Martin there was a painting of the BV, now D. Saillens mentions another 15 C. painting in the museum where the Virgin is grey and pink with a black veil.

(4) BV reported at Monastery of l'Esvière near Angers.

6 *Angoulême* Charente; 72 (13)(14); A BV has been reported but its whereabouts is uncertain.

Apchon   See Font-Sainte.

7 Aragnouet Hautes-Pyrénées; 85 (19); 9 km S of St Lary-Soulan on D. 929; N-D known as The Throne of Wisdom, late example of the St Savin type of madonna, related to BV of Dorres; date problematic; hands and Child missing; stolen 15 years ago from Templar Ch. nearby to SW; by village of Plans. Curé says not a BV.

8 Arbois Jura; 70 (4); N-D de l'Ermitage on hill-top hermitage outside town; BV carved from Miraculous oak of Montaigu, brought back by old soldier *c.* 1700; hidden at Rev. by hermit; rediscovered 1856; pilgrimage 1st week in July; Feast of wine 1st Sun. in Sept.; Earlier statue N-D de Montserrat late 15 C.; D.

9 *Arcachon* Gironde. 78 (2) (12). In La Chapelle des Marins (Basilica of N-D); N-D d' Arcachon; Franciscan, Thomas of Illyria, in retreat at Arcachon after six years of preaching missions in France (1516-22) prayed for two ships he saw sinking in a storm; the sea became calm and the waves brought the statue (13/14 C.) to his feet; Chapel destroyed by storms and buried in sand over the centuries but was always rebuilt; for the last time in 1722; it was untouched at Rev. and the Annunciation was celebrated there at the height of the Terror under the protection of the National Guard; statue has clearly been repainted and restored (probably 1973) but Curé says it is not a BV (despite Saillens, who claims it as 'earliest replica of BV of Loreto in France'); living cult, miracles, ex-votos.

10 **Arceau** Côte d'Or; 66 (12); 12 km NE of Dijon; N-D de Bon Secours; *c*.1300; 60 cm; very light wood (cork?); found 1227 by ox near green tussock; cures eyes; candles; ch. open Sun. Wed. Sat.; Chapel to St Anne.

11 **Arconsat** Puy-de-Dôme; 73 (6); 4 km NE of Chasbreloche by D 86 beyond E end of B 71 Autoroute at frontier of Auvergne, Bourbonnais and Forez in the Bois Noirs, a continuation of the Mts de la Madeleine; N-D d'Arconsat; 12 C.; 70 cm; in village Ch. on altar of Blessed Sacrament to rt of choir; Pag.; water; windows to St Anne, St John the Baptist, St Roch and St Louis. Stolen by men of

Forez, she assisted her recovery and punished the thieves. Remarkable statue in that only the faces, very black, are sculpted, the body of the Child being limbless and pear-shaped, which suggests it was intended to be robed from its origin, though many authorities attribute this custom to a much later date. Mural of 1976 behind the statue illustrates its legend. The area was the centre of paganism and fairy-lore until very late. A monster called the Ré du Sol was slain by a Templar. It was the custom to climb Montoncel to watch the sun rise on St John the Baptist's Day.

12 *Ardes* Puy-de-Dôme; 76 (4); 73 (14); La Vierge de la Récluse; painted stone; quoted as BV in *Atlantis*, Curé vehemently states this is not the case.

13 **Arfeuilles** Allier; 73 (6); 38 km NW of Roanne by D 26; N-D d'Arfeuilles or des Houx (hollies); 12 C.; standing; 95 cm; heavily restored and repainted in flesh tints in 1938. Drochon writes in the late 19 C.; 'one of the most interesting images that Christian art has bequeathed to us . . . she was formerly completely black. God preserve our churches from these ill-advised restorers.' Miracles: the resuscitation of unbaptised babies and the healing of blindness and paralysis. According to Saillens, Arfeuilles was successively a centre of Druidism and the cults of Bellona and St Roch. St Roch normally shares his feast day, 16 Aug., with St Joachim, the

husband of St Anne, but at Arfeuilles it was apparently the custom to celebrate it on 3 Feb., the feast of St Blaise and the morrow of Candlemas.

14 *Arles* Bouches-de-Rhône; 83 (10); N-D de Grâces presented to Ch. of Alyscamps 1203; removed to St Trophime; disappeared 1915 (see Barbegal); Pag; Mer; the first revolutionary who tried to pull down the statue was knocked over, broke his leg and limped till his death in a poorhouse 40 years later. Prayers for rain by 7,000 in 1868 answered. Arles was the capital of the later Roman Empire, of which les Alyscamps was the biggest cemetery. Cult of Isis and Cybele (altar to Bona Dea found 1758), whose Temple is now N-D la Major. St Radegonde, wife of Merovingian King Clotaire I, left Anjou for Arles in 6 C. Arles one of four main starting-points for Compostella and Grand Commandery of the Temple.

15 *Arpajon* Cantal; 76 (12); 4 km SE of Aurillac; miraculous N-D des Grâces; wood; 140 cm; 17 C.; replaces BV of Crusades; D; Pag. called 'City of Tombs' (Gallo-Roman). Temple of Jupiter. BV took the place of the female sacristan who left for Aurillac to be with her lover, performing all her duties until her return (a similar tale is told in Buñuel's film *The Milky Way*).   Home of Kipling's French translator.

16 Aspet Haute-Garonne; 86 (2); 18 km S of St Gaudens of D 5; in chapel of N-D de Miège-Coste (ask for key at presbytery); N-D de Meijo-Costo or Miège-Coste (half way up the hill); 160 cm, *c*.1680 replacing BV of 4 C.; only heads sculpted; hands sewn on to sleeves of dress; BV of La Daurade at Toulouse is similar; documented as BV 1682; hidden at Rev.; invoked against war, plague and famine, miracles of healing (including blindness 1753); Aspet has never known the horrors of war; large white statue of Virgin on Ch. roof destroyed by lightning 1945.

17 Aureil-Maison Vosges. 62 (14); 2 km S. of Lamarche on N 460A; present 12 C. Virgin probably replaces earlier BV.

18 Aurillac Cantal; 76 (12); (1) N-D des Neiges, formerly d' Aureinques, in Ch. of the Cordeliers, 3rd chapel on left; 70 cm; original BV destroyed by Huguenots. Present statue of 1581 is a close copy of BV of Le Puy. BV helped defeat Huguenots at Aureinques Gate on 4/5 Aug. 1581 (Feast of Our Lady of the Snows), by miraculously advancing the hour of dawn and producing a snowfall.

(2) N-D du C(h)oeur, copy of painting attr. to St Luke; D Rev.; in first Ch. dedicated to the Immaculate Heart of Mary. Aurillac ('lake of gold' or 'boar's ear') on R. Jordanne in which fleeces were turned to gold is the town of

Pesco-Luno (moon-fishers) and of Gerbert, the first Frenchman to be Pope, who held office in the Year 1,000. He was a shepherd who studied with the Benedictines of Aurillac before being instructed in the occult arts and put on the path of advancement by the beautiful demoness Meridiana, probably in Spain (cf. Limoux). Another famous inhabitant was St Géraud, whose golden statue was as well-known in the Middle Ages as that of Ste Foy at Conques, and whose cult included a sacred fountain and tree. Aurillac was closely linked to Compostela, whose cockle-shells appear on its coat of arms.

19 Authezat Puy-de-Dôme; 73 (14); 23 km S of Clermont-Ferrand by N 9; N-D d' Authezat; 13 C. 40 cm; wood; now in treasury of Cathedral at Clermont-Ferrand (qv). Definitely a BV. Statues of Sts Anne and Roch. Formerly an important pilgrimage centre, especially on Good Friday. Gallo-Roman temple of Ceres discovered 2 km from Ch. No resident priest. To visit apply to M. Crapelet, 20 rue de l'Hôtel de Ville, Riom.

20 Auxerre Yonne; 65 (5); N-D de Chartres or La Brune formerly in crypt; D; Auxerre was the centre of a cult to Cybele and its Roman name Autricum was the same as that of Chartres. Relics of St Amadour of Auxerre (d.418) at St Nectaire (qv).

21 Auzers Cantal; 76 (2); NE of Mauriac by D 678 and D 22; 6 km N of Moussages; N-D du Mas; standing; wood; 75 cm; 17 C. replacing statue D by Huguenots; flesh tinted child (Saillens). Guide Noir mentions only fine 16 C. limestone pietà in village Ch. chambre vert — cave painted green.

22 Avignon Vaucluse; 81 (11) (12); BV, N-D La Brune D. at Rev. Large BV (1859) on Cathedral (no child) looks down on crucifixion and Palace of Popes. In Ch. of Black Penitents, angels carry head of John the Baptist. Cathar centre.

23 Avioth Meuse; 57 (1); N-D de Vie (life) or l'Epine (thorn) or de Luxembourg; 12 C.; 88 cm; SD; doll-like Child not part of original statue; BV whitened for many years but Nostra, 1983, shows photograph of her as dark; as old as BV of Chartres, may be copy of BV of Walcourt (Belgium); water. Found in a hawthorn bush in 1140 which blossomed, now in great 14 C. Basilica on original site above tiny village near Belgian frontier. BV turned red and looked sad during French invasions of 1657. Earlier she struck dead an impious Huguenot captain who used her altar as a manger for his horse. Unique architectural feature, La Recévresse at gate of former cemetery outside Ch., above underground spring, where offerings of dead babies were placed (last recorded offering 23 Feb. 1786).

Statue on it guillotined at Rev.; special miracle – restoring to life unbaptised babies (*les petits voleurs du paradis*) to enable them to receive baptism and avoid limbo, entering eternal bliss. Avioth — *a via* (without a way) or 'Ave O Theotokos Virgo' (Hail, Virgin who bringest forth a child), formerly St Brice (Briccia — Celtic goddess of springs). The spring under the Ch. has miraculous properties among which is the granting of fertility to women. St Bernard visited the site, just a few miles from Orval (which he founded in 1131) and encouraged the pilgrimage. Aviot has come to mean a pilgrimage for the purpose of restoring children to life. The village is 25 km from Stenay, one of the most important commanderies of the Prieuré de Sion, where the last reigning Merovingian King, St Dagobert II, was murdered in 679. Avioth 22 km from Carignan where a huge statue of Diana/Arduina was destroyed in 590.

24 **Ay** Ardèche; 76 (10); 5 km N of Satillieu by D 578A and D 6; N-D d'Ay or d'Ayde; 15 C.; 76 cm; replacing earlier BV known in 12 C. when Emperor Frederick Barbarossa took the shrine under his protection. Miracles include resuscitation of still-born children and the end of droughts and plagues. Impressive site high above the R. Ay, where the Virgin saved a shepherd girl from drowning. Mothers still take their children there to be blessed; relic of

Virgin's milk. Crowned Queen of the Haut Vivarais in 1890. Cousin of BVs of Lyons and Le Puy who used to visit her on 8 Sept. Shrine originally served by Benedictines and first granted a charter by Charlemagne in 776.

25 *Bagnères-de-Bigorre* Hautes-Pyrénées; 85 (18); BV reported by Durand-Lefèbvre; may have been Virgin of Médous now at Asté (7 km S by D 8); Curé of Asté says no BV.

26 Bailleul Nord; 51 (5); BV copy of N-D de Halle (Hella, German Persephone, Queen of the Underworld); in chapel of Allied Military Cemetery, where the battle-lines remained almost unchanged throughout the four years of the Great War. Family of John of Balliol (King of Scotland) originated here.

27 *Ballon/ StMars-Sous-Ballon* Sarthe; 60 (13); 21 km N of Le Mans by D 300; N-D des Champs, rare 15 C. terra cotta BV now in private collection; replaced in Ch. of St Mars-sous-Ballon by wooden standing statue of 19 C; 150 cm; this, too, now seems to have disappeared. Ballon may derive from the Celtic Mars, Belenus.

28 Banyuls Pyrénées-Orientales; 86 (20); N-D des Abeilles or dels Monts; in old Ch. in cemetery where all the statues come from the chapel of N-D des Abeilles W of Amont up the stream Baillaury near the Spanish frontier; dark

polychrome wooden statue; 100 cm; known since 1254; called black 'because of the Moors' according to sacristan; Ch. now usually locked, also · contains statue of Mary Magdalene with dark, smudged face. Large statue of Artemis stood on Cap l'Abeille, 4 km S. Abelio is the Pyrenean sun-god and bees are symbols of Ra, Demeter, Artemis, Persephone, Cybele, Deborah, Pharoah and St Bernard as well as of the Merovingian dynasty. Doors of old sanctuary, in which bees built their nest, were never closed as they opened by themselves. Feast was 10 Feb.

29 *Barbegal* Bouches-du-Rhône; 83 (20); NE of Arles by D 33b. Saillens reports BV which might be that of Arles; no Ch., but statue may be in private château (closed).

30 Le Barboux Doubs; 66 (18); near Swiss frontier and Chaux-de-Fonds, D 437 Morteau/Montbéliard rd, fork rt, 7.5 km S of le Russey for 2 km on D 211 or D 298. Copy of N-D d'Eisiedeln (Switzerland).

31 *Bargemont* Var; 84 (7); 21 km N of Draguignan by D 25; N-D de Montaigu; 10 cm; carved from piece of the Belgian oak of Montaigu/Scherpenheuvel; cures blind and resuscitates drowned children; saved at Rev.

32 *Le Barroux* Vaucluse; 81 (3); between Carpentras and Vaison-la-Romaine on D 938; N-D la Brune; cedar; whereabouts unknown; reported to be in vandalized hill-top chapel of St Christopher opposite castle above cemetery but not there; questioning aroused hostility; Benedictine monastery 11 C. has ancient German wooden statue of Virgin in crypt; Ch. of la Madeleine to E; Rock of Alaric to W; Crête de St Amand to N.

33 *Bastia* Corsica; 90 (3); N-D de Montserrat; Ch. of Holy Cross has rare black Christ found in sea by fishermen 15 C. and confraternity of St Roch.

34 **La-Bastide-de-Sérou** Ariège; 86 (4); 17 km W of Foix by D 117; N-D la Noire; 100 cm; new devotion 19 C. according to Saillens; Curé confirms BV's presence, but has no information concerning it save that it was venerated by pregnant women; in heartland of Catharism.

35 *Beaudricourt* Vosges; 62 (14); SW corner of Mirecourt aerodrome on N 66; N-D de Lorette; 1578; once much frequented; Robert de Beaudricourt, Captain of Vaucouleurs, was the first authority to whom Joan of Arc appealed when she set out on her mission; Curé says no BV.

36 **Beaune** Côte d'Or; 69 (9); N-D de Beaune; 12 C.; probably replica of original N-D du Port at Clermont-Ferrand; brought from Auvergne by Matilda of Turenne, wife of Hugh, Duke of Burgundy,

both friends and patrons of St Bernard; statue cleaned and lightened; saved at Rev. by school mistress; invoked successfully against cholera 19 C.; Child carries vine-branch (Beaune capital of Burgundy wine); Ch. and window of St Mary Magdalene. Beaune probably takes its name from Belena, a feminine form of Belenus, the Celtic Cybele in her warlike form, similar to the Roman Bellona, companion of Mars who figured on the original coat of arms of the city. A statue of Belen was discovered at Beaune in 1767. An ancient coin showing the sun and a wolf has also been found there.

37 Billom Puy-de-Dôme; 73 (15); *Nostra* 1983 mentions BV who heals children unable to walk. In Ch. of St Cerneuf (Sirénat) the story of Zacchaeus of Jericho (later the Amadour of Rocamadour) is depicted on the capitals. Ch. of St Loup now closed. Feast of Holy Blood (3 May), celebrated at the Chapel of the Black Penitents, a former Templar commandery. Druidic hanging stone near by, the Pierre des Fées.

38 Blois Loir-et-Cher; 64 (7); N-D des Aydes is reputed to have been one of the famous BVs of France until burnt at Rev., 24 Nov. 1793; found by sailors in Loire; 13 C.; 100 cm; Mer.; Joan of Arc invoked her aid 26/27 Apr. 1429. In 1588 Henri III convoked parliament under her protection. Louis XIII renewed the consecration of France to N-D at her altar. N-D des Aydes is mentioned as a healing BV in *Nostra*, 1983. Copy, not BV, according to ecclesiastical authorities, on altar of the Virgin in Ch. of St Saturnin. A second, ebony BV, N-D de Champbourdin, dug up while ploughing his field by the peasant, Bourdin, on the site of the present Protestant Ch. The statue is in the secretariat of the Blois diocese, 2 rue Porte-Clos-Haut, Blois, where it is not considered a BV. Although its date and fate are not mentioned by Brétigny and Deloux in their book *Rennes-le-Château*, they point to it as an object of quite special veneration and hint that it plays a part in the frequent choice of Blois by the Prieuré de Sion for their gatherings to elect a new Grand Master, known as Le Nautonnier (helmsman). Victor Hugo entered the Order there on 2 May 1824 under the mastership of his fellow littérateur, Charles Nodier, whom he succeeded there on the Feast of Mary Magdalene 1844. The recent Grand Master, Pierre Plantard, was elected at Blois on 17 Jan. 1981, reputedly the 1,300th anniversay of the arrival of his ancestor Sigisbert IV at Rennes-le-Château. The name of the inhabitants of Blois, Blésois or Blaisois suggests a possible derivation from the pagan god of wind and the underworld, Blez. Orchaise, 11 km, Orci Casa, house of Pluto, mouth of Hell.

39 Boëge Haute-Savoie; 74 (7); 29 km E of Geneva by D 903 and D 20; N-D des Voirons (local Mt and range); darkened lime; 50 cm; now in parish Ch.; Pag.; The gods of the Allobroges ruled in the Pays des Bois and on the Combe Noire until 10 C. when the Bishop of Geneva destroyed the Temple of Jupiter and burnt the idol. Thereupon a demoniac wild bear ravaged the countryside. Sieur de Langan, while hunting it, was wounded by it and only escaped with his life by invoking the Virgin. He built a chapel in her honour and installed a statue of her. Marauding Bernese Protestants destroyed the sanctuary in 1536 and one of them dragged the blackened Virgin with him on a cord, turning his head to taunt her until it remained stuck in that position and his shoulder and arm were paralysed. His descendants remained under the curse for 350 years. That night snow fell, hiding the statue and the bell of the chapel which they had planned to take with them. St François de Sales placed his missions under the protection of N-D des Voirons.

40 Boulogne-sur-Mer Pas-de-Calais; 51 (1); N-D des Anges or de Boulogne; Pag.; Mer.; standing; D at Rev. (one hand of original remains in a reliquary). The legendary origins of the cult date from 633 AD, in the reign of the Merovingian Dagobert I when, perhaps in his presence, a mysterious boat arrived without sails or crew, containing nothing but a copy of the Gospels in Syriac and a statue of the Virgin standing upright like Isis and surrounded by an extraordinary light. The cult became involved again with the Merovingian blood-line through Ida of the Ardennes, the Lady of Boulogne, the mother of Godefroy of Bouillon. Ida's crypt, the largest in France (though the earliest crypt of Boulogne was traditionally consecrated in 46 AD) housing her tomb and a copy of her son's, is built on the site of a Roman Temple of Mars and is highly impressive. The crypt museum contains an early 19 C. BV in a white dress standing in a boat. Boulogne, 'la ville de Nostre-Dame', ranked with Chartres as a place of pilgrimage and is mentioned by Chaucer in the same verse as Jerusalem, Rome and Compostela. The war-cry of the Counts of Boulogne was 'A la bataille Notre Dame!' and she and her city were indeed often embattled, a bone of contention between France, England and Burgundy. Joan of Arc prayed to her in 1429, and in 1477 Louis XI transferred the suzerainty of the entire Boulonnais to her. Most of his descendants paid her homage. Captured by the English in 1544 (when the crypt was filled in and lost until 1827) and restored, N-D de Boulogne was thrown on a dung-heap and then into a well by the Huguenots, re-emerging to be destroyed finally, save for one hand, in 1793. Boulogne was from 1104 the home of another

BV, Our Lady of the Holy Blood, reputedly a copy of N-D de Boulogne and venerated in the Ch. of N-D du St Sang, D. The cult of N-D de Boulogne took on a new lustre in 1945 when she acquired the title of N-D du Grand Retour, in honour of her succour of the refugees who returned safely from the war. Nicolas Flamel, the alchemist, who preceded René d' Anjou as Grand Master of the Prieuré de Sion, established various charitable foundations in the city.

41 *Boulogne-sur-Seine* Seine. N-D de Boulogne; 237 (17); 1319; D. at Rev.; In 1308 some inhabitants of the village of Les Menus in what is now the Bois de Boulogne in Paris went on pilgrimage to Boulogne-sur-Mer, and on their return built a Ch. to N-D de Boulogne-le-Petit. The original statue dates from 1319 as did a famous confraternity in its honour to which Joan of Arc and most French kings belonged. In 1469 a piece of the statue of Boulogne-sur-Mer was taken as a relic to Boulogne-sur-Seine under the protection and with the authorization of Louis XI, and was exposed once a year. In 1793 a silver statue was taken to the mint to be melted down. A new statue by Viollet-le-Duc was installed in 1853.

Bourbon l'Archambault Allier; 69 (13); see Vernouillet.

42 **Bourg-en-Bresse** Ain; 74 (3);

N-D de Bourg; standing; 80 cm; blackened elm or willow; found in hollow willow tree in swamp by shepherd in 13 C.; now in Ch., open 8-12, 14-19; saved at Rev. but badly burnt; Pag. The area was only Christianized gradually during the period 800-1200. Statue conveys little impression of its original appearance but probably only the faces were carved; SD; Saillens reports the existence of two BVs in this 'funeral city'; healed Aymon de Savoie 1343; statue's clothes and jewels now hidden; ex-votos; candles (despite efforts of clergy); images of Sts Anne, John the Baptist, Margaret, Catherine, James the Greater, Roch, Crispin and Crispinian, Andrew. Cult of St Margaret and Mary Magdalene.

43 *Bourganeuf* Creuse; 72 (9); N-D du Puy; 17 C., replacing earlier statue; given to the Templars by Raoul de Montgeniez, Lord of Le Puy, in gratitude for being freed from the Saracens by them during the Crusades; standing; no Child; stone; polychrome. Saved life of soldier on retreat from Moscow.

44 **Bourisp** Hautes-Pyrénées; 85 (19); on D 929 Auch-Lérida rd 1.5 km N of St Lary Soulan; standing; 53 cm; 13 C.; water; cattle; SD; in niche to right of entrance. An unknown architect traced the plan of the Ch. and disappeared. BV sits on black and gold throne in black dress with white veil and red flowers. The

Child sits centrally holding a closed book in his left hand. Indulgenced Feast on Ascension Day, when the statue was found. Stolen 21/11/82.

45 *Bredons* Cantal; 76 (3); 2 km S of Murat; N-D de *Sion*; wooden Majesté stolen recently. Bredons was a very important Benedictine Priory from 11 C. Reredos shows Adam and Eve with the inscription 'Death comes from wood', and Jesus and Mary with the inscription 'Life comes from wood'. Noel Verdier, an artist who made a Faustian pact with the Devil at Bredons in 1722, was saved because he had not finished gilding the tail of St Roch's dog.

46 *Briançon* Basses-Alpes; 77 (18); pre-14 C. BV, 'La Belle Briançonne'; Pag.; now at Tarascon (qv).

47 *Brioude* Haute-Loire; 76 (5); Romanesque BV now in Rouen museum; Brioude on the ancient Via Tolosana to Compostela.

48 *Le Buret* Mayenne; 232 (8) 64 (1); 15 km NW of Sablé-sur-Sarthe by D 21 towards Laval and D 285; N-D de la Ducraie; 25 cm; tiny white stone figure 12 C., blackened 17 C.; found on log. The statue now stands in a case over the altar in a small chapel, restored 1871-4, a few hundred metres W of the village. Ex-votos include children's clothes and shoes, many recent, testifying to her special protection and help for children who have difficulty in learning to walk. She also reigns over the mines of Chémeré-le-Roi near by. Neighbouring villages include St Loup and St Brice.

49 *Cambrai* Nord; 53 (3) (4); in the Cathedral of N-D; N-D des Grâces; a painting attr. to St Luke on cedar with a gold background, originally in Constantinople at Church of St Pulcheria, one of the chief originators of the cult of relics and images of the Virgin; brought back from Rome by Canon Fursy de Bruilles in 1440. The Palladium of Cambrai, it saved the city in many battles and was itself preserved at Rev. Visited by Louis XI.

50 Capdrot Dordogne; 75 (16); 2 km E of fine Bastide of Monpazier, 15 km W of D 710 Périgueux-Villeneuve road; N-D La Noire; wood; 50 cm; 19 C. signed J. Boullac. An original and attractive statue showing the throned and crowned Virgin with a small head, two braids, somewhat Indo-Chinese features and an empty right hand raised to her side. The Child stands by her left hip holding on to a plait. Statue stands on plinth behind altar. Nearest village to N St Marcory (Mercury?). Original statue hidden from Protestants in a wall.

51 *Capelou* Dordogne; 75 (16); 1.5 km W of Belvès by D 54; water; cattle; SD; N-D de Capelou or de Pitié was a small stone statue discovered by a herdsman in a thorn-bush thanks to the strange behaviour of one of his cattle. Taken to Belvès Ch. it returned three times to the thorn tree, where a chapel was built, mentioned by Pope Eugenius III in 1153. The present chapel was built by the man who destroyed it at Rev. The Virgin now venerated in the Ch. is a standing white stone statue without Child from the Abbaye de Fontgolfier replacing the BV D in 1793. There is a miraculous, never-failing spring near the entrance that heals the blind and dumb. The two side chapels in the Ch. are dedicated to St Anne and St Mary Magdalene.

52 *Carcarès* Landes; 78 (6),234 (46) (21); 2 km NE of Tartas; replica of BV of Guadalupe. Whereabouts now unknown.

53 *Carry-le-Rouet* Bouches-de-Rhône; 84 (12); 27 km W of Marseilles by A 7 and A 55; N-D du Rouet (oak); discovered underground and destroyed by Huguenots; patroness of sailors; major feast Candlemas. There is now a N-D des Marins NW at Martigues, near St Blaise and St Mitre.

54 Cases-de-Pène Pyrénées-Orientales; 86 (9); 14 km NW of Perpignan by D 117; water; N-D de Pène in hermitage 15 min. walk to hill-top above road where spring gushes from rock-face; old, dark wood, worm-eaten strange Virgin on shelf in lateral chapel to right of altar. Gilt standing Madonna behind altar with fine statue of St Catherine of Alexandria, to whom the neighbouring Ch. on the other side of the hills to SE is dedicated. Ch. open Easter Monday (and other major feasts) when the Dominican Fathers carry up a small travelling Virgin in a case for the veneration of the faithful, including many of the Black Penitents of Perpignan. The Ch. was once a barracks and the Salt de la Donzella commemorates a virgin who leapt from a rock to escape the unwelcome attentions of the soldiery. The ruins of the last Cathar stronghold of Quéribus, which did not fall until 1260 are just visible to the NW.

55 *La Cellette* Corrèze; 73 (12); 1 km S of N 89, 2 km W of Bourg-Lastic; BV brought from Paris 1830; 12 C. Benedictine Priory D by English 15 C. Cordelier Priory D at Rev., now mental hospital.

56 Les-Cerneux-Monnots Doubs; 66 (18); replica of BV of Einsiedeln; 10 km from Swiss frontier.

57 Champagnac-les-Mines Cantal; 76 (2); 20 km N of Mauriac (qv) by D 922 and D 112; N-D de Bon-Secours, a pre-Christian idol was donated by the Merovingian King Clovis and venerated as a BV. Saillens identifies it with the Frankish goddess, Hel, and describes it as a weird-looking object without a face or Child which a 19 C. curé hid in his loft. It has been replaced on the

altar by N-D de Lourdes. Saillens reports the presence there also of a black statue of St Anne known as La Bonne Dame (cf. Cybele). *Nostra* 1983 mentions the BV of Champagnac as a patroness of mines. On Zero meridian of Paris.

58 Champdieu Loire; 73 (17); 4.5 km N of Montbrison by D 8; BV; dark wood; 15 cm; standing; 15/16 C.(?); transferred from Sauvain in 1715; sometimes called Virgin of the Crusades; kept hidden for security reasons (apply to Curé).

59 Champels Haute-Loire; 76 (16); 2.5 km W of Monistrol by D 589; N-D des Tours or d'Estours; 60 cm; 11 C.; majesté; wood; cattle; SD: now kept at Monistrol; to see apply to Priest; photograph in sanctuary; veneration of St Mary Magdalene.

60 La Chapelle Geneste Haute-Loire; 76 (6); 6 km N of La Chaise-Dieu by D 499 and D 201; enthroned and crowned BV and Child; wood; 70 cm; faces very black with red lips and gleaming whites of eyes in contrast; beautiful fine features; statue difficult to date, but the devotion is immemorial. Cult and chapel of St Roch and statue of John the Baptist. Flat carved capitals like those of Thuret and Clermont-Ferrand.

61 Chappes Allier; 69 (13); 30 km N of Montluçon by D 33, 3 km S of Murat by D 543; 12 C.; wood; 93 cm; recently gilt; water;

saved at Rev. Statue, found in nearby fountain which heals fevers, has green veil and yellow robe with Merovingian-style buckle. Drochon calls it the most remarkable Virgin of the Moulins diocese after N-D de la Ronde. St Anne patroness of parish.

62 *Charlemont* Ardennes; 53 (9); citadel on W outskirts of Givet; Virgin sculpted in splinter of oak of Montaigu (Belgium); village of Mesnil-St-Blaise to E of frontier in Belgium; fortress built by Charles V; Beauraing (apparitions of Virgin 1932) 15 km E.

63 Charlieu Loire; 73 (8); N-D de Charlieu in Ch. of St Philibert; 16 C.; Chapel of St Anne; statue of St Crispin; Benedictine monastery.

64 Chartres Eure-et-Loir; 60 (7) (8); the BV of Chartres officially recognized as such by the Church is N-D du Pilier in the nave; 60 cm; early 16 C. replacing a 13 C. gilt statue. But it is N-D de Sous-Terre (underground) in the crypt, though probably exposed outside in the early centuries, D at Rev. and replaced in 1856 by the present natural wood statue of 80 cm, that carries the magic of the Chartres tradition relating to a pre-Christian image of the Virgin who will bring forth a Child. From photographs of the 17 C. replica in the Carmel of Lucé (Chartres) there seems no doubt that she was a BV. Huysmans, in *La Cathédrale*, 1908, claims that

Chartres is unique in having two BVs. Her altar stands next to the 'Puits des Saints Forts' well, the origin of Chartres and its most ancient thing, which was long lost. The largest image in Chartres and the oldest cult object in France known for certain to have been continuously black since its creation is the window of St Anne, the second patroness of the Cathedral, offered by St Louis in the 12 C. The *chainze* (shift or tunic) of the Virgin that had belonged to Charlemagne was transferred from Aachen (qv) to Chartres in 876, bestowing unique prestige on a pilgrimage already well-established in 600 when St Béthaire prostrated himself 'before the altar of the very glorious virgin Mary'. According to tradition, Chartres was the sacred capital of the Druidic world. Also 12 C. BVs in N Rose and S Transept windows.

65 La Grande Chartreuse Isère; 77 (5); 30 km N of Grenoble by D 512; BV; 16 C.(?); 85 cm; wood; majesté; similar to BV of Le Puy D at Rev.; in monastery; replica in museum of La Correrie. Durand-Lefèbvre quotes a sentence in Latin referring to a BV taken from 'the pagans in India'. Former cult of Cybele.

66 Chastreix Puy-de-Dôme; 73 (13); 20 km S of Le Mont-Dore by D 213 and D 88; in Ch. of St Bonnet; BV; 11 C.; stolen 1983; not yet replaced; has strange staring eyes and holds Child in her disproportionately large left hand. She repels enemies, heals all types of disease, and was once the centre of the pilgrimage which supplanted for a time that of Vassivières. Key at the bakery. There is a cult to St Anne who grants freedom to prisoners. Near by a Commandery of the Knights of St John and a menhir.

67 Châteauneuf-les-Bains Puy-de-Dôme; 73 (3); N-D de Châteauneuf in Ch. of Châteauneuf open daily; 13 C; 80 cm; tin or pewter (cf. Thuir); repainted, but priest confirms it is BV.

68 Châtillon-sur-Seine Côte d' Or; 68 (5); N-D de Toutes (les) Grâces, de Toute Grâce, du Château or de St Bernard; 12 C.; in École St Bernard and on Feast Days at Ch. of Vorles; 78 cm; Pag.; wood; water; BV revered for centuries as that from whose breast St Bernard received three drops of milk. Hidden at Rev. in garden of farm. Restored 1927; miracles include resuscitation of dead babies. The subterranean R. Douix gushes forth magnificently near by for its short journey to the Seine. A third river, the Ource (Orcus — Lord of the Underworld), rises on a hill near Châtillon once dominated by a Ch. of St Blaise, and flows through St Phal, a holy one not included in Butler's *Lives of the Saints,* between Châtillon and the Templar house of Voulaines.

69 Chatou Seine-et-Oise; 237

(17); Greater Paris, take N 186 from Paris towards St Germain-en-Laye, Chatou first town after crossing Seine at Nanterre; standing; 19 C.; 150 cm; plaster; old BV D at Rev.; Mer.

70 *Chauriat* Puy-de-Dôme; 73 (15); 20 km E of Clermont-Ferrand by N 89 and D 4; local priest says no BV in his Ch.; Saillens reports N-D du Clocher; majesté; 67 cm; 12 C.; no Child; chocolate colour over tape; in crypt; water. *Guide Noir* mentions that the parish Ch. of N-D with a well in the crypt is now a wine cellar and has masonic symbols on the tower but does not refer to any BV. Near by is miraculous spring of Ste Marcelle who successfully prayed to the Virgin to save the village from the plague, and whose remains are in the Ch. St Bonnet next village to W.

71 *Chenoise* Seine-et-Marne; 237 (20); 11 km NW of Provins by D 231; black marble plaque on mortuary cenotaph in grounds of former abbey of La Merci; but no BV or N-D de La Merci according to Priest of Chenoise, despite Durand-Lefèbvre and Saillens.

72 *Clairmarais* Pas-de-Calais; 51 (3); Cistercian Abbey now D had fresco of lactation of St Bernard and replica of N-D de Toutes les Grâces of Châtillon-sur-Seine.

73 **Clermont-Ferrand** Puy-de-Dôme; 73 (14); (1) N-D du Port; water; Pag.; wood; 29 cm; From 14 C. at latest there were two famous statues of the Virgin at N-D du Port, one in the crypt, one on the high altar, both probably BVs, but the BV cult belongs mainly to the crypt where there is an ancient well sacred from Gallo-Roman times, perhaps to Cybele of the fountains, in which the earliest BV may have been found. The present Virgin, an Oriental Vierge de Tendresse, whose image is known from 13 C., was saved by two women at the Rev. but stolen on 28 Jan. 1864. It cried so much that it was restored by the remorseful thief in 1873. 'Port', which evokes the idea of the Virgin guiding voyagers home to the safe haven, derives from the nearby market-place of Champl'Herm. The city was a Druidical centre and close to the site of the last stand of Vercingetorix. Gregory of Tours, who was born there in 538 or 539 called it the equal of Rome. Clovis the Merovingian captured it from the Visigoths in 507. The first Christian oratory in the Auvergne was dedicated to N-D d'Entre-les-Saints at Font-Gièvre (Fountain of the Jews — i.e., Syrian Christians). To Clermont belongs the first great feast of the Assumption, the first Mass 'Sancta Parens' in her honour, the first office of the Blessed Virgin Mary and the Council which decided on First Crusade under Pope Urban II who wrote the preface of the Virgin there. Cult of St Anne.

(2) N-D de Neyrat; standing BV; 17 C.; 58 cm; since 1981 in the

9. Clermont-Ferrand (5)

new Ch. of La Croix Neyrat, 78 rue du Solayer, Clermont-Ferrand 63100; standing; gold-draped robes.

(3) N-D d'Authezat qv.; 13 C.; 40 cm; wood; partially taped; in treasury of Cathedral of Clermont-Ferrand; saved at Rev; Priest says no longer there.

(4) BV de Vernols (qv.) in Musée Lecocq.

(5) Cathedral of N-D de Clermont, chapel of St Austremoine behind high altar, magnificent 10 C. Romanesque BV in majesty with gilt robes resembling Marsat BV. Discovered in the Cathedral in 1974.

74 **Cléry** Loiret; 64 (8); 15 km W of Orléans by D 951; N-D de Cléry; wood; 107 cm; 17 C.; replacing BV discovered by ploughing oxen 1280; D by Huguenots. Salisbury pillaged the Ch. and town in 1428 and shortly afterwards was wounded at Orléans and died at Meung, across the Loire from Cléry. Louis XI was a faithful pilgrim of Cléry

and is buried there. On his orders the practice of sounding the Angelus spread from Cléry to the rest of France. Dunois, the companion in arms of Joan of Arc, another pilgrim to Cléry, is also buried in the Ch. Many kings and saints have been numbered among the countless pilgrims of Cléry, the last famous visitor being Earl Mountbatten in 1976. Drochon reports instances of the miraculous statue weeping, sweating and changing colour, and states that it is black and escaped destruction. Perhaps he is referring not to the painted Virgin of the high altar, whose naked cross-legged Child holds a red pear in his left hand, but to the BV visible in the underground tomb of Louis XI. The present Curé knows nothing of any BV cult.

75 *Cluny* Saône-et-Loire; 69 (19); BV of St Jacques-la-Boucherie; wholly black faces and ochre robes; greatest Benedictine abbey in France; D at Rev.

76 Condé Nord; 53 (5); 5 km N; N-D de Bon-Secours: venerated in oak-tree 16 C.; possibly copy of N-D de la Chaussée (D 16C.) in Valenciennes; Basilica exactly on Belgian frontier in deanery of St Brice; oak-trunk in crypt; tunnels to Valenciennes (18km); living cult; castle of Belgian kings; cult of BV of Czestochowa here and Condé.

77 Conliège Jura; 70 (14); 17 C.; replica of N-D de Lorette

(Italy); 20 cm; SD; found by shepherd boy in cleft rock *c.*1600.

78 *Conques* Aveyron; 80(1)(2); included by A. Noguera i Massa in his list of eight famous French BVs at staging posts to Compostela and by M. Moreau. Do they mean Ste Foy?

79 Cornabey Doubs; replica of N-D d'Einsiedeln (Switzerland).

80 **Cornas** Ardèche; 77 (12), 93 (19), 76 (20); 6 km N of Valence by N 86; N-D de la Mûre from Abbey of La Mûre; in roadside Ch.; key available from Café des Pêcheurs (1st turning rt N of Ch.); 70 cm; wood; against back wall behind altar; opp. confluence of Isère and Rhône; remarkable ancient BV similar to Thuret, both perhaps copies of old BV of Le Puy; saved fishermen from drowning (mosaic). Huynen suggests 'Mûre' derives not from mulberry, blackberry or river-walls but from Myrrh (cf. Epiphany).

81 Corneilla Pyrénées-Orientales; 86 (17); 2.5 km S of Villefranche-de-Conflent by D 116; Beautiful Ch. houses three ancient statues of the Virgin; key from M. Houdayer, Villa al Soul; candles in cart-wheel ring of fire like Moulins and Marsat. For BV (now cleaned) N-D de Pésébré, see Cuxa.

82 *Coulandon* Allier; 69 (14); 6 km W of Moulins by N 145; BV now in seminary of Moulins (qv).

83 *Coulombs* Eure-et-Loir; 60 (8); 1 km across R. Eure E of Nogent-le-Roi on D 983; 14 C.; black stone statue in turban now transferred to the Louvre Museum. Saillens. mentions neighbouring spring of St Chéron (Chiron?; Charon?) (cf. Villiers-en-Désoeuvre); between Vacheresse and Vacheresses.

84 **Couterne** Orne; 60 (1); 4 km S of Bagnoles-de-l'Orne by D 916 and rd to rt before Couterne; N-D de Lignou; terra cotta and metal (Durand-Lefèbvre); blackened wood of 17 C. or 19 C. (Saillens); found in hawthorn-tree; SD; statue left Briouze, owing to wickedness of inhabitants, in favour of Lignou. Hidden in cemetery at Rev. — lost — revealed herself by great light. Very heavy. Living cult. Pilgrimages.

85 *Craponne* Haute-Loire; 76 (7); 30 cm; wood; now in private collection.

86 Crespin Nord; 53 (5); 13 km NE of Valenciennes by N 22 and D 954 on Belgian frontier; replica of N-D de Halle (Belgium).

87 **Cuiseaux** Jura; 70 (13); on N 83 25 km S of Lons-le-Saunier; N-D du Noyer in Ch. of St Thomas of Canterbury, Cuiseaux; 1236; 60 cm; found in walnut-tree; carved by shepherd; resuscitates dead children — 60 cases from 18 C. to 19 C.; living cult and pilgrimage; Mt Février 2 km SE.

88 La Cula Loire; 93 (16), 73 (19); 5 km NW of Rive-de-Gier by D 6; BV; D at Rev.; Ch. 11 C.; BV found near spring that never dries up early 13 C. Ch. and statue restored 1859.

89 **Cusset** Allier; 73 (5); 1 km E of Vichy; wood; 13 C.; head and hands saved from flames at Rev. by baker's wife, Geneviève Tuchard; faithful reconstruction; original 9 C. BV destined for Gannat, refused to go beyond Cusset; found in spring. Benedictine Priory from 882. Many royal pilgrims from Charles VII to Napoleon III include Louis XI who gave his arms to the town. Statue of St Anne. Ch. of Ste Madeleine 5 km.

90 **Cuxa** Pyrénées-Orientales; 86 (17); 2 km S of Prades by D 27; on zero meridian; Abbey of St Michel; N-D de Pésébré (crib) or La Maureneta, now at Corneilla (qv) due to be restored to its original home in 11 C. crypt where it has been known since 1040. First circular crypt with central palm-tree pillar in W Europe. Present statue 14 C.; 70 cm; saved by pious woman at Rev.; Child holds closed book in left hand. Abbé Guérin friend of Pope Sylvester II (see **Aurillac**).

91 *Dammartin-les-Templiers* Doubs; 66 (16) 19 km NE of Besançon by D 464 and D 112; BV; Templar Commandery.

92 **Décize** Nièvre; 69 (5); in

crypt (gen. locked 'owing to abuse') of Ch. of St Aré, N-D de Sous-Terre; 16 C.; springs; mines. A short distance from site of Château de Barberie, 'occult bastion of France', built by Bera IV of Merovingian blood-line in 10 C. and utterly destroyed by Mazarin in 1659.

93 **La Délivrande** Calvados; 54 (16); 16 km N of Caen by D 7 (Douvres); N-D de la Délivrande; standing; 100 cm; stone; 1580; original statue 4 C. (*Michelin Guide Normandy*); SD; most ancient and famous pilgrimage in Normandy; Ch. D by Normans 830; 200 years later (11 C.) statue found by sheep (fat without grazing); D by Protestants 1561. The largest known statue of the earth goddess was found locally in 1942 near the village known in Celtic times as Delle Yvrande (= land, water, boundary) — now in University of Caen museum. BV frees captives, helps sailors, grants fertility and easy births and looks after small children. Louis XI twice a pilgrim. Talleyrand was converted to Christianity by the prayers of the Archbishop of Paris there. Victor Hugo prayed there. British War Cemetery. Nearest town, Luc, commemorates sacred oak wood 'Lucus' and perhaps Celtic God, Lug. A quarter of it called Petit-Enfer (little hell). Statue saved at Rev. Three religious congregations founded under her protection. The cholera epidemic of 1832 halted from the moment the BV was processed round the village on 15 Aug.

Crowned 1872. Basilica 1895. Chapter of St Mary Major in Rome affiliate La Délivrande to their Basilica. Republic of Senegal officially consecrated to N-D de la Délivrande 1963 (welcomed in 1888 on account of her colour). Diocese of Martinique also consecrated to her.

94 *Digne* Alpes-de-Haute-Provence; 81 (17); BV reported at Digne, along with those of Toulouse, Le Puy, Lyon and Grenoble by Albert-Paul Alliès. Local authorities know of no BV cult at Digne but suggest author may be referring to that at Manosque.

95 **Dijon** Côte d'Or; 66 (12); Ch. of N-D; N-D du Bon-Espoir, d'Apport, du Rapport or du Marché; 12 C.; oak; 84 cm; Child of different period now D.; black 1591; polychrome 1820; 'sooty black' according to Huysmans (*c.* 1900); blackened 1945, now light wood colour; hands and feet cut off at Rev. Unlike any other BV — pendant breasts and prominent belly. Has been compared to Gallo-Roman statues of Cybele and Isis, but more like a Teutonic/Celtic good witch. Saved Dijon from Swiss 12 Sept. 1513 and from Germans 12 Sept 1944. The Sainte Chapelle (D at Rev.) was the home of the Order of the Golden Fleece founded at Bruges (qv) in 1429 by Philip the Good to undo Philip the Fair's destruction of the Order of the Temple. St Bernard born at Fontaines (qv) 4 km from Dijon. No postcards or

brochures of statue though acknowledged as one of the oldest and most renowned of French BVs, owing, according to hearsay, to policy of priest. Wall painting of crucifixion without Jesus. Carving of owl on N facade of Ch., rubbed smooth, brings good luck.

96 Dorres Pyrénées-Orientales; 86 (16); 10 km N. of Bourg-Madame by N 20, D 618 and D 10; N-D de Belloch formerly in Ch. of Belloch 2 km further on on mountain top up rough track, now in village Ch.; 11 C.; 46 cm; seated on plank jutting out from post; wears only a tunic and veil; described by Noguera i Massa as 'a Christian fetish'; wood; water. Remarkable oriental-looking BV and Child of great serenity, very thin and fine; BV has huge hands, the rt one outstretched, palm up. Child, too, has disproportionately large rt hand raised in blessing, and closed book under left hand. Almost impossible to visit except during Mass as local hotel hold key and refuse to lend it in any circumstances and the Curé is chaplain of the local rehabilitation centre as well as serving 5 parishes.

97 Draguignan Var; 84 (7); N-D du Peuple or La Bonne Mère; carved from a piece of the oak of Montaigu (Belgium) in Ch. of N-D du Peuple; walls covered with ex-votos; original BV of 1632 D at Rev. One of five old sanctuaries of the Virgin in Draguignan before Rev.; including N-D de Bethléhem, and N-D de Montserrat. Draguig-

nan has silver dragon on coat of arms to commemorate the one slain by St Armentaire of Antibes. Pierre des Fées (dolmen). Abbey of Ste Roseline 6 km S.

98 Droiteval Vosges; 62 (14); 5.1 km W of Monthureux-sur-Sâone in Forest of Darney on banks of Ourche in Ch. of 12 C. Cistercian Abbey (nuns, then monks). BV; late 15 C. replacing earlier BV; painted stone; 130 cm; nearby hamlets of La Sybille, La Grande Catherine, Le Hubert and Jerusalem; also Celtic camp.

99 Dunkirk   Nord; 51 (3) (4); N-D des Dunes or de la Fontaine; 32 cm; found 1403; date unknown; SD. Yolande de Bar, known as the Lady of Dunkirk, whose family produced two women Grand Masters or Nautonniers of the Prieuré de Sion (Jeanne de Bar 1136-51, Iolande de Bar 1480-3) died in 1395 leaving Dunkirk to her son Robert who obtained permission from Philip the Good, Duke of Burgundy, to rebuild the fortifications. As soon as the workmen started digging in the sand at the foot of the NE of the walls they struck a spring of pure fresh water, and a few days later found the statue there. Virgin saved Dunkirk in many battles, beginning with the siege of the English fleet in 1405. The vow to enlarge the Ch. after the city was preserved in 1914-18 was not kept, and Dunkirk fared less well in the Second World War, though the evacuation of the British was

considered a miracle. Statue saved at Rev.; shown as BV on banners, but not black now. N-D des Dunes, apart from protecting her town, frees prisoners and protects sailors. Scottish Catholics sent Our Lady of Aberdeen to Dunkirk for safe-keeping in 1625. Painting of Our Lady of Czestochowa in Ch.

100 *Les Écharmeaux* Rhône; 73 (9); at cross-rds of D 485, D 37 and D 10. Durand-Lefèbvre reports presence of BV still venerated here, possibly the stone statue by Molette *Le Sabottier* near the Col des Écharmeaux. Priest says no BV.

101 *Égliseneuve d'Entraygues* Puy-de-Dôme; 76 (3); 17 km S of Besse by D 978; BV one of four black sisters (Vassivière, Font-Sainte, Latour d'Auvergne) from the east asking the way to Mont-Dore.

102 *Embrun* Hautes-Alpes; 77 (17) (18); Mosaic in Cathedral is copy of miraculous painting of BV of Adoration on stone under the porch D at Rev.; 'good mistress' of Louis XI.

103 *Épinac* Saône-et-Loire; 69 (8); 18 km E of Autun by D 973 and D 232; N-D de Lorette; early replica of Italian BV.

104 **Err** Pyrénées-Orientales; 86 (16); 8 km E of Bourg-Madame by N 116 and D 33a; N-D d'Err found miraculously in tree by

cattle; heals contagious diseases of humans and cattle; controls rain; watches over mines; fairy grottoes; cemetery. Important live cult in special chapel next to parish church. BV seated; mature looking Child stands on what looks like funerary urn by Virgin's left knee. Both dark grey with silver crowns. Impossible to date statue, but Ch. was consecrated 930.

105 **Espalion** Aveyron; 80 (3); La Négrette; standing; 40 cm; wood; crowned and robed; no Child; in Ch. of hospital on D 920 towards Estaing; SD; weeps and when painted returns to her original colour; brought back 'from Crusades' by Lord of Calmont (ruins of castle at Espalion near remarkable Ch. of Perse with sculptures on exterior of Virgin and Child and Three Kings); saved from Ch. of Château at Rev.; perhaps originally part of Crucifixion scene.

106 Evaux-les-Bains Creuse; 73 (2); BV; wood; only head preserved after statue was mutilated at Rev. and thrown in well. Of the four profaners one cut his throat, one died falling from a rock, one who boasted of breaking the statue's jaw had his tongue cut out and one was struck by lightning.

107 Eygurande Corrèze; 73 (12); just N of N 89 8 km W of Bourg-Lastic; dark walnut statue, child on left arm, discovered in disturbed ground by parishioner called Lebros, 24 Sept. 1720.

108 *Eyne* Pyrénées-Orientales; 86 (16); Saillens mentions 13 C. statue in crypt of BV; the *Guide du Roussillon* refers to two very ancient Virgins in the Ch., one the Mare de Deu del Remey (remedy). The tiny village Ch. which now has no resident priest is in a bad state of repair and had no obvious access to any crypt. A statue with a sign 'Ns. Sra. Dél Remey, Eyne' stands to the right of the altar, crowned, freshly painted in flesh tints, doll-like, robed in white tulle, with baby on Virgin's left arm. On the other side is a tawny Virgin of Sorrows like that at Banyuls (qv), dressed in black with a slumped infant Jesus held between her knees. Next to cemetery. Sts Michael (or George) and Dragon, John the Baptist and Catherine. There is a path across the mountains (and frontier) to Nuria, site of the most venerated Virgin of the Catalan Pyrenees.

109 **Ferrières** Loiret; 237 (43); 12 km N of Montargis by N 7 and D 96; N-D de Bethléem; standing; late 15 C.; 35 cm; water; Pag.; Mer.; Sts Anne, Roch, Michael; confluence of R. Cléry and R. Loing; resuscitates still-born infants for baptism. Early Christian settlement 461 (366 inhabitants burnt in Ch.); D by Attila, rebuilt 499. Clovis, first Merovingian, met his Queen, Clothilde, there. Their son, Clodomir, was healed by N-D de Bethléem. Abbey founded by Clotaire II. Dagobert gave it the right to the arms of St Peter of Rome. Residence of the last of the Merovingians. Pepin fought a lion and a bull there. Louis de Blanchefort (Mer. bloodline), godson of Louis XI, abbot 1465-1505 restored the Abbey after Hundred Years War. Central window, presented by Louis XI, depicts his Queen, Anne of Britanny, as Mary Magdalene. Hot springs; underground galleries; Castle of St Luc. An English soldier who set fire to the Ch. in 1427 felt his entrails were on fire and jumped into the well, where his bones were discovered in 1607. Huguenots pillaged Ch. and Abbey 1569. Statue crowned 1898. The statue on display in the Ch. is an exact replica of the original which is kept in a safe hiding-place.

110 *Feurs* Loire; 73 (18); BV reportedly given by Counts of Forez (Abbé Prajoux, *Histoire du Côteau*, Roanne, 1924), presumably to Ch. of N-D, cf. Vernay.

111 **Finestret** Pyrénées-Orientales; 86 (18); 5.5 km S. of Vinça by D 25; BV from Spain in Ch. of Ste Colombe, who brought a bear with her from Spain and is depicted with it over the porch. The first mention of the Ch. is 1033. Oratory dedicated to St Anne, who also has a chapel on a mountain-top to S of village. BV holds Child on left arm, both haloed, with finely carved draperies and face (Child less so). Brétigny (*Nostra*, 31 Mar. 1983) stresses importance for Merovingian blood-line connection of its

situation near the Meridian. The last Count of Razès of Merovingian descent, Sigisbert VI, was known as Prince Ursus (bear).

112 **Font-Romeu/Odeillo** Pyrénées-Orientales; 86 (16); BV; standing; wood; 12 C.; 66 cm; water; cattle; spends summer (Trinity to 8 Sept.) at Font-Romeu (spring of the pilgrims), rest of year at Odeillo. Spring (at side of Ch.) and statue discovered by bull striking earth in 1113. Magnificent *camaril* (BV's private apartment) by J. Sunyer, 1707. Many naive 19 C. ex-votos.

113 **Font-Sainte/Apchon** Cantal; 76 (3); Apchon 3 km SE of Riom-ès-Montagnes by D 3 and D 49; Font-Sainte 4 km S of Apchon by D 249; N-D de la Font-Sainte; BV of the Crusades D 16 C. by Huguenots; ancient sacred springs; Druids; standing stones; 17 C. apparition of Virgin to shepherdess Marie Galvin asking her to restore sanctuary; present statue 40 cm; not a BV from that period; Ch. restored 1837 and 1886. Statue spends summer at Font-Sainte (main feasts Sun. after St Anne's Day and 8 Sept.), returning to winter in Ch. of St Hippolyte. Virgin's foot-prints on threshold stone of Font-Sainte and triple spring where she touched rock with three fingers. 'Spring of the Fairies' on other side of valley.

114 *Gérardmer* Vosges; 62 (17); N-D de la Grèse or de la Creuse, painted on rock 1 km from Gérardmer, repainted 19 C.; Ch. for pilgrims 1740.

115 **Gerzat** Puy-de-Dôme; 73 (14); 3 km NE of Clermont-Ferrand; N-D du Vignal; small, rustic BV; found near spring which heals fevers; moved from original site at Rev. to village Ch.; stolen *c.*1975; replaced by smaller replica; fine 12 C. Ch.; painting of original shrine; statues of Sts Anne, Blaise and Bonnet; city, once of 12 towers, belonged to Dukes of Bouillon.

116 **Ghissignies** Nord; 53 (5); 3 km S of Le Quesney by D 86; replica of N-D de Halle (Belgium); the Knight Jean de Cordes, captured by the Turks, invoked N-D de Halle. His chains fell off and on his return home he built the chapel. Annual candle offering.

117 *Gisors* Eure; 55 (8) (9); Window in Ch. of BV N-D de Liesse (qv); commemorating visit of Gisorcines in 1643. Gisors is at the heart of the mystery of the Templars (see Gérard de Sède, *Les Templiers sont parmi nous, l' énigme de Gisors*).

118 **Goult-Lumières** Vaucluse; 84 (2); 22 km W of Apt on N 100; N-D de Lumières or La Santo Vierge Négro; wood; 38 cm; stolen 1979 and replaced with replica; original statue, there in 16 C., lost in religious wars; rediscovered 17 C.; strong devotion; many ex-votos; heals blindness; much venerated by

Prieuré de Sion who held that the true title of Isis who became the BV is N-D de Lumière; BV in right hand crypt chapel; cult of Virgin at Goult since 4 C.; many apparitions and healing miracles in 1661. The local guidebook by Delarue refers to 'the touching and very mysterious Black Virgin'. Ancient chapel to St Joachim in crypt of St Michael's Ch. on rocky hill above. Tradition of early link with Cassianite monks from Marseilles.

119 Grandris Rhône; 73 (9) 91 (6); 4 km S of Lamure by D 485 and D 54; N-D de Grandris or de Rivolet (?); disappeared 1836; replaced. Drochon says N-D de Rivolet (on D 504 between Grandris and Villefranche) is invoked for rain and N-D de Grandris for fine weather. Sal de St Bonnet between Grandris and Rivolet; N-D de l'Hermitage from Noirétable (Loire) hidden at Rev. in Grandris and remained there until returned in 1979.

120 Gray Haute-Saone; 66 (14); N-D Libératrice; 11 cm; carved from oak of Montaigu (Belgium); brought back by widow in 1613; heals; saved at Rev. found in chest later; man who blasphemed her and carried her to the Hôtel de Ville died in despair a few years later.

121 Grenoble Isère; 77 (5); N-D de la Tronche (yule-log); standing; 60 cm; 1789/80; replacing earlier wooden statue; faces and hands blackened intentionally; water; cemetery; in hillside oratory; found on banks of Isère.

122 Guingamp Côtes-du-Nord; 59 (2); N-D de Bon-Secours, Itron Varia Gwir Zikour (Dame Marie du Vrai Secours), N-D de Halgoët (of underground, of the hollow wood or of the willow grove); 14 C. or 17 C.; 150 cm; wood; BV's head saved at Rev.; restored; procession of BV and Pardon 1st Sun. in July followed by bonfires and Midnight Mass; Ch. of N-D known at Guingamp since 1158. BV, claimed to be the only one in Britanny, saved her country from Prussian invasion, 17 Jan. 1871 (thanksgiving of 100,000 pilgrims 1874). Since the Rev. the statue dislikes being moved and, at its coronation procession, produced such a downpour of rain that no further attempt has been made. Labyrinth on floor reputed to be identical to that of Chartres. Statues of St Catherine and St James (important pilgrimage to Compostela); former chapel of St John the Baptist; windows of Sts. Mary Magdalene and Vincent de Paul; benefactors include the families of Luxembourg, Berry and Chambord (the Countess sent half her wedding gowns to N-D after her marriage to the heir to the throne). Pagan cult at Le Grand Rocher opposite the Basilica.

123 Le Havre Seine-Inférieure; 55 (3); N-D du Havre de Grâce; massive 3 metre dark bronze

statue overlooking the city and harbour from the park of the Abbaye de Graville in special enclosed garden. Many ex-votos and offerings, including baby shoe. Erected to fulfil vow of 1870 when the town was saved from the Prussians. Known as BV locally.

124 **Héas** Hautes-Pyrénées; 85 (18); 28 km S of St Sauveur by D 921 and D 922; rd closed Dec.-Apr.; N-D de Héas; wood; 16 C.?; 45 cm; found in rocks by shepherds with nearby spring where two doves had been drinking; painting of Ste Germaine de Pibrac; pilgrimage Ch. D by avalanche 1915; rebuilt; statue saved; known since 1415 but probably much older; at Rev. ex-votos taken; soldier shot at statue, killed a few hours later by Spanish sniper's bullet in same place where his bullet had struck statue.

125 *Hix* Pyrénées-Orientales; 86 (16); 1 km E of Bourg-Madame on N 116; N-D de la Cerdagne; wood; 68 cm; 13 C.; Child holds open book in left hand; typical polychrome Catalan Majestat in beautiful little Ch. (apply for key at house next door). Hix was the residence of the Counts of Cerdagne until 1177 when the capital was transferred to Puigcerdá. Statue was also moved to Puigcerdá in 1648.

126 *Honfleur* Calvados; 55 (3) (4); N-D de Grâces; original BV an 11 C. wooden statue D at Rev.; survived landslide which destroyed Ch. in 1538; present Ch. of 1615 contains many ex-votos, a brownish, 150 cm, 17 C. Madonna and a statue of St Anne carrying in her arms Mary who is in turn carrying Jesus. Honfleur was captured from the Saxons by Clovis the Merovingian. Original Ch. 1023. Pilgrimage procession at Whitsun from interesting Ch. of St Catherine, with its double nave, statues of St Anne, St Mary Magdalene and several Madonnas, up the hill to N-D des Grâces.

127 *Joinville* Haute-Marne; 62 (1); no one knows of the BV mentioned by Durand-Lefèbvre, but Saillens refers to a remarkable funerary chapel of St Anne which may have contained a black statue of the saint. The village of Blécourt (Blez?), 9 km SW has a 13 C. wooden statue of the Virgin and Child and is the centre of a pilgrimage dating to the time of Dagobert the Merovingian. 8 km SW is the village of Les Bons Hommes, one of the titles given to the Cathar perfecti.

128 *Josselin* Morbihan; 63 (4); N-D du Roncier (bramble); wood; found 808; SD; D at Rev.; modern replacement. When the original statue was burnt it caused such a stink that the soldiers fled. Drochon states that fragments of it have been preserved. Grand Pardon 8 Sept. The Ch. was rebuilt 10 C. after destruction by the Normans and the present town

and castle developed as a result. Priest says never a BV at Josselin.

129 *Jouhet* Vienne; 68 (15) 238 (37); 8 km N of Montmorillon by D 5; Saillens notes that 13 of the 17 figures in the 15 C. frescoes of the funerary chapel are black. In Montmorillon itself the crypt of the Ch. of N-D is dedicated to St Catherine and contains interesting frescoes depicting scenes from her life.

130 Jouy-en-Josas Seine-et-Oise; 237 (17) 60 (10); in the Grande Banlieue to SW of Paris, E of Les-Loges-en-Josas and W of Villacoublay aerodrome; Ch. open daily; N-D de Villetain (former abbey), known as 'La Diège' (Dei Genetrix); saved at Rev.; unusual 12 C. restored polychrome wooden statue of 150 cm in which the feet of the Child are held up by angels and his body wrapped in a toga-like cloak. According to Durand-Lefèbvre, it is universally cited as a BV. Now faces and heads are light wood colour. The priest neither confirms nor denies that it has been considered a BV. Once venerated in special chapel on Saclay plateau.

131 Jussey Haute-Saône; 66 (5); 19 km N of N 19 at Combeaufontaine by D 54 and D 3; in Ch. of Jussey (open daily) N-D de Jussey; wood; 7 cm; carved in 1613 from wood of oak of Montaigu (Belgium); standing; crowned; holds Child in left hand and sword in right; saved at Rev.

132 *Laghet* Alpes-Maritimes; 84 (10); 6 km W of Monte-Carlo; N-D du Petit Lac; sanctuary founded 1658 after Hyacinthe Casanova underwent a miraculous cure and BV was found in lake; statue saved at Rev. but in poor state of repair; now replaced; most ex-votos now in museum; feasts — Trinity, Our Lady of Mt Carmel (16 July;, Christmas (shepherds).

133 *Lantenay* Côte-d'Or; 65 (19) 66 (11); 10 km W of Dijon by D 10 and D 104; La Noire; wood; 80 cm; 12 C.; gift of a crusader; hill-top; Child missing; forgotten today according to Saillens; two nearby villages called Blaisy (Blaise?). Local Curé says no BV.

134 Laon Aisne; 56 (5); Durand-Lefèbvre refers to a BV given in 1818, a modern statue in which the Virgin is crushing the serpent; Saillens describes a new devotion to a BV in wood; 150 cm; 1848. Photograph in *Nostra* 1972 shows it to be based on N-D de Liesse. In the centre of the great rose window the hands of the Virgin and Child and the face of the latter appear to be black. Laon, Laudanum, which some say derives from the Paracelsian opiate, the Carolingian capital of France and former Merovingian stronghold, has a well-preserved Templar chapel containing a disembodied stone head evocative of Baphomet and a museum next to it with a triple goddess of the Gallo-Roman period with very large hands. Charles, son of the last Carolingian king, Louis V, known as Duke of Lorraine, though supported by Pope Sylvester II (Gerbert of Aurillac), was betrayed and brought down by the Capetian conspiracy. The Lorraine family later married into the Merovingian blood-line (Jean III d.1068/1072 married Beatrix of Lorraine). There was an important colony of Scots and Irish in Laon in the 9 C. which included John Scotus Erigena, the leading Neo-Platonist theologian of his age. The Cathedral, built with the aid of a magic ox, has remarkable statues of oxen. Relics of N-D taken to Bodmin in 1113.

135 *Laroque* Hérault; 83 (6); on D 968 between Ganges and the Grotte des Demoiselles (fairy grotto); standing; 17 C.; wood; replacement of local image which has been whitened. The Grotte des Demoiselles contains an impressive stalagmite known as the Virgin and Child.

136 Laurie Cantal; 76 (4); 15 km SW of Blesle (Blez?) by D 20 and D 109; N-D du Mont Carmel; wood; 11 C.; BV whitened in 1883; now polychrome; water; feast-day 16 July; heals plague; procession from Blesle to Laurie on Whit Monday in thanksgiving for end of plague in 14 C. Temple of Jupiter at Blesle and carvings of wolves as well as black marble altar donated by Pope in 870 and statue of St Anne in choir of Ch. Fontaine of St

Blaise at Espalem (5 km E) heals cattle.

137 Lempdes Haute-Loire; 76 (5) 91 (14); 19 km S of Issoire by N 9; N-D de Bonne Nouvelle; very old BV D at Rev.; replaced 19 C.; feast-day 2 July; mines. (There is also a N-D de Bonne Nouvelle in Lempdes, Puy-de-Dôme.)

138 Liesse Aisne; 56 (5); 15 km NE of Laon by N 377; N-D de Liesse or de la Joie (Liesse = joy); modern BV in ebony replacing BV of Crusades D at Rev. Liesse was the most important place of pilgrimage for the French Royal Family from 1414. Louis XI in particular had a great devotion to N-D de Liesse, whose medal he wore in his bonnet. Legend: Three Knights of St John (perhaps originally Templars), serving in the First Crusade under Foulques d'Anjou (see Angers) were captured and taken to Cairo. Resisting all attempts to seduce them into apostasy, they succeeded, with the help of angels, who carved a beautiful BV, in converting the Sultan's daughter, Ismeria (Isis + Mary?), and returning miraculously to their native land. At the spring of Liesse the BV became so heavy that they could carry her no further and a Ch. was built there in her honour. The chief miracles of N-D de Liesse are freeing captives and granting fertility. The Duchesse de Berry thanked her in 1821 for the birth of her son, the Comte de Cham-

bord, who nearly became King. The neighbouring Castle of Marchais, where Royal pilgrims used to stay, still belongs to the Lorraine family (Merovingian blood-line). Joan of Arc may have been a visitor, and in May 1940, Charles de Gaulle set out from Liesse to counter-attack Guderian's panzers. The Knights of Malta, heirs of the Knights of St John (and the Templars) have a chapel in the Ch., as does St Bernard. The mother of St Thérèse of Lisieux is said to have made the pilgrimage as a girl. The devotion has been spread by missionaries to many parts of the world, including Quebec, China, Japan, Ceylon, French Guiana and Madagascar.

139   *Ligny-en-Barrois* Meuse; 62 (2); 16 km SE of Bar-le-Duc by N 66; N-D des Vertus; miraculous painting; Durand-Lefèbvre states it is a 10 C. copy by Luca il Santo of Salus Populi Romani (attr. St Luke) in St Mary Major, Rome, but very dissimilar; presented to Charles d'Anjou, brother of St Louis, by Pope Urban IV when he anointed him King of Naples; painting in Capri until 1435; La Salle, emissary of René d'Anjou, miraculously saved from shipwreck by N-D des Vertus; in 1459, having rendered a signal service to Louis of Luxemburg, he brought the painting to Ligny. The houses of Anjou, Luxembourg and Bar are all closely connected in the Merovingian blood-line. Painting hidden at Rev., returned 1795. Curé says never a BV.

140   *Lille* Nord; 51 (16); Durand-Lefèbvre and Saillens report presence of BV in chapel of Hospital St Sauveur, copy of Our Lady of Tongres (Belgium). 11 C. N-D de la Treille, found in vineyard, Patroness of city (cf. Tournai).

141 **Limoux** Aude; 86 (7); N-D de Marceille; 11/12 C.; 55 cm; black hard wood; sanctuary known since 1011; attested as place of pilgrimage 1380; water; hill-top; cattle; heals blind; nearest BV to Rennes-le-Château (18 km S), refuge and centre of the Merovingian blood-line since the murder of Dagobert II, and of related mysteries. Another mystery concerns St Vincent de Paul's disappearance and 18 month sojourn in Barbary. It has been suggested that it was from Marceille rather than Marseille that M. Vincent was spirited away for his initiatic journey. Statue and cult of St Vincent de Paul. Many ex-votos include pieces of bridal veils.

142   *Lisseuil* Puy-de-Dôme; 73 (3); 4.5 km S of N 144 at Pont de Menat by D 109 on R. Sioule; Durand-Lefèbvre reports BV in wood many times repainted, with a reliquary placed in the body of the Child. 13 C.; healing spring; procession Sun. after 8 Sept.; cures on awakening from sleep as in Temples of Asklepios.

143 *Llo* Pyrénées-Orientales; 86 (16); 2 km S of Saillagouse by D

33; Saillens notes wooden 13 C. BV; this statue, the BV of Llo, belongs to a local family and is now in their private house at Canet Plage. Strange carvings above portico — skull with bats' wings, devils' heads, cats and Viking-like small heads carved in wall by pilasters.

144 *Loches* Indre-et-Loire. 68 (6) 238 (14); BV reported by Durand-Lefèbvre N-D de Beau-terre in Ch. of St Ours built by Geoffroi d'Anjou to house part of the girdle of the Virgin, has altar with mysteries of Attis and was twice visited by St Joan of Arc. No BV according to Tourist Office. Gipsies, 'very good Christians', first appear at Loches in 1427. Main prisons of Louis XI. Foul-ques Nerra built abbey there. Tomb of Agnès Sorel.

145 **Longpont-sur-Orge** Seine-et-Oise; 60(10) 237 (29); 1.5 km NE of Monlhéry by N 20 and D 133; (1) N-D de Bonne Garde; standing; wood; 200 cm; 19C.; replacement of local image D at Rev.; relics of old BV in new statue; a Virgo Paritura older than that of Chartres, originally a Druid image in an oak-tree. (2) N-D de Bénédiction; wood; 30 cm; 17 C.; brought from the Ch. of Les Filles du Calvaire, Paris; no longer on view to public; neigh-bouring parish of St Michel (Mercury?); miraculous water be-hind High Altar. Orge (Orcus?). Druids and cult of Isis. St Denis presented piece of Virgin's veil. Ch. visited by St Bernard.

146 **Lorient** Morbihan; 63 (1); N-D de Bonne Délivrance in Ch. of Kerentech; standing; 135 cm; 17 C. replica of N-D des Grès (Paris).

147 *Lupiat* Haute-Loire; 76 (5); 16 km NE of Brioude by D 588; Saillens mentions Romanesque BV.

148 **Luvigny** Vosges; 62 (8); S of N 392 between Raon-l'Etape and Schirmeck on borders of Lorraine and Alsace; N-D de la Maix or de la Mer in Ch. of Luvigny (key from Mme Marcel Lacher); wood; late Middle Ages; seated; resuscitates dead children who are then baptized in lake which was a pagan holy place; solar cult on nearby mountain; 7 C. priory of Abbey of Senones. Curé acknow-ledges it is often considered a BV but doubts it himself.

149 **Lyons/Lyon** Rhône; 74 (11) (12) 93 (15); (1) N-D de Fourvière; BV; standing; 100 cm; wood; 17 C.; replica of ancient local image; on High Altar. (2) N-D de Bon Conseil; 1630; on side altar facing entrance; Both BVs in Chapel of St Thomas à Becket next to basilica. Fourvière (old forum) the acropolis of Lyons (Lugdunum — city of Lug), Roman capital of the three Gauls and city of Cybele. According to legend, the porticoes of the forum crumbled in 840 and a chapel to the Virgin rose up out of the ruins

in place of the great Temple of Venus; 'sumptuous Ch.' of Fourvière 12 C.; Louis XI pays homage to N-D de Fourvière 1476; N-D de Fourvière protects Lyons from enemies and sickness though the sanctuary was occupied and ruined by the Calvinists in 1562. Lyons is the primatial see of France, founded by St Irenaeus (2 C.), and city of Mary since that period. When the cult of the goddess Ferrabo (Farrago) was finally abolished in 16 C. in Ch. of St Etienne, the cult of N-D de Fourvière took on new lustre. Confluence of Rhône and Saône.

150 *Mailhat* Puy-de-Dôme; 73 (15); 10 km NE of St Germain-Lembron; (1) N-D de Montgie; wood; 12 C. stolen 1972, not replaced.
(2) Replica of ancient French BV; interesting sculptures in porch including woman suckling serpents; staging point for Compostela; Curé says no BVs at Mailhat.

151 Mailhoc Tarn; 79 (20); near Cagnac-les-Mines just N of Albi on D 90; painting of N-D de Guadalupe called N-D la Noire brought back from Senegal 18 C.

152 **Maillane** Bouches-du-Rhône; 81 (11) (12); N-D de Grâces, de Bethléem or de Bételen; walnut; 12 C.; 60 cm; living cult; Ch. on site of pagan temple; BV hidden by priest till most of the inhabitants died of cholera; then brought out and stopped the epidemic 28 Aug. 1854; parish dedicated to St Agatha (cf. Cybele, 'the good goddess'); annual procession of BV on her feast-day, 5 Feb.; villagers still make her clothes; statue of St Roch and village 6 km SE; birth-place of Mistral (1830-1914), father of modern Provençal literature. (Maillane-Maia?).

153 *Malaucène* Vaucluse; 81 (3); N-D du Grozeau, de Consolation or la Brune; 1 km E of town on slopes of Mt Ventoux where seven springs gush out of the rock; 11 C., though original may have been brought by St Eusebius in 380 (cf. Oropa, Italy); chapel closed, no key, postcards, booklets or information available; Malaucène — Malaoussa = black earth; a legend states that rock opens when Gospel is read during Midnight Mass at Christmas to reveal gold behind; Ch. erected by Benedictines on site of pagan temple. Vaison-la-Romaine 9.5 km N city of Romans, Merovingians and Counts of Toulouse. Present Curé knows nothing of any BV.

154 **Manosque** Basses-Alpes; 81 (15); N-D du Romigier (bramble) or de Vie; 70 cm; unknown wood; 6 C. (Forsyth says 12 C.); buried in sarcophagus from Saracens; found by ox 9 C.; Child added 12 C.; 'doyenne of French BVs'; now kept in a safe hiding-place; copy in Ch.; Ch. closed for repairs for many years; no postcards, booklets or information; BV resuscitates dead babies, calms storms, rings Ch. bells, announces coming

misfortunes by weeping; pentagram of white stones set in black points to main door in Place de l'Hôtel de Ville; on Via Heraclea; Benedictines of St Victor of Marseilles at Manosque; gifts from Peter the Venerable; rediscovered statue taken to Mont d'Or (golden mountain) outside town by the Monteé des Vraies Richesses, but returned miraculously to altar of Ch.; Count of Provence on pilgrimage there 984; Knights of St John of Jerusalem took over from Benedictines.

155 **Marsat** Puy-de-Dôme; 73 (14); 3 km SW of Riom; N-D de Marsat; wood; 80 cm; 12 C.; walnut, painted gesso and gilt; cult known since 6 c.; statue of St Anne; visit and vow of Louis XI, 1465; Benedictines; annual pilgrimage from Riom in thanksgiving for saving town from Normans 916 and from the plague 1631, with a ring of wax on wooden wheel (cf. Montpellier, Moulins, Valenciennes); procession Sun. after Ascension; relics of girdle of Virgin and of St Martin (during Viking invasions). Gregory of Tours, 6 C., 'father of French history' in his *De Gloria Martyrum* describes how he came to Marsat by night and saw the whole building full of light. The door opened by itself and as he entered the Ch. it was plunged into darkness (allegory of *lux in tenebris*). The Ch. was built by three boys who materialized mysteriously when the builders laboured in vain. The remarkable beauty of N-D de Marsat has given rise to doubts concerning her date of origin. Marsat = valley of waters?

156 **Marseilles** Bouches-du-Rhône; 84 (13) 93 (14); (1) N-D de la Confession, du Fenouil (fennel) or Feu-Nou (new fire); walnut; 78 cm; 13 C.; in crypt of Basilica of St Victor built by St John Cassian in 416; tombs of martyrs, many sarcophagi including St Maurice and his companions (Cassian may have brought mummies from Egypt); miraculous well of St Blaise; unique green candles for BV (probably not the original, but lightweight processional statue); chief feast Candlemas (2 Feb.); *navettes* (barque of Isis pastries) on sale opposite Ch.; women and female animals not admitted to crypt as late as 17 C. lest they be blinded; Candlemas replaced torchlight procession of Persephone in 472 in Marseilles; Sicilian Persephone/Bona Dea/Agatha/Cybele — cures eyes, helps nursing mothers. Isis = Green Goddess; Cybele black under green mantle; but the patroness of every Massiliot from founding of the city in 600 BC was the black Artemis of Ephesus that the Phocaeans brought with them from Asia Minor; BV invoked in first hymn for Candlemas procession as 'Virgin of light'; site of Ch. on main Roman cemetery of city; first Christian religious foundation for men and women in the West.

(2) N-D de la Garde, La Bouéno

Méro Négro or La Brune; in ancient watchtower of the city from Phocaean times; chapel built 1214; BV D at Rev.; known as La Brune from 14 C.; statues to St Anne & St Roch 1714; retired sea-captain restored cult 1807 and installed wooden statue from Abbey of Picpus; several new statues; active cult in crypt; city and basilica saved from destruction 25 Aug. 1944.

(3) N-D de l'Huveaune (river from Ste Baume); wood; 34 cm; 11 C.; D.

157 Marvejols Lozère; 80 (5); N-D de la Carce (prison) or de la Corse; standing; wood; found 10 C. by shepherds; frees prisoners, including King of Aragon during Cathar Wars, 1213, and heals blind; from 1120 Marvejols belonged to the Counts of Barcelona; statue hidden at Rev. by sacristan, back on altar 1802; now large (400 cm) polychrome statue; two pairs of twin hills between Mende and Marvejols; half of town belonged to St Victor of Marseilles; town totally destroyed during Wars of Religion 1560-86, recaptured by Duc de Joyeuse (Rennes and blood-line) 1586; rebuilt 1638.

158 Mauriac Cantal; 76 (1); on zero meridian; N-D des Miracles; 114 cm; 13 C.; mutilated 1789, resculpted late 18 C. arms in pear wood, body in walnut, Jesus in oak; standing; found 6 C.; Mer; Pag.; cemetery; frees prisoners; Templar cross and masonic symbols on 10 C. font and three children in baptismal scene; town pillaged for two months by Huguenots; BV stopped rains 1816, cholera 1832. Mauriac was captured from the Gallo-Roman, Bazolus, by Thierry, son of Clovis in 507 and was given to Théodechilde, daughter of Clovis. She saw a great light in the forest there and discovered an image of the Virgin guarded by a lioness (Cybele?). She had a Ch. built to house the statue with stones taken from the temple of the Gallic Mercury and the Visigothic Saday, and ordered a light to be burned perpetually in front of it. This practice continued until the Rev. when the monastery which Théodechilde had given to the Benedictines of Sens was destroyed. Stone lions still guard the portico of the Ch. (the only other Ch. in the Auvergne with lions is at Aurillac, qv). The Ch. was situated in an important cemetery, and a rare lantern of the dead still stands outside. It was the custom in the 16 C. to perform mystery plays in the cemetery, including The Conversion of the Magdalen and Susanna and the Elders. The relics of St Marius (Mary) used to be carried in procession to Puy-St-Mary on the Sunday before 8th June, Feast of St Melanie (=black) the Elder. Saracen chains of liberated captives still hang on the wall of the Ch. St Dominic spent two days in prayer at the feet of the BV. An 11 C. priest who tried to enlarge his house at the expense of the BV's garden

died suddenly along with two of his workmen. The present splendid Ch. was built in reparation to her.

159 Mayres Puy-de-Dôme; 76 (6); 14 km N of La Chaise-Dieu by D 906 and D 38 on the confines of the Auvergne and the Velay above the gorge of the R. Dore; N-D de la Roche; Ch. in field at end of wood just S of Mayres to left of road; BV and (naked) Child, both crowned, in niche under middle of altar with Benedictine in adoration. This statue (a copy) commemorates the vision of a 12 C. monk of La Chaise-Dieu. At the end of the 18 C. the statue was stolen, but brought such misfortunes on the family of the thieves that they hid it in a cleft rock where it was found and the cult restored. Saved at Rev. by pious women and, to avoid further risk, the original BV now stands behind the altar in the village (key from bar/tabac on opposite side of square). It is small (50 cm); 14 C.; stone, very black and shiny, with golden crowns and red lips, while the praying monk who forms part of the group is painted in natural colours. Living cult, ex-votos, fresh flowers, villagers aware of the legends and traditions. Statue of St Roch, pointing to wound in left thigh, and of his dog. Sts Anne, Joseph, Louis of Gonzaga and Margaret.

160 Mazan Vaucluse; 93 (10); 7 km E of Carpentras by D 942; (1) N-D la Brune or La Sarcleuse;

wood; 14 C. Original found 11 C. by women weeding field (*sarcleuses*); SD; Ch. to E of town locked but BV visible through barred window; built on site of pagan temple; it became a leperhouse of Knights of the order of St Lazarus; Ch. sacked 1794; BV thrown into brazier which exploded; saved by women; BV damaged by fire and sabre, but Mazan and its inhabitants were spared in the Terror; BV restored 1954.
(2) N-D de Pareloup (wards off wolves) or du Puy, in midst of major cemetery dating from pagan times, up the Montée de la Madeleine and the Allée des Sarcophages; D. at Rev.; replaced by polychrome Virgin without Child taming a wolf; also in 11 C. Ch. life-size statue of the Magdalen. Belfry of main Ch. of Mazan built on Templar tower. To N of the town is the Ch. de St Roch on the Chemin de St Anne; between it and the Ch. of N-D la Brune is the Ruisseau de St Joseph. Mazan is the home of the de Sade family. The famous Marquis held the first festival of Provence there in 1772. On the arms of the town are the sun, the crescent of Islam and the hand of Fatima. The Frankish sword which used to hang above them in memory of Charlemagne's victory was suppressed by the ecclesiastical authorities.

161 *Meaux* Seine-et-Marne; 56 (12) (13); bronze standing statue of Virgin with Child on left arm and long hair was found in the

Gallo-Roman *castrum* and venerated in the Capuchin Ch.

162 Mende Lozère; 80 (5) (6); (1) N-D de Mende; in Cathedral; wood; 70 cm; no Child; red-painted robe reveals rounded breasts and prominent belly; brought back from the Holy Land by the Crusaders of the Gévaudan in first half of 13 C.; perpetual lamp from 1314; damaged by Huguenots; saved at Rev.; crowned 1894 Queen of Mende and of the Gévaudan; saved city from 2000 Germans, Feast of the Assumption 1944; in former Chapel of St Roch to left of choir; Chapels to Sts Anne, Blaise, Margaret, Gervase and Protase (Dioscuri?), Joseph; original Merovingian Ch. built above the crypt of St Privat which dates from Gallo-Roman times and replaced a pagan temple.
(2) N-D de la Fontaine or du Puits in glass-covered niche above water pump in rue Notre-Dame; mural above BV shows angel holding scroll with 'Nigra sum sed formosa' (I am black but beautiful); BV; 50 cm; naked Child on left knee with hand on BV's left breast and finger pointing upwards.

163 *Metz* Moselle; 57 (13) (14); N-D de la Rotonde or de la Ronde in Ch. now incorporated into the Cathedral of St Etienne (built on site of Temple of Diana) is now N-D de Mt Carmel and contains a popular Mater Dolorosa and a lamp-stand of a sow suckling two children. Metz, which means 'mother of the middle', was an ancient Druidic centre where the Druidess Arete, inspired by a dream, raised a monument to the god Silvanus and the nymphs, who no doubt constituted the pagan influence overcome in the form of the drac or wouivre called the Graouly by St Clement whose Merovingian throne is in the choir. St Bernard preached the Second Crusade there as well as at Vézeley and persuaded Louis VII to add two priories to Our Lady at Metz in addition to the two already founded there by his friend Cardinal Etienne de Bar. The Cathedral contained a statue of Isis until the 16 C. The octagonal Templar Ch. in the arsenal is unique in Lorraine. Durand-Lefèbvre reports a cult to N-D d'Einsiedeln (Switzerland) whose first abbot St Benno was a native of Metz.

164 Meymac Corrèze; 73 (11); N-D de Meymac; wood; 12 C. 48 cm; very black faces and hands, pink finger-nails, red lips, white and black eyes; BV has gold sabots and turban or toque, very large hands, red cloak and green dress; Child in red with bare feet sits between her knees holding closed golden book in left hand; throne light natural wood; one of the strangest and most interesting of BVs; once part of treasure of 11 C. Benedictine priory of St Andrew, originally a hermitage (with chapel to N-D) of Merovingian period. BV and Child gaze across to windows symbolizing Synagogue and Church with St John holding a closed gilt book, like that of the Child, and to the Station of the Cross in which Jesus is condemned to death. A statue shows St Roch accompanied not by his dog but by a woman in black. Windows to Sts John the Baptist and Michael. Statue of St James. Ancient carved water-stoup, former capital, recalls Laocoön. In porch, very dark wooden statue of woman with castle under her left hand (Tower of David?). Chapel of St Roch in village and Chapel of the Magdalen near by. The Plâteau de Millevaches, on which Meymac is situated, derives its name not from cattle but from its many springs (Celtic, batz = spring).

165 **Mézières** Ardennes; 53 (18); N-D d'Espérance; 60 cm; BV much venerated since it was found in the early 10 C. in the foundations of the ramparts; D. by Huguenots; replaced in 17 C.; BV carries purple bunch of grapes (cf. Cybele and Hecate); many ex-votos, including thanks for saving city in 1815 and 1918; Statue of St Joseph; near frontier (26 km from Bouillon); no postcards or booklets available; Mézières derives from the pagan god Macer (or vulgar Latin *macerias* = material or ruins) and was a Druidic centre. Louis de Gonzague, Duc de Nevers, Grand Master of the Prieuré de Sion, acquired the city in 1565 and in 1570 his son Charles IX married Elisabeth of

Austria in the Basilica. Charles built the new city of Charleville on the other side of the Meuse between 1606 and 1627.

166 *Mièges* Jura; 70 (5); 20 km NE of Champagnole by D 471 and D 119; N-D de l'Ermitage; tiny statue of 13 cm carved from oak of Montaigu (Belgium) 1602. An earlier statue of silver found 6 C. or 7C. preceded this one, which in its turn had succeeded the cult of pagan divinities. Present statue saved at Rev.; many miraculous cures; Priest says not a BV.

167 **Modane** Savoie; 77 (8); N-D du Charmaix; 40 cm; marble; SD; probably 14 C., though one authority says 6 C.; known to have been black since first document of 1623; originally under rock next to road and river; Ch. built 1401 (miraculous rescue of three builders); 1597, Huguenot officer Laplante vexed at being paralysed while engaged in loot-ing oratory shot at statue and was shot dead himself a few moments later; saved at Rev.; many miracles; ex-votos; living cult; BV visible through grille, locked except during services; Sts Anne, Michael, John the Baptist, Blaise, Roch, Mary Magdalene, Catherine, Margaret and Bernard all venerated in the High Valley of the Maurienne.

168 **Molompize** Cantal; 76 (4) (see also **Vauclair**); N-D de Molompize, in Ch. of Molompize, open all day; confirmed by Priest

as BV without details; 15/16 C.;
Virgin, wood; Child naked,
covered in stucco and painted
black; original statue may have
been brought back from Antioch
by Crusaders; links with Conques.

169 Mondragon Vaucluse; 81
(1); 6 km NW of Orange by N7;
N-D des Plans; wood; 12 C.;
cattle; now polychrome; in Parish
Ch.; on pedestal; background of
croix ancrées or moline crosses
with rosy hearts; Virgin in red
dress, green cloak; found in bush;
pilgrimage since 1200 established
by Benedictines; chapel of St
Blaise built to house BV on site of
finding; protects from plague and
cholera; taken to Orange to be
burned at Rev.; saved by man of
Mondragon; Ch. of St Ariès half
way between Bollène and Mondragon; Drochon confirms statue
was originally a BV, but already
whitened by mid-19 C.; Fête du
Drac, 23 May; impressive cemetery Ch. at Mondragon with
strange, ghostly statues of praying
figures on façade.

Monistrol d'Allier Haute-Loire;
76 (16); See **Champels**.

170 *Monjou* Cantal; 76 (12)
(13); 20 km ENE of Aurillac, 12
km SE of Vic-sur-Cère; in Ch. of
Pailherols; statue refuses to accept
paint. Monjou = Mountain of
Jupiter; Templars at Polminhac
(W of Monjou), even after dissolution; Jesuit found 15 C. Tarot
deck there with Joan of Arc as
Pallas Athene and other historical

characters including Dunois,
Charles VII and Pope John XXII.

171 Montaut Ariège; 86 (5); 6
km N of Pamiers; N-D des
Ermites; 1748, cult introduced by
Fr Voisard who was impressed by
the cures of Our Lady of Einsiedeln (Switzerland) of which this
BV is a copy; stopped plague
1752, cholera 1854; Cathar
country.

172 *Montbrison* Loire; 73 (17);
BV donated (presumably to Ch. of
N-D d'Espérance) by Counts of
Forez (Abbé Prajoux, *Histoire du
Côteau,* Roanne, 1924). Curé
knows of no BV tradition.

173 *Montciel* (Lons-le-Saunier).
Jura; 70 (4) (14); N-D de Montaigu (carved from oak of Montaigu, Belgium); cult established
1610; Mons Coelius was the
Roman city of Ledo and a centre
of pagan ceremonies Christianized
by St Desiderius, to whose Ch. the
statue was taken during Rev.;
statue was returned to Montciel in
1832 and prevented a cholera
epidemic in 1854.

174 Montluçon Allier; 69 (11)
(12); BV; wood; 9 C.; gilded 19
C.; near meridian zero degree;
windows of St Anne and of
Adoration of Magi and shep-
herds; St Victor to N; St Anne to
S. Quoted as former BV by
Durand-Lefèbvre, Saillens and
Atlantis. Tourist office denies pre-
sence of BV at Montluçon stating
N-D de Montluçon in Ch. of

Notre-Dame is 17C. seated gilt wood Madonna with Child.

175 **Montmerle-sur-Saône** Ain; 74 (1); 12 km N of Villefranche by D 993; N-D de Bon-Secours or des Minimes; sailors saw bronze statue in Saône which moved miraculously to site of present Ch.; pilgrimage and Ch. of St Mary well established by 1192 when Pope Celestine confirmed the claims of the Abbey of Cluny to its possession; pilgrimage there by Order of the Thistle (founded by Louis II of Bourbon at Moulins in 1370); much destruction at Rev.; Ch. rebuilt 1825; no information about the statue in the booklet *N-D des Minimes* by Abbé Renoud; present Curé neither confirms nor denies she is black, but she is known as such in the diocese. 1945 statue taken to visit N-D d'Ars (ex-votos with signature of Curé d'Ars). 1946 N-D de Boulogne paid her a visit.

176 Montpellier Hérault; 83 (7); N-D des Tables (Nostra Dama des Taoulas), La Nègre, or N-D de Substancion; one of the most famous BVs of France; D. at Rev.; replaced by 19 C. marble copy in 1881 and crowned 1889; cult and miracles since 878; original Ch. of N-D late 4 C.; miraculous BV brought back from Crusades 1143; wood; 83 cm; saved Montpellier from drought and plague; Montpellier greatest medical and healing centre in France; Rabelais studied medicine there; St Roch b.

in shadow of N-D des Taoulas c. 1293; Nostradamus practised there; coiled candle one foot thick and three times as long as the circumference of the ramparts offered to BV four times in 14 C.; Albigensians who renounced their faith had to make pilgrimage to BV; Ch. D. by Huguenots 1621; 1789 Ch. struck by lightning, hand of BV mutilated; Drochon claims that it was saved at Rev. and is still venerated; ruins of Temple of Vesta on hill called Le Verrou (bolt) connect with tradition that BV when hidden revealed her hiding-place by flames; Churches to St Anne, St Denis, St Roch and St Cleophas (one of the Emmaus disciples, husband of the Mary who stood with Mary Magdalen at Cross and father of St James); Chapels to St Blaise and St John the Baptist; BV visited by nine Popes and eleven kings.

177 *Montperoux* Allier; 69 (15); 38 km SE of Moulins by D 112 and D 53; BV noted by M. Mitton (*Revue d'Auvergne*).

178 **Montréjeau** Haute-Garonne; 85 (20); 13 km E of Lannemezan on N 117, ancient prehistoric road; N-D de Polignan, Ch. de N-D de Polignan in Gourdon-Polignan (village 1 km S of Montréjeau on other side of Garonne); 14 C. statue, not copy as stated in earlier editions; SD; discovered by bull; frees prisoners and broke her own chains to escape from Huos (1 km E) and return to Polignan;

to visit arrange with Curé of Montréjeau.

179 Montrésor Indre-et-Loire; 64 (16) (17); 17 km E of Loches by N 760; N-D de Lorette; 1542 copy of Italian BV; funerary Ch. founded 1521 by Counsellor of Louis XI; gilt wood; *Annunciation* by Philippe de Champaigne; statue of St Roch; castle of Foulques Nerra.

180 Mont-Saint-Michel Manche; 59 (7); N-D du Mont-Tombe, de Sous-Terre or N-D des Morts (site of Gallic cemetery); D at Rev. 1790; Abbey founded on site of Carolingian abbey by St Aubert, early 8 C.; who brought back piece of Archangel Michael's cloak from Monte St Angelo on Gargano Peninsula (see **Manfredonia,** Italy); Bernard le Sage might have brought BV back from Holy Land 867, but cult of Virgin in the Crypt of the Thirty Candles, the underground shrine of St Aubert, is probably older; an attempt to restore religious life and the cult of the BV 1863-70 was unsuccessful, but since 1966 some monks have returned; plaster BV in sacristy of Parish Ch. in the Grand-Rue; Louis XI founded Order of St Michael there 1469; Mont-St-Michel one of nine great commanderies of the Prieuré de Sion; Plantard motto 'Et in Arcadia Ego' quoted in 1210 by Abbot Robert; Mount surrounded in Roman times by Sessiacum Forest (Sessia = goddess of seeds and grains — cf Proserpina), home of priestesses who assured safety of sailors who vowed chastity to them; alternatively, islet where women celebrated the rites of Bacchus (as sacred prostitutes), crying Evau (cf. repeated refrain 'Aoi' or 'Evoe' in *Chanson de Roland*); newly-wed couples of Lower Britanny abstained from sex until purification at Mont-St-Michel (cf. Montserrat and Loreto); ancient name Portus Herculei or Tombelen (tomb of Belenus); on tin route to Marseilles from St Michael's Mount in Cornwall; cult of Cybele and Mithra (Temple of Cybele at Dol — 28 km — till 1802); the late 19 C. plaster BV in the abbey has been relegated by the Beaux Arts to a loft as of no artistic value.

181 *Montvianeix* Puy-de-Dôme; 73 (6); wood; 12 C.; 70 cm; cleaned 1931 transferred to private collection; nearby villages of St Victor Montvianeix and Bonhomme (Cathar Parfait).

182 **Moulins** Allier; 69 (14); (1) N-D de Moulins in Chapelle de la Vierge Noire in Cathédrale Notre-Dame; 12 C. substitute for the original brought back by St Louis from the Crusades; very dark wood; 80 cm; Child holds closed book in left hand; in same chapel sculptures of Descent from Cross and Burial of the Virgin; tablet of thanksgiving for preservation of Moulins in two world wars; copy of the original in white marble; Cathedral not begun until 1474 — Moulins originally part of parish

of Yzeure (1 km E), ancient Gallo-Roman spa whence an underground passage reputedly led to the castle of the Bourbons at Moulins next to the Cathedral; dragon grew unnoticed in the passage until slain by a hero; windows to St Mary Magdalene, St Catherine, Crucifixion (with angels collecting blood), St Elisabeth of Hungary, Tree of Jesse, St Apollonia (of Alexandria like St Catherine), St Louis; St Anne in Moulins triptych; St Joan of Arc prayed to BV of Moulins 1429; St Bonnet (Belenus) other old parish besides Yzeure on which Moulins depended; Ch. of St John at Yzeure likely original BV site;. from Robert de Clermont, sixth child of St Louis and Anne de Bourbon the eight Bourbon Kings of France were descended.
(2) BV of Vouroux or des Chartreux; 12 C.; in museum.
(3) BV of Coulandon in Seminary of Moulins. Louis of Bourbon founded Order of Our Lady at Moulins after his release from captivity in England and in 1370 the Order of the Thistle (emblem of Lorraine and Scotland); BV extinguished great fire of 1635; in Middle Ages the faithful burned a great wheel of light before the BV; Moulins important staging post for Compostela — pilgrims prayed to BV without fail; Moulins the N limit of the land of the Arverni.

183 *Mozac* Puy-de-Dôme; 73 (4); 1 km W of Riom nr Chapel of St Don (Dionysus?); Saillens notes BV reported by M. Mitton; Benedictine Abbey from 7 C.; remarkable capital — wizards on goats, marauder in vine, etc.; on lintel of cloister portico Virgin in majesty; Virgin on casket of St Calmin.

184 **Murat** Cantal; 76 (3); N-D des Oliviers (olive-trees) — title unique in France; in Ch. of St Martin; 14 C.; 83 cm; wood; standing; olive-wood blackened by fire of 1492, since when she has always protected the town from lightning; under her olive branch no citizen of Murat died during the Rev.; Candlemas procession in which BV and participants are dressed in green (cf. Marseilles); statues of Sts Roch, Blaise, Peter of the Cock-Crow, Mary Magdalene, Vincent-de-Paul and Dominic, but all chapels dedicated to the Virgin — Our Lady of Good Help, Mt Carmel, Victories, Snows, Seven Sorrows, Rosary; painting of the resuscitation of a roast cock at La Calzada on the road to Compostela, thanks to which St Dominic, who had been hanged as a thief several months before, came back to life; olive-oil lamp with miraculous properties burns before BV; town dominated by 14-metre statue in honour of N-D des Oliviers on the summit of the Rocher de Bonnevie; BV traditionally the gift of St Louis, who had many connections with Murat; twin heights with R. Alagnon between; Murat depended on the village of Bredons (qv) where there was a Benedictine Monastery and a BV, and for

centuries the parish was centred there (cf. Moulins and Yzeure) on its holy hill with caves. BV the patroness of butchers.

185 Murbach Bas-Rhin; 62 (18); 18 C. copy of N-D of Loreto (Italy); abbots of Murbach ranked as Princes of the Holy Roman Empire, and the monks as knights.

186 **Myans** Savoie; 74 (15); 10 km SE of Chambéry by D 201, N 6 or A 41; N-D de Myans, 'most ancient and stable pilgrimage in France' (van Gennep); Queen of Savoy; in the heart of the Savoy vineyard (Abymes, Apremont); in crypt of sanctuary; wood; 70 cm; chapel there since c.1100 with 'l'image de Notre-Dame, noire en éthiopienne' (historian Fodéré, 1619); Ch. framed in saddle between two mountains of uneven heights to W, with Mont-St-Michel visible across the valley. 27 Nov. 1248, earthquake, Mt Granier disintegrates, obliterating the town of St André (from which the Benedictines of the Priory of Apremont had been expelled that day) as well as 16 villages, killing over 5,000 people. The monks fled to the Chapel of Myans, the very place where the avalanche stopped as if by a miracle. The monks could hear the demons calling to each other 'Go on! Go on!' to be answered by their fellows, 'We can't because the Brown One, that is to say the Black One, is stopping us.' Ch., statue and ex-votos to St Anne. Brother of St François de Sales

(himself a pilgrim to Myans) saved from drowning by BV on the way to his marriage; Jean Grandris only survivor of shipwreck between Genoa and Leghorn 1534, having invoked BV.

187 *Nanc* Jura; 70 (13); E of N 83 2 km SE of St Amour; N-D de Bon-Encontre; 25 cm with base; box-wood; formerly venerated at Mt Orient in the Mts du Gouilla (throat); statue in lime-tree caught eye of passing horseman on an important business trip to Lons-le-Saunier, brought him good fortune; he built chapel, D at Rev.; statue saved by sacristan; resuscitates still-born babies.

188 Nancy Meurthe-et-Moselle; 62 (5); capital of House of Lorraine; (1) N-D de Bonsecours behind altar in Ch. of N-D de Bonsecours, built by René d' Anjou to commemorate victory over Burgundians (1477), rebuilt by King Stanislaus the Magnificent of Poland, who married there; carved from piece of oak of Montaigu (Belgium) 1505 by sculptor Mansuy Gauvin; Drochon suggests statue D at Rev. and restored thanks to engraving which survived.
(2) N-D de St Cirgues (Auvergne); 13 C.; 73 cm; museum.

189 *Nevers* Nièvre; 69 (3) (4); Durand-Lefèbvre gives N-D des Grâces (whose chapel, founded in 1620 at the instigation of St François de Sales, is now disaffected) as a seated wooden BV and states

BV of Coulandon (qv) is in Nevers museum; Nevers seat of Gonzaga family (Louis, Grand Master of Prieuré de Sion — see **Mézières**) whose 16 C. palace has bas-reliefs of legend of Lohengrin, from whom they claimed descent; St Bernadette of Lourdes died at Nevers, where her incorrupt body is venerated. Gypsies arrived at Nevers 1436 under Thomas, count of Little-Egypt.

190 Noves Bouches-du-Rhône; 81 (12); (see also Vacquières); BV of Noves stolen twice from Ch. of Noves; whereabouts unknown.

Odeillo Pyrénées-Orientales; 86 (16); See **Font-Romeu;** only Ch. in diocese still with cattle-grid.

191 **Orcival** Puy-de-Dôme; 73 (13); 17 km N. of le Mont-Dore by D 983 and D 27; N-D d' Orcival, de la Délivrance or des Fers; 12 C.; 70 cm; recently restored; unknown wood covered in silver except face and hands (very large); Child holds closed book in left hand; dolmen; water; funerary site; twin peaks near by, Rochers Tuileries and Sanadoire; BV attr. to St Luke; one of oldest and most famous Marian shrines in Auvergne; traditionally founded by St Ursin, disciple of St Austremoine (3 C.); priory dependent on Chaise-Dieu since 12 C.; one of 5 major Romanesque churches in Auvergne; pilgrimage pre-10 C.; miraculous spring saved inhabitants during Norman siege; Orcival = valley of Orcus,

Gallic divinity in form of devouring dog/wolf (Blez), temple to Pluto and Proserpine with statues on ebony thrones underground; or Valley of Bear (*ours*), cf. St Ours, companion of St Victor — formerly bearskins on Ch. doors; or *urs* (spring); BV found when workman's hammer was thrown to determine site of Ch. on hillock called le Chancel or the Tomb of the Holy Virgin; torchlight procession to ruins where she was found (and to which she returned three times) on Ascension Day when the multitude include the gypsies of central France; cures blind and barren, heals scabies; resuscitates still-born babies; has freed captives since Norman times (chains on walls); casts out demons; protects sailors (formerly ship ex-votos, chief hymn 'Ave Maris Stella'); protects from plague; grants victory (Charles VI, Duc de Berri et Bourbon, offered standard after defeating English at Roche-Sanadoire 1385); cult of Sts Anne, Blaise and Eloi (patron of smiths, Gallo-Roman friend of Merovingian Dagobert I); door of St John; next village to N St Bonnet (Belenus); neighbouring hamlet of Briffons has copy of N-D d'Orcival; Orcival included as important BV by Durand-Lefèbvre, Saillens, Huynen, Peyrard's *Histoire Secrète de l' Auvergne* and *Nostra,* though face and hands are no more than brownish; I asked the proprietress of the souvenir shop opposite the Ch. why she was called a BV and she replied in a tone that brooked of no contradiction, 'Because she is one.' Other Auvergnats, including priests, agree. Feast of Fools; Boy Bishop 28 Dec. Village of St Ours nearby.

192 Orléans Loiret; 64 (5); N-D des Miracles, de la Recouvrance or St Mary the Egyptian; standing; stone; 100 cm; 16 C., made of two unequal stones deliberately blackened, replacing ancient wooden BV burnt by Protestants 1562; described as Vierge Noire Couronnée on prayer card; Syrian quarter of city had oratory with ebony Virgin in 6 C., soon honoured by the inhabitants of the whole region; Syrians acclaimed Merovingian King Gontran 588, welcomed St Columbanus as their guest *c.* 600; in pre-Christian times Orléans navel of Gaul, capital of Carnutes; springs of goddess Acionna; 897 Norman siege, BV puts forth knee to protect defender from arrow, saves city; 989 wolf rings Ch. bell in warning of great fire; 1152 Order of Prieuré de Sion returns to France, 62 installed in Priory of St Samson of Orléans donated by Louis VII, 26 in Priory of Mt de Sion at St Jean le Blanc on outskirts of Orléans; remaining 7 incorporated into Order of Temple; 1429 Joan of Arc (Maid of Orléans) enters city, stays with Jacques Boucher whose house communicates to Ch. of St Paul where BV then was, hears Mass before BV daily; gives thanks to her after famous victory of 7 May; 1450 Charles VII institutes annual procession; 12 Nov. 1793 mob invade Ch.; locksmith Marsin tries to break BV with hammer blows, no impression; 1802 cult restored; 17/18 June 1940, Orléans attacked by Germans, everything in Ch. of BV burnt except her Chapel where nothing was touched by the fire; 120 pages of miracles in *N-D des Miracles* by Fr Delahaye; from 11 C. Orléans an important centre of St Mary Magdalene cult.

193 Ornans Doubs; 66 (16); (1) in Ch. of St Laurent, N-D des Malades; 1610; 13 cm; oak from Montaigu; considered Vierge Brune by Priest and made for leper house.
(2) N-D du Chêne (oak); 3 km NW of Ornans along valley of R. Loue; found in trunk of oak-tree which opened to reveal it after revelation to local girl in 1803; statue in special Ch.; bronze statue where oak stood; not considered BV by priest; living cult; pilgrimages.

194 Oust Ariège; 86 (3); 18 km SSE of St Girons by D618 and D32; N-D du Pouech; 10 C. and 13 C. replica; 1854, stopped cholera; reigns over mines (Nostra); in area known as 'Terro Santo'.

195 La Pacaudiere Loire; 73 (7); 24 km NW of Roanne by N 7; N-D de Tourzy, Salus Infirmorum; unknown black stone; 70 cm; standing; found in forest in hollow oak pre-11 C.; vast abbey there till Rev.; many cures; living cult; Tourzy now part of La Pacaudière (S) at N extremity of Mts de la Madeleine. St Bonnet next village to S.

196 *Palau* Pyrénées-Orientales; 86 (16); 2 km S of Bourg-Madame; painting of BV by J. Serra (Catalan 14 C.); Ch. of Ste Marie or Paladiso (Paradise = Palau); consecrated by Bishop of Urgel 949 in present cemetery; present Ch. built 1808; on Spanish frontier.

197 **Paris** (1) Above altar on left side of Ch. of Nuns of the Sacred Heart, 35 rue de Picpus, open daily 9.30-12, 2-4, 6-7, N-D de Paix; 16 C.; 33 cm; wood; standing; Child on left arm; on column behind high altar; most celebrated and venerated Madonna in Paris until Rev. The statue may have been a wedding gift from Jean de Joyeuse to his wife Françoise de Voisins in 1518. Its first home was with them in the Château de Couiza, two miles from Rennes-le-Château. Arques, site of the tomb of Poussin's *Les Bergers d'Arcadie* also belonged to the family. After a time in Toulouse, the BV was brought to Paris in 1576 by Henri de Joyeuse who took it with him to the Capuchins of St Honoré where he became a religious after his wife's death. His daughter's second husband was Gaston d'Orléans, brother of Louis XIII. Her daughter married Charles de Lorraine, Duc de Guise, and built a great new chapel for N-D de Paix. It has thus more

associations with the aims of the Merovingian blood-line in the 16th and 17th centuries than any other BV. Saved at Rev.; given to Sisters of Sacred Heart 1806.

(2) In Chapel of the Congregation of St Thomas of Villeneuve, 52 Boulevard d'Argenson, Neuilly-sur-Seine, open weekdays 7-7, Sun. 7.45-7.15, N-D de Bonne Délivrance, La Vierge Noire de Paris; 14 C. replacing earlier BV, probably of the 11 C., in Ch. of St Etienne des Grès (Greeks or steps) (cf. Tarascon); 150 cm; carved in a single block of hard limestone. St François de Sales was saved from the temptation of despair and found his vocation at her feet. St Vincent de Paul often prayed to her. Anne of Austria entered her son Louis XIV as a member of her confraternity in 1643. Saved at Rev. by Mme de Carignan who gave it to its present guardians.

(3) St Germain-des-Prés. Abbey built in 542 by Merovingian King Childebert I (511-558) on site of former Temple of Isis to house the treasures of Solomon. A black statue of Isis 'thin, tall, straight, naked or with some flimsy garment' was worshipped as the Virgin Mary in the Ch. until destroyed by the Abbot, Guillaume Briconnet, in 1514. A seal of the Abbey from 1138 confirms the description. Ch. contains only Merovingian relics in Paris (later burials at St Denis) and the tombs of Descartes and John Casimir, King of Poland. The Ch. of St Sulpice, built in the Abbey grounds for the seminary founded

by J.-J. Olier, disciple of St Vincent de Paul, contains a monolith with a red (or 'rose') line down the middle marking the zero meridian of Paris that runs through Rennes-le-Château. In her chapel at St Germain, St Genevieve holds what could be a spear and a grail. The only other statue in the chapel is of St Theodosia, who shares a feast (2 April) with St Mary of Egypt, like St Genevieve a successor of Isis. 13C. window of St Anne and modern copy of BV icon also in the chapel.

(4) In Ch. of N-D des Champs founded in reign of Hugh Capet, BV reported by *Atlantis*. No BV at present.

(5) In Abbaye du Val de Grâce, built by Louis XIII to celebrate the 'miraculous' birth of Louis XIV, BV reported by *Atlantis*. No BV now.

(6) In cellars of the Observatory belonging to the convent of the nuns of St Thomas de Villeneuve, rue Denfert-Rochereau, very dark Madonna and Child, not considered black by the congregation, recently destroyed owing to damage caused by the dampness of the cellar and other depredations.

(7) In Ch. of St Merri windows show St Mary the Egyptian (dark) next to St Mary Magdalene (fair).

(8) N-D de Coulombs (qv) in Louvre Museum.

(9) Durand-Lefèbvre reports another BV in Cluny Museum.

(10) N-D de Bénédiction transferred to Longpont (qv).

(11) Chapelle de l'Abbaye-aux-Bois, N-D de Toutes Aides; wood;

16/17 C.; copy of older BV, blessed by St François de Sales 1618, preserved there until beginning of 20 C.

(12) (13) (14) *Boulogne-sur-Seine*, Chatou, Joy-en-Josas, see under separate headings.

(15) Polish Ch., 236 (bis) rue Saint-Honoré, copy of BV of Czestochowa.

(16) Chapel of Russian Orthodox Seminary, rue de Crimée, replica of Moscow BV, N-D des Ibères, reported by Durand-Lefèbvre, 1937.

198 *Passais* Orne; 59 (9) (10); 12 km SW of Domfront by D 21; N-D de Liesse; St Mars next village.

199 **Peisey** Savoie; 74 (18); 15 km S of Bourg St Maurice by N 90 and D 87; in Chapelle de Pracompuet (always open), BV painted on silk; 110 cm by 170 cm; probably from BV of Oropa (Italy); cult of St James.

200 *Périgueux* Dordogne; 75 (5); N-D la Noire or La Vieille at St Front Cathedral; D. at Rev.; statue of St Anne venerated there; inscription *Virgo paritura* existed at Ch. of St Etienne in 1878; pagan Périgueux worshipped Cybele/Tutela, the remains of whose Temple is the Tour de Vésone.

201 **Pézenas** Hérault; 83 (15); N-D la Noire or de Bethléem; 12 C.; 60 cm; cult of BV known to have originated between 1311

(Templars superseded at Pézenas by Knights of St John) and 1340 (documentary evidence of statue). Origins: (1) arrives alone in a boat (cf Boulogne); (2) brought by Commander of Knights of St John from Crusade against Rhodes (1310), where he acquired two BVs, giving the other to the Ch. of La Daurade in Toulouse, his native city. Commandery D. at Rev.; BV saved by Mesdemoiselles Bézard and Vidal, though damaged. Venerated since on High Altar of Ch. of St Ursula (open 8-12, 2-7), home of the Archconfraternity that has served her for centuries. Napoleon III dedicated a lamp in her shrine to gain her support for his army assisting the Lebanese Maronites against the Turks in 1860. Many individual miracles of healing (ex-votos, candles), protection against epidemics (1852, 1854) and drought (1840, 1947 — date of last procession). Pézenas's patron is St Blaise; statue of St Roch in Ch. of BV stolen 1963. Except for a short time at Rev. a lamp has remained lit in front of BV night and day since 1340. Pagan cults in neighbourhood (Pézenas on ancient via Heraclea).

202 **Pignans** Var; 84 (16); 10 km E of N 97 at Pignans to highest summit of Massif des Maures (771m); N-D des Anges in large pilgrimage Ch. rebuilt 1846, 1900 and more recently, open Sundays May-Nov. (All Saints' Day); standing; no Child; found by shepherd and dog 11 C., pre-

sent statue 17 C.; SD; patroness of sailors; walls lined with ex-votos; darkish wood; water; Ch. built by order of Thierry, son of Clovis, to commemorate victory over Visigoths, 517. Abbey a dependance of St Victor of Marseilles; old temple on site of martyrdom of Ste Nymphe, companion of St Mary Magdalene. Megalith became altar stone of 11 C. chapel. Shortly after its foundation three peasant girls, seeing Our Lady was not in her usual place, looked for her and found her returning all wet. 'Beautiful Virgin where have you been?' 'I come from distant seas where I saved a sinking ship and all her crew.' BV preserved Pignans from plague in 1720 and from drought 1753.

203 *Poitiers* Vienne; 68 (13) (14); BV in Ch. of N-D la Grande, D. 1562; held keys.

204 Pontarlier Doubs; 70 (6); N-D d'Einsiedeln; 17 C.; Ste Colombe 8 km SW.

205 *Pouilly-en-Auxois* Côte d' Or; 65 (18); N-D la Trouvée or du Lait; 13 C.; 55 cm; wood; blackened and whitened three times; resurrects unbaptised children; in Ch. of N-D la Trouvée, 14/15 C., half-way up hill in cemetery; found in ruins of burnt Ch.; statue stolen 1980; pilgrimage; Bellenot (Belenus?) and Martrois villages immediately to N. Priest says not a BV.

206 **Pradelles** Haute-Loire; 76 (17); in chapelle N-D (open daily, when shut ask at presbytery); N-D de Pradelles; 14 C.; cedar; brought back from the east by Crusader; hidden during troubles; dug up by servant girl 1512; living cult; palladium of Pradelles where heresy never took root; saved from fire at Rev. by remorseful Jacobin; still in old Dominican Ch. till fire of 1857 which stopped short of BV; highest town in France — 1157m; near source of Allier; on boundaries of Ardèche, Lozère and Hte Loire; Croix d' Ardennes just W of town.

207   **Prats-de-Mollo** Pyrénées-Orientales; 86 (18); N-D d'El Coral (oak-tree), in sanctuary of same name down track E of frontier post with Spain at Col d'Arès, though now in custody of priest of Prats except on feast-days such as Easter and Whitsun; first mention of Ch. 1267; BV found in heart of oak 13 C. by herdsman attracted by the strange behaviour of his bull; Chapel of St Margaret near by, half-way up the mountain; Ch. of Sts Justa and Rufina (Feast 20 July, same as St Margaret) has modern (1936) dark wood statue, a replica of N-D del Coral, flanked by Sts Cosmas and Damian; Chapel of St Catherine has statues of St Anne, St Margaret and St Lucy; Chapel of St Eloi has statue of St Joseph; Chapel of St Michael has retable of Tobias and his fish as well as a scene of an arrow aimed at the rebellious bull of Monte Gargano

(Italy — see **Manfredonia**) returning to strike the archer; large whale-bone in Ch. entrance; Prats formerly noted for its vineyards; Fête de l'Ours in Feb., with blackening of faces and hands and kidnapping of girl with subsequent rescue is the continuation of a pagan bear cult.

208 **Préaux**   Ain; 74 (3); S of N 84 1 km W of Cerdon; N-D de Préaux (open daily); 15 C.; wood; 50 cm; standing; veiled; arms crossed on chest; found in a hollow oak.

209 *Pringy*   Seine-et-Marne; 237 (30); 8 km SW of Melun by N 372; standing; wood; 80 cm; found in tree; water; frees prisoners.

210 **Le Puy**   Haute-Loire; 76 (7); N-D du Puy; city of Anis pre-Roman capital of Velay; major Druidic centre; two impressive rocky peaks of unequal size dominate the city, the Rocher Corneille, where the Cathedral stands with the huge statue (16 m) of N-D de France on the peak above, and St Michel d'Aiguilhe, her consort, where a Romanesque chapel of St John replaces the temple of Gallic Mercury; Temple of Diana at foot; first apparition of Virgin traditionally AD 46; black stone from dolmen on Rocher Corneille, La Pierre des Fièvres, healed malignant fever of widow AD 430 who was told by the Virgin in a vision to lie on top of it; Bishop recognized cure; stag

ran out of woods and traced plan of Cathedral in July snow-storm; further miracles led to construction of first basilica, which was consecrated by angels (cf. Einsiedeln, Switzerland); Bishopric from 4 C.; fever-stone formerly on high altar, now in front of the Golden Gate at main entrance; Le Puy visited twice by Charlemagne; in 778, according to legend, he was besieging the chief Moorish stronghold N of the Pyrenees whose general submitted thanks to Bishop Rorice II of Le Puy where he was converted, giving to the fortress its new name of Lourdes after his own baptism as Lorus; Pope Leo IX (11 C.) writes, 'Nowhere does the Holy Virgin receive a more special and filial cult of respect, love and veneration than that which the faithful of all France render in this Church of Mount Anis, otherwise called Puy-Sainte-Marie'; 11/12 C., Romanesque Cathedral built; grinning face between two wolves, Porche du For; sacred may-tree and healing spring (behind High Altar) incorporated into structure; Arabic inscription on N door = 'Here is that which God has loved'; Bishop Godescalc visited Mozabaric monasteries 951; Great Jubilee at Le Puy whenever Lady Day and Good Friday coincide, first in 1065, oldest Jubilee after Rome and Jerusalem; Joan of Arc sent the knights, who accompanied her from Vaucouleurs to Chinon, to Le Puy along with her mother and two brothers to pray for victory at 1429 Jubilee; next

Jubilee 2005; Pope Urban II held council to prepare for First Crusade 1095; Crusaders march to 'anthem of Le Puy', the 'Salve Regina'; visits of five Popes in next 70 years; visits by at least fifteen kings, including Louis XI; first act of King of England on becoming Duke of Guyenne was to pay tribute to N-D d'Anis; pilgrim saints include Peter the Venerable (who had Koran translated), Dominic, and Antony of Padua; BV presented by St Louis (more probably Louis VII), though sacred image (Mer.?) already known to be there since before 1096 when Count of Toulouse ordered perpetual light before her; BV made by Jeremiah (Coptic monk probably, though believed to be the prophet), and was the great treasure of Grand Sultan of Babylon, then ruler of Egypt, who gave it to Louis; might have been statue of Isis or based on one; covered in layers of gummed cloth (see small replica in vestry); burnt at Rev.; red Isiac stone discovered near site where débris dumped; 1844 present BV taken from Chapelle St Maurice and placed in Cathedral; crowned by Pope Pius IX 8 June 1856 (Feast of St Melanie (Black) the Elder); image sponged in wine annually; paintings of Mary and other two Marys at tomb, St Catherine and St Michael; statues of Joan of Arc, St Louis and St Andrew; porch and baptistery of John the Baptist; one of four main starting-points to Compostela; pilgrimage of thanksgiving to Le

Puy for successful childbirth; many connections with warlike actions — N-D de France made from 200 Russian cannons taken at Sebastopol; one of nine most important commanderies of Prieuré de Sion; courts of love on 15 Aug. precursor of Jocs florals at Toulouse; horn sounded on May Day (Venus, St Amadour, St Joseph) then broken on cross; horn of St Hubert, Bp of Tongres (see Belgium), apostle of Ardennes, among relics; Confraternity of Cornards (horned men — Kernunnos?).

211 *Le Puy-Notre-Dame* (2) Maine-et-Loire; 67 (8), 232 (8S); 7.5 km W of Montreuil-Bellay; a wooden majesté statue of the Virgin was given to St Pierre le Puellier by Ste Monégande, the contemporary of Clovis, and passed from there to Le Puy-Notre-Dame, which possessed fragments of the girdle of the Virgin (cf. Bruges and Le Puy-en-Velay) which helped in childbirth; Louis XIV was born under its protection since a piece of it was taken to his mother Anne of Austria and applied to her body before his birth. Louix XI had a special cult for Le Puy-Notre-Dame. 12 C. Ch. built on site of older one; Christianized monolithic pillar in portico until 18 C. — unique in Anjou; Benedictines; pilgrimages.

212 Quézac Lozère; 80 (6); 22 km S of Mende (qv) by N 88 and D 31, on the Tarn; Early 11 C. ploughman Jacques Deleuze's oxen refuse to pass a certain point; he tells curé; they dig and find BV; SD; Ch. built 1052; BV D. by Huguenots; present polychrome statue 16 C.; twice saved Quézac from plague.

213 *Quinipily Castle*, Morbihan; 230 (36); 2km SW of Baud, Venus of Quinipily. Transition from Menhir to BV (?); from Castennec where it was twice thrown into River Blavet by church; recarved as ISIS 18C.

214 *Randan* Puy-de-Dôme; 73 (5); near Thuret (qv); BV reported in *Histoire Secrète de l'Auvergne*; Benedictines; solitary Templar lived in forest after dissolution of order; fairy-stone, patroness of butchers near the Rond des Fées by St Sylvestre. Mayor has 'no information'.

215 *Remiremont* Vosges; 62 (16); N-D du Secrey (secret — because formerly not exposed in Ch. but kept in sacristy) or du Trésor; 11/12 C.; dark wood; traditionally gift of Charlemagne; contained hairs of Virgin Mary which the Canonesses of Remiremont had already had in their possession for 200 years when they descended from St Mont to the plain in 9 C.; hairs stolen at Rev. but statue, stripped of its gold and silver, was saved by a servant-girl, who had been ordered to burn it, and placed in parish Ch. in 1803; saved city in 1638 (Turenne), 1682 (earthquake — annual pilgrimage Sun. nearest 12 May), 1871 (Prussians), 1886 fire; not considered a BV by local authority on the subject. Remiremont a Merovingian foundation; very relaxed convent est. 7 C.; only the Abbess, a Princess of the Empire, took vows, sisters talked of love and its charms. St Nabor (Neptune) next village as at Mt St Odile.

216 Remonot Doubs; 70 (7); 19 km NE of Pontarlier on D 437; elongated cedar BV in Ch. of Grotte N-D; miraculous spring heals eyes; Grotte du Trésor near by.

217 Ribeauvillé Haut-Rhin; 62 (18) (19); at Dusenbach 2 km W up path to right off N 416 to St Marie-aux-Mines; N-D de Dusenbach; ancient BV brought back from Crusades by Egelolf of Ribeaupierre, probably 1221; SD; Anselm of Ribeaupierre, freed from prisons of Emperor at Candlemas 1297, built third chapel as thanksgiving to BV after miraculous survival of leap on horse from great rock while hunting prodigious stag; chapels and all their contents destroyed and restored three times; present statue of 1494, N-D du Calvaire or des Douleurs, dark polychrome pietà, 53 cm, hidden in cleft rock during wars of religion, found by woman called Marie; Lords of Ribeaupierre were Kings of the Minstrels (Pfeifferkönige), and all the Minnesänger or *ménétriers* wore a silver medal of the Virgin as a badge of their craft and her patronage; statue of St Michael 1760; Chapel of St Catherine; near by St Blaise, Rocher du Reptile, Venuskopf, Chemin Sarrasin; Dusenbach = spring of dwarves or incubi; one of two great pilgrimages of Alsace along with Mt St Odile; numerous ex-votos give thanks for miracles including one of cow in labour surrounded by the herd; pilgrimage under care of Dominicans 19 C., now of Capuchins. Last Lord of Ribeaupierre was King of Bavaria.

218 Riom Puy-de-Dôme; 73 (4); N-D du Marthuret in Ch. of same name (shut 12-2) built in 14 C. replacing chapel of 1240; 17 C.; based on older prototype venerated by St Louis in 1262; 60 cm; cattle; saved by butchers at Rev.; older Basilica of St Amable (formerly St Gervais et Protais) has strange recumbent statue of St Mary Magdalene dreaming in front of an urn; Riom passed, from being the court of the Dukes of Berry, into Bourbon hands; Joan of Arc relied on the town (which still has her letter of thanks) for supplies of powder, saltpetre and other munitions for her siege of La Charité; neighbouring village of St Bonnet with temple of Belenus; Ch. of St Don (Dionysus) among the vineyards; Martres-sur-Morge just between Riom and Thuret (qv) evokes the Celtic triple goddess; interesting Ch. of St Victor at Ennezat has statues of St Blaise and St Joseph; Riom captured by Louis XI.

219 Rocamadour Lot; 75 (18) (19); N-D de Rocamadour; 12 C. (*Michelin* says possibly 9 C.); 66 cm; walnut wood; attr. to St Luke; still covered in some blackened silver strips; the most ancient image already in 8 C. 'routed the infidels everywhere' (Collin de Plancy); brought victory at Navas de Tolosa, 1212, to armies of Aragon, Castille and Navarre; Durandal, Roland's sword, hangs above portico of Ch.; BV resuscitates unbaptized babies, protects sailors (bell rings miraculously to calm storms when mariners in danger invoke her — one ship was carried miraculously to Compostela); frees captives; promotes fertility; druid stone under altar; many dolmens and menhirs; worship of goddess Sulivia, goddess of alders and the dead (Cybele, according to Saillens), a triple goddess (Sulevia, Iduenna, Minerva) to whom human sacrifice was offered in cave where Amadour placed BV; Amadour (lover) born in Lucca (home of Holy Face), owned field where grain grew miraculously to hide Holy Family in flight to Egypt, is also Zacchaeus who climbs sycamore in Jericho to see Jesus and entertains him the night before he arrives at house of Mary Magdalene in Bethany (story told only by St Luke — Luca); Zacchaeus and his wife St Veronica (true image or bearer of victory) land at Soulac (qv);

Zacchaeus/Amadour proceeds by boat to Souillac (= place of wild boars or hermits — same as Soulac) and on to Rocamadour (also in one tradition founding Le Puy and visiting Compostela); brings drops of Virgin's milk; Amadour's body found incorrupt by Benedictines 1166; first documents by Robert de Thorigny, Abbot of Mt-St-Michel 1170, Benedictine; Amadour's feast-day, 1 May, feast of Belenus and Venus (also St Joseph, and first day of month of Mary) changed to 20 Aug., feast of St Bernard (d.1174) who visited Rocamadour (as did a multitude of saints and monarchs including St Louis, Ramon Lull, St Dominic, Louis XI, Henry II and in 1172 Eleanor of Aquitaine). Zacchaeus venerated in Berry as Silvanus; Zacchaeus = 'pure' (cf. Cathar); Amadour — Amad Aour = 'just'; Chapels of St Anne, St Blaise, St John Baptist and St Michael, painting of St Roch; important stage on road to Compostela; Cistercian monastery built on site of community for women archers called Dianas, men excluded but relations with fairies; Saut de la Pucelle near by; Belcastel (Belenus?) next to well of St Sol and large miraculous grotto; Cathars sent to Rocamadour as penance. Poulenc converted to Christianity there, and composed a litany in honour of the BV.

220 La Rochette Savoie; 74 (16), 91 (24); 10 km NE of Allevard by D 525 and D 925; N-

D des Plaints; 13 C.; 120 cm; painted wood; in Ch. of St John the Baptist; SD; found by shepherd who heard tearful voice from bush; statue of St Joseph; retables of 'The Presentation in the Temple' and 'The Flight into Egypt'; arms of Louis de Seyssel and his wife, daughter of the Count of Auvergne and Boulogne, widow of Alexander Stuart, son of James II of Scotland.

221 Rochefort-du-Gard Gard; 80 (20); 11 km W of Avignon by N 100 and D 111; N-D de Grâce, la Brune or Ste Victoire; standing; 40 cm; gift of Charlemagne; D. 1567; replaced 17 C.; near Tavel vineyard; village to N Grand Belly (Belenus?); the Director of the Foyer de Charité states that the history of N-D la Brune has left few traces; strikingly black hair of Virgin and Child, otherwise flesh tints.

222 Rodès Pyrénées-Orientales; 86 (18); N-D de Domanova 2 km S of Rodès across N 116; standing; 81 cm; 13/14 C.; in 11 C. hilltop Hermitage; now polychrome; only open on certain feast-days (Lady Day, Easter, Whit Monday, etc.); Calvinists unable to burn statue. Rodès (Lérida, Spain) also has a Na Sra de Domanova found by shepherd and lamb in a juniper bush.

223 *Rodez* Aveyron; 80 (2); Durand-Lefèbvre mentions N-D de Passer, a copy of N-D de Guadalupe brought from Spain in 1283; statue of local goddess Roth, Ruth or Rodu still in Cathedral; *Nostra* refers to BV which 'reigns over the mines'; city founded by Ruthenians 600/700 BC; patron St Amans; Cathédrale N-D 1277 contains tombs of Merovingian period, chapels of St Anne (formerly of John the Baptist), St Joseph (formerly St Michael) and St Catherine; Place de la Madeleine next to Ch. of St Amans; Ch. of N-D des Jubés (formerly Ste Madeleine); Ch. of Ste Germaine (formerly Ste Catherine); Ch. of St Pignes de St Blaise; nearby villages of Luc and Ste Radegonde (Mer.); no evidence of any BV on visit 4/8/81.

224 *Romay* Paray-le-Monial; Saône-et-Loire; 69 (17); in Ch. of Romay, open daily, N-D de Romay; 12 C.; stone polychrome; 60 cm; in first sanctuary built by the Benedictines of Cluny; cures children; quoted as BV by *Atlantis,* local authorities deny this. N-D de Romay venerated by Catholic esoteric school, Hiéron (1883-1918), who saw it as one of four spiritual centres along with Rome, Montmartre and Lourdes. Druidical oath taken at Romay.

225 Ronzières Puy-de-Dôme; 73 (14); SW of Issoire by D 32 and D 34; N-D de Ronzières (brambles); wood; 13 C.; 60 cm; original found by cattle 11 C.; healing BV with enigmatic gaze miraculously saved from destruction at Rev.; Mass under lime-tree 8 Sept.; fairy spring found by St

Baudime 3 C. who placed statue of Virgin in Chapel there; ox-hoof imprint on rock; girls wanting husband put their foot in it and offer daisies; Ch. of St John the Baptist formerly at foot of hill in Pré de Sabios; nearest village Vodable — valley of the Devil (Druids).

226 Roumégoux Tarn; 83 (1); 25 km SE of Albi on D 86, linking D 99 and N 112, 10 km NE of Réalmont; N-D de la Brune; 15 C.; 30 cm; standing; wood (gilt); found by sheep; original dark stone statue perhaps destroyed by Protestants 1568; in Parish Centre; 17 C. copy in Ch.; apply for key to house nearest Ch.; taken to Spain at Rev.; near zero meridian; Statue of Ste Germaine de Pibrac; pilgrimages in May and 8 Sept.; candles; when village of Fauch deserted the Sanctuary, two years of disastrous hail; young children favoured by BV.

227 Rumilly Haute-Savoie; 74 (5); 17 km W of Annecy by D 16; N-D de l'Aumône in Chapelle des Soeurs, 8 avenue de l'Aumône; 15 C., replacing original of 13 C.; 74 cm; lime-wood; standing; large hands; recently restored and repainted in flesh tints; replica of 1982 in Sanctuary of N-D; statue saved at Rev.; called BV in *N-D de l'Aumône* by R. Bouvet, Rumilly, 1982, and by R. Salvat, *N-D des Voirons,* Boëge, 1981; at confluence of rivers Chéran and Néphaz; site of temple to Fortunate Mercury; chapels to St Anne and St Nicholas; images of Sts Mary Magdalene, Maurice, James, John the Baptist, Joseph; chapels to Sts Margaret and Mary Magdalene near by.

228 St Béat Haute-Garonne; 86 (1); 21 km S of Montréjeau by D 125 and N 618; N-D de l' Espérance; 13 C.; blackened polychrome wood; St Béat 'the key to France' frontier citadel.

229 *St-Bertrand-de-Comminges* Haute-Garonne; 86 (1), 85 (20); Chapel of Ste Marie de Comminges in Cathedral; Priest says no BV (*Nostra* reports one); Roman city of Lugdunum Convenarum with 60,000 inhabitants, including Herod (see tomb), who was banished there according to Josephus after the beheading of John the Baptist, Salome, who drowned while crossing a frozen river, and Herodias who, naked and dishevelled, still, as queen of magicians, leads her covens to their Pyrenean sabbaths; Visigoths and Merovingians; crocodile and unicorn horn in Cathedral, gift of Pope Clement V (Bertrand de Goth); also woodcarvings of St Michael and sibyls; Cathedral N-D, on site of Temple of Abelio, built by St Bertrand, 11 C. member of family of Counts of Toulouse; freeing of captives.

230   St-Christophe-les-Gorges Cantal; 76 (1); 11 km SE of Pleaux by D 6; N-D du Château; BV brought back from Crusades by Raoul de Scorailles 1098; 80

cm; intentionally black from origin; in Ch. of lower of two castles (both D) on hill; pilgrims used to climb rock staircase on knees; wolf-heads carved in porch of neighbouring Ch. of St Martin Cantalès; key from Curé; regional pilgrimage 12 Aug.

231 *St Cirgues* Haute-Loire; 76 (5); 53 km NW of Le Puy by D 590 and D 585; 12 C.; 73 cm; now at Nancy (qv); St Cirgues birth-place of St Odilo 962-1048 (feast 1 Jan.) who instituted prayers for dead on All Souls' Day.

232 *St-Denis-de-Cabanne* Loire; 73 (8); 4 km NE of Charlieu (qv) by D 4; 1870; wood; replacing BV D at Rev.

233   *St-Etienne-du-Grès* Bouches-du-Rhône; 81 (11); N-D du Château 8 km E of Tarascon by N 99, then up track to S; BV now at **Tarascon** (qv) except on certain feast-days.

234 *St Flour* Cantal; 76 (4) (14); Saillens mentions BV formerly in Ch. of St Christine, N-D de Frédière, who cured children; N-D de Pesgros ('dangers' or 'big feet') now in Lyons museum; beautiful 12/13 C. black Christ, 'le Bon Dieu Noir', in Cathedral; statue of St Anne; virgin city never taken 'except by the wind' ('Le Bon Dieu de St Flou' fait hou hou hou') perched 881 metres above sea-level on plateau dotted with dolmens and menhirs; St Flour

(feast 3 Nov., day after All Souls) in legend son of one of Three Magi and youngest of 72 disciples.

235 **St-Genès-De-Lombaud** Lot-et-Garonne; 71 (1), 234 (3); 3 km S of Créon on D 20, 30 km SE of Bordeaux; N-D de Tout Espoir; walnut; 14 C. or earlier; saved at Rev. but mutilated; in pretty Romanesque Ch.; if closed ask Curé of Créon or Mayor of St Genès; Druidic cult near by.

236 **St Geniez d'Olt** Aveyron; 80 (4); N-D de Lenne, Romanesque BV.

237   St-Georges-Nigremont Creuse; 73 (11); 10 km SE of Felletin by D 10; new statue of BV, ancient Celtic Earth-Goddess, constructed according to ancient ritual formulas and worshipped with druidic rites in 1982 and 1983.

238   *St-Germain-des-Fosses* Allier; 73 (5); 9 km N of Vichy by D 258; Durand-Lefèbvre reports 15 C. pietà.

239 **St-Germain-Laval** Loire; 73 (17); N-D de Laval by R. Aix; standing; wood; 68 cm; 13 C.; in Ch. of Baffy, open daily in summer; BV brought back from Crusades by St Louis, visited by Louis XI 1470. Ch. of St Mary Magdalene in town has pietà; near by 12 C. Commandery of Verrières (Knights of Malta) and Goutte-Belin.

240 *St-Germain-Lembron* Puy-de-Dôme; 73 (15); 10 km S of Issoire; N-D de Chalus in 11 C. hill-top Ch. of Chalus on site of ancient fortress replacing ruined village Ch. of St Mary Magdalene; statue of St Roch; Curé says no BV.

241 **St Gervazy** Puy-de-Dôme; 76 (4); 6 km SW of St-Germain-Lembron by D 141; wood; 11 C.; 77 cm; stolen 1983; in interesting Ch.; exact replica in plastic from the workshops of the Louvre has replaced the original since Aug. 1983; eight standing stones called 'Grotte des Fées' or 'Cabane du Loup'.

242 **St Guiraud** Hérault; 83 (5); 7 km N of Clermont-l'Hérault by N 9 and D 130e; in village, to see apply to Sacristan; N-D de Consolation or N-D de la Noire; wood; possibly original BV of 950; 70 cm; saved from Protestants and at Rev.; near St Guilhem-le-Désert and uranium mines.

243 **St-Jean-Cap-Ferrat** Alpes-Maritimes; 84 (10), 195 (27); at St Hospice; Madone de St Hospice or La Vierge Noire; 5 metres; bronze; 16/17 C.; in cemetery overlooking sea; crowned BV and Child; protects fishermen; under the photograph of her in the tourist leaflet is a message dated 1961 in the handwriting of Jean Cocteau, citizen of honour of St Jean and Grand Master of the Prieuré de Sion, that begins 'There is a mysterious youth in the oldest stones of St Jean'.

244 **St-Julien-des-Chazes** Haute-Loire; 76 (6); 11 km SE of Langeac by D 585 and D 48; in 10 C. Ch. on banks of Allier; N-D des Chazes; 12 C. majesté; restored to natural colouring (still described as BV by Abbé Lespinasse 1965); Virgin has short hair and red cushion under feet; site of Ch. determined by throwing hammer (cf. **Orcival**). Abbey of Dames Noires founded by Charlemagne on opposite bank of river.

245 **Les-Saintes-Maries-de-la-Mer** Gard; 83 (19); no BV but statue of Sara the Egyptian 'who gave birth to the cult of Black Virgins' (*La France des Pélérinages*); legendary cradle of Christianity in France where Mary (wife of Clopas Alphaeus and aunt of Jesus, mother of James the Less and Joses), Mary Salome (mother of James the Greater of Compostela and John), Mary Magdalene, Martha, Lazarus and others arrived in a frail bark from Palestine without sails or oars at the ancient city of Ra or Ratis where Isis Pelagia, Artemis and Cybele were already worshipped in 4 C. BC (cf. also Gallic triple goddess, Matres). Relics of two Marys discovered in 1448, by René d'Anjou, King of Provence, who in the same year founded his Order of the Crescent; in 1449 he demolished the nave to open up the crypt; site first called Ste Marie de Ratis or N-D de la Mer; large stone in crypt,

L'Oreiller (pillow) des Saintes (altar of Juno), powdered and mixed with water bestowed fertility and healed eyes; main pilgrimage of Gypsies in Europe; Sara, until 1686 simply presented as the servant of the Marys, became black and a saint as a cult object in the crypt where the Gypsy women elect their queen; since 1935 Gypsies are permitted to dip Sara-la-Kali in sea; Stes Maries an important stage on the pilgrim route to Compostela.

246 **St-Martin-de-Vésubie** Alpes-Maritimes; 84 (19); Madone de Fenestre 13 km E of St Martin by D 94; at 1903 metres; N-D de Fenestre, Ste Marie de la Mer; 75 cm; cedar; 13 C.; in legend attr. to St Luke; brought by St Mary Magdalene to France; Templars took over shrine from Benedictines; 4 km from Italian frontier; BV carried up from St Martin first Sat. in July, remaining there until second Sun. in Sept.; otherwise in Friary Ch. of St Martin; dressed in rich garments and lace; polychrome since 1974 restoration; river flowing from sanctuary to St Martin called Madone de Fenestre (fenestre = window, opening on to heaven, fines Terrae — mountain frontiers, or deformation of ferestra = bier); Templars took refuge and died in their Ch. there during persecution; veneration of Sts Anne and Roch.

247 **St Nectaire** Puy-de-Dôme; 73 (14); N-D du Mont Cornador;

12 C.; polychrome statue of wood covered in pasted cloth, considered a BV in the Auvergne; home of warrior maiden Madeleine de St Nectaire; major druidic centre; impressive dolmens and menhirs (one Christianized); relics of one of three St Amadours (see **Rocamadour**), Bp of Auxerre.

248 *St Pardoux* Puy-de-Dôme; 73 (13); 13 km S of La Bourboule by D 922 and D 203; N-D de Natzy (large statue of 1850 on neighbouring hill where there is a pilgrimage on 1st Sun. in Aug.) Saillens may refer to earlier BV of which there is no information; St Anne patroness of St Pardoux, noted for freeing prisoners; local Priest says no BV; statue of 1880; wood; 40 cm; kept at St Pardoux; copy of N-D du Sacré-Coeur of Issoudun.

249 **St-Paul** Alpes-Maritimes; 84 (9), 195 (33); in treasury of parish Ch.; restored 17 C.; standing; BV of 13 C.; oriental appearance; Tintoretto of St Catherine of Alexandria. Temple of Cybele at nearby Vence.

250 St Quentin Creuse; 73 (11); 14 km S of Aubusson by D 982; N-D de Sous-Terre; standing; wood; 125 cm; 17 C., replacing BV D by protestants; in 11 C. crypt; local pilgrimage; dolmen and uranium mines.

251 *St Saturnin* Puy-de-Dôme; 73 (14); 20 km S of Clermont-Ferrand by N 9 and D 213 (twin

village of St Amant); Pietà; 15 C.; stone; painted; in circular crypt; 12 C. Ch. with octagonal tower; Curé says no BV; St Saturnin seat of the La Tour d'Auvergne family to which Catherine de Medicis belonged; in the castle ancient ornaments given by St Vincent de Paul; near-by Benedictine Abbey of Randol and Commandery of the Knights of St John at Olloix.

252 **St Savin** Hautes-Pyrénées; 85 (17), 234 (47); 3 km S of Argelès by D 101; BV of the Crusades; 12 C.; 40 cm, Syrian; possibly copy of N-D de Confession at Marseilles (Abbey of St Savin a dependence of St Victor de Marseille from 1080); the original, ancient Madonna of the Abbey Ch., now removed to museum because of 'the depredations of tourists'; heads of Sts Catherine and John the Baptist in museum; see also Virgin of the Long Thumb and Virgin of the Big Hand; window and holy water stoup of the untouchable cagots, who lived in the Mailhoc quarter; Feast of St Savin, 9 Oct., day after that of two reformed harlot saints, Thaïs and Pelagia the Penitent.

253 *Salers* Cantal; 76 (2); in Chapelle N-D de Lorette, near Château de la Jordanne, N-D de Lorette; D at Rev.; replaced 1813, not BV. 17 C. tapestry in Parish Ch. of St Matthew of the Adoration of the Magi in which all the characters are dark; there is also a polychrome stone Entombment of Christ given to the Ch. in 1495;

ancient Pietà on N front of Ch.; annual celebrations on Feast of Our Lady of Pity (Fri. before Christmas) instituted by Helme de Salers in thanksgiving for safe return from Crusades with St Louis. At festival for Nativity of the Virgin, 8 Sept., fountains ran with wine. Templar Commandery, staging house for Compostela, now a school, has interesting sculptures on vault including androgyne. St Bonnet-de-Salers has alchemist's tower. Croix du Bataillou commemorates site of battle between Attila and Roman General Aetius by R. Mars (near Anglards-de-Salers) where the rock Malsarte, with a Ch. St Eloi on it, contains hidden the statue of Mercury from Mauriac, and on which children unable to walk are placed for healing.

254 Sarrance Basses-Pyrénées; 85 (16); 16 km S of Oloron-Ste-Marie by N 134 to Spanish frontier at Somport and road to Compostela; N-D de Sarrance, de la Pierre or La Sarrasine; 40 cm; difficult to date; black stone; cattle; water; SD; found by bull swimming in river 8 C.; hidden from Protestants 1569 in mountain cave; saved at Rev.; the damaged arms and head have been replaced; Virgin bestows fertility. Pilgrimage put in care of Premonstratensians 1345 (now Betharram Fathers); two visits by Louis XI; Marguerite de Navarre wrote much of *Heptameron* there; Gen. Camou presented to BV a

Russian icon of the Mother of God from the ruins of Sebastopol; Priest neither confirms nor denies statue is BV.

255 Saugues Haute-Loire; 76 (16); 21 km S of Langeac on D 585; N-D de Saugues; 12 C.; polychrome; Curé says not a BV; Durand-Lefèbvre and Saillens say painted over. Torchlight procession of penitents Maundy Thursday since 1150; octagonal tower; cemetery; 15 C. pietà.

256 *Saulzet-le-Froid* Puy-de-Dôme; 73 (13); 18 km NE of Mont-Dore by N 89 and D 74; Saillens reports 12 C. wooden BV in private collection.

257 Saumur Maine-et-Loire; 64 (12); (1) N-D de Nantilly; 12 C.; heavily restored in polychrome; found by peasants in lentil-field (hence name) among ruins of pagan temple on site of Druid cemetery; converted into Ch. of St John the Baptist 2 C.; Ch. known as N-D de Nantilly since 848, Mother Ch. of Saumur; Benedictines; Louis XI enlarged it and gave chapel his own name; miraculous statue with Merovingian crown still object of considerable cult; requiem for dead of the year said on St Roch's Day, 16 Aug. (for apparent transposition of St Roch and St Blaise cf **Arfeuilles**); statue saved from Protestants and Rev.; Child stolen early 19 C., restored 1887, both figures dressed in red; unblackened 19 C.; epitaph of René d'Anjou for his nurse Tiphaine; Tree of Jesse; statue of St Mary Magdalene guillotined at Rev. in Saumur.

(2) N-D des Ardilliers in Ch. on S bank of Loire 1 km upstream has many BV features: sacred healing stream in Golden or King's Wood; monk Absalon escapes from destruction of his monastery in 848, hides in grotto with statue which is discovered by labourers 1454; SD; tiny pietà behind grille on altar; pilgrims of this very active cult include Louis XI and Pope John XXIII; centre run by Sisters of St Anne.

258 *Sauvagnat-Ste-Marthe* Puy-de-Dôme; 73 (14); 7 km N of Issoire by N 9 and D 23e; BV reported by Brétigny and Sérénac; saved miraculously from destruction; Curé has no knowledge of any BV.

259 *Séderon* Drôme; 81 (4); N-D de la Brune, whereabouts unknown; ruins of very ancient chapel on hill-top with round crypt of 6/7 C.; marked as N-D de la Brune on map; 200 metres, above gorge; next parish to N St. Côme (Cosmas and Damian). Pilgrimage to pray for rain on Ascension Day at altar — massive stone block — up to 35-40 years ago.

260 *Sées (Séez)* Orne; 60 (3); Durand-Lefèbvre reports N-D du Vivier as standing painted, blackened stone statue of 14 C.; *France des Pélérinages* names N-D des Champs as the main cult

object in the Cathedral; *Michelin* refers to a pretty 14 C. Virgin, N-D de Sées; Tourist Office says statue in central chapel of the ambulatory seems white. Also in Cathedral sculpture of the Invention of the Bodies of St Gervais and Protais. When revolutionary tried to use statues of Virgin and saints from façade to build house, it fell down twice.

261 *Serrigny* Côte d'Or; 69 (9), 70 (1); 7 km NE of Beaune by N 74 and D 20; N-D du Chemin; 14 C. Spanish style Virgin with Child on knees now in parish Ch. of Serrigny; 15 C. Virgin, now disappeared, replaced by modern reproduction. Priest says no BV. 11 C. Chapel of N-D du Chemin now restored; Saillens says BV whitened 1860; restored life to unbaptised babies, helped in childbirth and healed eye complaints; Aloxe-Corton vineyard near by.

262 *Serverette* Lozère; 76 (15); 42 km NW of Mende by N 106; BV reported to Saillens by Abbé Costecalde; next village S on N 106 St Amans.

263 *Sévérac* Aveyron; 80 (4); N-D de Lorette; Italian statue of 1648 in Ch. S of town; Bellas (Bellona?) hamlet to E.

264 Seyssel Ain and Haute-Savoie; 74 (5); N-D du Pont or du Rhône; 14 C.; BV, formerly in sanctuary, brought back from last Crusade by Comte de Seyssel; on bridge joining two sides of town separated by the Rhône, one in France, one in the ancient Duchy of Savoy; BV now in Ch.; saved at Rev.; consists of two heads on uncarved block of wood; statue of St Blaise, window of St François-de-Sales who visited the shrine. Sanctuary on bridge replaced in 1886 by 3.5 metres statue of 4000 kg; Seyssel noted for its white wines.

265 *Sigy* Seine-et-Marne; 61 (3), 237 (32); 14 km SW of Provins by D 403; N-D du Puy; copy of BV of Le Puy presented by Antoine de Roux 15 C., removed by a descendant 1477; present statue 17 C.; Ste Colombe and St Loup to the N, St Brice the other side of Provins. Curé denies past or present existence of BV at Sigy.

266 Sion-Vaudémont Meurthe-et-Moselle; 62 (4); 37 km S of Nancy by N 57, N 413 and D 58; 'La Colline Inspirée' of Maurice Barrès and chief pilgrimage of Lorraine, where France confronts Germany; twin peaks on a horseshoe plateau of the deities of war and peace, Wotan, and Rosmertha of the prominent breasts and the short hair. The name links Jerusalem with the Teutonic high god (Vaudémont = Mt of Wotan); from the Middle Ages to the Revolution a Black Virgin reigned (Huynen). St Gérard de Toul (who shares a feast-day with St George, 23 Apr.) placed a statue of a nursing Madonna, who became the patroness of Lorraine, on the site of the pagan shrine c.994; on 26 Dec. 1393 Ferry I de Vaudémont founded the order of chivalry of N-D de Sion there; his son Ferry II married Iolande, Grand Master of the Prieuré de Sion, daughter of René d'Anjou, and defeated Charles the Bold at Nancy under the banner (now disappeared) of N-D de Sion; Marguerite, Duchess of Lorraine, great-niece of another Grand Master of the Prieuré de Sion, Louis de Nevers/Gonzaga, devoted great interest to the old sacred site, installing a cross and establishing a religious house and school there; an earlier Lord of Vaudémont, Hugues III, pillaged his own Ch. of Sion, and was killed in 1246 at the siege of Lucera, another BV and bloodline site (see Italy); ancient BV hidden in Saxon at Rev., betrayed out of fear by Roger, put on cart to Vézelise; horses stop in Bois de Villars; Petitjean beats them, blasphemes, falls under wheels and dies; two policemen chop up statue (expiatory chapel later erected on site); 15 C. Vierge à l'Oiseau (the alerion of Godefroy de Bouillon?) from Vaudémont (Ch. of St John the Baptist) replaces BV of Sion 1817; mid-19 C. Baillard brothers establish new order, Frères de N-D de Sion — new age of Holy Spirit and Mary, free love, sexual sacraments, magic; House of Habsburg solicited for support; twin establishment at Mt St Odile (Alsace); late 19 C., bronze hermaphrodite excavated; votive stone to Mercury and Rosmertha in thanks for cure; Domrémy 30 km W (Joan of Arc important figure in Baillard's new cult). It is curious that Sion, the capital of the Valais in Switzerland, which has important Merovingian connections, including their royal mint, with its twin rocky citadels of Valère and Tourbillon, and its main square of La Planta (one of the names of the Plantard family) also has a village called Saxon near-by (18 km down the Rhône).

267 Soissons Aisne; 56 (4); 19 C. wooden copy of N-D de Liesse crowned 1857; Clovis defeated Romans at Soissons, Capital of Clotaire and Chilperic; Merovingian tombs at St Médard Abbey; Cathedral of St Gervais and Protais contains Rubens's *Adoration of the Shepherds*; Thomas à Becket spent nine years at Abbey of St-Jean-des-Vignes.

268 **Sommepy** Marne; 56 (8); in Parish Ch., open 8.30-18.00, modern original BV 1937; 90 cm; black wood; standing; replaced statue D in the Great War; won prize at Paris World Fair of 1937.

269 Soulac Gironde; 71 (16); N-D de la Fin des Terres; St Veronica and her husband, St Amadour (Zacchaeus — see **Rocamadour**), landed here on their missionary journey, and Veronica ('true image' or 'bearer of victory') died and was buried here; major staging-post on road to Compostela; many pilgrims include

Eleanor of Aquitaine and Louis XI (three times — 1453, 1472, 1473); BV D by Protestants 1622; 1659-1744 Ch. and town gradually covered by sand; 1860 restoration begun; modern polychrome N-D de la Fin des Terres (the end of the lands) blessed 1891; ex-votos and candles; spring; capitals of Daniel and St Peter, who escaped from captivity.

270 **Tarascon** Bouches-du-Rhône; 81 (11); N-D du Château, La Belle Briançonne or La Vénérade; ancient; 60 cm; larch-wood; standing; Child on right arm; polychrome traces; formerly at *St Etienne-du-Grès* (qv — annual procession); now kept by priest of Tarascon in the presbytery of Ste Marthe for fear of theft; may be visited for 40 days following the Sunday before Ascension Day; brought from Briançon in 1348 by the hermit Imbert, fleeing the Vaudois invasion. St Martha, sister of Mary Magdalene, came to Tarascon from Les Saintes Maries de la Mer and overcame a dragon (the tarasque); René d'Anjou, who lived in the castle of Tarascon where N-D du Château was venerated in the chapel, organised great festivities in honour of the miracle, which are still celebrated annually on the last Sunday in June; body of St Martha discovered 12 C.; tomb in crypt next to well, fed from Rhône; La Belle Briançonne perhaps originally goddess Dana (Brigantia — Brigid-Anna?).

271 **Tarascon-sur-Ariège** Ariège; 86 (4) (5); N-D du Sabart or de la Victoire; Renaissance; 100 cm; standing in prayer; no Child; only head and hands sculpted; SD; Chapel of Sabart traditionally founded by Charlemagne 788 on defeating Saracens 8 Sept. (Nativity of Our Lady) after being saved from ambush by apparition of luminous lady; bronze statue found where she had appeared. Ch. ruined by Albigensians, Protestants and Revolutionaries. Before the fall of Montségur the Cathar bishop En-Marti sent four Parfaits out of the castle through the enemy lines carrying the 'treasure' of the Cathars to the safety of the grottoes to the S. of Tarascon; many Cathar symbols at Lombrive (where there was another terrible massacre of Cathars), Ussat, Bethléem and Ornolac attest to the powerful presence of Albigensians in the area; ruins of Ch. of St Michael on hill; uranium mines of Sabart; always a town of smiths and forges; Mercus to N; statue crowned 1884.

272 *Tauxigny* Indre-et-Loire; 64 (15) 232 (r.h. end-fold); 36 km SE of Tours by N 143 and D 82; N-D de Lorette; copy of 1542 (see **Loreto,** Italy).

273 **Thuir** (**Tuir**) Pyrénées-Orientales; 86 (19); N-D de la Victoire; 50 cm; late 12 C.; lead — 4 statues from same mould, 2 went to Catalonia, 2 to Massif Central; devotion from 13 C. but

first mention of statue 1567; first mention of Ch. of St Peter 957; original statue perhaps 7 C.; brought Charlemagne victory against the Saracens, produced spring to quench thirst of his army; lost for a long time, then found by shepherd in search of lost sheep on present site; BV already known as N-D des Victoires with her feast on 7 Oct. before victory of Lepanto, 7 Oct. 1571; dipped in the sea at Le Canet 21 Apr. 1571 and on other occasions to end a drought; many healing miracles, and examples of assistance in childbirth produced by touching people with pieces of her silk robe; she also wards off lightning; devotion to Sts Anne, Catherine, Michael, Mary Magdalene, John and Isidore, Chapel of St Roch; hamlet of Ste Colombe (Ch. mentioned 974) 2 km S, St Joseph 5 km N; Jewish colony 14/15 C.; witchcraft and sorcery trials 17 C.; wine-cellars of Byrrh reputedly the biggest in the world.

274 Thuret Puy-de-Dôme; 73 (5); 10.5 km SW of Randan (qv) on D 210 to Riom (qv) between Vichy (qv) and Clermont (qv); Vierge des Croisades; 13 C.; similar to Cornas and Aurillac, all perhaps influenced by ancient BV of Le Puy; Abbé René Chabrillat priest of Thuret and author of local guide is reminded of Blanche of Castille and the young St Louis (Blanche, wife of Louis VII, important in proving descent of Pierre Plantard from Dagobert II);

Merovingian sarcophagus discovered 1962; chapel of former Benedictine priory 11 C.; Chabrillat calls it 'a church of initiates'; holy water stoup has sculpted horse biting its tail which he connects with the mare-goddess Epona; outside above the S door a statue of a juggler, holding a mirror while somersaulting, warns initiates not to enter there (now the only way) but by the N Portico which features a Dionysian figure with grapes; the capitals are unique in their artistry and symbolism, including masonic signs (rosy-cross, apron), the phallus, the phoenix, a chained ape that Chabrillat calls the Baphomet, the rehabilitation of woman, and Christianity triumphing over (completing?) the religions of light — Mithraism, Mazdaism, Druidism, the cult of Isis and the faith of Moses; link with Louis VIII who died of dysentery contracted while fighting the Cathars; stone on which the Merovingian sarcophagus reposed represents a wild boar with the hair on its spine erect (cf. special physical characteristic of Merovingian monarchs) which Chabrillat relates to Teutates, Celtic god of knowledge, poetry and eloquence, but which also symbolizes the *solitaire,* the Celtic contemplative hermit; other associations with Thuret include Pope Clement VI, who as a student took refuge from brigands, Lavoisier, the greatest chemist of 19 C., John Law, the inventor of paper money who was Lord of

Thuret and godfather of the great bell of the Ch., 1720, and Bénilde, France's most recent saint (1962); as we drove into the car park (7/12/80) I was reading to my wife from the *Guide de l'Auvergne Mystérieuse* the story of a carpenter charged at the Rev. with the task of taking down the spire. At his death a black cat was seen to sit for a long time on his shroud. Simultaneously we noticed a black cat sitting on a large box on the back seat of the car next to us. Thuret is that sort of place. Something of its enigmatic fascination is hinted at in two verses of a poem called 'Eglise de Thuret' by Dr Jacques Jaudel, May 1971:

De l'abside royale et qu'illumine Sion
Où je te cherchais, Rose ésotérique et sûre
Que grava par amour le ciseau de Maçon
En haut du chapiteau sur une face obscure!

Quelle onde enfermes-tu, fleur à quatre pétales,
Par laquelle éclairée Isis crea les voiles,
Et par qui fut donné le signe magistral
Au templier vaincu par le secret fatal.

275 Tocane-St-Apre Dordogne; 75 (4) (5); N-D de Perdux; in chapel N of town on banks of Dronne to left of bridge; standing; wooden; crowned; chocolate-coloured BV; *c.* 95 cm; of un-

certain age (Saillens says modern devotion); crusader of local Fayolle family promised Ch. to Virgin on safe return; found statue in ruins of old chapel actually in the Dronne; 19 C. Ch.; windows of 1890 include the Ark of the Covenant, Mystic Rose, Tower of David, Tower of Ivory (from Litany of Loreto) and Mary with Joachim and Anne saying to High Priest 'The Lord is my portion'; many ex-votos; important dolmens at Tocane until sleep-walker reported treasure there and they were destroyed; St Victor 7 km downstream on N bank; Mass and torchlight procession on 15 Aug. Priest has key to chapel. Parish Ch., consecrated on Feast of St Vincent de Paul, 1864, has window to John the Baptist, statue of St Anne teaching Mary to read and 17 C. statue of standing Virgin with naked Child on left arm in vestry (formerly in crypt — fear of theft). Nerval left unfinished novel 'Le Marquis de Fayolle'.

276 Toulon-sur-Allier Allier; 69 (14); 5 km S of Moulins on N 7; Ch. of N-D, formerly St Martin; Saillens includes Toulon in his *repertoire* though elsewhere in the text he says the BV of Toulon was called N-D de la Ronde, simply mentioning that it was drawn to his attention by M. Mitton. Parish priest (6/12/80) says there was never a BV there. 16 C. standing stone statue of rather ghostly Virgin holding Child's foot with small hand and 17 C. statue of Sts

Anne and Mary; Celtic statue of Great Mother found at Toulon according to Pierre Nancray (*Nostra* 31 Mar-7 Apr. 1983). BV confirmed by d'Arès.

277 **Toulouse** Haute-Garonne; 82 (8); (1) N-D la Noire or de la Daurade in Ch. of La Daurade; wood; only head and bust sculpted; 1806, replacing very different older gilt statue with black hands and face D at Rev. (1799); earliest BV was a statue of Athene (?) found when Consul Cepio drained a lake in 109 BC searching for the famous 'gold of Toulouse' taken from Delphi by the Gauls (Volskian Tectosages — tribe of Rennes-le-Château); statue installed in Temple of Pallas and Christianized by Galla Placidia 415; temple became chapel of Visigothic kings, then beautiful Ch. of La Daurade, centre of the poets and initiates of the Company of Gay Science who continued the troubadour tradition and held their *jocs florals* on 3 May in honour of the BV. One of the major pilgrimage centres of France, especially for pregnant women; Ch. D and replaced 18 C.; statue of Venus found; BV of **Solsona** (qv), Spain, may give impression of La Daurade.
(2) N-D du Palais or La Noire, dark stone, formerly in niche on Château Narbonnais (Palais de Justice) now on front of Jesuit Ch.; Churches of St John the Baptist, Vincent de Paul, Sylve, Jeanne d'Arc, Joseph, Roch, Margaret and Germaine who was born at Pibrac 11 km W; Ch. of la Madeleine 5 km E; St Sernin (Saturninus, 1st Bishop) martyred by a wild bull 216, commemorated in romanesque masterpiece of St Sernin Ch. and N-D du Taur (bull); home of the Dominican Order, 1216, after defeat of Cathars; tomb of St Thomas Aquinas.

278 *Tournon* Ardèche; 77 (1); Durand-Lefèbvre reports statue sculpted from oak of Montaigu (Belgium); Hermitage wines.

279 **Tournus** Saône-et-Loire; 69 (20); N-D la Brune; 12 C.; cedar; 73 cm; gilt; water; in 15 C. side-chapel of St Philibert (feast day 20 Aug. with Amadour and Bernard); Curé told Durand-Lefèbvre statue still black at beginning of 20 C.; large hands; Child holds closed book in left hand; Saillens mentions cult of St Maurice, black Captain of Theban Legion who can send troublesome and unwanted parents to the next world; Chapel of St Michael; St Valerian martyred at Tournus 179; Ch. of La Madeleine.

280 *Tours* Indre-et-Loire; 64 (15); Durand-Lefèbvre refers to N-D des Miracles 12 C.; wood; gift of Ste Monégonde (feast day same as the Visitation 2 Jul.) who founded St Pierre-le-Puellier under the patronage of Queen Clotilde (Mer.). Statue hidden in walnut-tree during barbarian invasions; saved at Rev.; given to Sisters of Charity 1833; Louis XI did much

for the city and died there (as did that other improbable lover of BVs, Anatole France) praying to his 'good mistress', N-D d' *Embrun* (qv). Tours, like Ephesus, has its Grotto of the Seven Sleepers. The city was bestowed on Mary Queen of Scots and her husband, the Dauphin.

281 *Trois-Epis* Haut-Rhin; 62 (18); N-D des Trois-Epis; 15 C. pietà; D at Rev; 1491 apparition of Virgin surrounded by light to a smith named Thierry Schoeré as he prayed before an image of the Virgin fixed to an oak; Saillens relates the cult to that of the Corn Mother common in Austria and Germany; Trois-Epis on the linguistic frontier.

282 **Tudet/Gaudonville** Gers; 82 (6); 8 km E of St Clar by D 167; in chapel of N-D de Tudet (= protection); 15/16 C. replacing original of 1152; black marble; standing; 47 cm; ox, fat without eating, gazes into spring where young herdsman finds BV; damaged at Rev.; partially restored 1963; oldest pilgrimage in Gascony. Gaudonville = Town of Rejoicing (not of Godons — English soldiers). Ask for key at white house next Ch. (Mme Marquet).

283 *Tursac* Dordogne; 75 (16) (17); 5.5 km N of Les Eyzies by D 706 turn rt up unsigned rd opposite village Ch. 2.5 km to old restored sanctuary of Fontpeyrine; Saillens describes N-D de

Fontpeyrine (= pilgrims' spring) as a stone BV; standing; 15 C.; without Child; with veiled head; cattle; SD. Drochon adds that the statue was found by a ploughman near a spring by a dolmen, and was perhaps a pagan divinity; it was badly mutilated at Rev., head cut off, forearms lost; cult restored 1845. Today the pilgrimage is clearly active and there are three white stone statues, one in the Ch., one behind a grille by the spring, and one large one looking down on Ch. from other side of rd; hotel proprietress said Fontpeyrine a healing shrine like Lourdes; no mention of BV.

284 Vacquières Bouches-du-Rhône; 81 (12); 3 km S of Noves (qv) by D 30B; N-D de Vacquières or des Oeufs; 19 C. bare wood statue of 40 cm replacing ancient image discovered by cattle D at Rev.; reported to have disappeared in 1920 but the Curé of Noves writes (Jan. 1984) that the BV can be seen in the chapel, of which Mlle Marvotte is the proprietor. Shrine behind grille has statuette of N-D de Lourdes and wall-painting of Virgin in red dress; well and spring reputed to heal fevers; no sign of active cult. Eggs offered to Hecate at crossroads by night.

285 *Valenciennes* Nord; 53 (4) (5); the destructions wrought by wars and revolution in this frontier city and the great devotion shown to many BVs there, including those of Halle, Tongres,

Walcourt, Cambrai, Le Puy and Liesse makes the situation somewhat complicated. The earliest BV, N-D de la Chaussée (from Roman road), du Puits (found in a well) or du Puy (from BV of Le Puy) was donated in 756 by Pepin the Short, father of Charlemagne, in his attempt to stamp out the worship of Mars at Famars, Jupiter on Mt Ovois and Isis on the heights of Anzin; this image survived with blackened face the flames of Protestantism in 1566; the churches in which she was venerated are now destroyed, but there was an old copy of her at Bon-Secours just into Belgium beyond Condé. N-D du St Cordon in the Ch. of that title who saved the city from the plague in 1008 by tying a red cord round the walls (cf. Jericho) is the patroness of Valenciennes and still the object of pilgrimages. Saillens says it has replaced N-D de la Chaussée. Christianity was brought to Valenciennes by St Piat and in 367 the first Ch. of N-D replaced the Temple of Vesta. St Bernard preached there. Poetry competitions in honour of N-D du Puy, whose main feast was Candlemas; traditional pilgrimage to Ch. of St Roch on the outskirts of the city Sun. following 16 Aug.; Faubourg Ste Catherine. Syndicat d'Initiative says no BV in Valenciennes.

286 Valfleury Loire; 73 (19); 10 km N of St Chamond by D 2; N-D de Valfleury, La Vierge au Genet d'Or (golden broom) or La Vieille Dame; early 12 C.; 67 cm; wood; original found in flowering broom bush at Christmas 800 (coronation of Charlemagne); Burgundy/Rhône majesté; Benedictine priory dependent on Chaise-Dieu 1052-1687; Mission of St Vincent de Paul takes over 27 years after his death; Virgin enthroned and crowned has apron on which child sits centrally between her knees, staring black and white eyes, two snarling beasts under feet and her right palm held out towards the sky; Child holds closed book in left hand, whole figure completely reconstructed in 1869; statue black in 19 C., now dark natural wood with some traces of polychrome.

287 Vassivière Puy-de-Dôme; 73 (13); 8 km SW of Besse-en-Chandesse by D 978 and D 149; present BV *c.* 1805 replaces ancient N-D de Vassivière, D at Rev., whose relics are no doubt enclosed in the sealed cavity in the back of the statue; it is reported to be a copy of the ancient BV but is crudely carved with peasant features in peasant garb, most unlike the famous majestés of the Auvergne; it summers at Vassivière between 2 July and 21 Sept. (processions), and spends the remainder of the year in the Ch. of St André at Besse where there is also a replica; a BV also reigns in the *chapelounne,* behind a grille by the healing spring, built in 1550 and restored in 1747 on the site of a BV in a niche of a wall of the old Ch. of Vassivière, still left standing after its mysterious destruction along with the village that supported it in the early 14 C. In 1321 Bernard de la Tour gave permission to the canons of Clermont to take the stones of the Ch. of Vassivière to build a Ch. at Condat 33 km S in Cantal. There is a strong tradition that after the dissolution of the Order in 1307 (finally suppressed 1312) a Templar group took refuge in the Grottes de Jonas 8.5 km NE of Besse, and there may be some connection now forever lost between these two events. In 1547 when the first wave of Protestantism was strong in the Auvergne a merchant from Besse, Pierre Gef, passing the BV of Vassivière with two companions, failed to pray before her image and was struck blind. On promising to become her 'King of Devotion' he was healed, and so began the widespread fame of the BV, one of whose specialities was restoring unbaptised babies to life. The coat of arms of Catherine de Medicis, who was the Lady of Vassivière, can still be seen in the Ch., and the association with the Royal Family may be one reason why the feast of St Louis is so important there. The suggested etymologies of Vassivière include 'place of cattle', 'vas-y veire' (go and see for yourself — the marvels) and 'Vas Iver' (temple of water) recalling a Celtic cult of springs. The BVs of Clermont, Vassivière and Orcival shared a father who was the King of the East, while the Virgins of Vassivière, Font-Sainte, Lastour and Egliseneuve d'Entraygues were four black sisters from the east asking their way to Mont Dore. The pilgrimage to Vassivière was commended by several Popes and became the 'Roumagna' of the Auvergne. The original chapel of the BV in the Ch. was dedicated to St Joseph. Living cult, many ex-votos and large numbers of pilgrims.

288 **Vauclair** Cantal; 76 (4); 4 km SW of Molompize on N 122; N-D de Vauclair; in Chapelle de Vauclair; 11/12 C. majesté; 73 cm; wood with tints of green and ochre; traditionally brought from Antioch (cf. **Madrid**) but almost certainly local work; Virgin has large hands; Child holds open book in left hand; miracles include healing of blind (Vauclair = *valle clara*, valley of light, on the other side of the *gouffre noir* — black gulf — from Molompize). Feast-day 8 Sept. Ancient goldmines to E at Bonnac; Ch. du Bru dedicated to Sts Anne and James to N; Mt St Victor (former Ch.) and Ch. of La Madeleine to NE of Molompize; Wild Hunt along English Way on Mt ridge across R. Alagnon.

289 *Velars-sur-Ouche* Côte d' Or; 66 (11); Ch. of N-D d'Etang or N-D des Tans 13 km W of Dijon by D 10f on opposite bank of Ouche from Velars; 11 cm stone polychrome statue of Virgin found by peasants digging 2 July (Visitation) 1434 on Mt Afrique where the grass was always green

and the oxen halted; SD; 1529 Bp of Bethlehem consecrates new Ch.; Condé brings banners from victory of Rocroi 1643. Çuré says it is not a BV.

290 Verdelais Gironde; 79 (2); 48 km SE of Bordeaux by D 10 and D 120 or by A 61 (Langon exit); N-D de Verdelais, Consolatrice des Affligés, formerly N-D du Luc (sacred wood) or N-D de Viridi-Luco (green wood); chestnut wood; 13/14 C.; Drochon describes her as wholly black and Durand-Lefèbvre gives her as a BV; she has now been unblackened; Rector of Basilica says he knows of no document or oral tradition that statue is BV; Child holds a woodpecker (Mars) and seems to have a prominent penis; major pilgrimage of the Bordelais, Landes and Bazadais since 10 C.; first known chapel 1105; BV saved from wars and Rev.; bestowes fertility — Countess of Foix asked for 4 sons, BV gave her 5; hidden in hollow oak 1558, found by ox 1605; at Rev. mayor tried to remove her, was blinded and fell off ladder; Toulouse-Lautrec's tomb in cemetery. Pilgrimage and Basilica in care of Marist Fathers since 1838.

291 Verdelot Seine-et-Marne; 237 (21); 15 km W of Montmirail on N 33 and D 15; N-D de Pitié; 12/13 C.; chestnut; 112 cm; Byzantine throne; from SW France. Priest says not a BV.

292 Verghéas Puy-de-Dôme; 73 (2); 10 km W of Auzances by D 4 A; N-D de Verghéas; 69 cm; boxwood; BV of Crusades; 1250; saved at Rev. and from fire; protects from thunder and hail and heals all types of infirmity, especially the deaf and the lame thanks to miraculous waters; stolen 1976; replaced by 1979 copy in lime-wood; not black. Exvotos removed 1966; living cult.

293 Vernay Loire; 73 (7); 7 km S of Roanne by D 43 and D 84; in Ch. of Vernay (now a suburb of Roanne) open daily; Vierge de Vernay; 13/14 C. (rare, late example of seated Virgin); Child holds fish; BV probably given to Ch. by Counts of Forez who gave others to St Germain-Laval, Feurs and Montbrison. Living cult, 1,500 pilgrims on 8 Sept. Statue of St Roch.

294 Vernols Cantal; 76 (3); 6 km W of Allanche (named for the hip of John the Baptist) by D 9 and D 409; BV now in Clermont museum; wolf guarded hermit's body on orders of crusader; monks built chapel on spot now Ch. of Vernols.

295 Vernouillet Allier; 69 (13); 1 km N of Bourbon-l'Archambault; N-D de Vernouillet; 12 C. Majesté now transferred to Bourbon-l'Archambault; the two next villages to the NW are called St Plaisir (holy pleasure) and Couleuvre (serpent); just E is the Bois des Vesvres (wouivres?).

296 *Vézelay* Yonne; 65 (15); Durand-Lefèbvre refers in the past tense to the much venerated statue of the Virgin blackened by fire (presumably the great fire of St Mary Magdalene's Eve, 1120, in which more than 1,000 pilgrims perished); no doubt the BV was destroyed by the Protestants who devastated the abbey and Ch. in 1569, though it was also partially razed at Rev. Greatest shrine of the Magdalen, along with St Maximin. St Bernard preached the Second Crusade there and Richard Coeur de Lion met with Philip Augustus there before leaving for the Third Crusade. Abbey founded 9 C. by Girart de Roussillon, hero of Chanson de Geste; consecrated 878 by Pope John VIII. St Francis of Assisi established his first priory of Friars Minor in France there. One of the main starting-points for Compostela.

297 Vichy Allier; 73 (5); N-D des Malades, in Ch. of St Blaise; standing; no Child; head saved at Rev. and attached to new statue; statues of Sts Anne, Blaise, John the Baptist, Christopher; mosaics in the baptistery of the Queen of Sheba and the baptism of Clovis; excavations reveal local cult of Isis, Cybele, Pallas Athene, Venus, Proserpine, Jupiter Sabazios and Vichiaco, personified *mana* of the sacred springs; healing waters the home of a white fairy who came from Varennes-sur-Allier (between Moulins and Vichy) where the waters had been polluted by a woman (perhaps the advent of Christianity); Celestine monastery established above cavern of the famous Vichy Célestins source; one spring (*source des acacias*) is noted for promoting beauty and fertility in women.

298 Villavard Loir-et-Cher; 64 (5) 238 (1); 1 km E of Montoire in little Ch. of N-D — ask for key; 75 cm; standing; Child on left arm; SD; mutilated at Rev., much restored 1860; found in a clump of hazel trees by peasants; attempts to build Ch. on site fail when day's construction demolished each night (cf. **Walsingham** England); removed to drier site 100 yards away; the revolutionary who tried to burn BV died miserably of gangrene a few days later and his wife preserved the statue; BV saved Seigneur de Lavardin from drowning in full armour in the Loir by stopping his charger (cf. **Myans**). 2.5 km from Villavard former Templar priory of St Jean des Aizes where Merovingian tombs have been discovered; La Madeleine — E part of Montoire; village of St Anne to W and St Amand to SW. Sts Roch, Blaise, Mary Magdalene, Catherine and Margaret venerated in the district. Curé says no BV.

299 Villedieu Cantal; 76 (14); 6 km S of *St Flour* (qv) by D 10; N-D de Villedieu in Ch. of N-D; SD; tiny ancient statuette encased in the stand of the gilt Virgin; found in a hedge by oxen late 11 C.; taken to St Flour several times and returned; holy well; statues of St Anne and of St Michael and the Devil; village created by Templars; menhirs and dolmens near by.

300 *Villefranche-de-Conflent* Pyrénées-Orientales; 86 (17); 6 km SE of Prades on zero meridian of Paris; N-D de Vie or de Bon Succès, reported as a BV by Durand-Lefèbvre, is a polychrome statue of 1715 by the sculptor Sunyer; but there is also a 17 C. standing statue of a very dark-faced gilt standing Virgin without Child from the Ch. of Sant-Pere de la Roca which could certainly be considered a BV. The Ch. at St Pere is now dedicated to N-D de Vie and the natural grotto above the Ch. is called the Cova de la Madeleine. The Ch. of Villefranche also contains a 14 C. Virgin and child, another later Virgin, St Joseph of Arimathea and great iron wheels for candles. Most interestingly there is a special devotion to the relics of St Sulpice (see **Paris 3** — zero meridian) the Bishop of Bourges (zero meridian). Painting of St Isabel of Portugal, falsely suspected by husband, whose alms turned to roses (same story told at Rochefort near Orcival of Catherine of Bourbon). The Conflent is the confluence of the Têt, the Rotja and, down the Gorge de St Vincent, the Cady into which the Ours has already flowed; frontier bastion since the 11 C., completed by Vauban, Louis XVI and Napoleon III.

301 Villeneuve-sur-Lot Lot-et-Garonne; 79 (5); N-D de Liesse, de Gauch (joy) de Toute Joie et de Toute Grâce, now generally known as N-D du Bout du Pont, in Chapel of N-D du Bout du Pont (open daily 9a.m.-7p.m.); 40 cm; wood; possibly 17 C.; original venerated since 1289. Found in the R. Lot by a sailor who dived in to discover why his boat would not move. Many ex-votos, living cult. Ch. a dependency of the Parish of St Catherine, built 1642.

302 *Villiers-en-Désoeuvre* Eure; 237 (15) 55 (17) (18); on borders of Normandy and Ile-de-France 11 km NE of Ivry-la-Bataille by D 836 and D 148; brown Virgin blackened in 1930 without the priest's knowledge; standing; 60 cm; Chapel of St Louis in wood near by is object of great veneration; St Chéron next village to N.

GERMANY

Most Black Virgins in Germany are copies of Our Lady of Altötting. Many of the rest are copies of Our Lady of Loreto, though these may be original works of art by local sculptors simply inspired by devotion to the Italian Madonna, and not always black. Others are of Our Lady of Einsiedeln and other famous icons.

G1 Aachen North-Rhine-Westphalia; 987 (23) 203 (11); in Ch. of St Foillan (open weekdays 8.30-1, 3-7, parish office Ursulinerstrasse 1, 5100 Aachen)

Schwarze Madonna von Brünn; copy of painting in Brno, Czechoslovakia, 83.5 cm by 47.5 cm, on canvas, brought to Aachen in 17 C. by Augustinians; formerly in their parish Ch. of St Catherine; crowned 1736. From the Middle Ages there were close links between Aachen and the eastern parts of the Austro-Hungarian Empire, Bohemia, Moravia, Silesia and Hungary. Aachen, city of Our Lady, was from the time of Charlemagne until mid-16 C., capital of the Holy Roman Empire, and witnessed the crowning of 37 German Emperors. It still preserves the cloak of the Virgin for which Charlemagne built his chapel (Aix-la-Chapelle). Another precious relic, the Veil of the Virgin, was sent to Chartres in 876. As well as the Marienschrein, containing the sacred cloak, the Cathedral Treasury preserves the blue chasuble worn by St Bernard when he preached in Aachen in 1147. His statue is in the chapel of St Nicholas in the Cathedral along with a statue of the Virgin which used to be on the High Altar, replacing an older one c.1300. Chapels of Sts Anne and Michael. In Schnüttgen Museum of Christian Art, 2 BVs; 13 C.; and one black and white

G2 **Altötting** Bavaria; 987 (37); 93 km E of Munich by N12; in Heilige Kapelle (open daily 5.30a.m.-8p.m.); Unsere Liebe Frau von Altötting; c.1330; 65 cm; lime-wood; standing; Child on right arm; oldest and most important pilgrimage in Bavaria. Roman cross-roads settlement in 15BC. Temple Christianized by St Rupert 680, where the inner, Gnadenkapelle, the Heart of Bavaria, now stands with its candles, ex-votos and, on its altar, the BV.

G3 **Cologne/Köln** 987 (23) (24). (1) In Ch. of St Kolumba (corner of Kolumba and Brückenstrasse); Madonna in der Trümmern (ruins); stone; 1460-80 of Cologne school; 165 cm; standing; Child in right hand; above High Altar. Ch. totally destroyed in Second World War; after the worst raid all that was left standing was one pillar upon which stood the Virgin, hardly damaged, though the Child lost head and limbs. Interesting statue of St Anne, c.1500 with Mary and Jesus on her knees.
(2) In Ch. of St Maria in der Kupfergasse; Schwarze Mutter Gottes; standing; Child on left arm; brought to Cologne in 1630 by 6 Dutch Carmelite nuns seeking refuge from the Thirty Years War. Chapel of BV consecrated 1675; Ch. of St Joseph built above Gnadenkapelle 1715; BV crowned 1925. Total destruction of Ch. in air-raid of 31 May 1942. BV saved, returned to Gnadenkapelle 1948. Rebuilding of entire Ch. begun 1952.
(3) Two paintings of BVs in Andreas Kirche (Dominican), burial-place of St Albert the Great.

G4 **Freising** Bavaria; 987 (3);

in Diocesan Museum of Cathedral; Freisinger Lukasbild (painting by St Luke); early 13 C.; gift from Byzantine Emperor to Duke of Milan in late 14 C., in Freising in 1440; 27.8 cm by 21.5 cm; painted on lime-wood; restoration of 1964 revealed older painting of same type underneath (visible on x-ray).

G5 *Friedrichshafen* Baden-Württemberg; 987 (35) (36); BV reported by Saillens. No local confirmation.

G6 Gemünden-am-Main/Schönau Bavaria; 987 (25); 39 km NNW of Würzburg. In Minoritenkloster, Schönau; copy of BV of Altötting; 67 cm; wood; 1729; behind High Altar in choir of Monks.

G7 *Hamburg* 987 (5); Museum für Völkerkunde; charming, seated African BV admonishing tonsured, priest-like Child, dressed in black. Angolan; acquired 1914 from Congo estuary.

G8 *Hildesheim* Lower Saxony; 987 (15); Saillens reports a BV, and an old photograph of the Goldene Madonna in the Domschatzkammer, prior to the restoration of 1968 shows her to be very dark. The custodian of the Diocesan Museum simply states that the Golden Madonna does not have a black face. Lime-wood; 1007; after the Golden Madonna of Essen (where the Child has one black hand), it is the oldest statue of the Virgin in Germany, and possibly in the world. An example of a golden BV is to be found at Salamanca.

G9 **Hirschberg/Leutershausen** Baden-Württemberg; 204 (8) 987 (25); on the Bergstrasse 15 km N of Heidelberg; in Ch. of St Johannes, Vordergasse (open daily 8.30-6); Schwarze Madonna von Leutershausen; 1742 or earlier; 150 cm; wood; only faces and hands carved; placed in Chapel of Loreto, built 1742; new Catholic Ch. built 1905-7; window of St Anne.

G10 *Kevelaer* North-Rhine-Westphalia; 987 (13) 202 (4); between Nijmegen and Krefeld near Dutch frontier. BV reported by Saillens, denied by local authorities. ULF (Our Dear Lady) of Luxemburg, Consolatrix Afflictorum; yellowing paper picture; 7 cm by 10 cm; printed from a copper-plate in Antwerp 1640. On 13 Feb. 1642 Hendrick Busman, a pedlar, was passing a wayside shrine near Kevelaer when a voice said, 'Build a little chapel for me here.' Within the next fortnight he heard the same message in the same place on two occasions and gradually saved 100 guilders necessary for the chapel. His wife, Mechel, then had a vision of a picture of Our Lady of Luxembourg which two soldiers had tried to sell her, but had asked too much money. Mechel eventually succeeded in buying the picture which Hendrick stuck on a board and placed in the wayside shrine. From these humble beginnings Kevelaer became the major shrine in NW Germany, and the little shrine is still at the heart of the hexagonal Gnadenkapelle. With Lourdes and Altötting, Kevelaer has been since 1949 one of the three European shrines dedicated to Our Lady Queen of Peace. The BV of Avioth has sometimes been called N-D de Luxembourg, but the image of Kevelaer is copied from that of the Virgin 'in agro suburbano Luxemburgi'. The basilica of St Mary contains images of Sts Anne, Bernard, Blaise, Brigid, Cosmas and Damian, Eligius, Mary of Egypt and her fellow repentant harlots Pelagia and Thaïs, as well as Moses and the Burning Bush.

Ludwigshafen See **Oggersheim.**

G11 Mariaeck Eisenarzt-über-Traunstein, Siegsdorf; 987 (37) (38); 36 km W of Salzburg on autobahn. Copy of Salus Populi Romani in S. Maria Maggiore, Rome.

G12 **Neuerburg** 987 (23); 29 km W of Bitburg; Schwarzbildchen. 17 C.?; 46 cm; reported to be replica of Altötting BV; kept in oak-tree until 1984; now moved to Pfarramt (presbytery) and replaced by copy. Kuno von Falkenstein, a suitor of the beautiful Burgfräulein of Neuerburg, was attacked by jealous rivals and saved by a vision of the Virgin

pointing to a hollow oak, where he hid. In gratitude for his rescue, he placed the BV in the tree.

G13 *Nuremberg/Nürnberg* Bavaria; 987 (25); BV reported by Saillens. German National Museum has no knowledge of any BV as cult object in the city or surroundings, though acknowledging there are many copies of Our Lady of Altötting in both churches and museums.

G14 **Neukirchen-beim-Heiligen-Blut** (Holy Blood) Bavaria; 987 (27) (28); near Czech frontier 30 km E of Cham. BV; *c.* 1400; Bohemian; standing; 78 cm; Child on left arm; on high altar; many robes include one of gold velvet; attr. to St Luke by Lechner. A host was found in a tree stump in Lautschim across the border in Bohemia *c.*1400 and a chapel erected on the spot. The cult of the BV, which was placed there, largely superseded that of the host. Susan Halada rescued it from the Hussites at Martinmas 1419, took it to Bavaria and hid it in a hollow linden-tree. A Hussite called Krema in 1450 hurled it three times into a spring (near the right-hand altar of the present church). Each time it returned to its place. Finally he split its head with his sabre. Blood spurted out and Krema was rooted to the spot (cf. **Czestochowa,** Poland). He tore the four shoes from his horse's hooves in a vain attempt to break the spell. Finally he repented, renounced the Hussite creed, and became a faithful pilgrim of the BV. Ch. of St Anne near by.

G15 *Offenburg* Baden-Württemberg; 987 (34); BV reported by Saillens, denied by local authorities.

G16 **Oggersheim-Ludwigshafen** Rhineland-Palatinate; 987 (25) 204 (8); in Kapellegasse, Minorite pilgrimage Ch. of Maria Himmelfahrt, 1777, containing older Gnadenkapelle of 1729; Loretto Madonna or Gnadenmutter (mother of grace); 1729; 96 cm; wood; standing; Child on left-hand side; living cult; ex-votos. BV inspired by Our Lady of Loreto, but not a copy, carved by Paul Egell of Mannheim. Cult of St Elizabeth. Franciscan Convent in Oggersheim since 13 C. D with much else during Thirty Years War.

G17 **Regensburg** Bavaria; 987 (27); in Stiftskirche von Lieben Frau zur Alten Kapelle; Gnadenbild; 73 cm by 44 cm; painting attr. to St Luke; given to Emperor Henry II by Pope Benedict VIII in Rome 14 Feb. 1013; Henry gave it to the Stiftskirche 21 June 1014; silver and copper-gilt frame added 1752. No copies made until 1810 under the Napoleonic occupation when the original was removed until 1864. Its removal caused great unhappiness.

G18 *Singen* Baden-Würtemberg; 987 (35); near Swiss frontier; BV reported by Saillens, denied by local authorities.

G19 *Würzburg* Bavaria; 987 (25); BV reported by Saillens and Lechner, denied by director of tourism.

GREECE

The question as to which of the many dark icons in the Orthodox world are to be considered as BVs is beyond the scope of this book. Since the Catholic BV icons are Byzantine in origin, it seems worth indicating some in Greece that are mentioned as potential BVs.

Athens Byzantine Museum No T 388 Panaghia Galactotrophoussa, by Makarios the Monk, 1784. Painting of very dark, crowned Virgin in red dress suckling very dark Child at right breast (also dark).

Mt Athos Icon in Monastery of Dochiarou of totally Black Virgin and Child on left knee, holding key in left hand, blessing with right.

Salonika Basilica built 470 to house miraculous icon of the Virgin Hodegitria (Guide), painted by angels, *acheiropoieton* (not made by hand), model for various BV icons in the west. Saillens mentions mosaics in Ch. of St George black like negatives.

Tenos BV attr. to St Luke reported by Moss and Cappannari. Discovered 1822.

HUNGARY

Szekes-Fejervar (Alba Regia). In 1038 King Stephen, who had been crowned by Pope Sylvester II, declared the Virgin Queen and Patroness of Hungary, the first monarch so to dedicate his country. Szekes Fejervar (white see) where the Kings of Hungary were crowned was still named as the national shrine of the Magyars in 1629, and there is evidence of the presence of a famous BV at Bannonhalba near by. The Abbey no longer functions, and the BV has been gone 'for a long time' — possibly as early as the 17 C. According to one report it was taken to Czestochowa. When Hungary lost her monarch at the end of the Great War, the Government declared the Virgin Mary protectress of the nation. Hungarian stamps showed her holding Stephen's iron crown in her hands.

IRELAND

Dublin In the Carmelite Church in Whitefriar Street, in a pilastered niche above the High Altar, the Black Madonna, or Our Lady of Dublin, standing dark oak statue of the Virgin, with Child on left arm holding a pomegranate in his right hand; late 15 C. or early 16 C., possibly carved by student of Dürer for the Cistercian Church

of St Mary on the N side of the Liffey. During the Reformation the statue was partially burned, rescued, buried and used as a hog-trough according to popular belief. It is almost certain that the statue was venerated from 1700 to 1816 in the Jesuit Chapel in St Mary's Lane. It was then discarded at the construction of a new church and was bought from a second-hand shop in Capel Street in 1824 by a Carmelite priest, Fr John Spratt, who had it repaired and donated it to the renewed Carmelite Church built in 1827 on the site of the original 13 C. foundation. The fine gold crown of the statue is probably that used in the coronation ceremony of Lambert Simnel *c.* 1487, itself borrowed for the occasion from the statue of the Virgin in the Church of Santa Maria del Dam at the Damask Gate. The church is popular for weddings and the Black Madonna the object of a living and enthusiastic cult.

ITALY

There are almost certainly many more BVs in Italy than those enumerated here, and, quite possibly, some of those included are not BVs. I had relatively few replies from Italy to the questionnaires I sent out, and some of the responses were ambiguous. Furthermore, most Italian BVs are paintings rather than statues, and more difficult to assess.

I.1 *Anzio* Roma; 988 (26). Private report that there is a BV at the Ch. of Divino Amore, exposed annually with two other BVs, one from Sicily, one from N Italy.

I.2 *Bari* 988 (29). Moss and Cappannari report BV at Bari attr. to St Luke and note that Bari was the major seaport linking Italy with the Levant and abounds with Black Madonnas.

I.3 *Cagliari* Sardina; 988 (33); BV of St Eusebius (4 C.) reported by Mario Trompetto (see **Oropa**). Papal Bull of Pius XII, 24 Mar. 1957, confirms all three statues brought back from the Holy Land by St Eusebius *c.*345 were, according to tradition, black.

I.4 Collecchio Parma; 988 (14); BV of the Cappellina (wayside shrine) in the Strada Mulattiera, an ancient maestà, has now been replaced by a conventional Madonna. A gesso statue of the Madonna della Neve was exposed in front of the old town hall during the cholera epidemic of 1836, but has now disappeared. There is still an Oratory of the Blessed Virgin of Loreto (1709). St Anne — feast still celebrated in the vicinity. St Michael — medieval oratory at Aqualatula now D. St John the Baptist — bas-relief of 13 C. in Ch. St Blaise venerated at Talignano. St Roch — painting in Ch. of Madregolo. St Mary Magdalene — former oratory at Collecchio.

I.5 **Crotone** Cantanzaro; 988 (39) (40); on promontory of Capocolonna, 12 km from Crotone overlooking the Gulf of Taranto, where there was once a Temple of Hera Lacinia, protectress of women in childbirth, is the sanctuary of the Madonna di Capocolonna. It contains a copy of the painting attr. to St Luke, but probably early 13 C., the original of which is in the Cathedral of Crotone. The silver, gold and jewels adorning the painting were stolen in 1983. The standing Madonna is offering her right breast to the Child. The painting still shows signs of scorching from the flames of the Saracens which it miraculously survived. In the festivals of the 2nd and 3rd weeks in May the BV is carried from the cathedral to the sanctuary, returning at night by sea in a procession of torchlit fishing-boats.

I.6 *Custonaci* Trapani, Sicily; 988 (35); BV attr. to St Luke reported by Moss and Cappannari. In nearby Erice stood the great Temple of Venus and, possibly, Klingsor's castle, Kalot Enbolot.

I.7 Farfa 6 km from Fara in Sabina; 988 (26); in Benedictine Abbey, Madonna di Farfa; fragmentary 14 C. copy of original painting attr. to St Luke brought to Italy in 7 C. by St Thomas of Morienna; all that remains are four heads of the Virgin, Child and two angels. John the Baptist is the co-patron of Farfa. The goddess Vacuna was worshipped there. The present image is black, but in a MS of the 12 C. it appears normal.

I.8 Florence/Firenze 988 (15). (1) 16/17 C. copy of BV of Loreto with the Benedictines of the Via S. Marta.
(2) 13 C. image of Virgin and Child near the Ch. of S. Stefano al Ponte (by the Ponte Vecchio); blackened by age and elements.

I.9 Grizzana Bologna; 988 (14); 15 km SSW of Bologna; BV reported by Mr Robert Rietty.

I.10 Loreto Ancona; 988 (16); 31 km SE of Ancona. One of the most famous pilgrimage resorts in the world: the Holy House of Mary (Santa Casa) was transported from Nazareth by angels to a site near Rijeka in Istria in 1291 and then on to Italy in 1294 near a laurel grove (*loreto*), settling for the third and last time on its present site. The house first discovered by Dalmatian woodcutters in a field on the hill of Trsat, where there had been no building the evening before, contained a Greek cross on an ancient altar, a fireplace, a cupboard and a strange statue of a lady. The Governor of Dalmatia, Croatia and Illyria, Nicholas Frangipani, an important figure, sent three men to Nazareth who found that the Holy House, with exactly the same dimensions and contents and built of the same materials as the one at Tsrat, had indeed disappeared to the amazement of the

Moslems who had just taken the town and become masters of the Holy Land. The statue was accidentally destroyed by fire and replaced by a new standing figure, 3ft high, carved from the wood of a cedar grown in the Vatican. This happened in 1921, the year an image was placed in the Guilds Chapel at Walsingham, England's Nazareth, where a Holy House was built in 1061. St Louis heard Mass in the House at Nazareth in 1253, and the murals commemorating this event were on the walls of the Santa Casa after its miraculous flight. No BV has been more copied throughout the world. Richard Crashaw was a Canon of Loreto where he died in 1649. Loreto is a favourite place to be married and a pilgrimage for newly-weds.

I.11 Lucera Apulia; 988 (28); 18 km W of Foggia. Moss and Cappannari's interest in BVs began in 1944 when Leonard Moss, as a young soldier, wandered into a Ch. in Lucera and noticed in a niche adjacent to the altar a representation of the Virgin with black face and hands. He asked the priest why, and was told, 'My son, she is black because she is black.' The statue of S. Maria, protectress of the city, probably arrived at Lucera from Byzantium during the iconoclastic period. The Madonna, having healed many victims of the cholera epidemic of 1837, miraculously turned white and moved its eyes, since when, according to the

Mayor, it is no longer referred to as a Madonna Nera. Diomedes, a King of Etolia, journeyed to the Temple of Minerva at Lucera in the 10 C. BC according to legend, and built a temple to Ceres there. The goddesses changed their names under Phoenicians and Greeks and during the period of Roman colonization (from 318 BC) the cult of Isis was introduced. St Peter traditionally visited Lucera in AD 42 en route to Rome and installed Basso as bishop. The latter built a church on the site of the Temple of Ceres, dedicated to the Madonna della Spiga (wheatsheaf). Frederick II of Hohenstaufen installed the Saracens at Lucera and let them build a mosque on the same site. The BV is credited with the liberation of Lucera from the Moslems by Charles II of Anjou (ancestor of René d'Anjou) who built the Cathedral of S. Francesco on the site of the mosque and is buried there.

I.12 **Manfredonia/Siponto**
988 (28); 39 km NE of Foggia; in Cathedral of S. Lorenzo and now, also, of Pope John XXIII; la Sipontina or the Madonna dagli occhi sbarrati (staring eyes); wooden statue; late 11 C.; almost life-size; enthroned; Child held centrally; both figures have brown faces; in the crypt, where there is also an altar of the goddess Diana. In the upper church is the painting of the Madonna of Siponto. which after restoration has been found to be much more ancient than the 13 C.

as previously thought and is probably early Byzantine; painted on cedar-wood; 129 cm by 81 cm; crowned by Cardinal Roncalli (later Pope John XXIII) in 1955. Both images were formerly in the Basilica of S. Maria Maggiore in Siponto (3 km). Manfredonia is named after King Manfred, son of Frederick II (see **Lucera**) and the town became a stronghold of the House of Anjou. Monte Sant' Angelo where St Michael, Captain of the Heavenly Host appeared to some shepherds in a cave in 491 is 15 km NE. Part of the archangel's red cloak was taken to Mt St Michel (qv, France) by St Aubert. It is part of the rocky promontory of the Gargano, whose name sounds like a devouring throat. SW of Manfredonia flows the River Candelaro. Street of the Templars in Siponto.

I.13 *Messina* Sicily; 988 (37) (38); BV reported by Moss and Cappanari and Lechner.

I.14 *Milan(o)* 988 (3); BV reported by Saillens.

I.15 *Milazzo* Sicily; 988 (37); BV reported by Saillens. Port for Vulcano.

I.16 *Millesimo* 988 (12); 20 km NW of Savona on Turin/Genoa motorway; Durand-Lefèbvre reports 17 C. blackened painting of Nostra Signora del Deserto.

I.17 *Casale Monferrato* Alessandria; 988 (12); 23 km S of Vercelli; in Santuario di Crea 4 1/2 km SW; Durand-Lefèbvre reports cedar-wood statue, Nostra Signora di Crea; 70 cm; long olive-brown face of oriental type and proportions; attr. to St Luke; one of 3 BVs brought back to Italy by St Eusebius from the Holy Land c.345, the other two being at Oropa (qv) and Cagliari (qv). Good area for wine and grappa, Gonzaga stronghold (Prieuré).

I.18 *Montenero*   Livorno/ Leghorn; 988 (14); 8 km S of Leghorn; in Santuario di Montenero, La Madonna di Montenero, Mother of All Graces, Patroness of Tuscany. On 15 May 1345 the altar painting of the Madonna from the island of Euboea (Greece) appeared miraculously at a crossroads at the foot of Montenero. It was found by a shepherd who carried it up the hill until it became too heavy. On that spot the Sanctuary was built. Since the recent restoration, the painting no longer looks dark, and the Benedictines of Vallombrosa who are the custodians say she never was a BV, but a beautiful painting of the school of Giotto. The Madonna has a goldfinch perching on her left wrist. There is a magnificent collection of naive ex-voto paintings thanking the Virgin for miracles. Durand-Lefèbvre ranks her as a BV.

I.19 **Montevergine**   Avellino; 988 (27)(28); 56 km E of Naples.

In Santuario di Montevergine, Benedictine Abbey open 6a.m.- 8p.m.; Madonna di Montevergine, di Constantinopoli, Madonna Bruna or Mamma Schiavona (Slav); very large painting on pinewood; 460 cm by 230 cm by 6.4 cm; of the Hodegitria type; c. 1290; probably by Roman painter Pietro Cavallini, though Moss and Cappannari describe La Madonna di Constantinopoli as a portrait in two parts, the bust in brown wood by Montano d'Arezzo, 1340, the painted head, the work of St Luke in Antioch, brought from Constantinople by Catherine of Valois, wife of Philip of Anjou. Dom Giovanni Monzelli OSB of the Abbey dismisses this claim as pure legend, as he does the tradition that the present shrine is built on the site of a temple to Cybele (Moss and Cappannari say Ceres). Christianity, however, was probably established late on the mountain, since William of Vercelli dedicated it to the Virgin in 1119. There is another, older icon in the Abbey museum, c.1180, of the Galaktotrophoussa (suckling) type. The Abbey was visited by Swinburne, who noted the image's gigantic proportions and commented on so-called Virgins of St Luke: 'There are in Italy and elsewhere some dozens of black, ugly Madonnas, which all pass for the work of his hands.' Chapel of St Michael in the Basilica, cult of St Roch in the countryside at the foot of the Mt and of St John the Baptist in Mercogliano, where there is a Ch. dedicated to him.

I.20 **Naples** 988 (27); In Basilica-Santuario del Carmine Maggiore, open daily; La Madonna Bruna; 12 C.; on wood; 100 cm by 80 cm; many miracles; living cult. The Anjou dynasty was established in Naples in 1303 and René d'Anjou was titular King.

I.21 **Oropa** Biella; 988 (2) 26 (15); 11 km and 750 metres above Biella by N 144 at 1200 metres above sea level, the sanctuary comprises a vast complex of buildings; BV, La Madonna di Oropa; statue of 132 cm; carved in resinous wood (cedar?); faces and hands coloured black; standing; Child on left arm holds dove in his left hand, evoking the ceremony of the Purification and Presentation (Candlemas); attr. to St Luke; statue ancient but shows no sign of age; traditionally brought from the Holy Land by St Eusebius of Vercelli *c*.345 (he brought 2 other statues, one for the Sanctuary of Crea near Monferrato, one for his birth-place, Cagliari). Mario Trompetto supports the traditional origin of cult and statue. The oldest extant building is the Cappella del Sasso or del Roc, by a stone bridge, built by the inhabitants of Fontanamora *c*.700. Inscribed on the rock which forms the chapel's foundations is the date, 369. Eusebius would have placed the statue there to counter the pagan traditions of site — the woods were sacred to Apollo and the waters and rocks to the Celtic Mothers. BV in 13 C.

Basilica on High Altar; windows to Sts Mary Magdalene and Michael; Galleries of Sts Anne, Mary Magdalene and Joachim; fountain in centre of square; BV invoked against pestilence and drought; many miracles; Biella and its surrounding districts suffered no damage during Second World War. St Anne appeared to a Cistercian nun on 25/26 July (Feast of St Anne) 1620, telling her it was pleasing to heaven that the statue should be crowned and it has now had four coronations, 1620, 1720, 1820 and 1920. The House of Savoy has always had a great devotion to Our Lady of Oropa.

I.22 *Orvieto* 988 (25); in Cathedral, oral report, unconfirmed, of BV by Lorenzo Maitani; 1325/30; imitated from French style of 1235/40.

I.23 **Padua/Padova** 988 (5); in Basilica del Santo (Anthony of Padua) in Chapel on N side of High Altar close to Shrine of St Anthony, whose tomb was originally in the Chapel of the Madonna Mora, (1) La Madonna Mora; ascribed to Rinaldino Puydarrieux; 1396; standing statue; Child on left arm; skin soft beige-brown; ruby ear-rings; Virgin's left hand, holding sceptre, slightly larger than right.
(2) On High Altar, bronze Madonna and Child by Donatello 1445/50. It is a matter for debate whether this statue should be considered a BV or not. There is some

evidence to suggest that Donatello was inspired by an old BV, possibly the original venerated in the Cappella della Madonna Mora, which may have been brought from France by St Anthony himself. St Bonaventure, who developed the cult of St Anthony in the Basilica del Santo is credited with taking a BV to Aix-en-Provence in 1274.

I.24 **Patti-Tindari** Sicily; 988 (37)(38); in Santuario Maria Santissima del Tindari; La Madonna Nera; attr. to St Luke; 'one of the two most revered Sicilian images of the madonna' (Moss and Cappannari); Ch. built on ruins of Temple of Cybele mentioned by Strabo and Pliny. BV washed ashore in casket.

I.25 *Ragusa* Sicily; 988 (37); Durand-Lefèbvre reports BV, painting attr. to St Luke. Formerly city of Hybla, sacred to Hera.

I.26 **Rome** 988 (26); (1) Santa Maria Maggiore — painting attr. to St Luke, Salus Populi Romani, possibly copy of 13 C.
(2) S. Maria Nova, miraculous madonna reported by the Director of Monuments at the Vatican to be the oldest in Rome. On site of Temple of Venus.
(3) S. Maria in Ara-Coeli. On the Roman Capitol. Emperor Augustus had a vision of a beautiful lady standing upon an altar of heaven. BV attr. to St Luke — probably 10 C. Home of Santo Bambino. Temple of Cybele.

(4-8) S. Maria in Trastevere, S. Maria in Cosmedin, S. Maria del Popolo, SS Domenico e Sisto are all reported by Durand-Lefèbvre to contain BVs attr. to St Luke.
(9) S. Maria di Loreto on site of Trajan's Temple has on High Altar an unusual Madonna of Loreto between Sts Roch and Sebastian.
(10) S. Maria di Montserrato in Ch. Built in 1518 for a confraternity of Spaniards founded by Alexander VI in 1495. Many other possible BVs.

I.27 **Siena** 988 (15); in Duomo, Cappella della Madonna del Voto; Madonna del Voto, Madonna delle Grazie or Advocate of the Sienese called Madonna Nera as was its predecessor Madonna dagli Occhi Grossi (large eyes) now in Opera del Duomo; painting of Hodegitria type from the school of Guido da Siena; c.1280; commemorates Battle of Monteaperti; adapted for processional use 1448. Bernini Maddalena in chapel. Black Libyan sibyl on paving of Duomo. Duccio's Maestà (opera del Duomo) succeeded the other two Madonnas as the Votive Virgin of Siena.

I.28 *Spoleto* 988 (16)(26); La Icona di Spoleto, Byzantine, suggested as BV by the Director of Monuments at the Vatican.

I.29 **Venice** 988 (5). (1) In S. Maria della Salute, open 7-12, 3-7, La Madonna della Salute, Mesopanditissa, 12 C. icon.

(2) In S. Marco side-chapel, BV icon.
(3) BV reported in Torcello by Saillens, denied by local priest.

LITHUANIA

Vilnius/Vilna/Wilno At this corner claimed by three nations, the Virgin of Ostra Brama (sharp corner) looks down on the street, behind glass above an arch at one of the old fortified gateways of the city. People still kneel in the streets to venerate her.

MALTA

Durand-Lefèbvre reports 4 BVs (1) St Mary of Damascus, painting attr. to St Luke; (2) Città Vecchio; (3) San Lorenzo Burgo, painting attr. to St Luke; (4) Mdina/Notabile; in Dominican Priory, Sanctuary of Our Lady of the Grotto, one mile S of the old city there are images of Our Lady of the Grotto, commemorating the apparition of the Virgin to a hunter c.1400. The locals placed an icon of the Virgin in the cave or crypt and later the Dominicans decorated the walls with various paintings. They replaced the original image c.1600 by a Sansovino-style figure in alabaster. In the second half of the 18 C. a statue carved in Maltese stone was added (now in the chapel of the Dominican studentate in Rabat). In Valletta are also Chs to N-D de Liesse, Na Sra del Pilar and St Roch. The Prior of St Dominic's, Rabat and the historian of the Province know of no traces of shrines in Malta dedicated to a BV. There is a Madonna of St Luke in the Cathedral of Mdina.

MEXICO

Guadalupe In Cathedral of Nuestra Señora de Guadalupe; painting; standing; almost life-size. Within 10 years of the conquest of Mexico by Cortez (1521), a poor Indian, Cuatitletoatzen, or Juan Diego, experienced an apparition of the Virgin on top of the hill Tepeyac, and was told by her to go to the Bishop of Mexico and announce that it was her will that a temple be built to her on that site. The Bishop told him to return when he had some proof of what he was saying. The same thing happened a second time. On the third occasion he found roses blooming in profusion on the hilltop, although it was mid-December, which he picked at Our Lady's bidding and carried to the Bishop in his maguey cloak. When he unfolded it to present the blooms, the cloak was seen to be imprinted with the image of the Virgin with Indian characteristics. Scientific investigation has revealed some later features added by natural means — the golden rays, the moon, the tassel at the waist and the angel at the feet. The major portion of the image, however, remains inexplicable, showing no signs of sizing or preparation of the material and no under-stitch. The figure, standing, in prayer, without a Child, wears a blue cloak over a white dress, and the blue is a natural pigment which apparently cannot be reproduced. Maguey, woven cactus, generally disintegrates within 10 years. Patroness of All the Americas, she is above all the emblem of Mexican nationhood. She inherited the devotion formerly accorded to Kwatlikwe, the mother of life, and Texcatlipoca, 'smoking mirror', the dark sun-god. Tomatin, mother of the gods, worshipped on top of a mountain of human victims sacrificed on a black stone, became Tonantsin, Our Lady and Mother. Pope Pius XII said of Our Lady of Guadalupe, 'Brushes not of this world painted this most sweet icon.'

THE NETHERLANDS

Few ancient images of Our Lady escaped the wars of religion and national liberation of the 16 C. and 17 C. The sisters of the Virgins of Vilvorde and Hal at Haarlem and s'Gravesande disappeared, though one BV was taken by Carmelite nuns to Cologne.

Amsterdam In Rijksmuseum, copy, probably 17 C., of BV of Altötting (qv Germany). Catalogue No 828.

Breda   1(5) 408 (17) 409 (5). In open chapel in Lovendijkstraat

painting of BV of Czestochowa, placed there by Polish community after Second World War.

Dordrecht 408 (17). BV reported by Saillens. Local archivist knows of no BV in the area.

Huijbergen   408 (16) 409 (4); 8 km SE of Bergen-op-Zoom on Belgian frontier. Formerly in chapel of Carmelite convent, Broomstraat 9, rare and interesting copy of N-D de Sous-Terre, Chartres; plaster; brown; 50-60 cm. Noted by both Durand-Lefèbvre who dates it from the 17 C., and Saillens. Now in Instituut St Marie, Staartestraat 8, part of the collection of *c.*120 images of the Virgin belonging to Fr Renatus Verschuren OFM which includes more than a dozen BVs.

THE PHILIPPINES

Antipolo Near Manila. In Ch. begun 1632, Our Lady of the Philippines; national shrine of the Virgin; statue installed 1653; carved of wood which has discoloured over the years; on top of solid silver shrine. Also of interest is the Black Nazarene of Quialpo.

POLAND

Cracow Durand-Lefèbvre reports a painting of a BV attr. to St Luke in Carmelite Ch.

Czestochowa   Since the events of

the last few years there can be no image of Our Lady so famous throughout the world as the Black Madonna of Czestochowa, Queen of Poland, who reigns from the Basilica in the Jasna Gora monastery that is the national shrine. Its origins are, nevertheless, shrouded in some mystery. According to legend it was painted by St Luke on a table made by Jesus, discovered by St Helena in Jerusalem and taken to Constantinople where it was venerated in a church built for the purpose until the iconoclastic troubles of the 8 C., when it was hidden in the forest of Belsk in E Poland. During the Tartar invasion of 1382 the chapel housing the icon was enveloped in a cloud. After the departure of the Tartars the Prince of Belsk was told in a dream by an angel to take the painting to Czestochowa, where the monks of St Paul of the Desert have guarded it to the present day. Another tradition states that Charlemagne gave it to the Prince of Russia, whence it came into the possession of the Jagellonian family of Lithuania, which furnished the monarchs of Poland, Hungary and Bohemia. King Wladislaw (1386-1434) established the Paulite monks at Jasna Gora in 1382 from Hungary, and it is possible the icon came with them. In 1430, during the Hussite troubles, a robber-band removed it, but abandoned it in the mud at the outskirts of the village, covered in earth and blood, when their horses refused to move any further. A miraculous spring dates

from that time. All the victories and deliverances that have occurred since are attributed by the Poles to the intercession of their patroness. Czestochowa was besieged by the whole Swedish army for six weeks in 1655 until its withdrawal on 26 Dec. The following year the Virgin of Czestochowa was declared Queen of Poland. Jan Sobieski and his knights dedicated themselves to her at Czestochowa before riding to save·Europe from the Turks at Vienna. At another great siege, by the armies of Catherine the Great in 1770/1 victory was granted to Casimir Pulaski at Candlemas. Later deliverance from the Russians attributed to the BV took place at the Vistula on 15 Sept. 1920, feast of Our Lady of Sorrows. Her influence on the spirit of Polish independence since 1945 needs no comment. The painting was examined in 1952. It was found to be on lime-wood, not cypress as previously believed, and to have been restored by western painters in Byzantine style 1433, but ever since 1430 she has borne on her right cheek the ineffaceable sabre scars inflicted on her. She carries the Child on her left arm; he holds a closed book in his left hand. There are paintings at Jasna Gora of St Mary the Egyptian, Thaïs, a mysterious St Dythna, Princess of Scotland, and St Anthony being tempted by a naked woman. Algermissen notes a bee and black knight motif on the garment of the BV, though reproductions show a fleur-de-lys pattern. Triptych of Sts Catherine and Barbara in chapel of St Anne. Moss and Cappannari link the BV of Czestochowa somewhat cryptically with Bona Sforza of Bari, 'a nondivine queen of Poland' *c.*1515.

Kodek Old copy of O.L. of Guadalupe, Spain. Pope has replica in Vatican.

Koden BV; 17 C.; without Child, reported by Durand-Lefèbvre.

Lublin BV reported by Durand-Lefèbvre, Our Lady of Claremberg, attr. to St Luke.

Tivinskaya BV reported by Durand-Lefèbvre — 'very brown, intentionally darkened'.

Warsaw BV reported in pillar of cathedral by Marcel Moreau (*Atlantis,* no.205, p.100).

Wilno See Lithuania.

PORTUGAL

Lamego BV reported by Saillens. He may be referring to Nossa Senhor dos Remédios in the pilgrimage Ch. of 1750-60, which also has a chalice of Mithra.

Lisbon 18 C. BV, Nossa Senhora com Tiara or Aparecida; standing; Child on left arm; 18 C.; in possession of the Carmelite Third Order. Also cult of N-D de Rocamadour. In Museu Nacional de Artes Antigas, 2 BVs, nos 1761 (12C) and 1290 (13C).

Moncorvo BV reported by Saillens. Precious Gothic triptych in mother Ch. of the marriage of Anne and Joachim, with the presentation of Jesus in the Temple.

Nazaré Nossa Sra de Nazaré (Nazareth) or Pederneira (black stone). During the persecutions of the 4 C.. runs the legend, a Greek monk, Kyriakos, took an image of the Virgin nursing Jesus to St Jerome in Bethlehem, who sent it to St Augustine, who in turn transferred it to the monastery of Cauliniana (12 km from Mérida, Spain) (cf. **Chipiona**). After his disastrous defeat by the Moors at Guadalete in 711, King Rodrigo (who was almost certainly killed in the battle), reputedly fled to the present site of Nazaré with Abbot Romano of Cauliniana, taking with them the BV, already known as Na Sra de Nazaré. They arrived at the ocean on All Souls Day 713 on a hill with a cross and some tombs and separated to lead an eremetic existence, communicating by smoke signals. Romano died on 26 Mar. 716 (day after Lady Day) and was buried by Rodrigo who hid the BV in some rocks and went his way. It was discovered by some shepherds in 1179. On 14 Sept. 1182 (Feast of the Holy Cross), D. Fuas Roupinho was hunting a white stag in a fog and, misled by the devil, nearly went over a cliff. He prayed to the Virgin, and was saved.

When shortly after he built a chapel in her honour, relics were found, including those of St Blaise. Statue carved by St Joseph, painted by St Luke.

Oporto BV reported by Saillens. Cult of N-D de Rocamadour. Tomb of St Amator near Oporto, according to Huynen.

ROMANIA

Braşov BV reported in 1983 by the episcopal press office in Essen as an example of the genre along with Czestochowa and St Maria Maggiore. It was once the imperial city of Kronstadt.

Bucharest BV reported by Durand-Lefèbvre, Saillens and Huynen. According to Durand-Lefèbvre there was at St Vinera a Holy Virgin of silver, with a face as black as coal who welcomed amidst the sweet-smelling smoke the vows addressed to Venus and Ceres.

RUSSIA

The problem of eliciting up-to-date information concerning BVs in the USSR and the present state of the cult being considerable, I can do little more than repeat the list of Marie Durand-Lefèbvre. I am indebted to Mr Richard Temple of the Temple Gallery for his view that if there is a cult of the Black Virgin in the Orthodox world it is late and probably due to the influence of Catholicism. The earliest icon painters in Byzantium did, however, use pagan models, such as Isis and Horus. The description Black Virgin is foreign to the Orthodox Church. Marcel Moreau claims to have seen BVs in USSR (*Atlantis* No. 205).

Ghelat 14 C. copy of BV attr. to St Luke.

Kakhouli 12 C. painted BV attr. to St Luke.

Kazan Painted BV. Kutuzov and his army prayed to her before victory of Borodino. Inspired Rasputin. Now in USA (?).

Khopi 14 C. copy of older painting.

Kursk see New York.

Moscow (1) In Tretiakov Gallery on public view, Our Lady of Vladimir; icon; Child on right arm presses his cheek against the Virgin's; brought to Russia from Constantinople 12 C.. first to Kiev, then to Vladimir and finally to Moscow. She saved Moscow from Timur by appearing to him in a dream and ordering him to leave Russia. The Czar used to announce the results of elections of church dignitaries facing the icon which was brought to the balloting room for the occasion. (2) Our Lady of the Iberians (replica in Russian Orthodox seminary rue de Crimée, Paris in 1937).

Novgorod   Painting of BV praying.

Smolensk   14 C. painting of BV.

Vilna   see Lithuania.

SPAIN

There is no up-to-date work on Black Virgins in Spain, so the following list is inevitably incomplete. A book on the lesser-known Black Virgins of the provinces of Badajoz and Cáceres (qv) is awaiting publication.

Sp.1 **Los Arcos** Navarra; 990 (7) 42 (14); 19 km SW of Estella (qv); in parish Ch., open mornings, Sta María de los Arcos; 14 C.; polychrome; oak; Virgin enthroned with Child on left knee holding closed book in left hand; Virgin's right hand holds apple; known as Virgen Morena (dark); cult of Sts Michael, John the Baptist, Blaise, Roch, Anne and Catherine.

Sp.2 **Alaró** Majorca; 43 (19); 17 km NE of Palma; in parish Ch. Na Sra de Ayort (old name of Alaró) 6 ft; wood; standing; no Child; 17 C (?); displayed once a year on 15 Aug.; Virgin of dead; babies passed over her to protect them from illness; Sts Roch and Anthony; twin mts; BV hidden in sacristy; main cult is of Virgin del Castillo.

Sp.3 Ávila 990 (14); in Ch. of San Pedro, painting 24 ins by 18 ins of Our Lady of Czestochowa, Queen of Poland, is the only BV according to the local authorities. Saillens may have been referring to Na Sra Soterránea, de las Vacas, de Son Soles or Guía.

Sp.4 Ayerbe Huesca; 43 (2); 28 km NW of Huesca; in sanctuary 5 km from Ayerbe, Na Sra de Casbas. BV arrived miraculously from Toulouse; hidden during Moorish occupation; rediscovered at liberation.

Sp.5 **Baget/Beget** Gerona; 990 (20) 43 (8); 14 km E of Camprodón; in 12 C. Ch. of San Cristófol; Verge de la Salut; 11/12 C.; wood; grey hands and faces; seated; Virgin in blue carries on left arm Christ in green who holds closed book in left hand; Virgin's hands very large. Communist who cut off hand of Virgin during Civil War drowned within the week in the Beget River. Frontier village just across mountains from N-D del Coral (**Prats,** qv France).

Sp.6 *Barcelona* 990 (20) 43 (18); the Museo de Arte de Cataluña on Montjuich contains the finest collection of BVs in the world.

Sp.7 *Berbegal* Huesca; 43 (4) 42 (18); 15 km SW of Barbastro; Sta María la Blanca (cf. Toledo); D in Civil War, 1936.

Sp.8 Cáceres There were once

at least 12 BVs in the provinces of Cáceres and Badajoz (Extremadura). Fr Fernández of Cáceres reports that, with the exception of Guadalupe, all have now been whitened. One has been totally covered from head to foot in a costume surmounted by a mask. Na Sra de la Montaña, the patroness of Cáceres, also known as de Montserrat, is not a BV, and has nothing to do with the Catalan image.

Sp.9 Calatayud Zaragoza; 990 (17); in main Ch. and in ancient sanctuary on rock, Virgen de la Peña or La Morena; painted wood; traditionally brought by first apostles. Moorish castle built on site of Roman city of Bilbilis. San Sepulcro was the most important Templar Ch. in Spain. Cistercian Abbey 1194. Bath of Diana near by.

Sp.10 Candelaria Tenerife, Canary Is.; 990 (31); in Basilica of Na Sra de Candelaria BV who is patroness of the Canary archipelago. Statue found near beach of Chemisay in 1390 by two Guanche shepherds who reported the matter to their chief. She became the object of a pagan cult in a grotto. 50 years later a Christian Guanche, Antonio de Guimar moved the statue to the grotto now known as San Blas (Blaise), revealing to the people who the dark lady with the Child in her arms really was. The area was a Guanche burial-ground. In 1464 the statue was stolen by the inhabitants of Fuerteventura, but daily turned towards the wall and worked nothing but illness and despair until returned to her home. The islands were subdued during the course of the 15 C. by the Knights of Christ, the Portuguese continuation of the Templars. Candelaria means Candlemas and mysterious lights in the darkness were reported in the legends of the cult's origins. The statue, perhaps washed up by the sea, was swept away by it during a storm in 1826 and had to be replaced.

Sp.11 Chipiona Cádiz; 990 (3); in Franciscan Sanctuary de la Regla, open 8-1, 4.30-8, Nuestra Señora de la Regla; 12/13 C.; small wooden statue, Virgin black, Child white (see painting of it in Bruges, Belgium); BV formerly offering pear to Child; mutilated in late 16 C., though head, bust and much of the legs were saved. Sanctuary contains the key with which the Virgin freed the prisoners of Rota and the cave where she was buried (el Humilladero). Many miracles, especially involving sailors. St Michael is the patron of Chipiona where there was formerly a very important cult of St Anne. There are two versions of the origin of the cult. (1) The BV was carved in *León* (qv) whence the Augustinian canons took her in 1329 to the castle built at Chipiona by Gúzman the Good, and converted to a monastery in 15 C. (2) St Augustine sent the image to Tagaste, whence, during the Vandal invasions it was transferred to Chipiona and buried in a cave. In the 14 C. a canon of Léon had a vision in which the Queen of Angels told him to seek her image hidden by Christians during the Moorish occupation. Sleeping under a fig-tree above the cave he had a dream telling him to dig there and found the BV. Augustinians expelled 1835, Ch. D., BV profaned, Franciscans take over sanctuary 1882. BV crowned 1954. Living cult. Hercules worshipped at Cádiz, Venus at Sanlúcar de Barrameda (home of manzanilla sherry).

Sp.12 *Cillas* Huesca; 43 (3); within town boundaries of Cortillas; 13 C.; crowned, smiling, polychrome majesty with Child on left knee; both figures hold apples.

Sp.13 Ciudad Rodrigo Salamanca; 990 (13); Saillens reports statue of N-D de Rocamadour. Huge, very dark, old-looking painting of O.L. of Czestochowa in Cathedral.

Sp.14 *Covadonga* Oviedo; 990 (4); in Picos de Europa, Spanish national sanctuary, fountainhead of Spanish nationality, monarchy and re-Christianization. More than 2,000,000 pilgrims annually; in Basilica de Na. Sra. de la Cueva (Covadonga = Cave of the Lady or Deep Cave), la Santina, Virgin of the Battlefield, Patroness of Asturias; crowned 1908 when the present statue in natural wood replaced earlier versions; 8,000 jewels in crown; carries golden rose; waterfall from cave. Pelayo, descendant of the Visigothic kings, won a great victory over the Moors at Covadonga in 722 and began the reconquest of Spain. He is buried here with his family. The abbot says the statue is not considered a BV. Fernández thinks it is.

Sp.15 **Daroca** Zaragoza; 990 (17) 43 (11); in Iglesia Colegiata de Sta María (open daily) Na Sra La Goda (Goth); ancient; gilt wood; stern expression; Child, on left knee of Virgin, without crown and not entirely seated. Reputed to be the work of the Goths, the first conquerors of Daroca, or of their descendants, though its date is given as *c*.1300. Retable and 12 C. Ch. of St Michael. Gothic tombs.

Sp.16 **Estella** Navarra; 990 (6) (7) 42 (15); in Real Basilica de Na Sra del Puy, opens 8-8, Na Sra del Puy; 8 C., or 12 C.; 80 cm; polychrome wood covered in silver; smiling, crowned Virgin and Child seated on stool; large crescent moon under feet; Virgin holds flowering thorn-twig; BV found in cave after apparition to shepherds in 1085. Pilgrims from all over Europe stopped to venerate Our Lady on their way to Compostela. Ch. of St Michael in town.

Sp.17 **Fuenterrabía** Guipúzcoa; 990 (7) 42 (15); in Ch. of Sta

María; Na Sra de Guadalupe (qv) (also carved on Puerta Sta María, the gate through the 15 C. ramparts); 15 C.; wood; standing. Frontier fortress against France. BV delivered town from two-month siege by French in 1638. Louis XIV and María Teresa married there. BV appeared to 2 children on Mt Jaizkibel (hermitage); carved from their description.

Sp.18 *Gerona* 990 (20) 43 (9); in Cathedral; La Virgen de la Seo may originally have been a BV; wood; no polychrome; Child holds closed book in left hand. Province of Gerona has a number of BVs. 36 Romanesque statues of the Province have disappeared, mostly destroyed in 1936, the first year of the Civil War.

Sp.19 **Guadalupe** Cáceres; 990 (24); in the Camaríin of the Monastery Ch., La Virgen de Guadalupe, Our Lady of Silence, Patroness of Extremedura and All the Spains. When Don Rodrigo, Visigothic King of Spain, was defeated by the Saracens in 711, some of his knights took with them a statue of the Virgin given to Bishop Leander of Seville by Pope Gregory the Great. They placed it in an iron casket and buried it in Guadalupe. In 1326, after the reconquest, a cowherd, Gil, found it following an apparition of the Virgin, perfectly preserved after 600 years in the earth. The custody of the shrine was entrusted to the Franciscans, one

of whose number, Zumarago, Bishop of Mexico, named a new shrine on the hill of Tepeyac, Guadalupe, a daughter that was to outshine her mother. BV crowned 1928. Guadalupe = 'hidden river' or 'wolf river'. Maria Prophetissa in camarín. Cult of Sts Anne, Blaise and Mary Magdalene.

Sp. 20 *Huesca* 990 (18) 43 (3); Na Sra de Salas or de la Huerta; seated; Romanesque; in sanctuary of Salas near Huesca. The province is rich in BVs.

Sp.21 *Jaén* 990 (35); Na Sra de la Capilla. On 11 June 1430 the Queen of Heaven visited Jaén. The Bishop built a chapel on the place where she halted, in front of the Ch. of St Ildefonso where the bells rang for matins. The photograph of the statue that commemorates her visit, standing with a naked Child on her left arm, shows both faces to be dark in relation to the Child's body colour.

Sp.22 *Lánaja* Huesca; 43 (13); La Virgen de Lánaja; wood; seated majesty; Romanesque/ Gothic; Child on right knee.

Sp.23 *Léon* 990 (11); Na Sra de la Regla (cf. Bruges, Belgium and Chipiona) reported to be still venerated in the area. Also copy of Virgin of Guadalupe. Na Sra del Camino, patroness of city, reported to be BV.

Sp.24 **Lluch Majorca**; 990 (29)

43 (19); (1) Na Sra de Lluc or La Moreneta; in monastery Ch.; standing; stone; 61 cm; 13 or 15 C.; found in cleft rock by shepherd boy and hermit 1240; hidden from Moors 9 C.; SD; returned twice (6 km) from Ch. of St Pere; water; nigra sed formosa sum on head-dress (stolen 1978 and replaced); Child on left arm with open book; fleur de lys on mantle; repaired for 1884 coronation; Queen and patroness of Majorca; ex-votos in museum attest blackness and miracles; Templars; Sts Anne, Mary Magdalene, Bernard, John the Baptist, Louis Gonzaga, Magi; BV known as black since 15 C. (2) In museum (open daily 10–5) 14 C. alabaster Virgin; standing; 40 cm; Child and bird on left arm; flower in right hand; turned black during journey from Belgium with José Amer in 1518.

Sp. 25 **Madrid** 990 (15); in Ch. of Na Sra de Atocha, Julián Gayarre 1, Madrid 17, Na Sra de Atocha (Antioch), co-patroness of Madrid with Na Sra de la Almudena; 25ins; very black; 12 C.; already in Madrid before reconquest; Ch. D. in 1808 and in Civil War, BV saved. Legendary origins: Sts Peter and James bring to Spain BV sculpted by St Luke, Peter carries it to Mantua (Madrid), James goes to Zaragoza (qv). BV disappears during Moorish occupation while Don Gracián Ramirez de Vargas is praying at her shrine. He organizes search-party for the statue on the hill of St Blaise where it is found in a tussock of grass (*atocha*). Gracián starts building new Ch. which Moors mistake for a fort and attack. Gracián's wife and daughters beg him to defend the BV to the last and prepare to sacrifice themselves to the Saracens. Gracián stabs them all in the neck to prevent capture and leads successful counter-attack. On his return to give thanks to the Virgin for victory and ask pardon he finds his family alive. Since 1523 the hermitage has been a Dominican Priory. Favourite Virgin of the Spanish Royal Family.

Sp.26 *Martinet* 990 (19) 43 (7); 25 km SW of Puigcerdá; Na Sra de Bastanist, twin BV of Nuria, now reported to be in museum in Barcelona; no cult since *c*.1975.

Sp.27 **Montserrat** Barcelona; 990 (19) 43 (17); La Virgen de Montserrat or La Moreneta, patroness of Catalonia. The documentary evidence for the origin of the devotion to Our Lady of Montserrat dates from 932 when the Count of Barcelona confirmed and renewed an endowment made to the shrine by his father in 888, soon after the BV was found among the rocks. This gift was confirmed again in 982 by Lothaire, King of France. According to legend, the rocks of Montserrat, formerly smooth, became serrated at the Crucifixion, after which the statue, carved by St Luke, was brought from Jerusalem to Barcelona by St Peter. It was hidden on the Sierra de Montserrat to save it from the Moors, and was found by shepherds guided by a choir of angels, possibly in the 8 C. (Moss and Cappannari state it is known to have been black since at least 718). When the Bishop of Manresa tried to move it to his cathedral it refused to budge. The present statue is a 12 C.(?) majesty; 38 ins; seated with the Child held centrally. Montserrat is the home of Catalan nationalism and scholarship, where the language has always been preserved thanks to the great monastery library of the Benedictines and the famous boys' choir, the Escalonia. The *sardana* is danced regularly in front of the Ch. The BV is concerned with fertility and marriage, 'No es ben casat qui no dun la done a Montserrat' (He is not well wed who has not taken his wife to Montserrat). St Ignatius of Loyola received his vocation there and hung up his sword. Wagner was inspired to compose *Parzival* there (Montserrat as Grail Castle). Goethe and Schiller both attributed great importance to Montserrat, and the house where Beethoven died was an ancient fief of the Abbey. Former Temple of Venus.

Sp. 28 *Nájera* Logroño 990 (6) 42 (13); in Santuario de Sta María la Real, Sta María de Nájera, de la Rosa, de las Azucenas or Lirios (lilies); 11C.; original brought according to legend by St Peter; found in 1023 by King García VII of Navarre who saw a light shining in a cave while hawking.

Abbot says statue now restored to polychrome and not a BV.

Sp. 29 **Nuria** Gerona; 990 (20) 43 (7); access by rack railway from Ribes de Fraser 9-8.15. The cult of the famous BV of Nuria (56 cm, no veil, rustic and archaic) began according to legend with an anchorite called Gil and his companions. The statue was hidden during the Moorish occupation and lost until 1032, when a lover of the Virgin in Damascus, called Amadeus, was told by an angel to go to the Pyrenees where he was to build a temple in a place where a white stone stood between two rivers. If he dug there he would find a great treasure. When he arrived at the site local shepherds watched him and understood when he addressed them in Syrian. A bull was seen digging in the mountainside and roaring. A cave filled with light was discovered on the spot. Inside they found a bell, cross, cauldron and the statue that became the Virgin of Nuria. In 1075 an attempt to carry her to Caralps failed when she became immovably heavy, though on the return journey she seemed to weigh nothing. The sanctuary was destroyed in the Civil War, but the statue was preserved in a bank in Geneva. In 1956 she was proclaimed principal patron of the diocese of Urgel and in 1967 she was crowned and stolen 'provisionally' for political reasons by a Catholic nationalist group. Nuria remains an important pilgrimage centre and ski-ing resort, as well as providing the second most popular girl's name in Catalonia (after Montserrat).

Sp.30 **Olot** Gerona; 990 (20) 43 (8); in Santuari de la Mare de Déu del Tura, open daily 8a.m.-9p.m.; (1) Mare de Déu del Tura; 11/12 C.; 60 cm; wood; Child D 1936 and replaced; legendary origin 872 when dug up on the spot where a bull was roaring strangely; photographs of different periods show some discrepancies; in photograph of 1943 similar to the BV of Ujué. Now seems to have been restored. Bull beneath feet. Cult of Sts Anne and Roch. Olot, in volcanic country, is noted for its cattle fairs, sacred polychrome statues and barretinos (Catalan red caps). In 1980 a local sculptor was engaged in creating a large statue of the Virgin in black stone for the swimming-pool.
(2) In private collection of Martí Casadevall, who sculpted the Child of (1); BV; early 12 C.; both Virgin and Child have exceptionally severe expressions.

Sp.31 **Palencia** 990 (15); Na Sra de la Dehesa Brava or Sta María de Husillos; 12/13 C.; 26 cm; Child on left knee holds closed book in left hand; gilt and enamelled copper, possibly from Limoges; in the Episcopal Palace; may be returned to Abbey of Husillos, now under restoration, or placed in the Diocesan Museum. Sancho the Great, King of Navarre, while hunting in 1035, was led to a cave by a wild boar, which sought asylum by the relics of St Antolin, a Visigoth from Toulouse who converted his compatriots in Old Castile. The King's spear arm was held back by a supernatural force, and he subsequently re-founded the shrine around which grew the city dedicated to the Virgin. BV probably a gift to the Abbey. Local veneration of Sts John the Baptist, Blaise and Anne. Dehesa means 'enclosed wood', or, perhaps in old Spanish, 'defence'.

Sp.32 *Panzano* Huesca; 990 (18) 42 (18) 43 (3); La Virgen de Arraro; 11 C.; 40 cm; Child holds closed book in left hand; discovered at reconquest in village totally destroyed by Moors, between Rivers Formiga and Falcón. Images of Sts Cosmas and Damian venerated in Cave of St Cosme.

Sp.33 **Peña de Francia** Salamanca; 90 (13); 75 km SW of Salamanca, 15 km W of La Alberca, on highest mountain of range where the sees of Salamanca, Coria and Ciudad Rodrigo meet, in Dominican shrine of Na Sra de la Peña de Francia, La Virgen Morena, Queen of Castile (priory and hostelry occupied in summer only). According to legend, French knights came to fight against the Moors in the time of Charlemagne, found the statue, attacked and won the day. A French bishop consecrated the mountain as Monte Sacro. The image disappeared and all who

10. Peña de Francia

Virgin, throned and crowned, suckles Child from right breast (medieval cult of Virgin's milk — cf. Halle, Belgium, Châtillon and St Bernard). The title of Sacristy was substituted for Milk out of modesty in 1585. Saillens states that the BV of Puigcerdá is N-D de *Hix* (qv France), which may have been sent to Puigcerdá during Second World War. Frontier town.

Sp.35 **Salamanca** 990 (14); in the Old Cathedral since 1945, Na Sra de la Vega; 12 C.; wood plated with copper and Limoges enamel on throne; Virgin leans forward; outstanding example of Romanesque art; venerated as patroness of city since 1150, first in Augustinian Ch. on banks of Tormes. Ch. of St Catherine.

knew its whereabouts died. In 1434 Simon Vela, a French Franciscan from Paris, found it in a cave after the Virgin appeared to him by night and told him to go to Peña de Francia.

Sp.33a Puerto de Sta María Cádiz; 990 (33). Sta María de los Milagros reported to be BV.

Sp.34 **Puigcerdá** Gerona; 990 (19) 43 (7); In Dominican Ch. to rt of high altar Virgen de la Leche (milk) or de la Sacristía; original disappeared 1936; 13 C; 85 cm; looks highly restored and shinily metallic compared with the photograph of 1943, but the sacristan says she is not modern.

Sp.36 *Sangüesa* Navarra; 990 (7) 42 (16) 43 (1); Na Sra de Rocamador, seated majesty dissimilar to French BV of Rocamadour; face of Child whiter than that of Virgin who holds curious horned sceptre in rt hand. Also, in Ch. of Sta María la Real, silver statue of Virgin, statues of Sts Mary Magdalene, Mary Salome, Michael, and Judas Iscariot hanging from the tree.

Sp.37 **San Marcos** Tenerife, Canary Is.; 990 (31); near Icod de los Vinos NW of Mt Teide on the sea; in small chapel, BV; standing; sleeping Child on right arm; staff in left hand; moon beneath feet; both figures crowned and dressed in flowing robes and cloak.

Sp.38 Santa Olaria Huesca; 43 (3); on C 138 12km W of Boltaña; la Morena; now gone; ch ruined.

Sp.39 Santiago de Compostela Galicia. 990 (2); in Cathedral copy of BV of Montserrat placed in Chapel of St Louis by Catalan pilgrims in 1971. Also statue of Our Lady of Walsingham. At the Monastery of San Pelayo in the portico of the Ch. of St Mary Salome, statue of the Virgin in advanced stages of pregnancy. Cult of St Roch throughout Galicia.

Sp.40 *La Selva* Gerona; 43 (9) (it is not clear which of various localities of this name in the province is referred to — but probably La Selva de Mar). In sanctuary 2½ km from La Selva, Na Sra de la Pared Delgada (Thin Wall). Shepherd found statue in roots of holm-oak which were damaging a wall.

Sp.41 *Sesa* Huesca; 990 (18) 42 (18) 43 (3); in Oratorian Hermitage; Na Sra de la Jarea; standing; dark wood; Child on left arm; crown with solar rays; many ex-votos.

Sp.42 Seville 990 (33); 14 C. painting of N-D de Rocamadour reported by Durand-Lefébvre in Ch. of San Lorenzo. Also copy of Na Sra de Guadalupe, which came originally from Seville.

Sp.43 **Solsona** Lérida; 990 (19) 43 (6); in Cathedral; La Mare de Deu del Claustre; 12 C.; stone;

probably carved in Solsona by Gilabert of Toulouse, it is a masterpiece whose beauty may reflect that of La Daurade D at Rev. (Toulouse). It was designed to stand originally against a pilaster in the cloister. Hidden in the well from the Count of Foix and the Cathars *c.*1200, it became the patroness of city and venerated inside the Cathedral. Face of Child D by fire caused by Napoleon's troops in 1810. Crowned 1916. Various confraternities in her honour include La Minerva (1574). Many miracles; living cult. Taken to Vic during Civil War.

Sp.44 *Sopeira* Huesca; 990 (15) 43 (5); Na Sra de Sopeira, de la O or de Alaón. The Monastery of San Pedro contained various relics left there by the Goths. In 835 Count Vandregisilo founded a monastery to Our Lady near Sopeira. A document of 12 Feb. 845 of Charles the Bald, King of France, grants privileges to Na Sra de Alaón. The 'O' is the cry of parturition celebrated in the Great O antiphons of longing sung at Vespers from 17-23 Dec. The first line of the hymn at Lauds in the Office of Our Lady is 'O Gloriosa Domina'.

Sp.45 Tarragona 990 (19) 43 (16); in Cathedral, copy of La Moreneta of Montserrat, 1935.

Sp.46 **Tarazona** Zaragoza; 990 (17); in Chapel of the Virgin of the Rosary in the Cathedral, Na Sra del Rosario; 13 C.; Gothic;

polychrome wood BV; cult of Sts Blaise, Roch and Catherine.

Sp.47 *Tauste* Zaragoza; 43 (1); Na Sra de Sancho Abarca in chapel in Tauste (copy in mountain sanctuary of Sancho Abarca, 10 km NW); found by shepherd in cave with supernatural light 1569 near ruined 10 C. castle of King Sancho Abarca. Cult fostered from 1666 by French hermit, Jean de Noballas.

Sp.48 Toledo 990 (25); in Cathedral, La Virgen Blanca, 15 C., standing, is considered a Virgen Morena (cf. Berbegal). See also in Cathedral statue of La Esclavitud de Na Sra del Sagrario, very dark patroness of Toledo, in chapel to left of entrance.

Sp.49 *Úbeda* Jaén; 990 (25). Copy of Virgin of Guadalupe reported.

Sp.50 **Ujué** Navarra; 990 (7) 42 (16) 43 (1); in Parish Ch.; Sta María la Real or de Usúa (dove, in Basque), Patroness of la Ribera (Ebro Valley) de Navarra; 11 C.; 90 cm; alder-wood; similar to Na Sra del Tura in Olot. Ruins of Ch. to St Michael.

Sp.51 *Valvanera* Logroño; 990 (6) 42 (13); in Benedictine Monastery, Na Sra de Valvanera; Patroness of Rioja; 11 C.?; 80 cm; cherry-wood; polychrome; attr. to St Luke and traditionally brought from Palestine by Sts Onesimus and Dositheus (name of a noted 2

C. Gnostic); hidden in oak on peak by Arthur the hermit; found in 10 C. surrounded by bees by thief who was moved to repentance. Abbot says not a BV. Living cult; many miracles. Valvanera = Valley of Venus.

Sp.52 Veruela Zaragoza; 990 (17); in Ch. of Abbey founded by French Cistercians in 1146 (guided tours 9-1, 3-5, closed Suns and holidays); Na Sra de Veruela; mid-15 C.; Burgundian; 24 cm; both faces 'somewhat dark'. See also Black Cross of Veruela.

Sp.53 Vich Barcelona; 990 (20) 43 (8); in Cathedral, replica of BV of Montserrat. In Episcopal Museum magnificent collection of Romanesque Catalan majesties.

Sp.54 *Vilajoan* Gerona; 43 (9); near Garrigas 5 km SW of Figueras; marble, standing, Gothic statue in Ch.; black faces and hands. Not on map.

Sp.55 **Zaragoza/Saragossa**
990 (17) 43 (12); in Zaragoza's second Cathedral of Na Sra del Pilar; Virgin of the Pillar; 15/16 C.; standing; 40 cm; marble covered in silver. On 2nd Jan., 40 AD, while St James (Santiago) was walking along the Ebro with seven disciples, he was visited by Our Lady, borne on a throne by angels from Jerusalem. She took from one of the angels a small jasper column on which was placed a wooden statuette of herself, and told Santiago to build a chapel for

it. Zaragoza is thus the premier Marian sanctuary of Spain. Pilar is one of the most popular Spanish girl's names. Her feast day, 12 Oct., was ordered to be celebrated throughout the Spanish dominions by Pope Clement XII.

SWITZERLAND

S1 **Ascona** Ticino; 26 (7); 2 km W of Ascona in a small wayside shrine, La Capella Nera, always open, half way up the Via Collinetta, on the slopes of the Monte Verità; BV in ceramic of the type of the Madonna of Loreto; 16 C.?; called La Donna della Verità (The Lady of Truth); standing; Child on left arm. According to tradition she will turn white when a virgin dances before her. A local pottery was still producing figurines of her some 50 years ago. Considered by some authorities to be a copy of the BV of Loreto or of Einsiedeln.

S2 **Einsiedeln** Schwyz; 21 (19); in the Abbey Ch. of the Benedictines, Our Lady of the Hermits, Die Schwarze Madonna, Madonna in the Dark Wood, Our Dear Lady of Einsiedeln (Einsiedeln = hermits); *c* 1466; 4 ft; wood; standing; naked Child on left arm carries bird in left hand; Virgin's dress painted in strawberry and gold, but always shown in sumptuous robes and mantle ('the best dressed Madonna in the world'). The Swiss national shrine in the heartland of the confedera-

tion (each canton presents a great candle), Einsiedeln also attracts pilgrims from Alsace, Lorraine, the Jura and S Germany. The original hermit was a monk of Reichenau, St Meinrad, who retired from teaching to lead a solitary life on the Etzel peak (birthplace of Paracelsus) overlooking the Lake of Zürich (N) and the present site of Einsiedeln (S). After 7 years, in 835, he penetrated deeper into the dark forest and settled by the Fountain of Our Lady (perhaps already consecrated to the Germanic deities) in front of the future Abbey. He was clubbed to death on 21 Jan. 861 and two ravens whom he had befriended (cf. Wotan's Hugin and Munin) brought the murderers to justice. His head now rests in a golden casket beneath the feet of the Virgin in the black marble Chapel of Grace, and is annually used to bless the people. The Abbey was founded by St Eberhard in 934. When St Conrad, Bp of Constance, came to consecrate the Ch. and Chapel in 948 he witnessed a miraculous light and heard the singing of angels as Jesus and the four Evangelists offered the sacrifice of the Mass before the statue of Our Lady brought by St Meinrad. Jesus altered the word of the Sanctus to 'Sanctus Deus in aula gloriosa Virginis, Miserere nobis. Benedictus Mariae filius in aeternum, regnaturus qui venit in nomine domini.' This practice has been preserved in the monastery. As Conrad was about to perform the act of consecration a voice said in Latin 'Cease, cease, brother, the chapel has been divinely consecrated.' The angel-choir then sang Psalm 16. The miraculous consecration (Engel-weihe) is celebrated on 14 Sept. There were five disastrous fires in the Abbey, which dates in its present magnificent Baroque form from the 18 C. The French invaders of 1799 were under orders to capture the statue, but it was a hastily constructed duplicate that was sent to Paris, while the original was smuggled to the saddle of Alpthal under the impressive, unequal twin peaks of the Mythen, and thence over the mountains to Bludenz in Austria where it was whitened. It was restored to its pristine blackness before being exposed once more to public veneration in 1801/2. St Maurice is one of the patrons of the Church and there is a chapel to St Anne. Every five years there is a performance of Calderón's *The Great Theatre of the World* in the square in front of the Abbey. Every afternoon the monks walk in procession to the Chapel of Grace to sing the 'Salve Regina' to Our Lady. The Abbey has been a famous centre of horse and cattle breeding since the 15 C. Visited by Goethe. C.G. Jung is reported as saying that the BV of Einsiedeln is Isis.

S3 Fribourg 70 (9); in Ch. of Cordeliers (open daily), N-D des Ermites; 112 cm; wood; skin painted black and dress white;

1690 copy by Josef Kälin of Einsiedeln of BV of Einsiedeln (but some differences, including sterner expression, hint at memory of older version — also compare position of Child). Daily Salve procession.

S4 Great St Bernard Pass Valais; 26 (2); (1) in Chapel of the Hospice (open daily 8-8) Virgin of Jasna Gora, painting of BV of Czestochowa (much darker than the original) of 1956 by Kosmowski; 117 cm by 77 cm; blessed by Pope Pius XII; placed in Ch. 26 Aug. 1956, the day 1,500,000 pilgrims heard Mass at Czestochowa and Cardinal Wyszinski prayed 'May our Queen of Poland become the Queen of the Universe.' The pass is the same height, 2,499m, as the highest mountain in Poland, Rysy Tatra.
(2) N-D de Lorette in Ch. of Lorette N of Bourg St Pierre on the road up from Martigny. At the foot of the pass, near Martigny is St Maurice where the Theban Legion, commanded by St Maurice, and including Sts Victor and Ursus, was massacred for refusing to worship the gods of Rome (at the top of the pass there was a cult to Jupiter). To the E along the Rhône lie Saxon and Sion (see Sion-Vaudémont, France) with its important Merovingian connections.

S5 Lenz/Lantsch GR; 24 (4); 23 km S of Chur; in Parish Ch.; Einsiedler Muttergottes; c. 1745;

120 cm; wood; Pag.; Sts Catherine, Margaret, John the Baptist, Lucius, Nicholas; Ch. of Cassian nearby; old Marienkirche 831.

TURKEY

Efes Meryemana (Ephesus) In small, simple shrine of the Holy House of Our Lady, standing statue on altar, black, modern. Ephesus was traditionally the last home of Our Lady on earth. The visions of Catherine Emmerich of the Holy House were confirmed by the excavations of 1891. Our Lady's cult at Ephesus succeeded that of the black Artemis, Diana of the Ephesians.

USA

There must surely be numerous copies of great BVs of the world venerated by Catholics of Belgian, French, German, Italian, Polish, Spanish and Swiss descent in the United States, but the task of finding them is beyond the scope of this book.

Doylestown Pa. Copy of BV of Czestochowa.

New York At the chapel of the Synod of the Bishops of the Russian Orthodox Church (but travels continuously), Our Lady of Kursk. Found in 1295 at the foot of an old oak-tree near Rilsk. Fountain sprang up. Log chapel built. Later, icon placed in Kursk Cathedral; escaped undamaged when revolutionaries threw bomb; found at bottom of well in 1918; reached Istanbul 1920; taken to Yugoslavia; escaped destruction in Second World War; found in Munich 1945; taken to New York.
BVs have been reported at the Metropolitan Museum and the Cloisters, but from eye-witnesses' accounts it seems doubtful whether they can be proved to be so.

Addenda to the Gazetteer

AUSTRIA

Grinzing 987 (40). In this village on the northern outskirts, famous for its *heurigen* (new wine), the BV of 1983 has replaced the weeping BV whose cheeks were slashed.

BELGIUM

Poperinge 213 (13). In Ch. of St Bertin tiny BV and Child halfway up an oak-tree, dedicated to N-D de Foy, confirming that the original was a genuine BV (see *Dinant*).

CANADA

Vanier Ontario. BV, Our Lady of Africa (see Algiers) has stood outside the city hall and library welcoming everyone since 1955. Now subject of an appeal for much needed rehabilitation.

CROATIA

Hvar Island of Hvar. Our Lady of the Smoking Cell is a BV.

CUBA

Havana The Catalans and their descendants honour in their church a copy of the BV of Montserrat.

Nuestra Señora de Regla de Cuba In Regla. On the other side of the bay from Havana. BV is the most worshipped image in Cuba. Annually she is taken down to the sea like the Afro/Latin American black goddess, Jemanja, or Sara at Les-Saintes-Maries-de-la-Mer (qv).

Virgen de Cobre La Caridad; near Santiago de Cuba in the mountains; miraculous BV. It inspired Thomas Merton to write what he felt was his first good poem about the white girls and the black girls, just before he entered the religious life.

EGYPT

El Sourian Monastery Wadi El Natrun (local authority El Beheira), between Cairo and Alexandria, BV from Syria painted by St

Luke. In 1981 some enthusiastic students on a pilgrimage put their candles too close to the icon and burnt it. Since then the Coptic Church, which had experienced something of a renaissance since the apparition of the Virgin on the roof of Zeitoun Basilica in 1968, has gone through hard times.

ENGLAND

Aylesford Aylesford Priory, Kent; 5B 32; (1) BV, known as the Black Madonna, carved by Clare Sheridan in the 1950s from a piece of Galway bog oak. It was venerated in the chapel at nearby Allington Castle, adorned with a Spanish silver crown, until 1993, when it was transferred to Aylesford. It is about 4 ft high.
(2) Baroque Flemish BV of Our Lady bestowing the scapular of the Carmelites, with the promise that whoever died wearing it would be saved, on St Simon Stock (d.1265). His relics were brought from Bordeaux, where he died, to Aylesford, his old home. The Virgin and Child are both crowned, and the group measures about 2 by 3 ft. It turned up in an antique shop in East Anglia in the 1950s and forms the centre-piece of the Carmelite Chapel.

Buckler's Hard   Hants; 3C 16; in Chapel of the Blessed Virgin Mary created in 1886 by the Rev. R. F. Powles. French BV of pol-

ished dark wood with a hollow back and a moveable hand, the gift of a local resident, Lady Ward Poole. Estimates of age vary from 330 to 600 years.

Cambridge 2D 54; in RC Ch. of Our Lady and the English Martyrs, corner of Hills Rd and Lonsdale Rd. Dark oak BV from former Dominican priory on site of Emmanuel College.

Epwell Oxon; 3A 52; 8 mls W of Banbury; modern, dark metal BV; standing, almost dancing, on wall to left of altar; springs and wells, possible connection to Epona and Lady Godiva.

Upper Brailes Warwicks; 4H 51; 3mls E of Shipston-on-Stour; in RC Ch. of Sts Peter and Paul; small standing wooden BV on table at entrance, reputedly based on BV of Downside (qv) on instructions of the Benedictine monk who was the incumbent at the beginning of the century, but very different in detail. The church in an upper room was used during penal times and was reached by a ladder, which could be raised in case of danger. Henry VIII, who dissolved the monasteries, used to stay near by in Compton Wynyates. The vestments embroidered by his first wife, Catherine of Aragon, for the chapel can still be seen there.

LONDON

City St Etheldreda's Church; Ely

Place, EC1. Modern BV in crypt sculpted in polystyrene by May Blakeman in the 1960s. Former chapel (1290) of the Bishops of Ely, oldest RC place of worship in London.

Mayfair Church of the Immaculate Conception; Farm Street. A fine replica of Our Lady of Montserrat, presented by the Casal-Agrupacio Catalana of the UK, dedicated on 8 December 1991. She commemorates the fifth centenary of the birth of St Ignatius of Loyola, the founder of the Jesuits, who found his vocation on the holy mountain and dedicated his sword to La Moreneta. The image stands in a place of honour in his chapel, to the left of the high altar at the heart of the Company of Jesus in England.

Streatham St Leonard's Church; Tooting Bec Gardens; SW16 1RB. In this interesting church, dating from the 14 C., where Dr Johnson used to receive Holy Communion, and the Master of the Revels lies buried, there is a BV who came through the fire 'and was not consumed'. She once formed part of a group including Jesus and St John on the Victorian rood-screen. In 1975, after a disastrous fire in which everything else in the interior was destroyed, the Rector discovered her charred form in the ashes. She is now installed in the Lady Chapel where she stands out in dramatic contrast against the whiteness of the new, bare church. Services daily.

Willesden Church of Our Lady. Large seated limewood BV was installed in 1972 in St Catherine's Chapel, replacing the most famous BV in London, burnt in Chelsea in 1535. It had probably been there since the foundation of this mother church of Willesden ('hill of the spring') in 938 and may have perpetuated the cult of the goddess Brigantia, whose name lives on in the R. Brent, of which the spring that flows under the high altar of the church forms a tributary. Certainly the BV of Willesden was worshipped by pilgrims with an uninhibited licence reminiscent of joyous paganism until the Reformation and attracted the censorious fulminations of the Dominicans.

FINLAND

In the Amos Anderson Museum in Helsinki is an interesting 16 C. painting of the BV of Montserrat with the colouring of a Native American, holding a sphere from which a lily is sprouting. The whole mountain is depicted as her throne of wisdom. It is very similar in style to a painting by J. A. Ricci in the Museu de Montserrat.

FRANCE

Bélesta 235 (47); 35 km E of Foix; 15 km from Montségur. In the heart of Cathar country, N-D du Val d'Amour is on a cliff sanctuary called La Coste d'Amour, over the caves of Hell where the R. Amourel rises and on 23 June 1821 destroyed the half of the town that had not prayed to the BV. Major feast on 16 Aug., St Roch, when flocks are blessed. Shrine destroyed 1567.

Bermont   Peter Dickens has drawn my attention to a book, *Joan of Arc* by Pierre de Sermoise, in which the author lists N-D de Bermont along with the famous BVs of France at Chartres, Le Puy and Liesse. Unfortunately I have not been able to track her down.

Ercé 235 (46); 25 km SE of St Girons. BV N-D la Noire, whose photograph we saw in an exhibition of BVs in Tarascon (qv). The town was famous for bear training.

Fécamp Seine-Maritime; 52 (12); 2 km N by D 79. BV of the sailors in N-D du Salut Chapel, fine view. Famous tree cult in Fécamp.

Houppach Haut-Rhin; 66 (8). On the Route Joffre between Masevaux and Thann the Chapel of N-D d'Houppach, also known as Klein Einsiedeln, houses a replica of the famous Swiss BV.

Lourdes Hautes-Pyrénées; 85 (18). In crypt of parish Ch. of the

Sacred Heart. Replica of BV of Montserrat.

Montségur Ariège; 86 (5). A tiny, seated, gilt BV adorns the parish church and dominates the altar from an elaborate white tabernacle. She is flanked in niches on either side of the altar by a standing BV and St Roch. The statue of a third black, rather sinister, female figure is to be found in the body of the church. Montségur is famous for the last stand of the Cathars in 1244 and is a prominent new-age and Grail centre.

Palau del Vidre Pyrénées Orientales; 86 (20); 4 km S of Elne on D 50; in parish Ch. *c.*15 ft up on E wall. Unique Vierge Ouvrante BV opens to reveal bearded figure inside; Child on left shoulder.

Palladuc Puy-de-Dôme; 73 (6) in small modern Chapel of N–D de la Lizolle on D 64 between Arconsat and Palladuc; 14 C. BV; 140 cm; wood; right hand missing.

Vic d'Oust 235 (46), 14.5 km S of St Girons (not Oust as in earlier entry). The BV is now kept in a box by the Curé, except during the Aug. festivities, when she is carried in procession.

Further BVs reported at Auxerre, Chalons-sur-Marne, Moutiers-en-Puisaye and Nogent-sous-Coucy. No details.

GERMANY

Augsburg 413 (21). BV reported in Cathedral.

Magdeburg 987 (16); in Cathedral. Miraculous standing sandstone BV, 1270/80, to right of choir; polychrome since 19 C.

GREECE

Argalasti on the Pelion peninsula; in a tiny chapel on the path down to Kalamos. BV icon (original in museum in Athens). After midnight on the feast of the Nativity of the Virgin the chapel was still open and full of lighted candles. The priest was non-committal on the subject of BVs.

Athens In Orthodox Cathedral; BV Myrtosa; miraculous icon.

Crete near Herakleon, Iera Moni Palianis; BV icon in myrtle tree in churchyard. Living cult. Successor to Aphrodite.

Leros In chapel of castle in main town of island; icon BV. Living cult.

Zakynthos/Xante BV St Maura.

HUNGARY

Budapest BV in Ch. of St Matthew.

IRELAND

Thomastown Co. Kilkenny in parish Ch. BV, O.L. of Thomastown.

ITALY

Bari 988 (29); Lucan BV S. Maria de Constantinopoli in Cathedral.

Bologna 988 (14/15). Birnbaum reports the Madonna de la Guardia as a Lucan BV. This is presumably in the sanctuary of the Madonna di San Luca, a famous viewpoint to the SE of the city.

Bovino 431 D 28; BV reported by Birnbaum.

Brixen/Bressanone 988 (4) (5); 429 B 16. BV reported, from 19 C.

Cagliari 988 (33); BV in Santuario di Bonaria.

Conversano 988 (29); 431 E 33; ancient BV stolen recently from Cistercian Abbey.

Elba 988 (24); BV in sanctuary of the Madonna of Monserrato, built by the Spaniards in 1606, replica of La Moreneta.

Foggia 988 (28); Incoronata 6 km on S 16. Birnbaum reports an interesting BV, l'Incoronata dei Povere (of the poor), who appeared in an oak-tree on the last Sunday of April in 1001 in the Forest of Cervaro. (Cervaro is also the name of a village and of the river which flows south of the town.) She was first seen by a hunter and then by a peasant, who together with his oxen fell to his knees. About 800,000 pilgrims visit the shrine annually, circling it three times before entering, singing ancient litanies to the accompaniment of bagpipes. The same pilgrims converge, according to Birnbaum, on May Day at neighbouring Cerignola for a communist celebration.

Genoa   988 (13): BV reported in Ch. of San Lazzaro and S. Stefano.

Grottaferrata   430 Q 20; BV reported by Birnbaum — appeared 1230.

Matera   431 E 31; BV la Madonna Bruna in Ch. of S. Maria di Constantinopoli. Many pagan remains including a sanctuary of Persephone.

Molfetta   431 D 31; BV, Vergine dei Martiri, brought by Crusaders in 1188, reported by Birnbaum.

Palmi   431 L 29; BV in Duomo, Madonna della Sacra Lettera e della Varia. Her title refers to the letter sent by the Virgin to Messina in AD 42, adopting its people, while the Varia is the heavy construction carried by the men of the town on the feast of the Assumption from which the girls chosen to personify the BV enact her Ascension.

The people of Palmi adopted the Madonna of Messina, who gave protection against pestilence, earthquakes and 'atrocious dominations'. During the Great Plague of 1571 they took in refugees from Messina. The Messinese, in gratitude, gave Palmi a black hair of their Madonna (now in another church in the city) said to have been sent by Mary from Jerusalem. The painting was undergoing restoration when we visited but was due back in August 1995. Will she still be black, crowned and encrusted with silver? We were able to examine an inexact copy in the Chapel of the Blessed Sacrament.

The Museo Calabresi di Etnografia e Folklore in the town has sections devoted to religious life and popular superstitions.

Pisa   988 (14); BV reported in Ch. of San Francesco.

Pomigliano d'Arco   431 E 25. Madonna dell'Arco, shown in ex-votos as black, though the images the Church authorizes are white. The statue herself is currently greyish. Hundreds of thousands of people visit the shrine, especially on Easter Monday, dancing out of Naples and the surrounding villages with candles and flowers. The Church tries to curb the enthusiasm of these *fujenti*, of whom in 1972 one thousand required treatment in the first-aid station. One ex-voto noted by Birnbaum 'depicts Catholic priests of the Inquisition interrogating and torturing two women as witches, while the Black Madonna watches'.

Positano 988 (27); in main Ch. of S. Maria; undergoing repairs when we visited in 1993. Painting of BV in vestry in gold frame. The name Positano is derived from *Posa Posa*, the words uttered by the BV indicating to the crew of her ship that she wished to disembark here. When she landed, her path was strewn with flowers.

Ravello 988 (27); BV, la Bruna, in triptych under pulpit, stolen in 1974.

Rome 988 (26). Further BVs reported in the Borghese Chapel, the Pantheon and St Peter's (right-hand chapel near door).

Seminara 431 L 29. Seminara is not well signposted. As you leave Palmi for its motorway exit go under the motorway E of the crossroads on the outskirts of the town and follow a winding road through groves of what must be the biggest olive-trees in the world.

The BV in the Duomo, which was destroyed in the earthquake of 1908 and then beautifully restored and reopened in 1933, is called Maria Santissima dei Poveri (of the poor). She was found in a bush by a poor peasant and refused to be transported to a place where only the wealthy could venerate her. The statue of the Madonna with the Child

standing on her right knee — both in gold skirts — is very black, a darkness enhanced by the gold and silver crowns and canopied throne with angels. The church was made a basilica by Pope Pius XII in May 1955.

Tellaro 428, 429, 430 J 11; 4 km S of Lerici. BV in Ch. of St George, removed from Candia in 1670 before its capture by the Turks.

Vicenza 988 (4) (5). BV reported by Birnbaum (perhaps in S. Maria dei Servi?).

SICILY

Sicily has long been famous for its Black Virgins. The most notable and indisputable is the Madonna of Tindari, with the replica at Tono. The problem with most of the others is that the cult, typically that of a BV in most cases, dates back to the earliest centuries of Christianity, whereas the cult object, owing to earthquakes, eruptions, invasions and the vicissitudes of time, is usually much more recent. The hazard of periodic cleaning of 'dirty' paintings adds to the difficulty of determining what is a genuine BV. When in doubt, we have given greater weight to the ancient tradition belonging to the cult than to the Madonna's current appearance.

The BV sites of this beautiful and interesting island can easily be covered by car in one week and will lead you well off the beaten track.

Acireale 432 O 27; Maria Santissima di Loreto. The Church of 1553 is dedicated to the famous BV of Loreto (qv) and contains a black wooden statue of the Madonna, donated in 1925 by the bishop of Acireale, as well as frescoes of three Sicilian saints with a pagan background — Venera, Agata and Lucia.

Biancavilla 432 O 26. In the *chiesa matrice* (mother church) there is a BV, Maria Santissima dell'Elemosina, a Greco-Byzantine icon (67 by 85 cm), painted in tempera on cedar wood. It was brought to Biancavilla in 1482 by a group of Albanians fleeing the Turkish invasion. Until 1948, when the painting was restored, it was certainly a BV, and preserved Biancavilla from plague, earthquakes, eruptions of Etna and the destruction of the Second World War. Her crown, jewels and silver covering were stolen in 1978, but much of the sacrilege was made good the following year. Perhaps because of the theft, the church is usually shut.

Brucoli 432 P 27. Santa Maria Adonai, one of the most ancient Marian sanctuaries in Sicily, dates back to the third century. It is, as far as we know, the only dedication in the world that links Mary and the Hebrew word for Lord. The little church, beautifully situated by the sea, is surrounded with walls and gates and is not open to visitors. So, we were unable to ascertain the nature of the current image. The original appeared, miraculously painted, deep inside a cave on the wall. Many hermits lived in the caves that can still be seen in the dry gorge leading down to the sea.

After the railway bridge, before entering the town, turn sharp left towards a holiday village signposted Valtur. Just before you reach the gates of the estate take a dust-track to the left, which will lead you to a dead end, where the sanctuary is signposted to the right.

Caltabellotta 432 O 21; in the Church of Sant' Agostino. Maria Santissima dei Miracoli, also called Madonna del Acqua. The feast and procession of the crucified Christ and his mother, which, usually, are combined, takes place on the last Sunday in July and is one of the best preserved and richest in folklore of Sicily. Her treasure — no fewer than six baskets full of golden jewellery, the gifts from devotees from all over the world — accompanies her on her procession. The small (70 cm) Christ of c.1300 is undoubtedly black and oriental. the Madonna is less dark, more, we were told, like a mulatta; though our friend, the hotelier of Erice, who came from these parts, assured us she was considered black. She was discovered in a fig-tree in 1546 by an artisan whose attention was attracted by mysterious and strange movements of the trunk. She was credited with saving Caltabellotta from both cholera and drought and in 1601 was declared protectress of the town. The church is usually open but we happened to arrive both on market day and the feast day of the Crucified (3 May) in the next village of Sant' Anna, which attracted the presence of the Caltabellotta clergy. So, we were unable to see the BV for ourselves.

Caltabellotta, though lit up like a cruise-liner by night on its mountain-top, is a magical and secretive place. It was the first Christian diocese of Sicily and the bishop, San Pellegrino, was sent by St Peter to free the area from the depredations of a dragon — usually a symbol for paganism. During the Arab period religious objects were no doubt hidden in trees and rocks, as in other parts of Europe. Its Norman castle, of which only one ruined tower remains, is the most probable home of the magician Klingsor who, after sleeping with the wife of a neighbouring king, was castrated, and turned to black magic, as Wagner recounts in *Parsifal* — though the locals make little of this.

In 1302 the peace of Caltabellotta, ending the long war of the Sicilian Vespers, was signed here between the Angevins and the Aragonese. Curiously, it does not figure in the comprehensive *I Santuari Mariani Di Sicilia*. Its olive oil is reputedly the best in Sicily.

Chiaramonte Gulfi 432 P 26; 4 km NW of Chiaramonte Gulfi; the Santuario della Madonna di Gulfi. According to legend, a statue of a BV, which was placed on a ship without sails in the Levant to preserve it from the iconoclasts, landed in 732 at Camarina (18.5 km SW of Vittoria). The statue was carried 30 km on a cart to Chiaramonte Gulfi, where a sanctuary was built for it. The statue of Christ that accompanied her chose to stay in Vittoria. At Gulfi, as in so many places, the cult of Mary is much older than the present image, a white marble Madonna, dating back no more than 300 years, when her predecessor was blown over and destroyed during the annual procession on the Sunday following Easter. Some experts consider that the cult originated in 4 C. and the first Virgin of Gulfi was visited by St Gregory the Great in 576, before he was elected Pope. the whole region has suffered heavily from earthquakes, and there is no way to discover what the earliest image looked like, but Birnbaum has no doubt that she is a BV and neither do we. On the day we arrived the Virgin had been taken to Gulfi for her annual stay of a week in the Cathedral of Chiaramonte, where we were able to see her.

Custonaci 432 M 20. Maria Santissima di Custonaci is the sanctuary at the top of the town. According to a tradition often found in Sicily, she was landed from a storm-beleaguered ship bound from Alexandria (home of Gnosis) to France. She was crowned by the Vatican in 1752 because of her many miracles. Her great speciality is freeing the country from drought, for which reason she is also known as the Madonna of the Water. In fact, she is a Madonna of Milk and is depicted seated on a throne offering her breast to the naked Christ Child. Both are crowned, and the Virgin's halo resembles the moon surrounded by stars. The picture is painted on wood and surrounded by a rich, silver frame. It has been erroneously attributed to Perugino or Raphael, but seems to be of the Flemish school.

The image was often taken to Erice (qv) in time of emergency, but that city now has its own version of the BV. Murals on the wall show her landing as 'Star of the Sea' — a title she shares with Isis — and the procession bearing her up to her new home. Her feast is the last Wednesday in Aug. The church was built in 15 C., enlarged in 1625 and restored in 19 C.

Erice 432 M 19. From her precipitous mountain-top castello, once the greatest temple of love in the west, the great goddess in her most sexual form gazed down on her access ports of Trapani and Custonaci. Both the images of Erice and Custonaci are called the Madonna of Custonaci, and the inhabitants of each town claim they have the original, although the Virgin at Custonaci seemed the older to us. Now she is represented in Erice by the painted BV in the *chiesa matrice* (mother church) in the chapel to the left of the High Altar.

The acropolis has disappeared into the Castello Pepoli, but the present hill-town, with its narrow cobbled streets, is well worth a visit, especially if you can stay at the Elimo Hotel, whose proprietor is a knowledgeable lover of BVs.

Giarre 432 N 27. In the church, dating from the end of the eighth century, there is a painting of the Madonna della Strada (of the street) surrounded by angels, with St John the Baptist pointing to the infant Jesus. The quarter of the town where the church stands is famous for its well, between the Malogrado and Trainara rivers. It was here that the Virgin saved Count Roger the Norman from a Saracen ambush.

Messina 432 M 28. Birnbaum states that the Madonna of Messina, although painted white, is, in vernacular belief, considered black. The Virgin Mary, according to legend, wrote a letter to the Christians of the city in AD 42, stating 'We bless you and your city,' and evidently enclosing a lock of hair, some of which was sent to the BV of Palmi (qv) in gratitude for the generosity of its citizens in taking in refugees during the Great Plague of 1571. There are at least five ancient churches in Messina and its surroundings dedicated to the Virgin, in addition to the cathedral with its Madonnina, the twin of the Palmi BV. There is also the gigantic statue by the harbour that greets all voyagers from the sea. Despite the Virgin's blessing, Messina has suffered more disasters in its history than any other city in Europe of similar size, but has always re-emerged triumphantly. Cybele and Rhea were popular carnival figures in Messina in 15 C. The real BV of Messina is the Madonna di Montalto, who arrived by sea and told one of the sailors she wished to be placed in a new church on the hill of La Capperrina. The painting is covered in silver except for the faces.

Milicia 432 N 22; 9 km E of Palermo off A 19. Take exit Altavilla Milicia and follow signs to Santuario. Go up the hill, turn left at the beginning of the town by the war memorial and park in front of the church.

The Madonna della Milicia is in a 19 C. church with fine views of the whole coastline from Cape Zafferano to Cefalù. According to a legend, a 7 C. painting of the BV was placed in the church in 1077 by the Norman conqueror Robert Guiscard. It came from a Saracen pirate ship in difficulties off Palermo. the crew, be-

lieving the image brought them bad luck, threw it overboard — they had been using it as a porthole lid. The Christians on shore put it in a cart drawn by two bulls, who stopped at the site of the present sanctuary and refused to move. She is credited with protecting the area around Palermo from pirates.

Historically, the origins of the sanctuary are linked to a pirate invasion on the night of 14/15 July 1636, which caused the celebrations of Santa Rosalia in Palermo to be abandoned. The militia were dispatched to Milicia, where they drove out the pirates, who managed to strike the Madonna on the neck with an axe before they left.

Experts have stated that the painting is in 15 C. Catalan style. The painting that you can see today was cleaned in 1990 because, according to the sacristan, it was 'dirty'. It is very different from the older photographs of it. In the original the faces of the Virgin, the Child and St Francis are definitely black, and the Virgin's body is covered in jewelled gold-plate, while her hands and the body of the Christ Child are covered in silver. In the restored version all the gold and silver have been removed, the Virgin is seated, the Christ Child is standing, and St Francis is introducing a boy, who did not figure in the earlier version, to Mary and Jesus. Milicia means 'blessed by Zeus Milichios', who had an important cult here.

The shrine is open daily 7-12 pm and 3.30-7 pm. Feast days 7-1 pm and 3.30-8 pm.

Noto 432 Q 27. We came to Noto following Birnbaum's list of prestigious sites linking BVs and Jewish communities, which includes Venice, Bologna, Naples, Siena and Rome. The information office is permanently closed but, asking around in Noto, we discovered no memories of any BV in the town, although one sanctuary of Noto, Montevergine, has the same name as a BV site on the mainland. This is how the confusion might have arisen. There are, however, eight sanctuaries to the Virgin in Noto and its surroundings.

Palermo 432 M 22; for Monte Pellegrino, see town plan of Palermo on the Michelin map.

The capital of Sicily has no BV, but its miraculous patron, St Rosalia, is sometimes depicted as black, certainly in the statue on the staircase outside her shrine on Monte Pellegrino. Rosalia, who died in 1160 aged about 35, was the daughter of Sinibaldo, probably Duke of Quisquina and of the Roses, where there is also a grotto associated with her (O 22). Her name is a combination of two flowers sacred to the Virgin — rose and lily. The place of her burial was not discovered until 1625, and then through a dream granted to Girolama La Gutta in 1624, when Palermo was being devastated by the plague. The bones of the saint were found in the grotto that is now her shrine, 4 m below the surface, together with a silver cross inscribed with the name 'Rosalia'. When her relics were carried in procession through the city, the plague ceased and within one year of their discovery not a single case could be found.

The beautiful altar of the saint was a gift of the Senate of Palermo in 1683. There is an exquisite statue of a reclining Rosalia in golden dress, and a crown beneath it behind a glass encasement. Golden necklaces, brooches, bracelets and hundreds of rings and coins fill the walls and the space around the figure — gifts from worshippers from around the world, but above all from the girls of Palermo.

Piazza Armerina 432 O 25. The BV is attributed to St Luke, painted on a rectangle of raw silk. Known as Our Lady of Victories, she was the war banner given by Pope Nicolas II to Count Roger the Norman when he entrusted him with the task of freeing Sicily from the Saracens. She is normally to be found in the Duomo, but we just happened to arrive during the week of her festival (30 Apr.-3 May), when she is transferred to her original sanctuary, now the Church of the Guardian Angels in Piazza Vecchia, where we were able to visit the portable version of her, ensconced in a niche behind and below the altar.

The Duomo in Piazza Armerina is easy to find, but if you wish to visit Piazza Vecchia (2 km W), follow signs to Villa Romana del Casale (Mosaici). The ancient hermitage is signposted up a hill to your right.

Ragusa 432 Q 26. We came to Ragusa to amplify the earlier entry (qv). We think that Durand-Lefèbvre must have been referring to nearby Chiaramonte Gulfi (qv). Everything in the area was destroyed in the great earthquake of 1693. In the cathedral of the old town, however, a statue in black schist of St John the Baptist (1.8 m), patron of the Duomo, from 1513, survived and is now well hidden behind the High Altar, covered by a heavy brocade curtain. It is only exposed for public veneration on 29 Aug., when the death of the Baptist is commemorated.

In the large wall-painting to the right of the statue his mother, Elizabeth, is shown as very much darker-skinned than the other figures. But there is today no cult of the BV in Ragusa itself.

Randazzo 432 N 26. BV, Madonna del Pileri, 10 C. Byzantine fresco on the north portico, antedates the present church of 1230, which is constructed from black blocks of lava so closely joined that no mortar is visible. Another painting inside the church shows the Virgin begging her son to save her devoted city from the fires of Etna. The church is open during normal hours but does sometimes close earlier for lunch.

Tindari 432 M 27. Update (see **Patti-Tindari**). From Messina on A 20 motorway take the Falcone exit and follow the S 113 (Messina-Palermo road) as it winds steeply up to the imposing new sanctuary (1957-80) on its mountain-top site. Signs try to persuade you to park at the bottom of the hill — ignore them out of season and drive on up until you reach the top, or somebody stops you.

As you enter the church your eyes will at once be attracted to the figure of the Madonna Nera and Child dominating the nave from their angel-borne throne above the High Altar. The wooden statue, about 1 m high, with *Nigra sum Sed formosa* inscribed underneath, shows a strong family resemblance between Mother and Child, both sumptuously crowned and robed in white and gold. Her face recalls that of a dark gypsy or a good witch, not dissimilar to her sisters of Dijon and Guadalupe.

Her legend is as follows: She was brought from the east on a ship forced to seek safe haven in the bay, which was once the splendid ancient harbour of Tyndaris. After the storm the ship would not move until the sailors disembarked the image in the place the Madonna had chosen. She was carried up the hill to the small church that had been built on the ruins of the Temple of Cybele, since when her cult has never ceased to flourish.

One famous miracle attributed to her concerns a mother whose daughter had been saved from sickness by the Virgin of Tindari. She brought her daughter to the shrine to give thanks but was disappointed to discover the image was black like that of an Ethiopian. When she gave voice to her dissatisfaction, her daughter fell from her arms from the high cliff to an almost certain death in the sea below. At the moment the child landed the sea was transformed into soft sand. So the Madonna saved the little girl twice, and the sea has never returned to cover the beach of Marinello. There are, however, in this miraculous *dry sea* strange lagoons whose shapes are constantly shifting. In 1982 one of them assumed the shape of a woman so perfectly that it was seen as the shadow of the Madonna of the Sanctuary above. On feast days the faithful carry replicas of the BV up to the sanctuary and the daughters have black dolls in their arms.

Tono 432 M 27. From the town centre of Milazzo take directions to Baja del Tonno, to the end of the beach where you find the small chapel. The Black Virgin, which I and other writers have situated in Milazzo, is actually to be found in this nearby small fishing village. The name means *tunny*, which once formed the

main industry for its fisheries. The BV is a smaller copy of the Tindari Madonna and is in the charming *chiesetta* of 1686, dedicated to Saints Philip and James.

The chapel is normally open on Sunday evenings, but a copy can be seen in a window niche on the street opposite the restaurant La Tonnara. There is a well opposite the church next to the old fishery. Between Milazzo and Tono is the cave of Polyphemus, the one-eyed giant from whose clutches Ulysses and his men escaped.

Trapani 432 M 19. There is some confusion about the existence of a BV at Trapani. The beautiful, famous and miraculous Madonna of Trapani in the Church of Annunziata is a white marble statue by Nino Pisano (*c.*1350). Many miracles of healing were attributed to her, especially against the plague, and she was the first Madonna in Sicily to be crowned, in 1734. She is now considered too precious to be carried around town during the celebrated Mysteries of Trapani, which take place on Good Friday, and now it is a black-clad Virgin of Dolours who seeks her son, sorrowing. Birnbaum states that there is an alternative procession in which women and workers carry a Black Madonna, bearing pine cones, in whose honour black rice is cooked. We could find no trace of such a practice on our visit in 1995. Nevertheless, it seems from the familiar legends of a statue arriving by sea, performing miracles of healing and travelling in an ox-cart to the place she designated, that there is a cult of the Virgin in Trapani that is older than the Pisano statue.

During the terrible plague of 15 C. the convent of the Carmelites next to the Church of the Annunziata was used as a hospital and later anything that might carry contamination was burnt, including all the records of the cult of the Virgin.

What is certain is that echoes of the past remain strong in this north-western corner of Sicily. The Madonna seeking her son on Good Friday comes not from the Gospel but recalls Demeter's hunt for her daughter, Persephone, who had been taken to the Underworld (cf. Caltabellotta). Presiding over the city and its surroundings is the Great Goddess of Eryx, under her various names — Astarte, Aphrodite, Venus.

Valverde 432 O 27. The arcaded Church of the Discalced Augustinians is the home of one of the most ancient Marian sanctuaries of Sicily. In 1038 a humble traveller, Egidio, found his way barred by a brigand, Dionysius, who was about to strike his victim when a mysterious voice bade him: 'Dionysius, Dionysius, do not touch my devoted servant! Lay down your arm and cease this life of brigandage.' It was the Virgin Mary. Egidio was

saved; Dionysius was converted and lived a life of penitence in a grotto. He constructed a sanctuary on the orders of the Virgin, who caused a healing spring to flow for him. On the last Sunday of August in 1040 Dionysius had a vision of the Madonna, surrounded by angels, who assured him of her protection. On the following day the celestial vision imprinted itself on a pillar of the temple. The church was destroyed in the earthquake of 1693 and soon rebuilt. The image, divinely painted, is clearly of Byzantine style. Feast day last Sunday in August.

Vena 432 N 27. Vena is 8 km SW of Piedimonte Etneo but is not well signposted, so you should enquire there.

Of the necklace of half a dozen BV sanctuaries which surround Etna none is more beautiful and peaceful than Maria Santissima della Vena. What is more, it is open most of the day.

The BV is painted in tempera on a very ancient table of cedar of Lebanon (170 by 67 cm) and is believed to date from the first centuries of Christianity. The site was given by St Silvia to her son, Pope St Gregory the Great, in 597 to build a monastery on, amongst the oaks and chestnuts 735 m above the sea. A mosaic in the church shows the painting being greeted by monks on its arrival on the back of a mule. The animal stamped on the ground, and a spring, from which pilgrims still drink, gushed forth miraculously. And here they built their monastery. As you enter the church the painting above the High Altar is strikingly — almost eerily — black. When you turn the lights on, the image changes to a tender, dark, Byzantine representation of Mary, holding Jesus, their faces touching gently. The child's feet are delicately shod in sandals. There are two statues of the Madonna in the church. One, which is black, is based on the painting. The other reminds us that the Virgins around Etna still perform their ancient function of halting its streams of molten lava. This is the Madonna of the Fire who came from Gieretto (2 km above Vena) on 6 February 1865, when she was placed in front of the stream of lava, blew on it and thus extinguished the fire. At nearby Zafferana, where we stayed, the Virgin there performed a similar function as recently as 1992.

La Vena, the vein, refers to the miraculous spring, but could equally well represent the flowing tide of the red lava, destructive but fertilizing, flowing from Etna and depicted in another mosaic in the fine new church dating from 1930. The next-door village is Santa Venera commemorating the goddess Venus.

LUXEMBURG

Schwarze Muttergottes 404 (26). In Ch. of St Jean in the Ville-

Basse or Grund, outside the city walls across the River Alzette to the E. Superb statue of BV, which came here in 1805 from Abbey of Marienthal (Mersch); walnut, standing; 1.2 m; probably late 14 C. from Cologne; invoked against Black Death; also known as Stella Coeli; statue of St Roch.

MEXICO

Guadalajara Miraculous and much venerated BV, La Virgen de Zapopan.

PORTUGAL

Madeira Funchal. BV, O. L. of Dolours in sacristy of Cathedral. In another Ch. on the island there is a BV from South America.

SCOTLAND

Roslin Michelin 401 31 K 16, S of Edinburgh. In Scotland's most mysterious building, Rosslyn Chapel, there is informed speculation that before the Reformation a BV in the crypt and in the triangular niche under the high altar was venerated.

SPAIN

The great increase in entries for Spain is due in part to the travels and researches we have undertaken for our books *On the Trail of Merlin* and *In Search of the Holy Grail and the Precious Blood*, but mainly to the books by Juan G. Atienza, especially the two-volume *Guía de la España Mágica* (Martinez Roca, 1981) and *Nuestra Señora de Lucifer* (Roca, 1991), and Rafael Alarcón Herrera's *La Otra España del Temple* (Martinez Roca, 1988). Atienza has maps for most of his itineraries with many symbols, including one for Black Virgins, without specifying the criteria adopted for this designation. Alarcón, as the title of his book indicates, is particularly interested in sites where the Black Virgin — past or present — is linked to the Templars, and gives little information about the actual images. There is also the authoritative and invaluable work, with maps and photographs, by Antoni Noguera i Massa, *Les Marededeus Romàniques de les Terres Gironines* (Artestudi Barcelona, 1977), though this refers only to images in the province of Girona, most of which are no longer in situ.

Finally, an exhaustive and definitive guide, lavishly illustrated, to all the Marian shrines of Spain, with a volume for each province, is being published by Ediciones Encuentro. The most recent volume appeared in 1995. Unfortunately, this massive work came to our attention too late for the information it contains to be included in this edition.

We were tempted to update earlier entries as our knowledge increased, but have mostly resisted the temptation in the interest of brevity and simplicity. We were increasingly struck by the number of Templar and Grail connections to BV sites and agree with Atienza that the Celtic god Lug is often to be found in references to St Luke, St Lawrence, St Lucia, Luz (light) and various place-names. We also concur with his views on the difficulty of determining what a Black Virgin is. A current (June 1995) exhibition in the museum of Montserrat (qv) demonstrates how many forms the most famous of all, La Moreneta, has assumed over the centuries. Throughout Spain, some images were created black, some were blackened later, some lost their polychrome or are in natural wood (often called Brown Virgins), many are now whitened, some are white but have typically 'black' stories and shapes.

Ágreda Soria   442 G 24. In the Ch. of Na Sra de los Milagros. BV of the Templars of Ágreda reported by Alarcón. In the nearby Cave of Ágreda, Cacus stole from Hercules the cattle of Geryon.

Agres   445 P 28. BV disappeared in the Civil War, replaced by flesh coloured copy in 1940. When fire was destroying her original church in Alicante, she flew away to Agres and landed near the castle, where her present shrine was built.

Alaquás   445 N 28. Na Sra del Olivar, BV found in 1300, destroyed in 1936, replaced by a black copy.

Almenar de Soria   442 G 23. BV Na Sra de la Llana formerly belonged to the Templars of Villaseca. She rescued a youth held captive in a chest from his Moorish prison in Almería, as well as his guard.

Aránzazu   Arantzazu Guipúzcoa 990 (6); 442 D 22. Above High Altar in Franciscan basilica, Andra Mari de Arantzazu, patroness of Guipúzcoa. In 1469 a shepherd, Rodrigo de Balzategui, received a vision, whose elements included a star in a hawthorn tree, a dragon in the great abyss below the tree and a sheep-bell. He discovered the statue in the branches, which, together with the bell, still form part of the Madonna's *mise en scène*. Through her intervention wars and droughts were brought to an end. St Ignatius of Loyola's pilgrimage to Aránzazu in 1522 signalled the start of his religious vocation. Huge modern Ch. and priory on edge of canyon 700 ft above sea level. Miracles include resuscitation, healing, freeing captives, calming storms and saving from shipwreck. Arantzazu is said to mean, in Basque, 'In the thorn, you?' Generally considered a BV.

Los Arcos   442 E 23; 13 C. Atienza considers her the only certain BV in La Rioja.

Astorga   441 E 11. Na Sra de la Majestad in the cathedral is considered a BV by Atienza despite her present colour. Early 12 C., 1 m, a favourite cult object of pilgrims to Compostela.

Astraín   442 D 24, 12 km SW of Pamplona. BV La Virgen del Perdón venerated in a hill-top hermitage since the 14 C.

La Avellá   445 K 29. Just N of Cati. BV of the Hazel Tree (*avellano*) where she was found next to a healing spring.

La Balma   Castellón; 445 J 29. Remarkable sanctuary built into the side of a cliff above a river housed a BV destroyed in the Civil War, though memory of her as black has now faded in La Balma (cave) itself. She was discovered by a one-armed shepherd and repeatedly returned from Zorita to the place that she designated. The area was once frequented by hermits dedicated to St Mary Magdalen. The particular miraculous quality of the shrine, until quite recently, was the cure of madness. It was fief of the Knights of Montesa, an order founded in 1316 as a continuation of the Templars.

Barcelona   443 H 36. In the Ch. of Na Sra de la Merced, just off the Paseo de Colón on the old port, the Princess of Barcelona, la Mare de Deu de la Mercé. Veneration since 13 C. It was she who inspired the youthful St

Peter Nolasco, who had left his home in Languedoc, which had been devastated by the Albigensian Crusade, to found the Order of Mercedarians, dedicated to offering themselves as prisoners to the Moors in substitution for those already captive. It was on 2 August 1218 that the apparition occurred, and the next day he sought out his confessor, the future saint, Raymond of Pennafort, who told him that he had also received this commission from the Virgin. They told the king, Jaime I, who had had the same message, and on 10 August, feast of St Lawrence, the order was duly founded. The statue today is polychrome, after the description of his vision given by Peter Nolasco, but Alarcón, drawing our attention to Jaime I's predilection for BVs, includes her in a list of eight of his favourites that are more or less black. Peter Nolasco received his inspiration to seek his vocation in Barcelona from a retreat he made at Montserrat. Locals we have consulted do not consider Na Sra de la Merced, *pace* Alarcón, to be a BV.

Benavente 441 F 12. In the Ch. of S. Juan del Mercado, the statue of St Catherine is also known as La Virgen Mora. Benavente was a Templar possession. (Alarcón.)

La Bien Aparecida 442 B/C 19. Na Sra Aparecida appeared to shepherds in a prodigious light. The BV sweated and shed tears on 30 March 1919. Each time

there was an attempt to move the Virgin it was prevented by great storms. (Atienza.)

Burgui 442 D 26. (1) Off C 137, between Burgui and Salvatierra de Esca. BV Virgen de la Peña in mountain-top hermitage marking the borders of Aragon and Navarre. BV noted by Atienza, first of a series of six in the area.
(2) Between Burgui and Roncal (qv) on the C 137 and the R. Esca, Na Sra del Camino (way), another BV mentioned by Atienza.

Burguillos del Cerro 444 Q 10, 24 km ENE of Jerez de los Caballeros. S. María de la Encina (holm-oak) originally a BV, whose cult was introduced by the Templars, whose property this was.

Cáceres 444 N 10. (1) 14 km N of Cáceres on N 630, second turning on left to end of track. Hermitage of La Virgen del Prado or Tentudía, who appeared in superhuman splendour to give victory to the Christians against the Moors. (Atienza.)
(2) 25 km W of Cáceres by N 521 and C 523. Hermitage of Na Sra de la Luz (light), whose miraculous lights brought victory to the Christians. She is also commemorated in the nearby Well of the killing. Celtic and megalithic remains. (Atienza.)

Calatrava la Vieja 444 O 18. In the Ermita Santuario de la

Encarnación 8 km N of Carrión de Calatrava. BV reported by Atienza. Here the R. Guadiana (Wadi = river, of the goddess Aau or Dana), arising in the lakes of Ruidera by the cave of Montesinos and Merlin, re-emerges from its underground journey. Near by are the ruins of the Castle of Calatrava — originally Qala'at Ribbat, stronghold of Muslim warrior monks, forerunners of the Templars, who later ruled here. The Order of Calatrava took on their mantle after the suppression of 1307.

Carrea 441 C 11. Na Sra del Cebrano, BV, with Grail cauldron in her Ch. (now stolen). Templar foundation. (Alarcón.)

Carrizo de la Ribera 441 E 12. Na Sra del Villar, BV venerated in a hermitage, which is all that remains of what was once a village and a Cistercian monastery. There is a popular pilgrimage procession on Whit Tuesday. The BV is invoked against storms and hail.

Carrizosa 444 P 21. Hermitage of Na Sra de la Carrasca (pineoak), BV near the Celtiberian sanctuary of Balazote and the Templar castle of Alhambra guarding the approaches to Merlin's cave at Ruidera, where until the Civil War there was a Grail cauldron particularly effective against sterility and diseases of the head. (Alarcón.)

Ceinos de Campos 442 F 14, 19.5 km NW of Medina de Rioseco on N 601. Na Sra del Temple or del Claustro, originally a BV who held a Catherine wheel in her hand. Her successor may be in the National Archaeological Museum in Madrid, but there is still a version of her in the parish church. Ceinos was once one of the richest Templar commanderies in Spain, and its stones were used to construct the Civil Guard barracks. An enchanted Moorish princess, Juanina, lived in Templar times at the bottom of a well, guarding a treasure, and sometimes appeared at night to tempt the knights. There is also an association of black cats who speak to each other in human language at the feast of St John the Baptist. Juanina is derived from Xana, a White lady or fairy, no doubt the origin of the BV cult. (Alarcón.)

Cornella del Terri 443 F 38; 10 km N of Gerona. Byzantine-style wooden BV burnt in 1936 by the Communists.

Cuenca 444 L 23. In Ch. of San Antón on N Bank of River Júcar by bridge on N 400 Madrid road. La Virgen de la Luz (light), standing on moon, Child on left arm, shepherd's crook in right hand. BV found by shepherd in cleft rock by river after apparition of light. The BV delivered the city to the Christians after a siege of nine months, in which the Templars were prominent. Statue of St Roch;

pagan and heretical traditions. Atienza calls Cuenca the City of the Grail and considers it derives its name from the sacred vessel.

Deyá/Deiá 443 M 37. A friend assures us that she has recently seen a BV in the parish church. Deiá is where Robert Graves (qv), the prophet of the Black Madonna, spent the last few decades of his life, and where he lies buried.

Garabandal 442 C 16 S. Sebastián de Garabandal. We have twice been drawn back to this not very accessible site by dreams and meaningful coincidences. In 1961 the Archangel Michael and later the Blessed Virgin Mary appeared to four little girls — Conchita, Mari Loli, Jancinta and Mari Cruz — aged between ten and twelve. Many miracles were associated with the visions, but the Church has evinced little enthusiasm for the cult that derived from them, perhaps because the Virgin's messages were unfavourable to new developments in the Church and favoured old-fashioned devotions like the Rosary.

In the circular grove of pines above the village you will see, high on a tree, as well as a glass-encased statue of the Madonna, a primitive wooden BV, which encapsulates something of the pagan magic of the site.

Garde 442 D 27. Na Sra de Zuberoa on borders of Aragon and Navarre. Romanesque BV brought from France, healer of the possessed. Country of the outcast, heretical Cagots.

Garriguella 443 E 29. Mare de Deu del Camp, BV who by a miracle of light helped Charlemagne to win a victory over the Saracens.

Girona/Gerona 443 F 38. (1) The Mare de Deu de la Seo now stands impressively on its own at the entrance to the Treasury Museum, but no longer as a cult object. Carved in box-wood by a stonemason in the mid 12 C., she was once covered in gold or silver and is 48 cm high. The cathedral has been dedicated to the Mother of God since its foundation at the end of the 3 C.
(2) Her place has now been taken by the Virgin who presides over the magnificent retablo on the High Altar, clad in gold, with a dark silver face and crowned by twelve stars.
(3) The Museu d'Art next to the Cathedral contains a splendid collection of Romanesque and Gothic statues of the Virgin. Some of them are black, many are brown, but they are all, sadly, reminiscent of caged tigresses in a zoo — beautiful but impotent and desacralized.
(4) Na Sra de la Pared Delgada or de la Selva (qv) is now said by Atienza to be currently in Girona, but our researches proved negative, and she is not mentioned by Noguera i Massa (see introduction to Spain). Atienza describes

her as strange and oriental-looking, wearing a bonnet of Byzantine appearance.

Gordalizo del Pino 441 E 14. Local tradition of a BV of the Elm, who prevented herself from being carried to Gordalizo by becoming impossibly heavy. She left behind her a stream of pure water, which flows around the village. (Atienza.)

Greixer 443 E 35. Once in Ch. of St Clement, consecrated in 839, BV has now disappeared after being, in Noguera's words, 'excessively and poorly painted late in the day in polychrome.' Held a very adult-looking Jesus with a closed book in his left hand on her left knee. Both figures crowned.

Güesa 442 D 26. Na Sra de Arburua between Güesa and Izal (Itzal in Basque) noted by Atienza as a BV, one of six in the immediate vicinity.

Hernani 442 C 24. the Virgin of Zikuñaga is reported by a local resident to be a BV.

Huesca 443 F 28. In Grail Ch. of S. Pedro el Viejo, BV Na Sra de las Nieves (snows).

Isaba 442 D 27. Na Sra de Idoya with her eternal smile noted as a BV by Atienza.

Jerez de la Frontera 446 V 11. Na Sra de la Merced in Santiago, the gipsy quarter, is a BV who

plays an important part in the traditions of southern Spain.

Jete 446 V 18; 8 km N of Almuñecar on old Granada road. A BV known as Our Lady of the Waters has been placed near the Río Verde, where an ancient river deity was once worshipped. (Information from the *Market Place*, a magazine of the Eastern Costa del Sol.)

Jimena 446 S 20. Na Sra del Remedio ranked as a BV by Atienza. Just to the south is the Cueva de la Graja (jackdaw), a prehistoric sanctuary, where there are many strange wall-paintings.

Jódar 446 S 20; 4 km S on C 325, 4.5 km W on C 328, turn left before village of Bedmar to la Ermita de Cuadros. A BV according to Atienza and one of the most venerated and ancient shrines in the region.

Lascellas 443 F 29. BV, Na Sra de la Alegría (joy), reported by Alarcón.

Leboreiro 441 D 4. BV, S. María de Leboreiro (of the hares), with a nearby spring, which emits light by night and a sweet perfume by day. The hare is associated with Hecate and the moon. The BV returned to her spring every night until a local artist sculpted a replica of her and placed it in the tympanum of the church, after which the original consented to stay in her temple. (Atienza.)

Lurdes 443 H 27 (not on map). Continue 3 km W up sandy lane from the centre of Arenys del Munt (signposted). BV in cave, credited with healing miracles. Ranked as a BV by Atienza, surprisingly, if she really is a replica of N-D de Lourdes. The images in the grotto were destroyed in the Civil War, but there is no memory of any of them being black. Ex-votos, living cult, sanctuary set amidst children's park, playgrounds and restaurants. Image brought from France in 1922.

Madrid 990 (15); (1) Na Sra de los Milagros is definitely a BV.
(2) Na Sra de la Almudena, the patroness of Madrid is brown, natural polished wood.

Mellid/Melide 441 D 5. BV reported by Atienza in an area surrounded by megaliths and near an important dolmen.

Meranges 443 E 35; 14 C.; wood; 80 cm. BV Mare de Deu de l'Ajuda suckling Child from left breast, both figures holding a dove. Disappeared 1936.

Mijas 446 W 16. BV, La Virgen de la Cueva, in a chapel adapted from a natural cavern. Miraculous cures. (Atienza.)

Mogrony 443 F 36 (not on map). Continue W up the GE 402 from Gombren until you see the now isolated Ch. of S. Pere (1138) on a small plateau on a cliff, which has a hermitage halfway down it. This was the parish church of the now abandoned and vanished village of Mogrony, the Covadonga (qv) of Catalonia, whence the *reconquista* of the nation began in the 8 C. The staircase leading to the sanctuary was constructed in 1915. The BV, called a *moreneta* by Noguera, was discovered by two oxen at the foot of the spring, with a vase of lilies, at the site of the present sanctuary. It is 12 C., wood, 50 cm, with the Child sitting centrally, blessing with his right hand. Excessively restored after 1939, but still black, and venerated in the Ch.

Monfragüe 444 M 11. In the Castle of Monfragüe, the headquarters of the order of chivalry of that name founded in Jerusalem after the First Crusade and now converted into the sanctuary of what Atienza calls 'a very curious BV'. Sculpted by St Luke and brought back from Jerusalem by Rodrigo, Count of Sarria. The Monfragüe National Park is notable for its birds, ancient forest and spectacular scenery. Sanctuary closed when we were there.

Morcín 441 C 12. Na Sra del Monsagro in octagonal Templar hermitage, La Ermita de Arriba, accompanied by Sts Catherine of Alexandria, Mary Magdalene and James (of Compostela).

Murcia   445 S 26. Alarcón notes Templar BV Na Sra de Gracia or la Real (royal) in the city.

Muskilda   442 D 26; in Santuario de Muskilda 2 km N of Ochagavía. BV, celebrated with strange pagan dances on 8 September. Found in oak by shepherd. Templar   sanctuary. (Alarcón.)

Navas de San Juan   446 R 19/ 20. Na Sra de la Estrella in sanctuary of that name marked on map 3 km S of Navas. BV of great popular   devotion   noted   by Atienza.

Oropesa   444 M 14. Na Sra de las Peñitas, tiny BV found among rocks by a herdsman, who noticed one of his cows pawing the earth. He placed the statue between the horns of the cow and took her to the town.

Ozón   441 C 2. Virgen de la Ozón noted as BV by Atienza — rare in Galicia. His directions for once are rather vague — he calls the place Ozas, perhaps the Gallego version — but from the map this must be the location he intends.

Paderne   441 C 5. Na Sra de Pedernere (black stone). BV in small hermitage between Paderne and Betanzos replaces the pre-Christian cult of a black meteorite by the Luso-Celtic worshippers of Lug. Important Templar commandery in Betanzos. (Alarcón.)

Pájaros de Lampreana   441 G 12; 36 km N of Zamora. Na Sra del Templo is one of the few images of the Virgin of the Temple which has come down to us. Originally a BV, or at least *morena*, her face and that of her son seem to be covered by doll-like masks. She helped a local Templar to overcome a monstrous serpent that was ravaging the surrounding territory belonging to the order. When the knight deposited a black stone in the lap of the Virgin, the serpent disappeared into a lake and was never seen again. (Alarcón.) The BV was hidden in a well during the French invasion, which is why, they say, she lost her dusky colour.

Parlavà   443 F 39; late 12 C.; wood. A Mare de Deu *Brune*, which had lost all its polychrome, once in Ch. of St Christopher, sold, and in 1977 still in private hands, though the Archaeological Museum in Girona would like to acquire it. Child missing, BV very worm-eaten, with eyes seemingly closed in blissful contemplation.

Peralada   443 F 39; 15 C. Formerly in Parish Ch. Seated BV with Child on left arm, Child's arms and Virgin's left hand missing, black faces. Now in Art Museum   in   Girona,   much cleaned up.

Ponferrada   441 E 10. The Templars were granted the ancient ruined fortress of Ponferrada in

1178 and, to repair it, cut down the wood on the hill there. When they struck one of the aged holmoaks with an axe, it split open to reveal a BV, which they named Na Sra de la Encina del Bosque Sagrado (holm-oak of the sacred wood). S. Toribio of Liébana in the Picos de Europa brought the BV back with him from Jerusalem, along with a piece of the True Cross. This he gave to the monastery there that bears his name. He placed the BV in the Cathedral of Astorga between León and Ponferrada. When the Muslims captured the town in 714, three centuries after the donation of S. Toribio, Christians hid it in the forest of Ponferrada. After her recovery she was placed in the church built by the Templars next to their castle, where she became the mother of the whole of the Bierzo. She disappeared when the new church was built in 1573, to be replaced by a version from the 16 C. She may have been returned to Astorga Cathedral, whose diocesan museum is rich in Romanesque Madonnas. Ponferrada is named for the iron bridge built in the 11 C. across the Sil to help pilgrims on their way to Santiago de Compostela. Fifty kilometres further along 'the Milky Way' is the pass of O Cebreiro, where Galician legend has Sir Galahad discovering the Holy Grail — by which name the chalice is still known. We visited Ponferrada and bought Alarcón's invaluable book there, to which we are indebted for much of this information. The castle is one of the most mysterious buildings in Spain.

Puendeluna 443 F 27 ('moon bridge'). In May 1987 thieves stole a decoy in place of the genuine BV, which is still there and well protected.

El Puig 445 N 29; between two motorways; half-way between the Grail city of Valencia and Spain's Masada, Sagunto. Templar BV carved from one of the stones from the cover of the Blessed Virgin Mary's tomb at Ephesus, home of the mother of all BVs. She appeared in the time of King Jaime I the Conqueror. (Alarcón.) Ch. erected on site of temple to Phoenician goddess, Tanit. St Peter Nolasco (see Barcelona) found the BV buried inside a bell, thanks to a path shown him by seven stars in the sky. Tradition has it that the image was engraved by angels.

Quadres 443 E 35. In hill-top sanctuary by the R. Segre in the parish of All (neither of them on map), SW of Puigcerdá, 12/13 C. wooden statue, now disappeared, which the cautious Noguera hints was a BV badly repainted in polychrome.

Requena 445 N 26. Very interesting, standing 14 C. BV, La Virgen de la Soterraña, found in a crypt, totally black face, destroyed in 1936.

Requesens 443 E 39 (not on

map). It is an exciting four hours' walk up the valley of the R. Anyet from Sant Climent Sescebes and four hours' walk back again. Join the *romería* at 6 am on the first Saturday after Easter. Dolmens along the way proclaim an ancient origin for the pilgrimage and the Església Vella (old church), now a heap of ruins, dates from 844. The beautiful, very old, wooden BV, 90 cm, was last described in 1657, and Noguera speaks of her in the past tense. There is, however, a rare representation of a late-Romanesque Virgin and Child with two angels on the tympanum above the entrance to the chapel of the castle.

Riglos   443 E 27. Two BVs in Ch. at highest point of village under the impressive sugar-loaf rocks of Los Mallos, haunted by Egyptian vultures. Ask for Sr Antonio, the sacristan, or contact the priest of Ayerbe.

El Rocío   446 U 10. The Virgen del Rocío (dew) is the goal of the greatest *romería* in Spain, attracting 500,000 pilgrims annually on the first Monday after Whitsun — a million when the Pope joined the throng. She was discovered by a shepherd in the 15 C., in a tree where she had no doubt been hidden centuries earlier to protect her from the invading Moors. But the tale has pre-Christian origins in tales of wood-nymphs, and Atienza goes further in seeing in the Virgen del Rocío 'a pagan deity in its deepest meaning', the mother of the superabundant world, nature naturing in the great nature reserve of the Coto de Doñana. Just to the north was the Templar stronghold of Villalba. Whatever the colour of her face today, this is surely a BV.

Roncal   442 D 27. Romanesque statue of the Virgen del Castillo, brought across the Pyrenees from France to escape the iconoclasm of the Huguenots to an area where Cagots and Cathars had already sought asylum. Atienza's photograph shows the image as whitened, but demonstrates what he calls the perfect structure of a BV.

Salinas de Añana   442 D 21; in parish church. (1) Na Sra de Villacones, 13 C. BV.
(2) Na Sra de la Redonda, or de la O (cry of parturition?), also a BV of slightly more recent date.

Santa Coloma de Farners   443 G 37. In hermitage by castle to W of town 12 C. Mare de Deu miraculously discovered by a shepherd boy and an ox. Wooden, 65 cm, badly damaged in the Civil War and tastelessly modernized in its restoration.

Santa Colomba de la Somoza   441 E 11. La Virgen de la O, a BV who represents the restoration of an ancient cult to the Great Mother, instituted by the Templars. The present statue dates from 15 C.

Sant Joan   443 N 39; 1 km outside village on a hill. BV Na Sra de la Consolación or the Mare de Deu Trobada (found). Strange lights in the night led shepherds to find her in the trunk of a wild olive-tree. Her first guardian was a young shepherd, who was also a Moorish slave. One recalls that on the nearby sacred mountain of Randa, Ramon Llull, Cataluña's greatest mystic, was enlightened by a Moorish shepherd-boy. The next door village of Montuiri was a Templar fief.

San Sebastián/Donostia   442 C 24. BV known as Kero reported by local inhabitant.

San Vicente de la Sonsierra   442 E 21. Don Ramiro, the Infante of Navarre, distinguished himself in the capture of Jerusalem under Godefroy de Bouillon, winning the Pool of Bethesda, famous for its healing waters, and traditional childhood home of the Virgin Mary, which is now the Church of St Anne. On his return Ramiro built the Church of Santa María de la Piscina, next to a druidic pool, hewn out of the rock, surrounded by a stone necropolis. In it he placed the BV, carved by St Luke, containing a fragment of the True Cross which he had brought back with him. (Alarcón.) On a neighbouring eminence are the remains of a hillfort. San Vicente has strong Templar and Grail connections, as well as a remarkable Holy Week procession of bare-backed penitents, who whip them selves until the blood flows.

Serinyá   443 F 38; 13 C.; wood. In tiny Ch. of Sant Miquel de les Vinyes S. of the town, BV Mare de Deu de les Vinyes (vines), made by local craftsman. Child on left knee; disappeared in the Civil War (1936); photograph shows black faces.

Seville   446 T 11/12. Some Sevillanos say their real BV is Our Lady of the Monarchs, given by St Louis of France to his cousin St Ferdinand of Spain, who lies buried below the altar of the Chapel Royal of the Cathedral over which the robed statue of the Virgin presides.

Sigena   443 G 29. Virgen of Sigena included by Alarcón in a list of 'more or less black' Virgins 'discovered' by King Jaime I, as great an admirer of BVs as Louis XI of France. Templar associations.

Siones   442 19/20 (not on map). Take the C 6318 SW from Bilbao, turn left at Villasana de Mena, follow the narrow road to Vallejo (interesting Hospitaller Ch.) to the former Templar stronghold of Siones and the Ch. of S. María under the rocky Sierra de la Magdalena. Ask for the key at the farmhouse next to the Ch. designed for initiates (cf. Thuret, France, also Templar). One capital shows a Grail-bearer. The BV has now been whitened. 'Siones' in the *langue des Oiseaux* means 'Thou art Sion'.

Soriguerola 443 E 35 (not on map); 12 C. BV; wood. Between Puigcerdá and Urtx, to which district it belongs, on right-hand bank of R. Segre in Ch. of St Michael (worth a visit). Now disappeared. Child seated centrally, right hand raised in benediction. Photograph shows black faces with whites and pupils of eyes in sharp contrast.

Tiscar 446 S 20. BV outside village in la Cueva del Agua, carved by St Luke and brought from Palestine by Bishop S. Isicio, a disciple of St James (Santiago) and by the sound of his name an initiate of Isis. Since there were only pagans in the land, he placed the statue in a cave to do her own work of conversion, which she has continued to do, with many miracles, since the first century, even among the Muslim conquerors who approved her cult. When the Christians returned she refused to be transferred to a church, preferring to remain in her grotto. Living cult, many ex-votos.

Tolosa 442 C 23. Virgin of Zaskeen reported as BV in Ch. of S. María.

Torme 442 D 19. BV reported by Atienza in the best preserved Romanesque church of the district of Butrera. Theme of heads, serpents, the Magi and the Great Mother saluting man.

Torreciudad 443 E 30. In a hill town with a wonderful situation, overlooking the Embalse (reservoir) of El Grado, strikingly visible from the C 138, which leads S from the Bielsa tunnel. Torreciudad and its BV have been a popular goal for pilgrims for over 800 years. José María Escrivá de Balaguer, who founded the influential Order of Opus Dei in 1928, was taken there on mule-back by his parents as a dying child of two years, a scene that reminded a shepherd of the arrival of Joseph and Mary with the Christ Child. They recited the rosary at the foot of the statue, and the mother offered her son to the service of the Virgin if his life were spared. A new basilica to house the miraculous image was built in 1975. Alarcón confirms that it is a BV.

Ugijar 446 V 20. Painting of BV La Morenita in apse of 16 C. Church of Our La ly of the Martyrdom. Crowned, standing on the moon, surrounded by white roses. (Photograph in the *Market Place*, a magazine of the Eastern Costa del Sol.)

Valdeavellano de Tera 442 G 22. BV Virgen de las Espinillas in a hermitage difficult to reach; reported by Atienza.

Vallivana 445 K 30. BV who is the patron of Morella, the city she saved from an epidemic. Her feast takes place every six years, when she is carried in procession the 24 km to the city.

Zocueca 446 R 18, 6 km W of Bailen (= Bethlehem, Belenos or both?). BV reported by Atienza in the sanctuary of la Virgen de Zocueca.

SWITZERLAND

Minusio 427 K 7. Ticino on E outskirts of Locarno. Wall-painting in a room of a house belonging to the Tognetta family of the Madonna di Walda (Einsiedeln qv) standing on a sort of palisade of candles, dating from mid 19 C.

USA

Eureka Missouri; 35 mls W of St Louis; Black Madonna Shrine and Grottos. This shrine, in honour of the BV of Czestochowa, was the life's work of Brother Bronislaus Luszcz of the Franciscan Missionary Brothers. This first chapel of cedar-wood was completed in 1938 but destroyed by vandals twenty years later. Now there is a remarkable complex of manmade grottoes in a park, with the BV in a fine open-air pavilion chapel. Open daily 8 am-8 pm during spring and summer.

NEW YORK

Lexington In Ch. of St John the Baptist, BV behind the altar doors, and another on the exterior portico.

New York Cathedral of St John the Divine, BV icon.

Santa Fe New Mexico. Friends tell us of a renewed cult of the BV of Guadalupe (Mexico) in the south-west, with a number of BV shrines.

Bibliography

Adams, H., *Mont-Saint-Michel and Chartres*, London, 1913, 1980.

Alexander, W. L., *The Ancient British Church*, London, 1889.

Algermissen, K., *Lexikon der Marienkunde*, Regensburg, 1957.

Allegro, J. M., *The Sacred Mushroom and the Cross*, London, 1973.

Alliès, A.-P., *Pézenas une ville d'États*, Montpellier, 1951.

Alvárez de la Braña, R., 'Palencia monumental y la Virgen de Husillos', *Boletín de la Sociedad Castellana de Excursiones*, año 1, no. 4, 1903.

Apuleius, *The Golden Ass*, trans. Robert Graves, London, 1951.

Aradi, Z., *Shrines to Our Lady*, New York, 1954.

Arès, J.d', 'Les vierges noires en France', *Atlantis*, no. 266, pp.123-32, 1972.

Arès, J. d'., 'A propos des vierges noires', *Atlantis*, no. 266, pp. 184–92, 1972.

Ashe, G., *The Virgin*, London, 1976.

Attwater, D., *The Penguin Dictionary of Saints*, Harmondsworth, 1965.

Auden, W. H. and Taylor, P. B. (trans.), *The Elder Edda*, London, 1969.

Bac, H., 'La vierge noire des Atlantes', *Atlantis*, no. 266, pp.147-55, 1972.

Bader, K., *Pfarr- und Wallfahrtskirche Leutershausen*, Ottobeuren, 1977.

Baedeker, K., *Northern Italy*, London, 1913.

Baigent, M. and Leigh, R., 'Virgins with a pagan past', *The Unexplained*, no. 4, pp.61-5, 1980.

Baigent, M. and Leigh, R., 'The goddess behind the mask', *The Unexplained*, no. 6, pp.114-17, 1980.

Baigent, M. and Leigh. R., 'Guardians of the living earth', *The Unexplained*, no. 8, pp. 154–7, 1980.

Baigent, M. Leigh, R. and Lincoln, H., *The Holy Blood and the Holy Grail*, London, 1982.

Balme, P. and Crégut, R., *La Basilique Notre-Dame du Port*, Clermont-Ferrand, 1971.

Bardy, B., *Les Légendes du Gévaudan*, Mende, 1979.

Barrès, M. *La Colline inspirée*, Paris, 1913.

Bauer, W., *Orthodoxy and Heresy in Earliest Christianity*, London, 1934, 1972.

Beaufrère, A., *Notre-Dame du Château à St Christophe*, Aurillac, undated.

Begg, E., 'Gnosis and the single vision', in M. Tuby (ed.), *In the Wake of Jung*, London, 1983.

Begg, E., *Myth and Today's Consciousness*, London, 1984.

Beicht, W., *Maria Himmelfahrt Ludwigshafen-Oggersheim*, Ludwigshafen, 1977.

Belot, V., *La France des pélérinages*, Verviers, 1976.

Benoit, P., *L'Atlantide*, Paris, 1920, 1974.

Berland, J., 'Meymac et son abbaye', *Bulletin de la Société des Lettres, Sciences et Arts de la Corrèze*, pp.5-77, 1975.

Bernard, J.-L., *Histoire secrète de Lyon et du Lyonnais*, Paris, 1977.

Bertrand, M., *Histoire secrète de la Provence*, Paris, 1978.

Bible. Various translations.

Blanc, P., *La Charité à Espalion*, Rodez, 1973.

Blanquart, H., 'La basilique hermétique de Guingamp', *Atlantis*, no. 253, pp.402-30, November 1961.

Bodeson, J., *Verviers Notre-Dame des Récollets*, Liège, 1972.

Bordenove, G., *Histoire secrète de Paris*, Paris, 1980.

Bouvet, R., *Notre-Dame de l'Aumône*, Rumilly, 1982.

Bouvier-Ajam, M., *Dagobert*, Paris, 1980.

Boymann, G. and O., *The Basilica at Kevelaer*, Munich, 1978.

Bradley, M., *The Mists of Avalon*, London, 1984.

Brétigny, J., 'Les vierges noires et le mystère de Rennes-le-Château', *Nostra*, March 1983.

Brétigny, J. and Deloux, J.-P., *Rennes-le-Château capitale secrète de l'histoire de France*, Paris, 1982.

Briffault, R., *The Mothers*, New York, 1977 (abridged), 1927.

Bril, J., *Lilith ou la mère obscure*, Paris, 1981.

Brion, M., *Frédéric II de Hohenstaufen*, Paris, 1978.

Bridge, W., *The Gods of the Egyptians*, London, 1904.

Buenner, D., *Notre-Dame de la Mer et les Saintes-Maries*, Lyons, undated.

Buisson, P., *La Vierge Noire du Charmaix*, Modane, 1984.

Burri, M., *Germanische Mythologie zwischen Verdrängung und Verfälschung*, Zürich, 1982.

Butler, A. (ed. Kelly, B.), *The Lives of the Fathers, Martyrs and Other Principal Saints*, 5 vols, London, 1959.

Campbell, J., *The Masks of God*, New York, 1964.

Campbell, J. (ed.), *The Mystic Vision, Eranos Yearbooks*, vol. 6, London, 1969.

Canseliet, E., 'Notre-Dame de dessous-terre', *Atlantis*, no. 266, pp.155-63, 1972.

Carny, L., 'Les vièrges noires en France', *Atlantis*, no. 206, pp. 163-8, 1962.

Cauvin, A. *Découvrir la France Cathare*, Verviers, 1974.

Cazes, A., *Tuir*, Prades, undated.

Cazes, A., *Le Roussillon sacré*, Prades, 1977.

Cazes, A., *Prats-de-Molló et sa région*, Prades, 1978.

Chabrillat, R., *Thuret son eglise d'initiés son saint*, Clermont-Ferrand, 1979.

Chagny, A., *Notre-Dame de la Garde*, Marseilles, 1949.

Champagnac, J.-B., *Dictionnaire des pélérinages*, Paris, 1850.

Champion, P., *Le Roi Louis XI*, Paris, 1936.

Charles, R. H. (trans.), *The Book of Enoch*, London, 1912.

Charpentier, J., *L'Ordre des Templiers*, Paris, 1977.

Charpentier, L., *Les Mystères templiers*, Paris, 1967.

Charpentier, L., *Les Jacques et le mystère de Compostelle*, Paris, 1971.

Charpentier, L., *The Mysteries of Chartres Cathedral*, London, 1972.

Chartuni, M., *Nossa Senhora de Aparecida*, São Paolo, undated.

Chevalier, J. and Gheerbrant, A., *Dictionnaire des symboles*, Paris, 1969.

Chevallier, B. and Goulay, B., *Je vous salue Marie*, Paris, 1981.

Cirlot, J., *A Dictionary of Symbols*, London, 1962.

Clarke, C., *Everyman's Book of Saints*, London, 1914, 1956.

Coadic, J.-B., *Notre-Dame de Bon Secours de Guingamp*, Guingamp, 1933.

Cohn, N., *Europe's Inner Demons*, London, 1975.

Colin-Simard, A., *Les Apparitions de la Vierge*, Paris, 1981.

Colquhoun, H., *Our Descent from Israel*, Glasgow, 1931.

Colson, J., *Sion-Vaudémont ou la colline inspirée*, Paris, 1978.

Comte, L., *The Cathedral of Le Puy and its Environs*, Colmar, 1978.

Cooper, J., *An Illustrated Encyclopaedia of Traditional Symbols*, London, 1978.

Croix, M., 'La vierge de Châtillon-sur-Seine dite du miracle de la lactation' *Aesculape*, no. 1, January 1932.

Cross, F. L. (ed.), *The Oxford Dictionary of the Christian Church*, London, 1958.

Dailliez, L., *La France des Templiers*, Verviers, 1974.

Daniel-Rops, H., *The Church in the Dark Ages*, London, 1959.

Darcy, G. and Angebert, M., *Histoire secrète de la Bourgogne*, Paris, 1978.

Davidson, H. R. Ellis, *Gods and Myths of Northern Europe*, Harmondsworth, 1964.

Davidson, R., *Astrology*, London, 1963.

Dawson, L., *A Book of the Saints*, London, undated.

Delaporte, Y., *Les trois Notre-Dame de la cathédrale de Chartres*, Paris, 1965.

Delarue, L., *Notre-Dame de Lumières*, Lyons, 1973.

Delsante, U., *Collecchio: Strutture Rurale e Vita Contadine*, Parma, 1982.

Denis, N. and Boulet, R., *Romée ou le pélérin moderne à Rome*, Paris, 1935.

Dereine, G., *La Légende de Notre-Dame de Walcourt*, Namur, 1975.

Devore, N., *Encyclopaedia of Astrology*, New York, 1947.

Drochon, J. E., *Histoire illustrée des pélérinages français de la Très Sainte Vierge*, Paris, 1890.

Duchaussoy, J., 'Vierges cosmiques et vierges noires', *Atlantis*, no. 226, pp.164-8, 1972.

Duhoureau, B., *Guide des Pyrénées mystérieuses*, Paris, 1973.

Dumas, F., *Histoire secrète de la Lorraine*, Paris, 1979.

Dumoulin, J. and Pycke, J., *La Cathédrale Notre-Dame de Tournai*, Tournai, 1980.

Dupuy-Pacherand, F., 'Les vierges noires et les déesses pré-chrétiennes', *Atlantis*, no. 205, November, 1961.

Dupuy-Pacherand, F., 'Du symbolisme cosmique aux vierges noires', *Atlantis* no. 266, pp.133-46, 1972.

Durand-Lefèbvre, M., *Etude sur l'origine des Vierges Noires*, Paris, 1937.

Eales, S., *St Bernard*, London, 1890.

Escot, J., *Fourvière à travers les sièclᵉs*, Lyons, 1954.

Fanthorpe, P. and L., *The Holy Grail Revealed*, North Hollywood, 1982.

Faux, A., *Notre-Dame du Puy*, Le Puy, 1979.

Fernández y Sánchez, P., *Mariología Extremeña*, awaiting publication.

Fisher, C., *Walsingham Lives On*, London, 1979.

Fleury, R de, *La Sainte Vierge*, Paris, 1878.

Foatelli, N., 'La vierge noire de Paris Notre-Dame-de-Bonne-Délivrance', *Atlantis*, no. 266, pp.180-3, 1972.

Forsyth, I., *The Throne of Wisdom*, Princeton, 1972.

Foucher, E., *Notre-Dame de la Délivrande*, La Délivrande, 1983.

France, A., *Thaïs*, Paris, 1890.

France, A., *La Rôtisserie de la Reine Pédauque*, Paris, 1893.

Franz, M.-L. von, *Aurora Consurgens*, London, 1966.

Franz, M.-L. von, *Apuleius' Golden Ass*, New York, 1970.

Franz, M.-L. von, *C.G. Jung: His Myth in Our Time*, London, 1975.

Franz, M.-L. von, *Alchemy*, Toronto, 1980.

Fraser, J., *The Golden Bough*, 1922.

Fröhlich, H., *Ein Bildnis der Schwarzen Muttergottes von Brünn in Aachen*, Mönchengladbach, 1967.

Fsadni, M., *Our Lady of the Grotto*, Rabat, 1980.

Fulcanelli, *Le Mystère des cathédrales*, London, 1971.

Furneaux, R., *The Other Side of the Story*, London, 1971.

Gage, M., *Woman, Church and State*, Watertown, 1893, 1980.

Gascuel, E., *Notre-Dame de la Brune*, Roumégoux, 1958.

Gilardoni, V., *I Monumenti d'Arte e di Storia del Canton Ticino*, Basle, 1979.

Gordon, P., *Les Vierges Noires*, Essais, Paris, 1983.

Gordon, P., *Les Fêtes à travers les ages*, Paris, 1983.

Gostling, F., *Auvergne and its People*, London, 1911.

Graves, R., *The Greek Myths*, Harmondsworth, 1955.

Graves, R., *The White Goddess*, London, 1961.

Graves, R., *Mammon and the Black Goddess*, London, 1964.

Graves, R. and Patai, R., *Hebrew Myths*, London, 1964.

Grigson, G., *The Goddess of Love*, London, 1976.

Groningen, G. van, *First Century Gnosticism*, Leiden, 1967.

Guirand, F. (ed.), *New Larousse Encyclopedia of Mythology*, London, 1959.

Guirdham, A., *The Cathars and Reincarnation*, London, 1970.

Gumppenberg, G., *Atlas Marianus*, 1657-9.

Gumppenberg, M. von, *Unsere Königin*, Munich, 1955.

Gustafson, F. R., 'The Black Madonna of Einsiedeln: A Psychological Perspective', Diploma Thesis, C. G. Jung Institute, Zürich, 1973.

Halevi, Z. ben S., *Tree of Life*, London, 1972.

Hall, N., *The Moon and the Virgin*, London, 1980.

Hamlyn, P., *Egyptian Mythology*, London, 1965.

Hamon, A., *Notre-Dame de France*, Paris, 1861.

Harding, E., *Women's Mysteries*, New York, 1955.

Harrison, J., *Themis*, London, 1911, 1977.

Helmbold, A., *The Nag Hammadi Gnostic Texts and the Bible*, Grand Rapids, 1967.

Herolt, J. (ed.), Power, E., *Miracles of the Blessed Virgin Mary*, London, 1928.

Hillman, J. (ed.), *Facing the Gods*, Dallas, 1980.

Hurwitz, S., *Lilith die Erste Eva*, Zürich, 1980.

Huson, P., *The Devil's Picture Book*, London, 1972.

Hutin, S., *Les Prophéties de Nostradamus*, Paris, 1972.

Huynen, J., *L'Enigme des Vierges Noires*, Paris, 1972.

Huysmans, J.-K., *Là-Bas*, Paris, 1908.

Huysmans, J.-K., *La Cathédrale*, Paris, 1908, 1955.

Jalenques, L., *Salers*, Clermont-Ferrand, 1970.

James, B., *Saint Bernard of Clairvaux*, London, 1957.

James, M. R., *The Apocryphal New Testament*, London, 1924, 1953.

Jean, R., *Nerval*, Paris, 1964.

Jonas, H., *The Gnostic Religion*, Boston, 1963.

Josy-Roland, F., *Notre-Dame de Walcourt*, Walcourt, 1972.

Josy-Roland, F., *La Basilique Notre Dame à Walcourt*, Walcourt, 1979.

Jung, C. G., *Psychology and Alchemy* (Collected Works, vol. 12), London, 1953.

Jung, C. G., *The Undiscovered Self*, London, 1958.

Jung, C. G., *Psychology and Religion: West and East* (Collected Works, vol. 11), London, 1958.

Jung, C. G., *Aion* (Collected works, vol. 9, part 2), London, 1959.

Jung, C. G., *Mysterium Coniunctionis* (Collected Works, vol. 14), London, 1963.

Jung, C. G., *Civilization in Transition* (Collected Works, vol. 10), London, 1964.

Jung, C. G., *Two Essays on Analytical Psychology* (Collected Works, vol 7), London, 1966.

Jung, C. G., *Symbols of Transformation* (Collected Works, vol. 5), London, 1967.

Jung, C. G., *Alchemical Studies* (Collected Works, vol. 13), London, 1967.

Jung, E. and Franz, M.-L. von, *The Grail Legend*, London, 1971.

Kerenyi, K., *The Heroes of the Greeks*, London, 1959.

Kerenyi, K., *The Gods of the Greeks*, London, 1961.

Kerenyi, K., *Hermes Guide of Souls*, Zürich, 1976.

Kerenyi, K., *Goddesses of Sun and Moon*, Dallas, 1979.

Kininmouth, C., *Traveller's Guide to Sicily*, London, 1965.

Klossowkski de Rola, S., *The Secret Art of Alchemy*, London, 1973.

Kluger, Schärf R., *Psyche and Bible*, Zürich, 1974.

Koestler, A., *The Thirteenth Tribe*, London, 1976.

Küppers, L., *Das Essener Münster*, Essen, 1963.

Lacordaire, H., *Saint Mary Magdalen*, London, 1880.

Lanson, G., *Histoire de la littérature française*, Paris, 1894.

Lauras-Pourrat, A., *Guide de l'Auvergne Mystérieuse*, Paris, 1976.

Layard, J., *A Celtic Quest*, Zürich, 1975.

Lechner, M., *Schön Schwarz bin ich: zur Ikonographie der Schwarzen Madonnen der Barockzeit*, Heimat-an-Rot w. Inn, 1971.

Legros, J., *Le Mont Sainte-Odile: Une énigme*, Paris, 1974.

Le Roy Ladurie, E., *Montaillou*, London, 1978.

Lespinasse, J., *Chroniques du Brivadois*, Brioude, 1965.

Lewis, C. S., *The Allegory of Love*, Oxford, 1936.

Lubicz, I. S. de. *Her-Bak Disciple*, Paris, 1956.

Macadam, A. (ed.), *Northern Italy*, Blue Guide, 1924, 1978.

MacDonald, G., *Lilith*, London, 1895, 1969.

MacGowan, K., *Our Lady of Dublin*, Dublin, 1970.

Magnusson, M., *Hammer of the North*, London, 1976.

Marie, F., *La Résurrection du Grand Cocu*, Paris, 1981.

Markale, J., *Women of the Celts*, London, 1975.

Martinet, S., *Laon, ancienne capitale de la France*, Laon, 1966.

Masson, J.-R. (ed.), *Guide du Val de Loire mystérieux*, Paris, 1980.

Matthews, J., *The Grail*, London, 1981.

Mead, G. R. S., *Fragments of a Faith Forgotten*, London 1900.

Michelin, *The Green Guides*.

Michell, J., *The Earth Spirit*, London, 1975.

Miller, D. L., *The New Polytheism*, Dallas, 1981.

Montaigu, H., *Histoire secrète de l'Aquitaine*, Paris, 1979.

Moreau, M., 'Origine des vierges noires', *Atlantis*, no. 205, November 1961.

Moreau, M., 'Les cultes de lumière, la déesse noire et la source', *Atlantis*, no. 206, pp. 147–61, January 1962.

Moritz-Bart, L., *Notre-Dame des Dunes et sa petite chapelle de Dunkerque*, Dunkirk, 1977.

Moss, L. and Cappannari, S., 'In Quest of the Black Virgin: She is Black because She is Black', in *Mother Worship*, ed. Preston, J., Chapel Hill, 1982.

Mylonas, G., *Eleusis and the Eleusinian Mysteries*, Princeton, 1961.

Nancray, P., 'Les déesses noires venues d'orient', *Nostra*, 31 March 1983.

Nelli, R., *Le Phénomène Cathare*, Toulouse, 1964.

Nelli, R., *L'Érotique des Troubadours*, Paris, 1974.

Neumann, E., *The Great Mother*, Princeton, 1963.

Nichols, S., *Jung and the Tarot*, New York, 1980.

Nicoll, M., *The New Man*, London, 1950.

Nicoll, M., *The Mark*, London, 1954.

Noguera i Massa, A., *Les Marededéus romaniques de les terres gironines*, Barcelona, 1977.

Nutt, A., *Studies on the Legend of the Holy Grail*, London, 1888.

Oken, A., *Complete Astrology*, New York, 1980.

Oldenbourg, Z., *Le Bûcher de Montségur*, Paris, 1959.

Oliver, G., *Breve Historia del Santuario y Colegio de Nuestra Señora de Lluch*, Palma, 1976.

Oursel, R., *Le Procès des Templiers*, Paris, 1955.

Ousset, P., *Notre-Dame de Miège-Coste à Aspet*, Comminges, 1959.

Pagels, E., *The Gnostic Gospels*, London, 1980.

Parker, D., and J., *The Compleat Astrologer*, London, 1971.

Perera, S. B., *Descent to the Goddess*, Toronto, 1981.

Pernoud, R., *Vie et mort de Jeanne d'Arc*, Paris, 1953.

Pernoud, R., *Les Hommes de la Croisade*, Paris, 1982.

Pertoka, A., *Recherches sur le symbolisme des Vierges Noires*, Zürich, 1974.

Peyrard, J., *Histoire secrète de l'Auvergne*, Paris, 1981.

Plancy, C. de, *Légendes des saintes images*, Paris, 1862.

Pomeroy, S., *Goddesses, Whores, Wives and Slaves*, New York, 1975.

Pourrat, H., *Histoire des gens dans les montagnes du centre*, Paris, 1959.

Preston, J. (ed.), *Mother Worship*, Chapel Hill, 1982.

Purce, J., *The Magic Spiral*, London, 1974.

Quispel, G., *The Secret Book of Revelation*, London, 1979.

Raeber, L., *Our Lady of the Hermits*, Einsiedeln, 1975.

Rákóczi, B., *The Painted Caravan*, The Hague, 1954.

Ravenscroft, T., *The Spear of Destiny*, London, 1973.

Rawson, P., *Tantra*, London, 1973.

Rawson, P., *The Art of Tantra*, London, 1973.

Reid, V., *Towards Aquarius*, London, 1969.

Renoud, G., *Notre-Dames, des Minimes à Montmerle*, Bourg, 1946.

Reynouard, J. and Sabatier, P., *Riom le Beau et ses Fleurons*, Clermont-Ferrand, 1973.

Ribón, A., 'Breve historia de la virgen de la Vega, patrona de Salamanca', *El Adelanto*, 30 August, 1981.

Riklin, F., *Jeanne d'Arc*, Zürich, 1972.

Rivière, J., *Saint-Savin en Lavedan*, Lourdes, 1982.

Robine, J., *Notre-Dame de la Garde*, Paris, 1978.

Robinson, J. (ed.), *The Nag Hammadi Library in English*, Leiden, 1977.

Ross Williamson, H., *Historical Whodunits*, London, 1955.

Rougemont, D. de, *Passion and Society*, London, 1940, revised and augmented 1956.

Rougier, M., *Notre-Dame de Paix à Picpus*, Paris, undated.

Roy, Y. *Le Testament des Templiers à Chinon*, Paris, 1974.

Runciman, S., *The Medieval Manichee*, Cambridge, 1947.

Saillens, E., *Nos Vierges Noires, leurs origines*, Paris, 1945.

Saintyves, P., *Les saints successeurs des dieux*, Paris, 1907.

Salvat, R., *Notre-Dame des Voirons*, Boège, 1981.

Sánchez-Pérez, J., *El Culto Mariano en España*, Madrid, 1943.

Sandars, N. (trans.), *The Epic of Gilgamesh*, Harmondsworth, 1960.

Saxer, V., *Le Culte de Marie-Madeleine en occident au Moyen Age*, Paris, 1959.

Schmitt, F., 'Vom Geheimnis der schwarzer Madonnen', *Königsteiner Jahrbuch*, Königstein i.Taurus, 1957.

Schnell, H., *Köln St Kolumba. Madonna in der Trümmern*, Munich, 1981.

Scholem, G., *On the Kabbalah and its Symbolism*, London, 1965.

Schonfield, H., *Secrets of the Dead Sea Scrolls*, London, 1956.

Schonfield, H., *The Essene Odyssey*, Shaftesbury, 1984.

Sède, G. de, *Les Templiers sont parmi nous*, Paris, 1962.

Sède, G. de, *Le Sang des Cathares*, Paris, 1966.

Sède G. de, *La Race fabuleuse*, Paris, 1973.

Sède G. de, *La Rose-Croix*, Paris, 1978.

Sèdir, *Les Rose-Croix*, Paris, 1953.

Sérénac, P., 'Les pouvoirs surnaturels des vierges noires', *Nostra*, 31 March 1983.

Seznec, J., *The Survival of the Pagan Gods*, New York, 1953.

Singer, J., *Androgyny, Toward a New Theory of Sexuality*, London, 1976.

Singer, (ed.), *The Jewish Encyclopedia*, London, 1901-6.

Sisters of St Thomas de Villeneuve, *La Vierge Noire de Paris*, Paris, 1982.

Smith, M., *The Secret Gospel*, London, 1975.

Smith, M., *Jesus the Magician*, London, 1978.

Sole, A., *La Mare de Déu del Claustre*, Solsona, 1966.

Stadler, J.-K., *Altötting Heilige Kapelle*, Munich, 1982.

Stewart, D., *The Foreigner. A Search for the First Century Jesus*, London, 1981.

Stone, M., *When God was a Woman*, London, 1976.

Stroud, J. and Thomas, G. (ed.), *Images of the Untouched*, Dallas, 1982.

Strub, M. and Moullet, M., *L'Eglise des Cordeliers de Fribourg*, Fribourg, undated.

Sykes, E., *Everyman's Dictionary of Non-Classical Mythology*, London, 1968.

Talbot, L. 'Sarah, la vierge noire des Saintes-Maries-de-le-Mer', *Atlantis*, no. 266, pp.169-79, January 1972.

Taylor, F., *The Alchemists*, London, 1951.

Thomas, P., *Notre Dame de Liesse*, Liesse, 1976.

Thompson, W., *The Time Falling Bodies Take to Light*, London, 1981.

Tournier, M., *The Four Wise Men*, London, 1982.

Toury, H., *Gerzat*, Clermont-Ferrand, 1964.

Toynbee, A. (ed.), *The Crucible of Christianity*, London, 1969.

Trible, P., *God and the Rhetoric of Sexuality*, Philadelphia, 1978.

Trompetto. M., *Storia del Santuario di Oropa*, Biella, 1979.

Turberville, A., *Medieval Heresy and the Inquisition*, London, 1920.

Ulanov, A., *The Feminine in Jungian Psychology and in Christian Theology*, Evanston, 1972.

Vacandard, E., *Vie de Saint Bernard*, Paris, 1895.

Vaes, H. and Schmitz, M., 'Le grand oeuvre de l'Abbaye d'Orval', *L'Action et les Arts Liturgiques*, nos 2 and 3, 1947.

Valléry-Radot, I., *Bernard de Fontaines*. Paris. 1963.

Vanderspeeten, H.-P., *Notre-Dame de la Consolation à Vilvorde*, Brussels, 1879.

Vazeille, A., *La Tour d'Auvergne et sa Région*, Clermont-Ferrand, 1977.

Verkest, I. and Coppens, C., *Het Eeuwfeest van Onze Lieve Vrouw van Affligem*, Affligem, 1946.

Vielva, M., 'La antigua abadía de Husillos (Palencia)', *Boletín de la Sociedad Castellana de Excursiones*, 1903, pp. 19-20.

Vigneron, C., *Grandes heures de l'histoire de Stenay*, Bar-le-Duc, 1978.

Villette, J., 'Que savons-nous de Notre-Dame de Chartres?', *Notre-Dame de Chartres*, no. 21, pp. 10-15, 1974.

Voragine, James of, *The Golden Legend*, ed. Ellis, London, 1900, 1255-1266.

Voragine, J. de, *La Légende de Sainte Marie Madeleine*, Paris, 1921.

Warner, M., *Alone of All Her Sex*, London, 1976.

Weston, J., *From Ritual to Romance*, London, 1920.

White, V., *Notes on Gnosticism*, London, 1969 (Guild of Pastoral Psychology Pamphlet no. 59).

Whitmont, E., *Return of the Goddess*, London, 1983.

Wilkins, E., *The Rose-Garden Game*, London, 1969.

Willems, J.-B., *O.L.V. van Affligem*, Brussels, 1924.

Wilson, E., *The Dead Sea Scrolls 1947-1969*, London, 1969.

Wilson, R. McL., *The Gnostic Problem*, London, 1958.

Wimet, P.-A., *Notre-Dame de Boulogne-sur-Mer*, Colmar, 1976.

Woodman, M., *Addiction to Perfection*, Toronto, 1982.

Yamauchi, E., *Pre-Christian Gnosticism*, London, 1973.

Yates, F. A., *Giordano Bruno and the Hermetic Tradition*, London, 1964.

Zingg, T., *Das Kleid der Einsiedler Muttergottes*, Einsiedeln, 1974.

Zuckerman, A., *A Jewish Princedom in Feudal France*, New York, 1972.

Index

Only references within the main text are given.